The Rest of Forever

by Alexa Land

The Firsts and Forever Series #16

Books by Alexa Land Include:

Feral (prequel to Tinder)

The Tinder Chronicles (Tinder, Hunted and Destined)

And the Firsts and Forever Series:

1 Way Off Plan

2 All In

3 In Pieces

4 Gathering Storm

5 Salvation

6 Skye Blue

7 Against the Wall

8 Belonging

9 Coming Home

10 All I Believe

10.5 Hitman's Holiday (novella)

11 The Distance

12 Who I Used to Be

13 Worlds Away

13.5 Armor (novella)

14 All I Ever Wanted

15 Take a Chance on Me

15.5 Once Burned (novella)

16 The Rest of Forever

Dedicated to

Terri H.

Friend and Reader

A special thank you to Terri

for coming up with

the title of this book!

Acknowledgements

Many thanks as always to my fantastic team:

Melisha, Kim, and Ron

Thanks Jera for the late-night company and all the laughs!

Thank you Aimee M. for the archive review

Thank you Kylee for the Hoff ☺

I appreciate your help and support!

And thank you as always to my Firsts & Forever group on Facebook for your friendship and enthusiasm!

Contents

Chapter One

"Dad, what does bukkake mean?"

I glanced at my youngest son Mark, who'd just asked that question around a mouthful of toast. Since MJ, my twelve-year-old, nearly choked on his orange juice when his brother said that, I was going to guess it wasn't good, but I actually had no idea what it meant. Instead of admitting I was clueless, I asked Mark, "Where did you learn that word?"

The nine-year-old pointed at his brother. "From MJ."

"Oh my God! This is why I never let you hang out with me and my friends! You're such a snitch!" MJ crossed his arms over his chest and glared at his sibling.

"Am not!"

"You totally are!"

"We don't have time for this," I said. "Finish your breakfast, both of you. If we don't leave in four minutes, you're going to be late for school." As I loaded the dishwasher, I looked around and asked, "Where's Mitchell? Why isn't he eating?"

MJ muttered, "He says he's doing a juice cleanse."

"Why is a ten-year-old doing a juice cleanse? Never mind, don't answer that. Just finish eating." Mark picked up his plate and scraped the scrambled eggs into his mouth with the side of his fork. We didn't have time for a lecture on table manners either, so I let that go and called, "Mitchell! Come here, please!"

He appeared in the doorway a few moments later with our dog tucked under his arm. All three of my sons were dark-haired like me, but while the youngest and oldest boys shared my olive complexion and were tall for their age, Mitchell was pale, short, and reed-thin. The last thing he needed was some sort of weird diet, so I said, "I never signed off on a juice cleanse." I picked up his toast, wrapped it in a napkin, and handed it to him as I added, "We have to leave in three minutes, so you can eat that in the car. Where are your shoes?"

He frowned as he pushed his glasses up the bridge of his nose and said, "It's my body. I think it's kind of dictatorial to tell me what I can and can't do with it." Mitchell was ten going on forty-seven.

"We can talk about it in the car. Go find your shoes please, and put Gizmo in his crate," I said as I dodged around Mark, who was carrying his plate to the sink. The dog flung himself around and grabbed the toast, which he choked down like a seagull with a fish. Mitchell grinned a little and held the napkin out of the dog's reach.

I sighed as I wiped Mark's crumbs from the sand-colored granite surface of the kitchen island and said, "There are granola bars in the cupboard. Grab one and keep it away from Gizmo." Mark slung his backpack over one shoulder, and when he grabbed his skateboard and helmet, I asked, "What are you doing with that?"

Mark stuck the helmet on his head and said, "You told me I could take it today, because Romi Mendez and a bunch of us are going to the skate park after school. Remember? Her mom's driving me to Nana's house after, because you said we're having dinner over there."

"Oh. Right. Well, be sure to keep it in your locker this time. I don't want another call from the principal about you skateboarding in the halls."

Mark looked exasperated. "That happened *one time.*"

I took MJ's plate as he started to put it in the sink and asked him, "Did you put your math homework in your backpack?"

"I don't remember." He unrolled the top of the brown paper bag with his name on it and looked inside as he said, "Nobody in junior high brings a sack lunch, Dad. Why can't I eat the cafeteria food like everyone else?"

"We tried that," I said, as I looked around for my glasses. "After a week, you admitted all you were having for lunch every day was five cartons of chocolate milk."

I found the glasses a moment later, beside the coffee maker that I'd somehow failed to use that morning, and put them on as MJ said, "So? Milk is good for you." He opened the sack labeled 'Mark' and peered inside.

I got the dishwasher going and gathered up the three sack lunches as I said, "Please go check your backpack for your math homework, and find Mitchell. We need to leave in two minutes!" I looked down at myself and brushed a dog hair from my navy blue tie, then patted my pockets for my keys. They were right where they should be, but I felt like I was forgetting something.

Mitchell appeared in the doorway, still shoeless, and announced, "Gizmo ate the latch on his travel crate, so now the door won't close. If you want, I can hold him on my lap on the way to school."

I paused in front of Mitchell and bent down to take a look at the panting, squirming animal in his arms. The dog was white with brown and black markings, and he was allegedly part Havanese and part Shih Tzu. But I was pretty sure Gizmo lived up to his name and was actually a gremlin. "Did he swallow it? If so, I probably need to take him to the vet."

Mitchell shrugged, and his green hoodie slid off his skinny shoulders, revealing a stain on his T-shirt. Normally, I would have asked him to change, but since we were almost late, the fact that my middle child looked like a hobo was the least of my worries. He said, "I think he mostly just chewed on it."

I heard the all-too-familiar sound of tires on hardwood in the front hallway and yelled, "No skateboarding in the house, Mark!" Then I looked around and asked, "Where did MJ go?"

Mitchell said, "I think he's already in the car."

If only. I took the dog from him and tried to keep the little beast from stuffing himself into the sack lunches as I said, "Go find your shoes and backpack. Actually, wait a second." I opened a cupboard and grabbed a granola bar, which I handed to him as I said, "Okay, now go find your stuff."

I grabbed my dark blue suit jacket and held it at arm's length in an attempt to keep the dog hair off of it. Then I headed toward the front of the house, herding my two youngest sons ahead of me. Mitchell was carrying his shoes, and for some reason he'd put on a green knit cap with a big pompom on top. Close enough. When I reached the connecting door to the garage, I glanced down at the SUV. Big surprise, MJ wasn't in there. I propped the door open with my foot and peered back down the hall as Gizmo struggled in my grasp and really tried to go for the sack lunches. After a beat, I yelled, "Michael, Junior! We're leaving! Get over here!"

A few moments later, I heard my oldest son barreling down the stairs. He appeared in the hallway and jogged past me as he said, "I hate it when you use my full name."

As if he hadn't told me that a million times before. "I had to go for the heavy artillery," I said, as I locked the connecting door and followed him down the stairway to the SUV. "We were going to be late."

He grumbled, "We'll be fine. You always get me there ten minutes early, and then I just have to stand around and wait for the bell to ring."

"Because after I drop you off, I still have to make it to the grade school on time." I glanced at the black concert T-shirt he was wearing under his red warm-up jacket and asked, "What happened to your polo shirt?"

"I had to change it. I looked like a dork."

"It's because he likes a girl," Mark chimed in, as he stuck his head out the window of the SUV, "so he wants to look sexy for her."

I stopped what I was doing and asked, "What girl?"

"There's no girl! Oh my God! I just didn't like that shirt, so I changed it."

Mark smirked and said, "Oh really? Then why were you staring at Janet Leno during my basketball game last week?"

MJ muttered, "You need glasses."

"Does Janet Leno go to your school," I asked, "and are you inviting her to your birthday party? I'd like to meet her."

The twelve-year-old looked mortified. "Just let it go, Dad."

As MJ climbed into the passenger seat, I offloaded the dog into the backseat with Mark and Mitchell. Then I deposited my coat in the trunk before climbing behind the wheel and handing the sack lunches to MJ. A moment later, I realized what I was missing and exclaimed, "Oh, my briefcase!"

As I tumbled out of the big Ford, Mark exclaimed, "We're going to be late, Dad!" I fought back a sigh.

Less than a minute later, my briefcase was loaded in the trunk and I was back behind the wheel. I hit the remote for the garage door, but nothing happened. Mitchell said, "Maybe the battery's dead."

In the next instant, Gizmo leapt out of the ten-year-old's arms, clambered onto MJ's lap, and crammed his head into one of the sack lunches. I grabbed the animal, who was wolfing down anything and everything he could sink his teeth into, and fought him for a ripped baggie of dog-mashed strawberries. I ended up flinging them onto the front of my light blue shirt. Awesome. Mark said, "Maybe we're not feeding Gizmo enough."

"We're feeding him exactly what the veterinarian told us to feed him," I said, as the dog began to lick the strawberry pulp off my shirt. "He had a good breakfast this morning, but it doesn't matter, because he's totally food-fixated."

As I returned the dog to Mitchell, MJ held up the smashed paper bags and said, "These have all been stomped on. Now can I have cafeteria money?"

I handed him my wallet, and then I shook the remote as I said, "Give your brothers lunch money, too. Five dollars each should cover it." I smacked the remote on my palm, pointed it at the garage door opener, and clicked it about a dozen times. Finally, the door opened with a mechanical whir and a rattle, and I muttered, "Thank God."

MJ said, "You only have two twenties and a ten."

I looked over my shoulder and backed out of the garage as I said, "Fine, use that and bring me the change." When I reached the driveway, I shook and smacked the remote again. To my relief, the garage door actually closed behind us.

My oldest son distributed the bills, and predictably, the kid who ended up with the ten exclaimed, "No fair! MJ and Mitchell got twice as much as me!"

"It's called the trickle-down effect," Mitchell explained. "You're the youngest, so you get less. It's basic economics." Where did he get that stuff?

I twisted around again and waited for some cars to pass while Mark and Mitchell bickered. The Outer Sunset was one of the quieter neighborhoods in San Francisco, but traffic was still a fact of life. While I was doing that, MJ began to chuckle, and he asked, "Why do you have this in your wallet, Dad?"

"Why do I have what?" My gaze was still on the traffic.

"This rubber. Hey, do you know it expired last September?"

My eyes went wide, and I turned to my oldest son and snatched the foil package from his fingers. "Never mind why I have that," I said, as I crammed it into my pocket.

"It's been like, a year since you broke up with Marie," MJ persisted. "Has that been in there the whole time?"

I looked over my shoulder again, then swung onto the street and muttered, "We're not talking about this."

"I miss Marie. She was fun," Mark said. "She said she was going to stay in touch, but she never did." Great, now I felt guilty.

"Grownups always say junk like that," Mitchell told him, "because they think we'll get upset if they tell us the truth. Like, if Marie had been honest and said she never wanted to see us again because Dad dumped her, then you might have started crying and stuff, and she would've felt bad."

"I'm not the one who would've started crying," Mark insisted. "You're the sensitive one."

"Am not."

"Are too. Yesterday, you started tearing up at a beer commercial!"

"So? The baby Clydesdale was lost, and it was sad."

"It was still a beer commercial. Plus, you'd seen it before, so you knew the horse was going to find its way home."

Mitchell shouted, "It's okay for boys to cry! Just because you have the emotional depth of a petri dish doesn't mean there's anything wrong with me having feelings!"

"Dad, Mitchell called me a petri dish!"

"I did not!"

My two youngest sons bickered all the way to the junior high school. When I pulled to the curb, MJ shot me a look and said, "Kids. Am I right?" Then he handed me the mangled lunch sacks and jumped out of the SUV.

I called, "Have a good day," and he gave me a little wave as he slammed the door. I watched as he jogged up to the building, and once he was inside, I pulled back into traffic.

The grade school was only a few blocks away, but I watched the time on my dashboard and chewed my lip as I made my way through the congested city streets. We were cutting it close. I pulled into the long line of cars in the roundabout at the front of the school with just a minute to spare, and then we ground to a halt. I leaned over to see who was holding up the line and sighed in exasperation as a mom in a white sedan got out of the car and went to the trunk with her kid. "Oh come on," I complained. "That's not how you do it! You're supposed to drop off and go, not drop off and doddle!" The mom opened the trunk for her daughter, who picked up a violin case, and I said, "That is not a two-person job." Finally, the parent got back behind the wheel.

"We can just hop out here," Mitchell said.

"No, wait, we're moving," I said, and then I crept forward a car length. The next car in the number one position turned out to be another doddler, so I sighed and took the dog from Mitchell as I said, "Maybe you should hop out here. Oh wait, no, we're moving again." I pulled forward another car length, this time with a squirming dog on my lap. I had to remember to buy another travel crate ASAP.

A harsh buzzing sound echoed through the roundabout, and Mitchell exclaimed, "That's the first bell, Dad, we gotta go!"

I said, "Yeah, okay," even though the cars ahead of me all pulled forward. Mitchell and Mark piled out of the backseat as the van behind me honked. I yelled, "Have a good day, kids!" The door slammed and my sons took off running. I rolled forward slowly, watching until they were safely in the building, then scowled at the minivan in my rearview mirror and muttered, "Yeah, you know what? You were even later than I was, so bite me." Few things made me as hostile as the daily school drop-off fiasco.

My next stop was doggie daycare. I'd learned the hard way that Gizmo really couldn't be left at home unsupervised, even in a crate. He was just way too high-strung. That was when the Pampered Pup Palace became an unfortunate but necessary part of my life.

The ten-minute drive to daycare was spent trying to keep the dog from devouring the sad, wadded-up lunches on the passenger seat. I was thrilled that I'd spent several minutes of my jam-packed morning preparing nice, healthy things for my kids to eat (even though they preferred the heinous swill served up by the cafeteria), and then it all just ended up Gizmoed. At least the dog appreciated the lunches, but then again I'd literally seen him eat cat poop, so he wasn't exactly a connoisseur.

As I pulled into the parking lot beside doggie daycare, Gizmo shifted his focus from the lunches to my leather wallet, which MJ had left in the center console. I tried to wrestle it away from him, which was great fun, as far as the dog was concerned. He wagged his stubby tail and really put his back into it. For a nine-pound dog, he was surprisingly strong.

Finally, I won the tug-of-war. While I was momentarily distracted, Gizmo lunged for the lunches and pulled a sandwich from the torn wrapping, which he choked down as quickly as he could. Fine, whatever.

I carried the dog into the building and tried to hand him to a new employee behind the counter. Just then, Gizmo made a disgusting retching sound, and the blond kid recoiled and said, "Dude, we can't take your dog if it has kennel cough."

"He doesn't have kennel cough. He just swallowed half a sandwich without chewing."

He shot me a look and said, "People food isn't good for dogs."

"Yeah, I know. Look, just take him. I promise he's healthy as a horse."

The kid countered with, "Dude, horses totally get sick."

My nerves were frazzled by that point, but I took a deep breath and said, "Check our file. It has copies of his vaccination records, including the one for kennel cough."

"I don't know what to tell you, man. We can't take sick dogs."

"He's not sick!" I took another deep breath and asked, as calmly as I could, "Can I speak to a manager?" The kid pointed to his name tag and grinned. Under the name "Dirk' was the title 'assistant manager.' Really? I tried again. "The dog has a grooming appointment this morning at ten, and we can't miss it. Your groomers are booked solid for a month, and his coat's gotten so long that he can barely see." I gathered up the hair over Gizmo's eyes to illustrate my point.

"The salon can't take sick dogs, either."

"Help me out here. What am I supposed to do?"

The kid glanced from me to the dog, and then he looked under the counter. After a moment, he produced a sparkly, purple clip in the shape of a butterfly and fastened it onto Gizmo's head, so the dog's bangs stuck up in a little spout. Gizmo panted happily, and the kid reached for some hand sanitizer, which he squirted liberally into his palm. As he rubbed his hands together, I exclaimed, "Seriously? He's a dog, not a plague rat!"

"Better safe than sorry, man."

"Look, I have appointments all day, and I'm going to be late for the first one. I really need to go, and he really needs to stay."

"Guess you have to take him to your appointments."

"I don't even have his leash with me."

The kid gestured at the wall of merchandise to my left and said, "You can buy one."

I glanced at the flimsy nylon leads and said, "Those won't work. He chews right through that kind."

"You should like, think about training your dog, dude."

My voice rose a little, despite myself. "I did! I paid for a whole year of private dog training! But at the end of it, the only person the dog would listen to was the trainer."

The blond kid shook his head. "That's no good, dude. That trainer needs to come back and like, show you how it's done."

"That's not going to happen. She and I dated for a while, and then we broke up, and she moved to San Luis Obispo, and...why am I telling you this?"

"Wish I knew, man. So, do you want a leash, or not?"

I shook my head. "It'd be bitten in half in less than a minute. Do you have any pet carriers?"

"Yup, right there." He pointed at an oversized pink purse with mesh sides. It was shaped like a castle and featured dimensional turrets with hot pink roofs in each corner. 'Pampered Pup Palace' was embroidered on both sides, beside a cartoon of a poodle in a tiara with a scepter in its mouth.

"Oh, come on."

"Take it or leave it."

I pulled the drool-soaked, slightly chewed wallet from my pocket and juggled the dog in my arms. "I don't really have a choice. How much is it?"

"It's on sale. Only one twenty-nine ninety-five." I stared at him for a long moment, and then I sighed and handed over my credit card.

*****

After the hang-up at doggie daycare, I was already late meeting my brother for coffee. Then I had to spend fifteen minutes trying to find a parking spot in the Castro. Once I finally wedged the SUV into a space several blocks from my actual destination, I put on my suit jacket and loaded

Gizmo into his new carrier. He stuck his head out through an opening at the front of the bag and panted happily.

I slung the carrier over my shoulder and hurried down the crowded sidewalk. Every fifteen feet or so, someone handed me a postcard-sized flyer advertising a sale or event. I took them just to be polite and stuck them in my jacket pocket. Eventually, I reached the elegant coffee house named for its owner, Sawyer MacNeil.

Like half the gay men in the city (or so it seemed), Sawyer was friends with my grandmother. Nana was a very enthusiastic supporter of the LGBTQ community, to say the least. She'd raised my brothers and me after our parents died, and when my oldest brother Dante came out, Nana decided to show her support in a big way. Somehow, it had spilled out to include the entire community.

When I stepped into the coffee house, Sawyer called out, "Hey there, Mike," from behind the counter. I didn't know him very well, but that didn't really matter. Since he was part of the extended family Nana had created, that sort of made us relatives, minus the DNA.

I said hello and waved, and when he asked if I wanted the usual, I nodded. Then I craned my neck to look for Dante and finally spotted him in the back corner of the café. I wove among the tables, most of which were full, and glanced around at the warm surroundings. The floor was honey-colored, the lighting subdued, and the exposed brick wall to my right was lined with gorgeous oil paintings done by local artists. It was one of my favorite places in the city, and that was even before you factored in the sensational coffee.

Dante was doing something on his phone, and I took a moment to study him as I approached. I always thought he and I couldn't be more different, although we looked a lot alike. Along with our brother Vincent, we were six-foot-four with a muscular build, black hair, dark eyes, and olive skin. Only our brother Gianni had broken the mold (like my son Mitchell), in that he was smaller and paler than his brothers and had lighter eyes. Genetics was a funny thing.

As was so often the case, Dante was dressed in a needlessly expensive dark suit, which he'd paired with a crisp, black shirt. He reclined in the booth with one long leg sticking into the aisle and an arm draped over the back of his seat, completely owning his space. When he got a look at me, he chuckled and snapped a picture with his phone.

Then he tapped his screen and said, "Nice pretty pink penis purse, Mikey. It really goes with the blood-stained shirt. Were they both included in some sort of mental breakdown starter kit?" The phone beeped, and Dante grinned and added, "Vincent likes it, too. He wants to know if the cock clutch comes in any other colors, because the pink peens don't really go with the suit from Accountants R Us."

I put the carrier on the table and slid into the booth across from him as I said, "They're strawberry stains, and is there some reason you've mentioned penises three times in the last thirty seconds?" Dante raised a dark eyebrow and gestured at the pet carrier. "What about it?" He traced one of the dimensional turrets at the corner of the bag, and I asked, "Are you saying that looks like a cock? Come on."

"You can't honestly tell me you don't see it."

"No. It's just a castle. Only you would turn it into something dirty."

Sawyer appeared at our table just then with my cappuccino and a paper cup of water for the dog, and Dante pointed at a turret and asked him, "What does that look like?"

Without missing a beat, Sawyer said, "A great, big dick."

He grinned and leaned over to pet Gizmo, who slobbered on his hand, and Dante asked me, "Are you responsible for the have-a-shit's hairdo? Because that's a lovely butterfly clip, Mikey."

I frowned at my brother and said, "As I've told you many times, a Havanese-Shih Tzu cross is called a

Havashu, not a have-a-shit. And no, the clip wasn't my idea. The dog had to miss his grooming appointment today, so that's just to keep the hair out of his eyes."

"And the dick purse? How do you explain that?"

"It's not a dick purse! You're just warped."

While Sawyer was petting the dog, I glanced at his outfit. He was tall and built like I was, and he had a habit of mixing traditionally masculine and feminine clothing into a style all his own. That day, he was wearing a simple, V-neck T-shirt with a snug miniskirt, opaque tights, and high-heeled boots, all in black. His red lipstick provided a pop of color and was an interesting contrast to his no-nonsense short haircut. The way he dressed always struck me as really bold and brave. I usually tried to blend in, but I secretly admired people who were that comfortable in their own skin.

As Dante took a sip of coffee, I turned my attention back to him and said, "Hey, speaking of dirty minds, do either of you know what bukkake means?"

A burst of laughter slipped from Sawyer, and Dante just barely stopped short of a spit take, like MJ and his orange juice earlier that morning. My brother put down his mug and chuckled as he ran a napkin over his permanent five o'clock shadow. "Where did you hear your new word, Mikey?"

"Mark asked me what it meant over breakfast this morning. He said he learned it from his twelve-year-old brother."

"And what did you tell him?"

"I couldn't give him an answer, because I didn't know, either. So, what does it mean?"

Sawyer was still smiling as he turned to walk away, and he said, "Have fun explaining that, Dante."

While our friend returned to the counter, my brother asked, "How are you this sheltered at thirty-two?"

"I'm not sheltered!"

"Oh no, you really are."

"You haven't answered me. What does that word mean?"

Dante stared at me for a moment, and then he picked up his phone and quickly searched the internet. A few seconds later, he turned the screen to face me and said, "It means this."

I exclaimed, "Oh my God!" The phone was playing a video of a naked woman, five naked men, and more flying semen than I'd ever seen, or ever wanted to. I felt myself turning red as I stammered, "Okay, I get the idea! Put it away!" Dante was grinning as he tapped the off-button and returned the phone to the tabletop. I frowned a little, and after a moment, I asked, "Wait, how did you know about that? It's not like you'd ever watch straight porn."

He shot me an exasperated look and said, "Can you honestly not imagine a gay version of that?"

"Oh. Right." I went to take a sip of coffee, but then I grimaced at the foamy, white surface of my cappuccino and pushed the cup away, which made Dante chuckle. After a pause, I muttered, "I hate the thought of MJ looking at porn. I have all the parental controls in place on our computers, so I don't even know how he's accessing it."

"At a friend's house, probably."

I nodded in agreement, and then I said, "How do I talk to him about this? I don't even know where to start. He's only twelve! I thought I still had time before something like this came up."

"He's turning thirteen in just a few weeks."

"So?"

Dante took another sip of coffee and said, "So, he's becoming a teenager."

"But everything's not supposed to change instantly. Just this morning, Markie was teasing MJ about having a crush on some girl. Before this, MJ never expressed the slightest interest in anyone. We've had the sex talk and all that, but I'm not mentally prepared for this to go from theoretical discussions to real life. Plus, now that I know he's been looking at porn, there's a whole added layer of complication. What's that teaching him about love, or relationships, or even realistic expectations?"

"My only piece of advice here is don't make it weird, but don't avoid talking about it, either. The consequences are way too real. Believe me, I know."

"What does that mean?"

"This weekend, I found out Joely's girlfriend Maya is pregnant." Dante and his husband Charlie were in the process of adopting two foster kids, brothers named Jayden and Joely. Jayden was fifteen, and Joely was barely nineteen, so that was definitely a surprise.

I asked, "Why didn't you tell me sooner?"

"Because you and I already had plans to meet here this morning, so I thought I'd tell you face-to-face."

"What are you going to do?"

"Maya is moving in with us until the baby comes, and then we'll figure it out. She says she wants to keep it, so we're going to help those kids any way we can."

"You're oddly calm about this." I finally took a sip of my cappuccino.

"Everyone keeps saying that. What good would it do to fly off the handle?"

I took another sip of coffee, and then I exclaimed, "I just realized this makes you a grandfather!"

Dante held up his hand, palm facing me. "No. We're not going there. I'm way too young to be anyone's grandpa."

I grinned and said, "Apparently not." Dante was only four years older than me and barely looked a day over thirty. Still, given how much he teased me, I was more than happy to return the favor.

As I took the dog out of the carrier and held him on my lap, my brother changed the subject with, "I want to talk to you about doing something special for Nana's upcoming birthday."

"Since she made us stop counting when she turned eighty, how do you think that'll go over?"

"Nana might like to pretend she's eighty and holding, and she may claim to be over the whole presents and candles bit, but she loves parties more than anyone I know," he said. "So, we just won't mention the birthday part. Instead, we'll call it...hell, I don't know, Nana Appreciation Day or something."

"Good idea." I held the cup of water for the dog, and Gizmo splashed more onto my pants than he actually drank as he lapped at it.

"As part of the celebration, I think it'd be great if the whole family could take a trip together over spring break next month. Since your schedule's the most complicated, I wanted to talk to you first and find out if that might be a possibility."

I thought about it before saying, "I could make it work. The boys all had different ideas about what they wanted to do with their week off, so I hadn't actually booked anything yet. Where would we go?"

Dante asked, "What do you think about the idea of Catalina Island? Since we're trying to coordinate a large number of people, I don't want to go too far, but I still want it to feel like a getaway. I could rent a tour bus to drive everyone down to Los Angeles, and then it's just a short ferry ride out to the island."

"That could be fun. I remember Nana taking us there when we were kids."

"That's what made me think of it. Nana loved that vacation and talked about it for years afterwards. She always said she wanted to take us back there, but she never got around to it."

I asked, "Do you think you'll be able to find a place that can accommodate all of us during spring break?"

Dante picked up his phone again and said, "Actually, I know a guy named Ren Medina, who owns a ranch just outside Avalon. I mentioned we might be interested in renting the entire property, and he was all for it."

He showed me a picture of an attractive, Spanish-style resort with a corral, and I said, "Mitchell will be so excited when I tell him they have horses."

"I think Nana will like this place, too."

"Definitely. So, how do you know this guy?"

"We used to be neighbors, and we played poker a couple of times a month before he moved south. He ran a successful tech company, and when he sold it, he used the money to build the ranch. But I don't think it's worked out the way he wanted it to."

"It looks great, though. It also looks pretty spacious, so do you think it'd be okay if I brought a friend?"

My brother exclaimed, "Have you been holding out on me, Mikey? I didn't know you were seeing someone. Who is she?"

"No, I literally mean a friend. I told you I was through with dating, and I meant it."

"How can you be through with dating? You've only dated two people in your entire life."

"That's not true. I went on some blind dates before I met Marie," I said. "Then I took a chance and got involved with her, but it didn't work out, and my kids got hurt. It's been over a year since she and I broke up, but just this morning they were talking about how much they missed her. I'm not doing that to them again."

Dante's expression grew sympathetic. "You're a great dad, and I respect the fact that you put your boys first, but they're fine. You raised them to be strong and resilient, and even if they miss your ex-girlfriend, they've dealt with it. So then the question becomes, what about your needs? Don't you want someone in your life? You must be lonely."

"How can I be lonely if I never even have a single moment to myself?"

"You can be lonely in a crowd, Mikey," he said. "Don't you miss the intimacy of being in a relationship? I don't just mean sex, but you must miss that, too."

"It doesn't matter," I said, as the dog began to lick my chin. "I just need to worry about raising my kids, running my business, getting through the ten thousand things on my to-do list, and—"

"This is just a thought, and feel free to tell me to fuck off. But maybe all of that's just an excuse to keep you from getting hurt again. I know what it did to you when Jenny was killed by that drunk driver. You barely even had a chance to mourn, because you had three tiny boys depending on you. But I know it tore your heart out, and even though it's been eight years, I don't think you ever really got over losing your wife so suddenly."

I told him, "I went out with Marie for close to two years. I *tried* to be in a relationship again. So, how am I making excuses?"

"Marie was utterly wrong for you. I have no idea what you even talked about, since you had absolutely nothing in common. In fact, I think the only reason you went out with her was because there was no chance of it developing into something serious, which meant you couldn't get hurt."

I frowned and said, "That makes it sound like I was leading her on."

"Not at all. I really don't think any of that was intentional."

I took a sip of coffee, then asked, "How did we get on this subject?"

"You said you wanted to bring a friend to Catalina. I assumed you meant a girlfriend, but apparently I was wrong."

"Yeah, you were. I was talking about Yoshi."

The corner of my brother's mouth quirked up into a smile, and he said, "Oh. Yeah, you should definitely bring Yoshi."

"Why are you grinning?"

"No reason." He picked up his phone and started writing a text. "I'm going to go ahead and tell my friend we want to rent that property, and we'll get the ball rolling on the rest of the plans for Nana's not-a-birthday party. I'll handle all the arrangements, since I know your plate is full."

"Can I bring the dog?"

Dante glanced at me. "Do you *want* to bring the dog?"

"Good point. I'll make a reservation at the Doggie Divas Pet Resort for that week."

My brother rolled his eyes and went back to his text. His phone beeped just a minute after he sent it, and he told me, "The ranch is reserved. Catalina, here we come."

We visited for a few more minutes, and I finished my coffee, despite Gizmo's best efforts to finish it for me. Then I slid out of the booth and said, "I have back-to-back appointments all day, so I need to get going. Um, my kids took all my cash…."

"Don't worry, Mikey, I've got it. Are you coming to Nana's Valentine's Day party on Wednesday?"

I returned the dog to his carrier and slung it over my shoulder as I said, "No, I'm taking the boys to her house for dinner tonight instead. Her parties are a bit much on a school night."

Dante's teasing grin returned. "For you or your kids?" I sighed and headed to the door.

Chapter Two

"Oh, honey. Rough day, huh?"

Yoshiro Miyazaki got up from behind his desk and crossed the room to meet me when I entered his office. As my best friend drew me into an embrace, I murmured, "Rough week, and it's only ten a.m. on Monday." At around five-eleven, Yoshi was five inches shorter than I was. I also outweighed him by probably fifty pounds. But his hug still managed to totally envelop me, and I sank into it.

He chuckled when Gizmo started licking him, and he let go of me and scratched the dog's ears as he said, "Aw, look at you with your cute little hair clip."

The dog was beside himself with joy because he absolutely adored Yoshi, and when I pulled him from the carrier, he wagged his entire body. "Doggie daycare rejected him because he was making gagging sounds after scarfing down my kids' lunch. They thought he had an infectious disease and didn't buy my explanation that he's actually just a crazed eating machine. Now I get to haul him from client to client all day."

"You don't have to do that. Just leave him here and pick him up after your appointments." Yoshi took the dog from me, and Gizmo licked his face.

"I'm sure you have better things to do besides babysitting my gremlin. And you know he's getting hair all over you, right?" As usual, Yoshi was dressed all in black, so that really was going to be disastrous.

He shrugged and said, "I don't mind. Come on, let's take Gizmo outside so he can stretch those stubby legs."

I glanced at my friend as we headed to the back door of his tattoo studio. I'd always been in awe of Yoshi. He was strikingly handsome with flawless skin, expressive eyes, and enviable cheekbones, offset by a slightly prominent nose, which I thought gave him a regal profile. But even more remarkable than his good looks was the way he moved through life with ease and confidence.

I'd also always been struck by the fact that Yoshi functioned on a whole different level when it came to style and sophistication. He somehow managed to look pulled together and elegant all the time, even in just a T-shirt and jeans. His constant accessory was the black cityscape that sleeved his left arm from wrist to elbow, which I thought was perfection on him, and I wasn't usually a fan of tattoos.

I considered myself lucky to know Yoshi. He and my brother Gianni had been best friends since college, and I'd been their third wheel. But when Gianni left to sail around the world with his boyfriend, Yoshi and I grew closer. Over the last couple of years, he'd become the best friend I'd ever had.

He turned the dog loose when we reached the cement patio behind the building, and Gizmo raced around sniffing everything. The yard was mostly used by the other tattoo artists for cigarette breaks, and apparently, as a freeform art gallery. The cinderblock walls surrounding the patio were covered in paintings ranging from a six-foot-high woman's face to an alien-looking landscape, and all sorts of things in between. The furniture was just as eclectic, unlike the interior of the studio, which was sleek, modern, and totally coordinated in chrome and black leather.

My friend and I sat side-by-side on a vintage patio swing, and I leaned against Yoshi and admitted, "I'm so tired, and it's only the start of the week. I have no idea how I'm going to make it to Friday, or why I'm even thinking about that, since my weekends are even busier than the weekdays."

Yoshi rested his cheek against my hair and said, "You really need a vacation."

"Funny you should mention that. I was going to ask if you want to come with me, my kids, and about thirty of my relatives to Catalina next month. Dante's renting an entire ranch, and we're going to celebrate Nana's birthday without letting her know that's what we're doing, because she likes to pretend she isn't getting any older. It's the last week of March, over spring break. Please say yes. You know how insane my family is, and I'd love having a rational human being to talk to."

"Absolutely. I'll have to move some things around on my calendar, but that's no problem. You know, I haven't been to Catalina since I was about ten years old."

"I was eight the one time I was there. I remember loving it. After that, I really wanted to move to an island."

Yoshi asked, "An island with or without people?"

"Without, for the most part. I wanted to bring my brothers and Nana with me, but that was about it."

"You know, you never mention your grandfather. Why is that?"

"He's a rotten human being. I know I'm not supposed to feel that way about family, but it's true. He barely wanted anything to do with my brothers and me when we were growing up. He used to say he'd already raised his sons, so he didn't feel he should have to raise his grandsons, too."

"What an asshole," Yoshi said. "It's not like you and your brothers had anyplace else to go after your parents were killed."

"Yeah, he's obviously a really compassionate individual. On top of that, we all found out a few years ago that he'd cheated on Nana throughout their marriage, and I'll never forgive him for doing that to her."

"It sounds like all of you are better off without him."

"We really are," I said. "It's a good thing he basically ignored my brothers and me when we were living under his roof, because I think he would have been a terrible influence. One of the best things Nana ever did was divorce him, and I'm so glad she's finally found herself a good man. She deserves every bit of happiness."

"Agreed."

"Anyway, enough about that. I'm glad you're coming to Catalina. Fair warning: there are horses, and at some point my kids will probably try to coerce you into sitting on one in the name of recreation."

Yoshi said, "So, you're a huge fan of horseback riding, obviously."

"Oh yeah. What's not to like about getting your balls mashed while trying not to topple off a giant, hooved mammal?"

He smiled at me, and after a moment he said, "Okay, I've made it this long, but now I really have to ask about the crime scene all over your shirt."

"You don't want to hear about my morning."

"Oh, but I do."

"Alright. Well, I dragged my ass out of bed at five-thirty and worked out in my super posh garage gym, and then I got the boys ready for school, which was a slow-motion train wreck, same as usual. Next, I went three rounds with the dog over my kids' sack lunches and lost, obviously, which is why I look like this and smell like Lotso Bear from Toy Story 3. You probably don't get that reference, but trust me, it's dead-on. Oh, I also learned what bukkake meant, and MJ found this in my wallet." I pulled the condom from my pocket. "So, all in all, it was a pretty typical morning."

"You didn't know what bukkake meant before today?"

"No, but thank God for my big brother Dante, who explained it by showing me a video I can never unsee while we were in a crowded coffee house."

Yoshi took the condom from me and glanced at it, and then he said, "Did you know this expired last September?"

"Yes, because MJ pointed it out to me. But the fact that it's expired isn't a problem, because my sex life is about as active as that of Tollund Man."

"Do I want to know what that is?"

"No, but I'm going to tell you anyway. Tollund Man is a naturally mummified corpse that was found in a bog in Denmark in the 1950s. And why do I know about this? Because this past weekend, Mitchell decided that mummified bog corpses would be a fun subject for a school essay."

Yoshi chuckled and said, "Let it never be said that conversations with you aren't educational."

I stood up and stretched, then said, "Okay, I'm going to shut up now and get to work. I'll be migrating your accounts payable and receivable to a new software platform today. And yes, that's every bit as exciting as it sounds."

"How long did you block off to do that?"

"Two hours."

"What's on your schedule the rest of the day?"

"I have back-to-back appointments with two of my regular clients every Monday afternoon."

Yoshi tossed his head to swing his glossy black hair out of his eyes, and his expensive haircut fell perfectly into place as he asked, "If you skipped those appointments today, what would happen?"

"There'd be more to do next week."

"An unmanageable amount?"

"No, but it's good to keep on top of things."

"I think you should cancel your appointments," he said. "Call and tell them you'll see them next Monday."

"Why?"

"Because if you don't take a break, you're going to run yourself into the ground."

"But—"

"Come on, Mike, you know you could use a day off. Do I need to kidnap you?"

I grinned a little and said, "How are you going to kidnap me? I'm a lot bigger than you."

"But I fight dirty, and I bet you don't."

"I might."

"Say yes, Mike."

I chewed my lower lip for a moment before saying, "It's kind of irresponsible to cancel those appointments, and ditching work sets a bad example for the boys."

"You're entitled to an occasional day off. When was the last time you had one of those?"

"I actually can't remember." He stared at me with an expression of exaggerated horror, and after a few moments, I said, "Okay. As long as I'm on time for after-school pickup, I guess it won't do any harm."

He looked delighted. "I'll catch the dog. You grab whatever the hell the pink thing with dicks is that you were using to haul him around. Then let's get you home, so the relaxing can commence."

"You're coming with me?" When he nodded, I said, "You should have led off with that. I would've said yes a lot sooner."

*****

When we got to my house, Yoshi turned the dog loose, and Gizmo ran off to molest his favorite stuffed animal. After I called my afternoon appointments and rescheduled, my friend asked me, "Have you eaten today?"

"I didn't have time."

"How do you have time to cook breakfast for your kids, but not yourself?"

"If I made myself something, I wouldn't have a chance to eat it."

He turned me around and gave me a playful push toward the stairs. "Go change. I want to see you in full comfort mode when you come back down here. That does *not* mean jeans and a polo shirt, Mike, because that shit's not comfortable. I'll make us some food while you're gone. Is there anything in the fridge you don't want me to use?"

"No, help yourself to whatever you want."

I turned and headed to the laundry room behind the kitchen, and Yoshi said, "Okay, so far you're totally failing at following instructions."

"I need to pretreat this shirt or the stains will set."

He stuck his hand out and said, "Give it to me."

I did as I was told, removing my suit jacket and tie before handing over the berry-blasted button-down. The stains had soaked through to the white tank underneath, so I stripped that off, too. His gaze flickered to my bare chest as he took the undershirt from me. I wrote it off as idle curiosity. Yoshi was gay, but he also had a very hot and very famous boyfriend, and people who dated rock stars didn't check out accountants. I scooped up my jacket and tie and headed for the stairs.

By the time I returned to the kitchen just a few minutes later, dressed in a baggy T-shirt and a pair of cotton shorts I normally reserved for working out, Yoshi was in full chef mode. He diced some vegetables so quickly that his knife was a blur, and then he swept them into a pan that was sizzling on the stove. When he glanced at me, Yoshi grinned and said, "Now that's what I'm talking about, maximum comfort."

"How are you this good in the kitchen?" I asked as I circled the island and watched him crack an egg into a bowl using just one hand.

"I don't like to half-ass things," he said as he tossed the shells into the sink and cracked another egg with one hand. "A few years ago, I decided I wanted to learn to cook, so I took a series of classes at a local culinary school." He added two more eggs, then whisked them with a splash of milk.

"Well, I'm certainly impressed."

As he poured the egg mixture over the sautéed vegetables, he said, "Well, now that I've raised your expectations, I hope the meal lives up to them."

Once the frittata was in the oven, Yoshi handed me a glass of orange juice and raised another in a toast, and I said, "To hooky Monday."

We took a sip and leaned against the island side-by-side as we waited for the egg dish to bake. He looked around at my traditionally-styled kitchen, which was mostly white except for the sand-colored countertops, and said, "I've always wanted to cook in here. Is that weird? Every time I come over, I'm drawn to your kitchen."

"I don't see why. The one in your loft is like something out of a magazine."

"Yeah, but all that stainless steel isn't very warm or welcoming."

"Well, any time you want to cook in a kitchen that's far less impressive than yours, you have a standing invitation."

He flashed me that radiant smile of his and said, "Though I disagree with the less impressive part, I'm totally going to take you up on that."

Once the frittata was done, Yoshi served it with a fruit salad, and we sat down at the kitchen island to eat. Not surprisingly, the dish was absolutely delicious. When I told him that, he seemed pleased.

A moment later, Gizmo came barreling into the room with a food-crazed gleam in his eyes. Yoshi pointed at the dog, who was just about to jump on him, and said, "No. Sit." To my amazement, the dog actually obeyed him.

"Wow. You're good at absolutely everything," I said. "I'm going to develop an inferiority complex."

"I'm most definitely not good at everything. For example, you really don't want to hear me sing."

"I've heard you, and it wasn't that bad."

"When?"

"Last week, when you came over for dinner and you and MJ started making up words to the Star Wars theme song."

He said, "Well, 'not that bad' is a long way from good."

After we ate, he sent me out of the kitchen with instructions to start relaxing while he cleaned up. I headed down the photo-lined hallway to the family room at the back of the house, where I dropped onto the denim-slipcovered sofa. I loved that room. It had pretty blue walls, and French doors that let in a lot of sunlight and led to a balcony, with stairs to the small yard below. To the right of the doors was our TV and the game console I'd finally broken down and bought for the boys, and to the left was an entire wall of built-in shelves, which were filled with books, board games, and lots of family photos.

When I glanced at the shelves, my gaze happened to land on a framed photograph of Jenny with our three sons. I'd taken that picture just a week before she died. The photo always made my heart ache whenever it caught my eye. But that day, it hit me particularly hard. I just didn't have the energy to keep up my usual façade of pretending everything was okay.

I studied the photo closely. Jenny had golden blonde hair and freckles and big, green eyes, and even though the boys didn't look like their mom, I saw so much of her in them. She was there in Mitchell's curiosity and quirky personality, and Mark's love of sports, and MJ's musical ability. Her kindness was in each of them too, and so was her zest for life.

Unexpectedly, a tear tumbled down my cheek. I took off my glasses and put them on the end table, at the base of a lamp shaped like a lighthouse with red and blue stripes. It had been one of Jenny's favorite things. I ran the back of my hand over my eyes and tried to make myself get it together, but the tears just kept coming.

When Yoshi appeared in the doorway a couple of minutes later and saw what was happening, he hurried over and sat beside me on the couch, and I sank into his embrace. He was so patient. He just held me and stroked my hair as my tears soaked into his T-shirt.

Eventually, I whispered, "Thank God the boys aren't here to see this."

"What would be so bad about seeing you cry?"

"I'm supposed to be strong for them, Yoshi."

He continued stroking my hair, and after a while, he asked, "What upset you?"

"I'm not sure. I was looking at Jenny's picture, which always hurts, but it doesn't usually bring me to tears. Not anymore."

"You must miss her so much."

"I do. She was my partner, in every sense of the word. But then, one day she was just gone. The boys were one, two, and four when that drunk driver ended her life. I hate the fact that MJ only has a handful of memories of her, and his brothers don't remember her at all. To them, she's just a face in pictures, like my parents are to me."

His voice was so gentle when he said, "I don't know how you got through it."

"I don't either. For a long time, I think I was just functioning on autopilot." I sat up and stared at that photo as I said, "We were a team. Jenny and I were supposed to raise our kids together. For the last eight years, I've been scrambling to do her job and mine, and I'm exhausted, Yoshi, mentally and physically."

"You never ask anyone for help, and I wish you would. You have me, and your brothers, and Nana, we're all here for you."

"That's just…hard for me."

After a pause, he asked, "Is Jenny's family in the picture?"

I shook my head. "There's no one left. She was an only child, raised by her widowed dad, and he passed away a few years ago. Jenny lost her mom when she was little. Since I'd lost my parents when I was three, it was one of the things that brought us together. Both of us wanted to give our kids what we never had, a stable home with two loving parents."

I sighed and added, "That makes me sound ungrateful. Nana means the world to me, and I was lucky to be raised by someone who loved me unconditionally. But losing my parents the way I did left me so insecure, and what I wanted for my boys more than anything was a sense of security."

Yoshi said softly, "You've provided that for them, Mike, that and so much more."

"I'm trying. God, I'm trying. But sometimes I wonder if I'm too damaged to ever really pull it off." I studied the red and blue area rug, and after a while, I asked, "Did Gianni ever tell you how we lost our parents?"

"He just said it was a home invasion."

"That's right. I was only three years old, so I'm pretty sure some of what I think I remember are actually manufactured memories, pieced together from the stories I've been told about that night. I know a group of men broke into our home when we were all asleep. They were there because of an old grudge, something stemming from my family's involvement in organized crime, which went back generations. They shot my parents and my baby sister in their beds, and then they came for my brothers and me." The story played in my head like a movie, showing me things I couldn't possibly remember, and I wrapped my arms around myself as a cold trickle of fear slid down my spine.

Yoshi whispered, "My God."

I took a deep breath and continued, "Dante heard them coming, and he woke my brothers and me. Then he held those men off with a shotgun so Vincent, Gianni and I could escape out a window." I paused for a moment before saying, "I think I really do remember this part. I remember the fear in Vincent's eyes as he lowered Gianni and me to the ground. I also remember I was barefoot, and the grass was cold and wet beneath my feet as we ran to the neighbor's house for help. It was dark, and I was scared and confused. I definitely remember the sound of the shotgun blast and the way it echoed through the yard. I thought Dante had been shot, and I tried to go back for him, but Vincent and Gianni told me I had to keep going. They pulled me by my arms, almost dragging me across the yard. I was crying and calling Dante's name. At least, I think I remember that."

I exhaled slowly, and then I said, "Later on, family members filled in some of the gaps in that story. I found out that Dante ended up shooting and killing one of the monsters that broke into our home. The shot woke my father's men, who were sleeping upstairs, and they saved Dante. Vinny, Gianni and I reached our neighbor's house, and they called the police.

"My brothers and I moved in with Nana and our grandfather, and we never went back home after that night. Apparently the house is still standing, and it's right here in the city. I've never gone and seen it. I'm afraid that if I do, I'll remember more about that night, and it's already too much to process, even after years of therapy."

Yoshi grasped my hand, and when I looked at him, his eyes were full of sorrow. He whispered, "I'm so sorry that happened to you and your family."

I wiped a tear from his cheek and murmured, "Sorry for dumping all of that on you." I'd stopped crying. Actually, I'd stopped feeling much of anything, which was almost always the case when I tried to talk about that night. It was just far too painful and overwhelming, so it usually ended up shutting down a part of me, in a way I both hated and welcomed.

"I'm glad you told me." I curled up on my side, and Yoshi sat on the edge of the couch and rested his hand on my arm. After a while, he said, "You should try to nap."

I nodded and murmured, "Don't let me sleep too long. Maybe just thirty minutes, okay? I can't miss picking up my kids after school."

"Don't worry. I've got you, Mike." I felt a surprising wave of relief as he draped a blanket over me and I let my eyes slide shut.

*****

The first thing I saw when I awoke was Mitchell, who was sitting cross-legged at the coffee table and drawing on a sheet of construction paper with a fat marker. I sat up groggily and mumbled, "Hey kiddo. What time is it?" When I scratched my cheek, I found my unrelenting five o'clock shadow was back with a vengeance.

He pushed his glasses up the bridge of his nose and said, "I'm not sure, but it's getting close to dinnertime. You slept a lot."

"How'd you get home from school?"

"Yoshi picked me up. He got MJ too, but not Mark because he's skateboarding with his girlfriend."

I echoed, "Girlfriend?"

"Oops, I wasn't supposed to tell you that. Mark thought you'd freak out if you knew he and Romi Mendez are a couple."

"Wait...my *nine year old* has a girlfriend? Since when? He and Romi have been friends since Kindergarten, and now they're dating?"

"You're freaking out, aren't you? That's exactly what Mark expected you to do."

"He's in the fourth grade!"

"Oh yeah, definitely freaking out. Do you want to breathe into a paper bag? I saw that on TV. I'm not sure what it's supposed to do, but I can get you one."

"No thanks." I looked around for my glasses. When I found them on the end table, I slid them into place and muttered, "When did I become the last person to know anything around here?" Mitchell shrugged, and I asked him, "Do you have a girlfriend?"

"Gross!"

"Does MJ?"

"No, but I think he likes somebody. He's all secret about it, though."

I stood up and asked, "What's he doing right now?"

"He and Yoshi are decorating cupcakes to take to Nana's house. They wanted me to help, but that sounded kind of boring, so I'm making a card instead. We stopped at the store on the way home from school and got her some flowers too, because I told Yoshi we're celebrating Nana's Valentine's Day today."

I followed the sound of laughter to the kitchen, and when MJ saw me he exclaimed, "I didn't think you'd ever wake up!"

"I hadn't planned on sleeping that long. It felt good, though." I squeezed Yoshi's shoulder and said, "Thanks for getting the kids."

"You're welcome. I know you only intended to take a short nap, but I thought you could use the rest."

"Yeah, I really needed that."

I surveyed the kitchen island, which was covered in cupcakes, red and pink candies, heart-shaped sprinkles, and pastry bags of pink frosting. MJ pointed to one of their creations and told me, "Yoshi and I thought we were doing a really good job frosting the cupcakes, but we just realized they look exactly like pink poop emojis."

They really did. "Nana will think it's hilarious. Definitely leave them like that." While MJ started fashioning eyes and smiles for the cupcakes out of candy, I said, "Be right back, I'm going to change my clothes. You should come to dinner with us, Yoshi."

"I'd never say no to dinner at Nana's."

I went upstairs and cleaned up a bit in my bathroom before exchanging my outfit for jeans and a white polo shirt. That was basically my off-work uniform. I'd left my suit on the upholstered chair near my closet, and I looked it over and decided it was ready for the cleaners. I went through the pockets and pulled out the stack of flyers I'd been given in the Castro, then flipped through them idly as I carried them to the trash can in the bathroom. Most of them advertised sales at local businesses. Some promoted events around the city. One caught me completely off-guard and made me freeze in my tracks.

It was the most erotic thing I'd ever seen. The flyer featured a black and white photo of two men. One of them was built a lot like me. He was naked and facing away from the camera, and his hands were bound behind his back. He knelt before a man in a suit, whose face was obscured by a shadow and the tilt of his head. The man in the suit was touching the kneeling man's dark hair, in a way that seemed tender, almost loving. Or maybe I was reading a lot in.

Red letters across the bottom said: *Join us at Kinx, the new, all-inclusive club for the BDSM community.* That surprised me. While the photo obviously depicted submission and bondage, I'd always imagined BDSM as much more hardcore, whips and pain as opposed to that kind of gentle intimacy. Admittedly, it was a subject I knew nothing about. But that picture connected with me in a way I couldn't explain, stirring something deep within and filling me with longing.

After a minute, I snapped myself out of it and threw away the stack of flyers. Okay, yes, I'd found that incredibly arousing, but there was no way on earth I'd go to a BDSM club. I didn't have an exhibitionistic bone in my body. In fact, I was uncomfortable even just talking about sex, so doing anything in a public space was absolutely not happening.

Dante's comment from just that morning came back to me: *what about your needs?* I hesitated for a long moment, and then I fished the flyer out of the trash can. Even though I had no intention of actually going to that club, I was willing to admit I needed that photo. I hid it on the top shelf of my closet, well out of reach of my kids. Then I exhaled slowly and headed for the stairs.

Chapter Three

I'd realized at an early age that there was no one on earth like my grandmother. Nana had always been quirky, but the older she got, the more she let her freak flag fly. Around the time she turned seventy, she decided she no longer cared what anyone thought of her, so she was free to do and say whatever she wanted. A decade later, she was more committed to that idea than ever.

Her huge Queen Anne Victorian had been my home from the time I was three years old. It had been white back then, but these days it featured a shimmering rainbow that covered the façade top-to-bottom. We let ourselves into the grand foyer, with its marble floor, symmetrical staircases, and giant crystal chandelier. When I glanced up, I noticed a big, dick-shaped balloon, which must have escaped from its owner and now rested against the high ceiling. Sure, why not.

Nana, her husband Ollie, and one of her friends were in the living room immediately to our left. All three were wearing huge wigs and were in full makeup. Mark was with them, and his face was painted to look like a tiger. I didn't bat an eye at any of that. Compared to some of the shenanigans I'd walked in on over the years, this was totally tame.

Nana called, "Hi boys! Mr. Mario was just giving me some makeup tips, and it turned into a full makeover! Ollie and Markie got in on the act, too. Don't they look cute?"

I'd been so happy when Nana and Ollie found each other a couple of years ago. The little old man had a heart of gold, and he adored my grandmother. He also rode motorcycles, jumped out of airplanes, and overall, was nearly as zany as she was. I thought they really proved the adage 'there's somebody out there for everyone.'

At the moment, Ollie was wearing a puffy, lavender wig and bold makeup, which was interesting with his green track suit. Meanwhile, Nana sported a Marie Antoinette-worthy white beehive, a ton of makeup, and a pink track suit. Her dear friend and hair stylist Mr. Mario was a drag performer on the side, and he was made up to look a lot like Ginger from Gilligan's Island, complete with a sparkly, white evening gown.

Yoshi and I called out a greeting, and as Mitchell and MJ went into the living room to present their great-grandmother with her card and gifts, I unclipped Gizmo's chain from his collar. He immediately took off like a shot and formed a pack with Nana and Ollie's dogs. One was a giant mutt named Tom Selleck, which looked like a Wookie. His buddy was a beige Chihuahua named Diego Rivera, a nod to Ollie's long career in the art world.

We'd brought a hell of a lot of Chinese food at Nana's request, after I told her we wanted to treat her to dinner for Valentine's Day. As Yoshi and I carried the two big cardboard boxes into the spacious, yellow and white kitchen, he said, "I was thinking we should make 'Hooky Monday' a weekly event. You only have three clients that day, and I'm one of them. Could you move us somewhere else on your calendar? I don't care when you get to my stuff, and you said the other two are long-time clients, so I bet they'd be fine with a change, too. That way, while the kids are in school, you'll have a little time to yourself."

"To do what?"

"I'm sure we'll think of something."

"We?"

He nodded. "I'll join you. Sundays and Mondays are supposed to be my days off, but I've let my business eat up way too much of my life lately. It'll be good for both of us to schedule in some down-time."

"That might be doable," I said, as I mentally rearranged my weekly schedule. "Mondays are my lightest days, so there's not much to move around. It obviously won't work during summer vacation when the kids are out of school, but until then, I think I can manage it."

"Wow, that's great. I really thought it'd be a lot harder to convince you."

"Well, after my mini meltdown earlier today, I guess I've realized how much I really do need a break. That's for my kids' benefit, as well as mine. I can't take care of them properly if I let myself get completely run down."

When we'd finished unpacking a sea of white take-out containers onto the counter, Yoshi asked, "What are you doing on Wednesday for Valentine's Day?"

"I'm totally embarrassing my oldest son by throwing a little party for the boys. We're going to order pizza, bake cookies, and watch a movie. It'll be super lame, just ask MJ. You probably have plans, but if not, would you like to join us?"

"Love to. What movie are we watching?"

"Whatever will embarrass MJ the most," I said with a grin. "I'm thinking 'Frozen,' the sing-along version."

"Perfect! Hey, did I tell you I learned to sing 'Let It Go' in Japanese?"

"Did you really?" Although he was second-generation Japanese-American, he rarely mentioned his heritage, so that was surprising on more than one level.

He nodded and said, "I was getting drunk by myself a couple of weeks ago while wading through the internet and found a video with subtitles. I had to watch it about twenty times, but I finally committed it to memory."

"Aw, that's both sad and funny. But I don't know if I should believe you, since I can't picture you doing any of that."

Yoshi took off his black leather jacket and tossed it over a barstool, and then he flung his arms out to the sides and began belting out the Disney song in Japanese. He was a terrible singer, but that just made it more endearing. A few moments later, all three dogs ran into the kitchen and started barking at him, and Yoshi and I burst out laughing.

"Tough crowd," he said with a smile, and we stepped around the dogs and headed for Nana's cheerful yellow, red and white living room.

Mitchell ran up to us so we could admire his ice blue lipstick and shimmering green eyeshadow, and MJ was standing behind the canary-colored sofa with his arms crossed over his chest, as if he thought Mr. Mario might try to tackle him and perform an ambush makeover. I hated the fact that he'd become so reserved and self-conscious over the last year, but I also totally understood it, because I'd been exactly the same way at his age.

"Are we ready for dinner?" I asked. "I haven't transferred the food to serving dishes yet, because I didn't want it to get cold."

"Oh now, don't worry about that, Sugarplum," Nana said as she came over to me. "We can just help ourselves out of the cartons. No need to get fancy." She was barely five feet tall, so she had to pull me down really far in order to plant a big kiss on my forehead. Nana patted my cheek and added, "You look happy. That's nice to see, since you've seemed pretty stressed out lately. Are you all mellow because pot's finally legal in California?"

MJ snort-laughed, and I told her, "Um, no Nana. I just had a nap this afternoon."

She shrugged her skinny shoulders and said, "That works too, I guess." Then she turned to MJ and asked, "What's new with you, Sugarplum, Junior? You've barely said a word since you got here."

He tilted his head forward, so his bangs fell over his eyes. Another recent change had been the desire to grow his hair out. I wondered if that was just so he'd have something to hide behind. "Nothing's new," he mumbled. "Junior high is kind of a nightmare, but whatever."

Mark came up to me with a big smile on his face and asked, "Do I look scary?"

"Terrifying." I pulled out my phone and snapped a picture of his tiger stripes while he mugged for the camera, and then I asked, "Want me to text a copy to your girlfriend?"

Mark whirled around and pointed at Mitchell. "You told!"

Mitchell put on his glasses and admired his makeup in a handheld mirror as he said, "It's in the past, bro. Let's put it behind us and move on."

I asked, "Do you want to invite Romi to our house for our mini Valentine's Day party, Mark?"

He looked mortified and muttered, "No, Dad. Just no. Oh my God."

I said, "Fine, but can we all just agree not to keep secrets from each other? I'm not going to lock you in a tower like Rapunzel if you do something you think I won't like."

Mark said, "I didn't think you were going to lock me up, Dad. I just thought you'd stress out about it and make it weird. Even though Romi and I decided to be boyfriend and girlfriend, it's exactly like before when we were just friends. The only difference is that now we get to use each other's skateboards." Okay, I could handle that.

"MJ is keeping a secret," Mitchell informed us. His older brother's eyes went wide, and Mitchell continued, "He told me not to tell anyone he really wants to audition for the talent show, but he's too scared. He's been singing Britney Spears songs in his room every night, and he actually doesn't suck, so I think he should do it."

MJ's look of panic turned to one of pure annoyance as he told Mitchell, "Dad wants us to tell him our own secrets, dork butt, not somebody else's!"

Before I had a chance to tell MJ not to call his brother names, Yoshi exclaimed, "Britney Spears is awesome! I bet you know the words to this song, MJ."

He pulled out his phone and tapped the screen a few times, and when 'Toxic' began to play, Yoshi put his phone on the coffee table and bounced to the beat. I chuckled and began filming when he started to lip sync, and he strutted around the sofa and grabbed MJ's hands. I was pleasantly surprised when the boy laughed and let Yoshi guide him to the center of the living room.

The two of them totally got into it, dancing with abandon while MJ sang along. Pretty soon, everyone joined in. My grandmother's go-to dance move was twerking, and she did it with the vigor of a twenty-year-old while her giant wig flopped back and forth. Meanwhile, Mr. Mario and Ollie started dancing the jitterbug, and Mark and Mitchell pretty much just jumped around and wiggled.

MJ and Yoshi owned that song. I couldn't remember the last time I'd seen my oldest son enjoy himself that much. He threw his skinny arms in the air and danced as he sang his heart out. Meanwhile, Yoshi lip synced and moved like one of Britney's backup dancers.

I glanced up from the screen and watched my friend. He was always graceful, so it wasn't really a surprise that he could dance, but it went above and beyond what I'd expected. When he turned around and swung his hips, my gaze shifted automatically to his ass in those tight jeans. As soon as I realized what I was doing, I quickly turned my attention back to the phone.

When the song ended, I told MJ, "You were amazing. You've always had a fantastic voice, and you'd be great in that talent show. What can I do to convince you to give it a shot?"

He studied the red and yellow area rug and muttered, "I want to, but what if I embarrass myself in front of the whole school?"

"You won't."

He glanced at me from beneath his dark lashes and said, "You don't know that. I could freeze up, or forget the words, or trip over my own feet, or who knows what else? It's all pretty terrifying."

"If you want to, we can video chat with Uncle Gianni's boyfriend," I said. "Zan has been performing since he was a kid, and I bet he has a lot of tips and tricks for overcoming those fears."

MJ shrugged and murmured, "Maybe."

It often struck me as odd that two people in my life were both involved with rock stars. It all started when my brother Gianni fell in love with a very famous singer named Zan Tillane. About three years ago, Zan headlined a concert for charity and invited our whole family backstage. That was where Yoshi met Gale Goodwin, lead singer of a successful band called Mayday.

But while Zan and Gale were both famous singers, there ended the similarities. Gianni and Zan were in a loving, committed, lifelong relationship, and they traveled the world together. Meanwhile, Gale treated Yoshi as little more than a booty call. They hooked up whenever Gale breezed through San Francisco, and the rest of the time, Yoshi sat around waiting for Gale to call. He deserved so much better than that, but it wasn't my place to tell him what I thought of his so-called boyfriend.

I returned the phone to my pocket and asked, "Is everyone ready for dinner?"

"Almost," Yoshi told me. "But first, we have to dance to one more song, and you need to participate instead of just watching."

"Oh no, I don't dance."

"Yes you do," Yoshi said. "But maybe not like that." He tapped his phone a couple of times, and as a slower Britney song called 'Everytime' began to play, he led me to the center of the living room. Yoshi slipped his arm around my waist and took my hand in his. Then we both tried to lead, which made us laugh.

He looked up at me with an amused sparkle in his dark eyes, and I said, "Go ahead."

It felt odd to let someone else lead, but after a few moments, we found our rhythm. Nana and Ollie began to slow-dance too, and Mark and Mitchell grabbed each other's hands and swung them back and forth as they did a jerky box-step around the living room. Meanwhile, MJ sang along, and Mr. Mario lip synced and acted out the song. Yoshi was watching me closely, and he said, "See? I knew you could do it. You just needed the right music."

"That and the right partner," I murmured, as he guided us confidently in a sweeping arc. That made him smile.

All too soon, the song ended. I was disappointed, maybe because that was more fun than I'd had in a long time. Mark said, "Can we eat now? I'm starving." When I nodded, the kids hurried to the kitchen, with Mr. Mario, Nana and Ollie right on their heels.

Yoshi and I hung back for a moment, and as he pocketed his phone, he said, "Thanks for inviting me tonight, Mike. I always have a great time with your family."

"I'm glad you're here. It's always twice as much fun when you're along." He probably thought I was just saying that, but I was perfectly serious.

*****

Later that night, after I'd dropped off Yoshi at his apartment and tucked Mark and Mitchell into bed, I knocked on MJ's half-open door and stuck my head into his room. "Hey," I said. "Can I talk to you for a minute?"

MJ was sitting at his desk in pajamas which were printed all over with Batman's bat signal. Twelve was a funny age. It seemed as though he both clung to and rejected his childhood in equal measure. I wondered how long it would be before he decided those pajamas were no longer cool, along with the Batman posters and toys that decorated his dark blue room. He looked up from his math homework and said, "I've been dreading this all day."

I crossed the room and sat on the corner of his bed, just a couple of feet from him. I'd actually been dreading it too, but I didn't tell him that. Instead, I said, "So, about that word you taught your kid brother…."

MJ's cheeks turned red, and he dropped his gaze to the blue and yellow Batman area rug. "I didn't teach it to him on purpose. My friend Caleb brought along his parents'

Cards Against Humanity game last time he came over, and we needed more than two people to play it, so we invited Mark and Mitchell to join us. But once we started, we figured out in like, ninety seconds that it wasn't a game for kids. I'm sorry. I didn't know that word either, and when Caleb looked it up online, it was super embarrassing. I didn't tell Mark and Mitchell what it meant, and I'd kind of hoped they'd forgotten about it."

"Well, good. I mean, you're right, that's definitely not a game for kids, but I thought you'd learned that word from watching porn. You're not doing that, are you?" I was nearly as embarrassed as he was, but I had to ask.

He looked mortified and murmured, "Oh my God, Dad."

"Is that a no?"

MJ glanced at me, and then he looked away and admitted, "One of the kids at school showed me a video on his phone once, and it was super embarrassing. I didn't get why anyone would do that for money, because it's just such a private thing. Then I wondered if there was something wrong with me, because he thought it was super hot, and I didn't. Like, at all."

"There's nothing wrong with you, MJ." He frowned and kept staring at the rug, and after a moment, I said, "I hope you know I'm here whenever you have questions or just need to talk about any of this stuff. I promise I'll always try my best to listen without judging."

"There is actually something I've been wanting to ask you." He glanced at me and said, "For my birthday this year, can we just get pizza and cake and invite Yoshi over, but that's it? I really don't want a party."

"You don't? I thought you were looking forward to celebrating with your friends."

"I'm not. Actually, I'm dreading it."

"How come?"

MJ picked up a pencil and began fidgeting with it. After a pause, he said, "I think I was friends with those guys out of habit, more than anything else. We all started hanging out in second grade, for no real reason, and I've realized I really don't have anything in common with them."

"You don't?"

He shook his head. "They're actually really mean. They think it's super funny to call everyone a fag or a homo, even though I've asked them to stop a bunch of times. I told them there were several gay people in my family, and I said I didn't think it was okay to use those words. Jeff Brewer made fun of me for it, and the rest of the guys laughed. That really bothered me."

"I'm proud of you for speaking up, MJ."

"I had to, but it didn't make a difference. They kept saying that stuff, and it made me super uncomfortable. So last week, I started eating lunch by myself, but that just made it worse. Jeff and Caleb and the rest of those guys started teasing me, and when I got upset, they said I had a stick up my butt and didn't know how to take a joke." MJ sighed and muttered, "I really hate junior high."

"I'm so sorry you're going through that. I think I should speak to Jeff and Caleb's parents and—"

"No! That would make it so much worse, Dad. Please, just let me handle it."

"Are you sure?" When he nodded vigorously, I said, "Well, okay, but you need to tell me if this keeps happening."

"I will." He added embarrassedly, "Thanks for listening, Dad."

"Always."

My son was quiet for a long moment before saying, "Remember what Mark said this morning? I wasn't looking at Janet Leno at the basketball game, Dad."

"It's fine if you were. You're almost thirteen, so if you've started becoming interested in girls—"

"Like I said, I wasn't looking at Janet." MJ met my gaze and said, so softly, "I was looking at her brother, Jude."

As understanding dawned on me, I murmured, "Oh."

"I know that shouldn't be a big deal, especially in our family, but I just wanted to be like everyone else, and I'm not. I can't stop thinking about Jude, and I don't know what to do. There's every chance he's straight, so if I try to ask him out, I'll probably embarrass myself. And what if he tells the kids at school? The teasing is already bad enough, and I can just imagine what would happen if Jeff and those guys found out I'm gay. My life would be hell." MJ sighed and slumped in his chair. "I should be talking to Uncle Dante about this, or Yoshi. They'd know what to do. I really don't expect you to understand what I'm feeling right now."

"Actually, I know exactly what you're going through," I said. "When I was in the eighth grade, I fell in love with my best friend, Greg Parker. I had no idea what to do, and I was terrified of how he'd react if he found out."

"How is that even possible? You like girls."

"Actually, I'm bisexual."

"Why didn't I know that?"

"The same way I didn't know you were gay. We just never talked about it before today."

He said, "But your family never mentioned it, either."

"They don't know."

My son asked, "Why would you keep that a secret? You have the most accepting family on the planet."

"It's not exactly a secret. I'm just a really private person, so I've always chosen not to talk about any aspect of my sex life with Nana or my brothers. If you tell one of them anything, then they tell the rest of the family. Next thing you know, your most private stuff is being openly discussed with anyone who'll listen. They assumed I was straight when your mom and I got together, and I never bothered to correct them."

MJ mulled that over for a few moments, and then he grinned and said, "You know what? We both just came out."

I grinned too. "You're right."

"So, what happened with you and Greg? Did you ever tell him how you felt?"

I nodded. "Right after eighth grade graduation. It didn't go well."

"Why? What happened?"

I muttered, "Let's just say, he didn't share my feelings."

"Come on, Dad. I know there's more to the story than that. You're always asking me to open up to you, so shouldn't you do the same with me?"

He had a point. "Okay. The rest of the story is this: he punched me in the jaw and cussed me out, and then he told me he didn't want to be my friend anymore. It was a relief that he and I ended up going to different high schools, because I think it would have been incredibly awkward to keep seeing him around after that."

"Bummer."

"I didn't want to tell you that part because my story probably seems discouraging," I said, "but it isn't the only possible outcome to a situation like that. I'm sure if you talk to my brothers or Yoshi, they'll have some good stories, along with a handful of bad ones from their past. That's true for everyone. No matter if you're gay, straight, bi, or whatever, there will be a few people who break your heart, and others who love you unconditionally."

"But nobody's going to tease you or beat you up for being straight."

"No, but then they'll find something else. I know that sounds pessimistic, but you've already learned the hard way that bullies don't need a reason to pick on you."

He murmured, "I guess that's true."

"The main thing is just to keep being yourself, despite them. I know that's easier said than done, by the way. But you're such a strong person, MJ. I might not have been able to take that advice at your age, but you're a lot tougher than I was."

"You think I'm tough?" When I nodded, he thought about it for a while, and then he said, "I'm afraid to tell Jude how I feel. It'll hurt if he rejects me, but at the same time, I don't know if I'm ready to openly date a guy and show the world who I really am."

"You're only in the seventh grade, and you have so much time to figure this out," I said, as I leaned forward and gently squeezed his skinny shoulder. "Maybe the first step is just to learn to accept this part of yourself. The good news is, you have me and the rest of our family behind you one hundred percent, so you won't have to go through this alone."

"Do you think you've accepted the bisexual part of yourself?"

I shrugged and said, "I guess so, although I don't think about it much. It's just a fact, like having brown eyes or big feet."

"But you've never actually gone on a date with a guy, right?"

"Right."

"Why not?"

"I've only dated three or four people in my life, and they happened to be women."

"How is it even possible to make it to your age and still be able to count the people you've dated on one hand?"

It was a fair question, and I said, "Your mom and I started dating in high school and got married right after graduation. After she was gone, it took a very long time for me to want to go out with anyone again. When I finally did, I got set up on a handful of blind dates, and then I started seeing Marie, but I could just as easily have dated a guy."

"Like Yoshi."

"No, not like Yoshi. He has a boyfriend."

"But his boyfriend is never here, and I've seen pictures of him kissing some guy in his band," MJ said. "What's that about?"

"I think he just does that for the attention." Gale Goodwin was a media whore, and he and his lead guitarist often made out onstage, probably because he courted controversy. He was also a dick, but MJ could figure that part out for himself.

"Well, it's not fair to Yoshi."

"I know." I got up and kissed the top of my son's head, and then I told him, "I'm glad we talked."

"Me too." He looked at me with a dead-serious expression and added, "If you find yourself crushing on a guy at some point and don't know what to do, you should come talk to me. My door is always open." I'd said that last part to each of my sons about a million times, and I couldn't help but grin as I left him to his homework.

Chapter Four

Every Wednesday afternoon, I had a standing appointment at the transition shelter my grandmother had founded. Rainbow Roost provided housing to LGBTQ young people, and it had only been open a few months. But from the moment the first residents moved in, it had become an extension of our family. That was true not only for the residents, but the staff and volunteers as well.

One of those volunteers hovered in the doorway of the director's office while I entered some figures into a spreadsheet, and I looked up from my laptop and said, "Hi Elijah. I like your new haircut."

Elijah Everett's blond hair spiked up on top in a way that didn't quite seem intentional, but it looked good on him. When his hair had been longer, it would often hide his face, the same way his baggy clothes still obscured his body. So in a way, the haircut seemed like progress, as if he was making an effort to come out of his shell.

He touched his hair self-consciously and said, in a soft voice tinged with a southern accent, "Thanks. Can I help you with anything? Nobody showed up for tutoring today."

"Sure. If you want to, you can sort through this box of receipts and separate the ones for food."

Elijah was a math prodigy, and he provided academic help to residents who were either in school or working toward their high school equivalency exam. He spent every Wednesday afternoon at the shelter, and since that was also when I came in to do the books, we'd gotten to know each other over the past few months. I'd always assumed he gravitated to me because we were both math nerds, and because he'd identified me as a fellow introvert.

He perched on one of the two chairs on the other side of the big desk and put the box on his lap, and as he began to go through it, I asked, "Are you having a good Valentine's Day?"

"No. I wish it was over."

"How come?"

Elijah peered at me from beneath his lashes. "I live with my ex-boyfriend Colt and his family, and his new boyfriend is coming to dinner tonight. It's going to be painfully awkward."

"I thought you were staying at a friend's house in the East Bay, near your university."

"I was, but when I finished my degree last month, I decided to move back to the city. That was a mistake," he said, as he pushed back the sleeves of his oversized, pale blue cardigan and revealed a delicate charm bracelet.

"Not that it's any of my business, but why do you live with your ex-boyfriend?"

"Colt's older brother Chance took us in when we were teens, and Chance's husband Finn became my legal guardian. They're the kindest people you'll ever meet, and they've always tried to make me feel welcome, but I don't belong there. Actually, I don't know where I belong."

At twenty, Elijah wasn't exactly a kid, but he still brought out my paternal instinct in a big way. Maybe that was because he always seemed so lost. I said, "Instead of enduring dinner with the new boyfriend, which really does sound awkward, come to my house for pizza tonight. I'm throwing a mini Valentine's Day party for my sons, and my friend Yoshi will be there, too."

He looked up from the receipts and chewed his full lower lip for a few moments. Finally, he said, "That sounds fun, but are you sure I wouldn't be intruding?"

"Positive."

"Okay then. Thank you."

As I sorted a stack of papers on the desk, I asked him, "So, what's the plan now that you've graduated?"

"I have no idea. My professors and academic advisor were really pushing me to go for my PhD. They said I'd be 'wasting my gift' if I didn't do that, but I needed to step back from academia for a while and figure some stuff out."

After another pause, he said, "The thing is, I never asked to be freakishly good at math, and I hate the idea of letting this random thing I had no say in dictate my future. I don't know what I want to do with the rest of my life, but I'd like a chance to figure it out on my own terms."

"If you ever need a sounding board, I'd be happy to listen and offer my two cents."

Elijah handed me a stack of receipts and said, "Can I ask why you decided to become an accountant?"

"It was a practical decision. I was married when I started college, and by the time I graduated, I already had three kids. This major and career were all about being able to support my family."

"If you didn't have to be practical, what would you have studied?"

It was nearly impossible to remember who I'd been before Jenny and the boys, back when my focus was solely on my wants and needs, and I murmured, "I really don't know."

"Do you like being an accountant?"

"I do, actually. It's orderly and logical, and I find that really satisfying. I also love the fact that I run my own business, so I can work around my kids' schedules and be there for them when they get home from school."

Elijah looked wistful when he said, "Your boys are so lucky to have a dad like you. I can't even imagine how different my life would have been if I'd gotten to grow up with that kind of love and support." My paternal instinct clicked up another notch. At that point, I would have adopted Elijah if I could.

"I'm lucky to have them, too."

After a pause, he asked, "Would you mind teaching me some basic bookkeeping? I had to work a register at my last job, and dealing with the public was miserable. I think this would be a much better fit for me."

It was tempting to say the same thing his professors had, that a job as a bookkeeper was a waste of his talents. But I got what he was saying about making his own choices, so I told him, "I'd be happy to." I opened a blank spreadsheet, and we got to work.

*****

At six o'clock that night, Yoshi let himself into my house with his key and called, "Happy Valentine's Day! Where is everyone?"

I yelled, "Hey! I'm in the kitchen."

He and Elijah appeared in the doorway a few moments later, and Yoshi said, "Look who I found on the porch."

"Welcome, you two. Make yourselves comfortable. I'm almost done mixing up this chocolate chip cookie dough."

Yoshi piled several canvas tote bags on the counter. Then he looked around at the cloud of red and pink heart-shaped balloons, the banner of hearts draping the island, and the cluster of cards on the windowsill and said, "It looks like Cupid blew up in here."

"I was just trying to make it festive for the holiday," I said, as I wiped my hands on my red apron. I was wearing it over a pink polo shirt, in keeping with the color scheme. "Want to help me with these cookies?"

Elijah pushed up the sleeves of his cardigan and asked, "What exactly are you doing here?" Two cookie sheets were lined up beside me, and each was topped with a dozen heart-shaped metal cookie cutters.

"I'm going to bake the cookies in the cutters, so they'll hold their shape," I explained.

Yoshi said, "And you just happened to have twenty-four identical cookie cutters?"

I shook my head. "I stopped by the dollar store before picking up my sons from school."

"You really don't do anything halfway when it comes to your kids," Yoshi said. "Where are they, by the way?"

"Upstairs, allegedly doing their homework. I hope they actually get it done, so we can watch a movie later."

Elijah asked, "How can I help?"

"You can deploy the nonstick spray, then help me pat the dough into the molds," I said, as I removed the bowl from my mixer.

Yoshi grinned at me and said, "The real question is, who gets to lick the beater?" He gestured at the mixer paddle while Elijah sprayed the cookie sheets and cutters.

"The dough has raw eggs in it," I told him. "It's unsafe." He raised an eyebrow, then took the beater from me and shared it with Elijah while I frowned and said, "You're taking a risk."

"Totally worth it." They both scooped up some raw dough and licked it off their fingers.

Once they finished contaminating themselves, they washed their hands, and as I deposited the dough into the molds with a small ice cream scoop, they pushed it flat with their fingertips. When I filled the same mold a second and then a third time, I shot Yoshi a look and said, "You're really pushing your luck."

He swallowed the mouthful of cookie dough, then flashed me a smile and said, "I have no idea what you're talking about."

"I have the world's biggest 'I told you so' cued up for later, when you're praying for death in the bathroom." That just made him chuckle.

Once the cookies were in the oven, I filled three glasses with nonalcoholic punch, and we sat down at the kitchen island. Elijah moved aside the elaborate fruit garnish, which was on a long skewer topped with a heart, and took a sip of his drink. Then he said, "You must really love Valentine's Day."

I just shrugged. "I try to make the most of every special occasion, for my kids' sake."

"You should see him on major holidays, like Christmas," Yoshi said with a smile. "He decorates every room in the house and goes totally overboard. It's so great."

I reminded him, "Last Christmas, you told me I was bat shit crazy. That's a direct quote."

"Oh, you are," Yoshi said. "You do way too much and totally wear yourself out in the process. But it comes from a place of pure love for your kids, so I think it's the sweetest thing ever. Besides, I know you really can't help yourself. You're just like Nana."

"I am?"

He nodded. "She can never do anything halfway either, and she looks for any excuse to celebrate."

I stirred my drink with the fruit skewer and said, "I always thought Nana and I couldn't be more different, but you're right. We do have that in common."

Yoshi asked, "What are you going to do about Easter? That's the day we're supposed to come back from Catalina."

"I'm bringing a bunch of stuff along and buying the rest on the island," I said. "We'll have time for brunch, Easter baskets, and the egg hunt before he have to head back to San Francisco. I wish the boys didn't have to be back in school the very next day, but we'll make it work." I turned to Elijah and said, "Hey, what are you doing the last week of March?"

He shrugged. "I doubt I'll find a job by then, so probably nothing. Why do you ask?"

"We're spending spring break on Catalina Island with about thirty friends and relatives, and you should come with us."

He looked surprised, and for just a moment, he seemed excited. But then he grew serious again and said, "Thanks for the offer, but I can't afford a vacation."

"It won't cost you a dime," I said. "My brother rented an entire ranch, and there's plenty of room. He's also getting a tour bus to drive all of us down to southern California. The ferry to the island is my treat, and food will be taken care of, since my family always makes sure there's enough to feed an army."

"That sounds amazing, but are you sure I wouldn't be in the way?"

"Positive."

"I'm coming too," Yoshi told him. "You should definitely join us."

Elijah was too cautious to simply agree, so he asked, "Can I think about it?"

"Sure. Take all the time you need," I said. "The bus is leaving at ten a.m. on March twenty-fourth, so you have until 9:59 that day to decide." He nodded at that.

A moment later, we heard two of my sons racing down the stairs. Mark and Mitchell appeared in the doorway a minute later with Gizmo bouncing at their feet, and Mitchell announced, "The whole house smells like cookies!"

"I made your favorite, chocolate chip," I said. "They're for dessert. The pizzas should be here any minute, so please take the salad to the dining room table and call your brother for dinner."

While Mark pulled the big salad bowl from the fridge, Mitchell turned and yelled, "Get your butt down here, MJ! It's almost time to eat!"

I sighed and muttered, "Because that's obviously what I meant."

"It's time-efficient. Oh hey, we have company. Not you, Yoshi, you're family." He went up to Elijah and stuck his hand out. "I'm Mitchell Dombruso. Please don't call me Mitch, I hate that. You look familiar, but I can't remember your name."

The blond shook my son's hand and said, "Elijah Everett."

"Now I remember. You volunteer at Nana's shelter. I think I've seen you at a couple of her parties, too. You're always hiding in a corner."

I thought that might embarrass Elijah, but he grinned a little and said, "Parties aren't really my thing, but every now and then, I let the people I live with convince me to go with them."

I took off my apron, brushed some flour from the leg of my jeans, and poured the boys their drinks. Mark and Mitchell clicked their glasses together, and I carried my drink and MJ's through to the adjacent dining room. Yoshi took one look at the red and pink tablescape and said, "I see now that I was premature with my earlier Cupid comment. The kitchen was where he began his death throes. Clearly, this was where the actual explosion took place."

"It's not even that elaborate," I protested. "I already had the red plates from Christmas and the pink tablecloth from Easter, and the centerpiece is just a bunch of Valentine's Day decor I've collected over the years."

"And the heart-shaped placemats and heart-festooned table runner?"

"Okay, those are new. You have to admit, they're kind of cute."

Someone knocked on the door, and a moment later, the timer went off in the kitchen. Yoshi said, "I'll take the cookies out of the oven, you get the pizza," and he and I went off in opposite directions.

By the time I returned to the dining room, MJ had joined us. I put the stack of cardboard boxes on the sideboard and lifted a lid, and Yoshi came into the room and said, "They're heart-shaped, aren't they?"

MJ answered for me. "Of course they are. My dad would never just get round pizzas on Valentine's Day. You know how much he loves his themes."

"I really do. Grab some salad, boys. That includes you, Mark," I said.

"It's not normal to eat leaves," Mark complained. "I'm not a koala."

"There's a lot more in there besides lettuce," I told him. "Pick out some cucumber and carrots."

MJ used a pair of tongs to fill his salad bowl and said, "The carrot slices are heart-shaped. You need an intervention, Dad."

Yoshi asked, "When did you find the time to make carrot hearts?"

"I made them last night, and it was actually pretty easy," I said. "You just make a few cuts to the whole carrot, and when you slice it, the pieces look like hearts. What? I saw it on Pinterest." Yoshi was chuckling as he sat beside me at the table.

After we ate our fill of pizza and I cajoled my sons into eating some salad, I stuck the leftovers in the fridge and served the cookies with milk. I also handed everyone a little gift bag, including Elijah and Yoshi. Elijah held the bag with both hands and asked, "Am I taking yours? You didn't know I was coming until a few hours ago."

I shook my head. "That's for you. I got carried away and bought enough for ten people."

As I watched him unpack the bag with wide eyes, I once again felt like adopting him. It just contained silly little toys, party favors, and a box of candy Conversation Hearts, but you would have thought it was a priceless treasure by his expression. He murmured, "Thank you so much," as he turned over a little, metal car in his hands, then tucked it in his pocket.

Yoshi put on a pair of novelty sunglasses with red frames and heart-shaped lenses, and he handed me a second pair, which had been tucked into the centerpiece. Then he smiled at me and said, "Thanks, Mike. I brought a few presents, too. Will you come into the kitchen with me and help me get them?"

I replaced my glasses with the sunglasses and said, "Absolutely."

When we reached the kitchen, he whispered, "Is it weird that I want to adopt a twenty-year-old? It is, isn't it?"

"I feel the same way. Elijah probably thinks I'm nuts for inviting him to Catalina, but he just trips all my caretaker switches."

Yoshi unpacked two of his canvas bags and said, "I'm glad you told me he was joining us tonight, so I could stop off and get him a gift. I would have felt terrible if I'd left him out." He stacked four small, heart-shaped boxes of chocolates on the counter and said, "Yes, I'm sugaring up your kids."

"I'm not complaining."

"This is for you." He handed me a very nice bottle of red wine and pulled a bottle of tequila from the bag. "And this is for me, after the kids go to bed, obviously. I don't want to drink alone, so is it alright if I spend the night here?"

"Of course. The couch is yours any time you want it, you know that." I put the wine on the counter and asked, "Are you alright, Yoshi?"

He took off his sunglasses and murmured, "Yeah. I'm just being stupid. Valentine's Day is basically a made-up holiday, right? And not everyone celebrates it, so…."

"You were hoping your boyfriend would call, and he didn't," I guessed, as I pushed the sunglasses to the top of my head.

"He still could. It's not even eleven p.m. in New York. That's where he is right now. He'll be headlining a show there on Friday, before flying to London."

"Did you try calling him?"

Yoshi nodded. "It went to voicemail. Nothing new there. I also sent flowers to his hotel, and I still didn't hear from him. But I bet a lot of men really aren't into receiving flowers. Or maybe he got so many from his fans that mine just got lost among them."

I said gently, "I can see why you're hurt."

"I'm not hurt. I just had some unrealistic expectations, which is on me, not him."

"I don't think it's so unrealistic to expect a call on Valentine's Day."

"But Gale never claimed to be a conventional boyfriend, and like I said, this is a made-up holiday. Not like it's Christmas or anything."

It would have been unkind of me to remind him Gale hadn't called on Christmas, either. Instead, I said, "Come on, let's move our party to the family room, pick a movie, and sugar up my kids. Trying to find something we all want to watch should be good for a few laughs."

"Okay. Just let me grab the rest of the gifts. I got everyone the same thing, so it wouldn't seem like I was playing favorites. Then I went back and grabbed one more for Elijah."

He handed me a dark blue, leather-bound journal, which was embossed with a bear and three cubs, along with a beautiful silver pen. "Yours is lined," he said, "because I couldn't quite imagine you drawing pictures. The kids' journals have blank pages. I doubt Mark will draw either, but maybe he'll think of something to do with it."

"Thank you. These are gorgeous. I got something for you too, but I'll give it to you after the kids go to bed." I left my pen and journal on the counter, well out of Gizmo range, and picked up the heart-shaped boxes.

We returned to the dining room, where Elijah and MJ were deep in conversation about music, and Mark and Mitchell were playing a game where the objective was to smack the back of the other person's hands before they could be pulled away. Yoshi gave Elijah and each of my sons a journal and a beautiful box of colored pencils, and I followed him and distributed the chocolates. My kids were enthusiastic, and they all thanked him, but Elijah looked like he was on the verge of tears as he whispered, "This is so beautiful. I can't thank you enough." His journal was pale blue, like his sweater, and its cover was embossed with a little bird in flight. I thought it was oddly perfect.

I said, "Let's head to the family room and get a movie going."

MJ said, "Eli and I will be there in a few minutes. You can start without us."

"Are you sure? That means Mark and Mitchell are picking the movie."

"I'm fine with anything but watching 'Frozen' for the thousandth time," he said. "I can't live through one more massacre of 'Let It Go' by my brothers."

We headed down the hall and got comfortable. Yoshi took his shoes off and curled up in a corner of the couch, and Mitchell climbed on him and put his head on Yoshi's chest. I settled in beside them and flipped through an onscreen menu, while Mark sat cross-legged on the area rug with the dog. After a few moments, I stopped what I was doing to listen. MJ and Elijah were singing, and they harmonized beautifully. I whispered, "What song is that?"

Yoshi said, "It's called 'Look Away' by Eli Lieb and Steve Grand. Wow, they're so good."

When they finished, MJ and Elijah joined us, but they both froze in the doorway when we all turned to look at them. Mark blurted, "You guys sounded awesome! I don't even like that kind of sappy music, but that was really good."

The color rose in Elijah's cheeks, and MJ said, "I didn't think you'd be able to hear us."

"That was extraordinary," I told them. "You really need to do the talent show, MJ."

The pair came into the room and perched on the loveseat to my right. Elijah still looked mortified, and MJ said, "I've been thinking about it. The deadline is this Friday, and I came super close to signing up this week, but I really don't want to make a fool of myself."

I said, "Want to call Uncle Zan for some advice, like we talked about?" When MJ nodded, I pulled my phone from my pocket and sent a text. A minute later, a call came through on video chat, and when I answered it, Gianni's face filled the screen.

My brother had always been handsome, but now he was absolutely striking. It wasn't just because of the tan he'd acquired while sailing around the world with his boyfriend. He looked happy and relaxed, and I said, "Hey, Johnny. Being in love looks good on you."

The nickname was our oldest joke. I hadn't been able to pronounce his name when I was a toddler, so I'd called him Johnny instead. The rest of the family had picked up on it, and they still used it more often than his real name.

"Hey Mikey! Happy Valentine's Day."

"To you, too. Where are you right now?"

"Baja." He and Zan had spent close to three years on a beautiful, vintage sailboat, in part so they could dodge the relentless paparazzi on their endless quest for photos of Gianni's very famous boyfriend. But it had also given the couple a chance to explore the world together on a never-ending honeymoon (minus the actual wedding, which was a bit conventional for those two). When Zan came up behind my brother and kissed his bare shoulder, I didn't have to ask how things were going. The love between them was impossible to miss.

"Hello there, mate," Zan said, as he pushed a strand of his long, salt-and-pepper hair out of his green eyes. "Did Gi tell you the news?" I'd always liked his British accent.

"I was about to." Gianni leaned back against his boyfriend and said, "We're meeting you in Catalina next month. Don't tell Nana, it's a surprise."

"That's fantastic! How long can you stay?"

"The whole week. After that, we're going to start house hunting in California. We haven't decided on an exact location yet, but we know we want to be close enough to visit my family and Zan's son regularly." Zan was a lot older than my brother, and his son wasn't much younger than Gianni, but I didn't have a problem with that. The important thing was that the two of them clearly adored each other.

"Wow, so you're finally giving up your seafaring lifestyle."

"Yes and no," Gianni said. "We're going to keep the boat, and we want to find a place close to the water, so we can sail whenever the mood strikes us. At the same time though, we've been talking about it, and we're ready to put down some roots."

"That's great! I can't wait to see both of you."

"We're looking forward to it, too," Zan said. "So tell me, what's this about an aspiring singer in the family?"

"MJ's thinking about signing up for the junior high talent show, but he's never performed before an audience before. I was hoping you might be able to give him a couple of tips for dealing with stage fright."

"I'd be happy to," Zan said. "Hand me over to the lad and I'll impart my Yoda-like wisdom."

I chuckled at that and gave the phone to MJ. Elijah leaned in and peered at the screen, and then he whispered, "Holy crap, that's Zan Tillane." He pulled back quickly and looked absolutely stunned.

MJ said, "Hi Uncle Zan. I'm sorry to bother you. I know a junior high talent show isn't a big deal or anything...."

"Of course it's a big deal," Zan told him, "and overcoming stage fright is an issue whether you're performing for five people or fifty thousand."

MJ said, "I keep thinking, what if I forget the words? Or what if I trip and fall on my way to the mic?"

"What if you do?"

"Everyone will laugh at me."

"But if you laugh at yourself first, then they're laughing with you, not at you," Zan said. "Do you know how many times I've embarrassed myself while performing? I once fell off the stage at Wembley Stadium, in front of a crowd of over ninety thousand people. Another time, I split my pants while trying to do an awkward kick. Also, on at least three separate occasions, I totally blanked on the words to a song in front of a sold-out crowd."

MJ murmured, "Oh my God, I would die."

"I had two choices in each of those instances: be mortified and run away, or laugh it off. I chose the latter.

When I forgot the words, the audience and I laughed about it together, and then I held out the microphone and they sang the song for me until I joined back in. I heard about that for years, not about how I'd screwed up, but how I and several thousand people shared a human, relatable moment. It became a favorite memory, both for me and the people in the audience."

"But...weren't you embarrassed?"

"Of course I was," Zan said. "I'm sure my face was crimson. I couldn't control that, but I could control what I did with my embarrassment. The key is being able to laugh at yourself, MJ. If you can do that, you take so much power away from the haters in the world."

MJ said, "Thank you for the advice, but I'm still not sure I can do this."

I was pleasantly surprised when Zan said, "Let's practice. Sing something with me."

MJ glanced up from the screen and said, "Um, my whole family is staring at me."

"Well, then let's give them something worth staring at," Zan said. "What shall we sing?"

"Um...how about 'Somewhere Over the Rainbow'? I know it's corny, but I've been practicing it." MJ turned to Elijah and said, "Will you sing it with us?"

"I…um…." Elijah looked like he might bolt from the room.

MJ turned the phone toward the blond and said, "Uncle Zan, this is my new friend Elijah. He has a great voice."

Elijah swallowed hard and whispered, "Oh my God, I can't believe I'm talking to Zan Tillane."

"It's a pleasure to meet you, Elijah. Now come on boys, sing with me," Zan said. "On three."

Yoshi held up his phone and started recording as the three of them broke into an absolutely beautiful rendition of that song. Elijah started off very quiet, but gained a bit of volume as the song went on. When they finished, I said, "I literally have goosebumps."

Zan exclaimed, "Wow! You two are naturals, and your harmonies are spot-on. MJ, mark my words: that talent show is just going to be the beginning for you with that voice."

My son asked, "Do you really think I can sing?"

"You both can. I'd tell you if it needed work, because it doesn't do you any good to be lied to. When's this talent show?"

"The Friday before spring break."

"Good, then we have time to get ready. I'm looking forward to passing on some of what I've learned," Zan said.

"I never actually said I was going to sign up."

"But you want to, don't you?"

MJ admitted, "Yeah. I really do."

"You've got this, MJ," Zan said. "Your only concern is going to be how badly you'll show up the unlucky kids who try to follow your act. What do you think you'll sing?"

"I haven't decided yet."

"Well, call me when you have it narrowed down. I'll help you pick a song, and we'll practice together," Zan said.

After MJ thanked him and they said goodbye and disconnected the call, I asked, "So, you're doing it?"

"Yeah. I mean, how many kids have a world famous rock star as their coach? I'd have to be crazy to pass up the opportunity to learn from one of the best. I just wish Eli could go up on stage with me."

"I can be in the audience if you want me to," Elijah said shyly.

"Definitely." MJ glanced at the clock on the end table and said, "We'd better get a movie started if we're going to finish before bedtime." We quickly decided on 'Cars' and settled in comfortably.

When Yoshi's phone beeped during the movie, he looked so hopeful as he pulled up the text. But then his face fell. I didn't have to ask what had happened. Obviously, he'd been hoping it was his boyfriend, and of course it wasn't. It seemed like all the joy drained from his body.

When the film ended and Elijah started to get up, MJ asked, "How about one more song for the road? What do we all know the words to?"

At that point, I would have done absolutely anything to make Yoshi smile again, so I leapt to my feet and said, "In continuing our Britney theme from the other day, how about this one?" I started badly singing 'Oops, I did it Again' and my boys fell over laughing. Then all three of them jumped up and joined in. We even attempted some of the dance moves, which was super awkward but hilarious. MJ took Elijah's hand and pulled him to his feet, and I did the same with Yoshi. All of this was a bit too exciting for Gizmo, who started yipping and racing around in circles.

We were all laughing by the time we finished. When Elijah caught his breath, he said, "Thank you so much for inviting me over tonight. I had a great time." I told him he was always welcome and offered to drive him home, but he said, "No thanks. My car's parked a couple of blocks over."

MJ said, "Can I walk him to his car?"

"Grab your coat," I told MJ. "We'll both go with him." Not that the Outer Sunset was a bad neighborhood, but just about anywhere in San Francisco, muggings were known to happen.

While Elijah thanked Yoshi profusely for the gifts, I pulled on my jacket and leashed the dog. Then I told Yoshi and the kids we'd be right back, and we stepped out into the cool, foggy night. Since our house was only a few blocks from the ocean, fog and dampness were regular occurrences.

As we walked Elijah to his car, Gizmo tugged on his leash and tried to pee on absolutely everything, and the boys talked about music. After a while, Elijah glanced at me and asked, "Were you serious about taking me along to Catalina?" He was clutching his gifts to his chest, as if they were precious to him.

MJ answered for me. "My dad is always serious. He's like, the most serious guy ever." So much for my delusion that I was actually a fun parent. My son added, "You totally have to come to Catalina with us. It's going to be so much fun! Plus, Uncle Zan will be there, so you and I can both get some vocal coaching from him, which is totally priceless."

"That's actually terrifying," Elijah murmured. "I've been a huge fan of his since I was about eight years old, so I know for a fact that I'm going to embarrass myself when I meet him. I'll probably start crying, and then he'll think I'm a dork."

"He wouldn't think that. Zan's a super nice guy, as you saw," MJ said. "Please come along. I feel like I made a new friend tonight, and I'd love having someone to hang out with besides my crazy family. No offense, Dad."

Elijah chewed his lower lip for a few moments before saying, "Okay. This makes me nervous, but I don't want to miss out."

MJ flashed him a huge smile and exclaimed, "Awesome!"

When we reached Elijah's compact car, he thanked me repeatedly. After he drove away, MJ turned to me and said, "I need you to be brutally honest with me, Dad. Don't just tell me I'll be great because you're my father and it's your job to build me up. Do you really think I can do the talent show without embarrassing myself? I'm not asking if my voice is good enough. Do you think I can get up on a stage and perform without choking? You know me better than anyone, so tell the truth. As much as I want to do this, I'll die if I mess up in front of Jude and the whole school."

"I know you can do this for an absolute fact. I don't think I could have done it at your age, even if I'd had a great voice like you do. But like I said the other day, you're a lot tougher than I was, and I honestly believe you can do anything you put your mind to."

"I hope I'm tough enough to take Zan's advice and laugh it off if I mess up. I'd never live it down if I burst into tears and ran off the stage."

"Let me ask you something. Are you putting yourself through all of this just to impress that boy you like?"

He glanced at me, and then he grinned a little and looked away. "Okay, so, maybe that's in the back of my mind. Right now, he doesn't know I'm alive, and I keep thinking, if I'm really good then he'll have to notice me. But that's not the only reason. I love singing, and if I ever want something to come of it, then I need to face my fears and get in front of an audience. Don't you think?"

"Learning to perform in front of people is definitely a part of it."

We started heading back home, and after a few moments, MJ said, "Thanks for the Valentine's party, Dad. I know you tried hard to make it fun for all of us, and I think you did a good job."

"Thanks, MJ. That means a lot."

After a minute, we rounded the corner onto our street. All the houses on the block were basically the same, and they butted right up against their neighbors on both sides. They were all vaguely Spanish-style, with no front yard, slightly curved façades, and two stories built above a ground-level garage. Our neighbors had tried to individualize their houses by painting them in Easter egg pastels. The house to the left of ours was pale terra cotta, and the one to the right was mint green. Ours was white. My kids thought that was boring.

I couldn't picture it any other color, though. It had been white ever since Nana bought the house for Jenny and me as a wedding present. I'd be forever grateful for that gift. We wouldn't have been able to afford living in San Francisco without my grandmother's generosity.

My son and I climbed the stairs to the left of the garage, and when I unlocked the door and we stepped into the foyer, MJ said, "I have a little homework left. I'm going to go upstairs and get it done." I nodded and freed Gizmo from his leash, and the little mop of a dog ran ahead of MJ to the second floor.

I continued down the hallway and into the kitchen, where I found Yoshi loading the dishwasher. He handed me a glass of the red wine he'd brought me and said, "Mark and Mitchell are putting on their pajamas. You should go and put your feet up. I know it's been a long day for you."

"You don't have to clean up."

"I want to. Go on now. I'll meet you on the couch in five minutes."

"Okay, I'm going."

When I reached the family room, I pulled a wrapped present from the cabinet beneath the bookshelves and put it on the coffee table. Then I sank into the comfortable sofa and took off my sneakers before sampling the wine. Not surprisingly, it was fantastic. Yoshi had excellent taste.

When he joined me a couple of minutes later, he too was holding a glass of red wine, and I asked, "What happened to the tequila?"

"As much as I'd like to drink myself into oblivion tonight, I decided that was a terrible coping strategy. So instead, I'll settle for a mild buzz and good company."

"And this." I gestured at the wrapped gift on the table.

"Aw, thanks Mike. You didn't have to get me anything."

"To quote you from five minutes ago, I wanted to."

He tucked his feet under him before unwrapping the gift, and then he murmured, "Oh wow." It was the Blu-ray version of a Japanese film I knew he'd been trying to find for quite some time. "You remembered. I only mentioned this in passing once, over a year ago."

"I'd been keeping an eye on eBay ever since. If you want to, we can watch it after the kids are asleep." All the lettering was in Japanese, but because the cover featured a car in mid-air with an explosion behind it, superimposed behind a muscular Asian guy holding two guns, it was pretty obviously not a family movie. "I made sure it would play on machines sold in the U.S., by the way, so we should be good to go." Yoshi tried to smile at me, but when he quickly turned away, I said, "Hey. Are you alright?"

He nodded. "It's really touching that you'd make the effort to find this for me. Obviously, my emotions are all over the place today."

"I'm sorry this Valentine's Day didn't work out the way you wanted it to."

"It's not just that. I haven't heard from Gale in days. I accept that when he's on the road, but I know he's had this week off. He's even in the U.S., so it's not like there's a massive time difference or anything." He was quiet for a few moments before saying, "He calls me his boyfriend and says he cares about me, but I wish he'd show it sometimes."

"I'm sorry, Yoshi."

After a pause, he said, "Gale told me right from the start that he wasn't going to be a typical boyfriend. For one thing, he's not a hearts and flowers kind of guy. Since he's on the road most of the time, he also said he needed a man who could deal with long absences and not take his busy schedule personally. I thought I could be that guy. In fact, it seemed ideal. You know how much time I devote to my tattoo studio, and it seemed like the best of both worlds: I could be a workaholic and still have a relationship. But after almost three years…I don't know. Gale's still Gale, but maybe I'm changing."

"Maybe you've realized you want more than he's willing to give."

He asked, "But is it fair to want to rewrite the script after all this time? I knew what I was signing on for when Gale and I got involved."

"If your needs aren't being met, then yes. Absolutely."

Yoshi fell silent. He seemed to be studying his left arm, the one that was sleeved wrist to elbow in a highly detailed cityscape rendered entirely in black ink. After a while, he said quietly, "I can't stand it when I'm like this. The last thing I want is to be needy, and I hate it when I don't have my emotions under control."

"It's okay to be upset."

He slid closer and leaned against me, and I wrapped my arm around his shoulder. "I'm giving myself five minutes for this pity party," he said, "and then I'm going to pull myself together, pretend Valentine's Day is over, and get on with my life." He curled up in the crook of my arm and put his head on my chest.

A couple of minutes later, we heard little feet on the stairs, and Mark yelled, "Daaaaad!" Neither of us moved an inch. Mitchell and Mark appeared in the family room dressed in matching Batman PJs, which I knew irritated both of them to no end. They'd picked out the same pajamas at the store, accused the other of copying, and finally reached an agreement to only wear them on different nights, because they didn't want to look like 'twinsies.' I was sure they'd come downstairs to rat each other out over the blatant violation of the Great Pajama Accord, but when they saw Yoshi curled up with me, they seemed to forget their mission, and Mark asked, "Whatcha doing?"

"We're having a pity party," I told him. "You're welcome to join us."

Both kids considered that for a beat, and then they climbed on top of us and snuggled with Yoshi and me. We gathered them in an embrace, and after a moment, Mitchell asked, "Why are we having a pity party?"

"Because sometimes we just need to feel sad," I said, "and that's okay." Mitchell nodded as he got comfortable on my lap.

A minute later, MJ wandered into the family room with the dog under his arm and asked, "What exactly is happening here?"

"We're having a pity party," Mitchell told him.

I added, "You're welcome to join us."

MJ opened the French doors so the dog could run down the stairs to the backyard, and he muttered, "You're all crazy."

"You say that like it's a bad thing." I flashed him a smile, and my oldest son frowned at me.

After Gizmo did his business, he came running back inside and jumped on my lap, and I said, "See? Even the dog's joining in. Come on, you know you want to."

MJ closed and locked the doors, and then he stared at us for a long moment. Finally, he crossed the room to the sofa, wedged himself right into the center of the group, and tried to put his skinny arms around all of us. After a beat, he said, "This is weird."

I chuckled and told him, "Yup. Just go with it."

Yoshi murmured, "I love you guys."

I said, "I love you too, Yoshi. I mean, we love you." In that moment, I finally realized how much truth was in those words.

Chapter Five

Everything and nothing changed after it dawned on me that I'd fallen in love with my best friend. February turned into March, I got my sons to school and their various activities every day, and I ran my business. I also took Mondays off and made up for it by working a few extra hours in the evenings, after my kids went to bed.

The biggest event during that time period was MJ's thirteenth birthday. We celebrated with our extended family, plus Elijah and Yoshi. I was sad that MJ didn't want to invite any friends from school to his party, but if he was upset about that, he didn't let it show.

While life went on around us, I made sure my relationship with Yoshi was just like it had always been. I didn't know what to do about the fact that I'd developed real feelings for him. But the last thing I wanted was to damage our friendship by making things weird or awkward between us.

On a random Monday morning in mid-March, I dropped off the boys and the dog before meeting Dante at the coffee house. My oldest brother glanced up from his phone as I slid into the booth across from him, and he said, "How do you manage to make even casual clothes look uptight?" He reached across the table and tried to unfasten the top button on my polo shirt, and I smacked his hand away.

"This from a man who wears suits every day for absolutely no reason," I shot back. "You don't even work." The one he was wearing that day was black and obviously obscenely expensive, as was his gray, open-collared shirt.

"I don't crunch numbers or spend my days making color-coordinated spreadsheets like you do, but I work."

"Kind of."

He really did, but it appeared so effortless that I liked to tease him. Dante owned businesses and real estate all over the Bay Area, from a furniture store and restaurant to an entire strip mall, but he paid people to manage them for him. He also handled the family's assets. The Dombruso clan had officially retired after generations spent doing some pretty shady stuff that was less than legal, but there was still money to manage, random business investments to keep an eye on, and the occasional fire to put out.

He took another sip of coffee, then asked, "How was your weekend? Did you do anything exciting?"

"It was a thrill ride, same as usual," I told him. "Mark had a basketball tournament in the South Bay, so that took up eleven hours on Saturday. Sunday, I re-grouted the boys' bathroom. The kids 'helped' so that went really well, obviously. Later on, while I was out back trying to get

Gizmo to stop eating the poo left behind by a cat who'd decided my yard was its litterbox, the kids decided to try a little experiment. They'd heard you can test spaghetti's doneness by throwing it against a wall. That wouldn't have been so bad, except that it was covered in marinara sauce at the time. Even after I scrubbed my white cabinet, it still looked like it was decorated in red fireworks. I ended up having to take the door off, and I plan to repaint it, but I haven't gotten to it yet."

My brother stared at me for a long moment, and then he said, "You're losing control, Mikey."

"The fact that you think I ever had control in the first place is hilarious."

"Well, at least you've had the sense to stick with taking Mondays off. God knows you needed that mental health break. What are you doing today?"

"I'm going to Yoshi's apartment, and he's making us brunch. I don't know what he has planned after that." Dante smirked, and I asked, "What was that for?"

"What?"

"That smirk."

"I didn't smirk."

Sawyer arrived with my cappuccino just then and said, "That was a total smirk. Hi Mike."

"Hey Sawyer. Nice timing." I took a look at my coffee and chuckled. He'd rendered a perfect, 3D representation of Gizmo out of foam. I snapped a picture, so I could show my kids later.

"I need to get back to work because I have two people out with the flu today, but it's good to see both of you." Sawyer flashed us a smile before turning on his stiletto heels and striding across the café. He was dressed in a V-neck sweater, a miniskirt, and tights, all black, and he looked fierce as ever.

"Thanks for the coffee art. This is way too cute to drink," I called after him. Then I turned back to Dante and said, "I want to know why you smirk every time you hear Yoshi's name. I thought you liked him. But whenever I mention him, I get this face." I curled one side of my mouth and tried to do an exaggerated imitation of my brother, which made Dante chuckle.

"I do like Yoshi. I also respect the hell out of him," he said. "You know that."

"So why the...oh my God. Is it because you know I have a crush on him?"

Dante looked surprised. "Wow, you finally figured it out!"

"What did I figure out?"

He took a sip of coffee, then said, "That you're crazy about your best friend."

"But I only realized it a few weeks ago, and you've been smirking for months."

Dante looked amused when he told me, "You and Yoshiro Miyazaki have been a couple for the better part of two years, but both of you seem bizarrely oblivious to that fact."

"Oh, come on. He has a boyfriend, and you know how I feel about cheating!"

Dante held up his hands as if to calm me down, and he told me, "I'm not saying the two of you have been messing around. I know you'd never do that. But you're still a couple, and you have been for a very long time."

"How do you figure, since you know we're not sleeping together? We've never even kissed."

"You're like an old couple who's been married for thirty years, so there's no physical intimacy anymore, but the love and mutual support remains. It's actually very sweet. That said, I wish he'd break up with that fucking asshole of a boyfriend already, because you really need to get laid."

"I never told you I was bisexual, so imagining us as a couple was a pretty big leap on your part."

My brother held my gaze steadily and said, "There was no need to tell me. I've always known you're bi."

"How? I never said a word to you or anyone else."

His expression grew surprisingly sympathetic when he leaned forward and said, "You sometimes seem to forget that I've been right here, every single day of your life, Mikey. When you fell in love with Greg Parker in junior high, I saw it in your eyes, maybe even before you realized it yourself. I also saw what it did to you when your friendship ended, right after eighth grade graduation. I've always assumed that happened because you finally told him how you felt."

"That's exactly right." I gave those revelations a moment to sink in, and then I asked, "Why didn't you say anything?"

"Because you've always been intensely private, and I figured if I brought it up, I'd only embarrass you. It's funny, Gianni would tell us everything that went on in his life to the point of oversharing, but you were the exact opposite. You always had this idea that you needed to handle everything yourself. You softened on that when you and Jenny got married. The two of you became a team. Now, you and Yoshi are the same way."

I murmured, "I never thought about that."

"Here's what I've come to realize: you're willing to let one person in and rely on them, but that's your limit. I used to hate the way you kept a wall between yourself and the rest of us. Now, I think I get it. After our parents were taken from us, we all developed different ways of coping with that loss. Yours was to move to an island, metaphorically speaking, and convince yourself you didn't need any of us to survive. I was glad when you figured out your island was big enough for a partner and kids. It would have broken my heart if you'd wound up alone."

Everything he'd said was dead-on, and it caught me totally by surprise. I told him, "I had no idea you saw so much over the years."

Dante took another sip of coffee before saying, "So, that's the past. Now let's talk about your future and what you're going to do about the fact that you're in love with your best friend."

"I only said it was a crush."

He waved his hand with a flourish and said, "Dante the all-seeing, remember?"

I grinned a little. "Yeah, okay. I had that lightbulb moment just last month. It was on Valentine's Day, actually."

"I take it you haven't told him how you feel."

"No, for a lot of reasons, including the fact that he's not available. Even though his boyfriend is an asshole, Yoshi must love the guy. Why else would he have stuck around all those years?"

Dante shrugged, and I continued, "Also, what if he doesn't feel the same way about me? Our friendship is as important to me as air, and finding out this isn't mutual could ruin everything. Even if by some miracle he feels the same way, what happens if we try to transition from friends to more and it doesn't work out? This is in the alternate universe where Yoshi doesn't have a boyfriend, obviously. But let's say he and the douche bag break up, and we try dating, and we fail. I can't imagine trying to go back to the way things were after something like that, so not only would I lose him, but my kids would too, and they absolutely adore Yoshi." I pointed at my brother and warned him, "Don't say I'm using them as an excuse, because I'm not."

"No, you're absolutely right. Your boys would be devastated, but I don't think Yoshi would ever turn his back on them, no matter what ended up happening between the two of you. He clearly adores those kids."

I picked up a teaspoon and finally stirred the deflating foam dog into my coffee as I said, "For the last month, my motto has been 'act casual.' I don't want to make things weird between Yoshi and me, which is pretty challenging since I'm a mess around him."

Dante asked, "So, what's the plan? I get that you have all kinds of reasons why you're afraid to start something. But what are you going to do, just wait forever and hope Gale Goodwin eventually dies of old age? I've watched Yoshi put up with a lot of shit over the years, and I'm starting to think he'll never break up with him. Gale probably isn't going anywhere either, since he's learned he can do whatever he wants, and he'll still have a hot booty call waiting for him whenever he breezes through town."

"I don't know what to do. If Yoshi loves that guy, I can't imagine he'd be very receptive to me telling him, hey by the way, your boyfriend is a total dick, so you should date me instead."

"You need to figure it out sooner rather than later. What are you going to do next time Goodwin comes for a visit? Can you really see yourself smiling and waving while the man you love goes off to be with someone else, especially a douche like Gale?"

"That would be devastating." I actually shuddered at the thought. "The good news is, his band's currently doing a series of concerts in the UK, so it's not like Gale's going to appear on Yoshi's doorstep tomorrow."

"But he will show up eventually, and you need to tell Yoshi how you feel before that happens."

"I know."

After a moment, Dante asked, "What are you more afraid of, telling Yoshi how you feel and finding out it isn't mutual, or finding out it is and opening yourself up to the first real relationship you've had since Jenny died?"

I didn't have an answer for that.

*****

My worries were replaced with raw desire when Yoshi opened the door to his apartment half an hour later. His hair was damp and tousled, and he wore a sexy pair of black shorts and a form-fitting tank top, which showed off his strong arms and shoulders. My brain fizzled out at the sight of him, and I began chanting to myself, *don't stare, don't stare, don't stare.*

He flashed a radiant smile and said, "Hey Mike. Perfect timing. I just got back from the gym. Two minutes earlier, and you would have caught me in the shower." My internal chant was replaced with *stop picturing that, stop picturing that...oh hell, you're totally picturing that.* I followed him inside, and when he turned to me and got very close, my heartbeat sped up. Yoshi unfastened the top two buttons on my polo shirt as he said, "You're so funny with the buttoned-up-to-your-chin thing. What do you think will happen if you show those extra two inches of skin?"

"Nothing." The word came out a bit choked. Okay, I really needed to get a grip.

"Exactly."

I followed him through his high-ceilinged living room to the open kitchen at the far end of the space. His home was a perfect reflection of him, in that it was gorgeous, flawless, and sophisticated. High-end furniture with clean lines, including black leather chairs and a matching sofa, mingled with modern artwork. The wall of windows on our left let in a lot of natural light, and the red brick on the opposite wall added warmth to the dark color palette. Immediately to the right of the kitchen, a spiral staircase led to his loft bedroom. I definitely didn't need to think about that.

When we reached the kitchen, he asked me if I was hungry. Since my stomach was in knots, I murmured, "Not really."

"Yeah, me neither. I think I'll just make us a couple of smoothies."

He tapped the iPod on the kitchen counter, and music began to play from a pair of wireless speakers. I used to tease him about his love of pop music, which somehow seemed incongruous with the rest of his aesthetic. But when he started dancing to an upbeat song I didn't recognize, I just thought it was adorable.

My gaze strayed to his swaying ass when he turned his back to me. I redoubled my efforts to get a grip and turned my attention to a piece of art in a corner of the living room. Since the abstract metal sculpture was of two men in a loving embrace, it really didn't help me refocus. Instead, it filled me with longing.

I leaned on the long, polished cement counter that separated the kitchen from the living area, and as he set up his blender and pulled some ingredients from the stainless steel refrigerator, I tried to make sense of the way my perception had shifted. I'd adored Yoshi for years, and the fact that he was strikingly handsome had never been lost on me. But realizing I was in love with him cast everything in a new light. He was still the same guy I'd known for years and the best friend I'd ever had, but he was so much more now, too.

He also had a boyfriend, so I really had to stop my ridiculous pining. I circled the counter and occupied myself by washing and slicing some fruit, while he talked animatedly about two of the artists at his tattoo studio and their ongoing efforts to out-prank each other. It took a lot of effort, but I managed to gather up all that longing and desire and push it aside, at least for the time being. I knew I'd have to deal with it eventually, but not right then. There really was only one objective that Monday, which was to calm the hell down and avoid ruining our friendship.

Once the smoothies were done, Yoshi turned off the blender and asked, "What would you like to do today? If you're tired and want to rest, I'm totally down with that. But if you feel like you have energy to burn, I had an idea that might be fun. There's a place that just opened a few blocks from here, and I thought we could check it out."

Since staying busy definitely sounded like the way to go, I said, "Let's do that."

"Don't you want to know what it is?"

I shook my head. "Surprise me."

That made him smile and say, "You're not really a 'surprise me' kind of guy."

"I'm not?"

"Nope. You're all about planning and preparation. But hey, I'm not going to argue with your new-found spirit of adventure. Why don't you pour the smoothies into a couple of travel containers while I change?"

I did as he asked while he bounded up the spiral staircase. By the time I located a pair of water bottles and filled them with the thick banana-mango-blueberry-kale concoction, Yoshi was back. He'd changed into a pair of track pants, sneakers, a T-shirt, and a hoodie, all black of course. I asked, "We're not going to a gym, are we? I know I told you to surprise me, but I worked out really hard this morning after taking the weekend off, and I'm feeling it."

"Where do you hurt?"

"My arms and shoulders."

He said, "You won't need those muscles for what we're about to do."

"I'm starting to regret that 'surprise me'."

We took the elevator to the ground floor of Yoshi's building and stepped out into the busy South of Market neighborhood. In recent years, SOMA had evolved into Silicon Valley North. The sidewalk was crowded with a lot of very busy-looking people in their twenties and early thirties, all apparently on their way to something vitally important. Yoshi and I were the only people not on a latest generation smartphone, Bluetooth headset, or Apple watch. I liked the fact that we stood apart from the crowd, though the kale smoothies were pretentious enough to keep me from feeling smug.

We started walking toward the cluster of huge buildings that made up the Moscone Center, and I asked, "Is that where we're going? Because I could get behind the idea of crashing a convention, as long as it's not about technology. I'm not into lusting over the latest and greatest gadget."

"Nope. I have something much more off-beat in mind."

"I can only imagine." I tried to suck some of the thick smoothie through the spout on the water bottle and ended up puckering my cheeks and making a weird slurping sound. Smooth. Yoshi grinned, then unscrewed the lid on his bottle and took a drink as we walked.

When we reached the convention center, a town car pulled to the curb, and a very self-important businessman on a cellphone breezed out of the backseat and almost plowed us over. Yoshi shot him a dirty look, but the man didn't even notice us. As the businessman hurried into the convention center, Yoshi stared after him and muttered, "My parents idolize that douche. How sad is that?"

"You know who he is?"

Yoshi nodded. "He and I were in the same high school graduating class, and now he owns a multi-million-dollar tech company. My parents read an article about him in the paper, and ever since then, they've been comparing me to him. It was already annoying when they kept comparing me to my cousin Stacey, who's a dentist. But now I also have to hear about how well Len Yakimoto is doing."

"I don't get it. You're really successful, Yoshi. Why can't they just be happy for you?"

"I'm not successful by 'Len Yakimoto' standards. Plus, let's not forget that I make my living tattooing people."

"So? You run a financially successful business, and your work is nationally recognized. What more do they want?"

"None of that matters to them. Maybe if I ran a different kind of business, they'd be okay with my income level. But they hate what I do for a living."

"Is it a cultural thing?"

"In part. Even though my parents were both born in California, they sometimes go a bit overboard with trying to hang on to their heritage, as evidenced by the fact that they named me Yoshiro. Their names are Bob and Cheryl, just to give you a point of comparison. Traditionally, tattoos aren't exactly celebrated in Japanese culture. That's starting to change, but to the older generation, there's still a stigma attached to it."

"It seems like they're looking for excuses to criticize you."

"Story of my life."

I said, "If you ever see me doing that to my sons, do me a favor and punch me in the face. There's so much I want for each of them, but I'd hate myself if I let that overshadow their own hopes and dreams."

Yoshi smiled at me and said, "You got it."

That made me chuckle. "You seem pretty enthusiastic about the idea of punching me."

"Nah. I'm just happy to hear you say you'll put their dreams first. I may end up reminding you of that ten years from now, when MJ wants to pursue a career as a pop star, Mark's trying for the NBA, and Mitchell...well, who knows what he's going to land on? Whatever it is, I doubt it'll be very conventional."

I stopped him in the middle of the crowded sidewalk with a hand on his arm, and when he turned to me, I said, "I'm going to say this because I think you don't hear it enough, especially from your parents. I admire the hell out of you, Yoshi. You're both a stunningly gifted artist and a shrewd businessman, and you found the perfect profession, one that brings together both of those talents. I'm also proud of you, and I'm glad you're a role model for my boys. If they end up doing even half as well as you, then they're going to be a huge success."

He pulled me down to his height and planted a kiss on my forehead before whispering, "Thank you." Then he playfully pushed me away and said, "Now stop trying to make me emotional in public, Dombruso. Look, we're nearly at our destination. Go ahead and tell me why you think we shouldn't go in there and act like idiots."

Yoshi gestured at a large building across the street, and I asked, "You mean that new trampoline place?"

"Yeah, have you been there?"

"Not yet, but I've been meaning to take the boys."

"Let's do that later this week. Today though, we're going to get a sneak preview."

"But it's just for kids, right?"

He shook his head and told me, "Children's hours on weekdays are three to eight p.m. The rest of the time, it's meant for grown-ups."

"That's...weird."

"And awesome. Come on, step outside your comfort zone."

"So...we're supposed to go in there and jump?"

Yoshi grinned and said, "It's much worse than that. There are also mazes, a giant ball pit, and an art room where you draw on the walls." His dark eyes were lit with excitement, but I looked skeptical. "You can do this, I promise you. Be silly. Have fun! Just for an hour or two, stop being a grown-up." I still hesitated, so he added, "Do it for me, Mike." That last sentence was the clincher. I would have done just about anything he asked of me.

When we got inside, I glanced up at the hundred random objects suspended from the high ceiling. They included several bicycles, a mannequin dressed like a scuba diver, and a big rainbow formed out of open, glittered umbrellas. The entire place was an onslaught of color, and I murmured, "It's like Willy Wonka's far less sedate brother decided to open a psychedelic gymnasium."

"I know. Isn't it great?"

Yoshi insisted on buying our tickets from the pink-haired young woman at the counter, and then he led me through the turnstile to a little room lined with neon-orange open shelving. As he took off his sneakers and stuck them on a shelf, I said, "Those are going to get stolen."

"Yours might, too. Or maybe not, we'll see."

I said goodbye to my fairly new sneakers and stuck them beside his twice-as-expensive pair, and then I followed him into a huge room lined with trampolines. Yoshi took a running leap and executed a surprising flip onto the nearest one, and then he bounced in place as he waited for me to join him.

I had a choice to make: hang back on the sidelines, or risk embarrassing myself and participate. I was well aware of the fact that I'd spent most of my life as a spectator, but I couldn't do that with Yoshi. If I was ever going to have a shot with him, I had to be willing to take some chances, and this was as good a place as any to start. I took a deep breath and leapt onto that trampoline.

*****

Two hours later, I grinned as I lounged in an enormous ball pit. We'd climbed and jumped and raced through mazes and made complete fools of ourselves, and it had been glorious. Fortunately, we'd had the place to ourselves, which had helped me lose my inhibitions.

I turned to Yoshi, who was floating beside me on a sea of brightly colored plastic balls, and said, "This was great. Thank you for bringing me here."

"Thanks for acting like a dork with me." When he reached out and brushed my hair from my eyes, my heart tripped over itself.

After a moment, I said, "I don't want to leave the ball pit yet because this is oddly enjoyable, but I just realized we lost our smoothie bottles at some point."

"That's not all you lost." He pulled my glasses from the pocket of his hoodie and said, "You didn't even know these were gone, did you?" I shook my head and took them from him, and as I polished the lenses on the hem of my polo shirt, he asked, "Why do you do that?"

"Do what?"

"You hide behind glasses you don't really need, and dress in what's practically become a uniform, and try to make sure no one notices you. But here's the thing, Mike: it's not working. You're stunningly gorgeous and impossible to miss, despite your best efforts to fade into the background."

I put on the glasses and murmured, "That's not what I'm doing."

"Sure it is. When the glasses were gone, you didn't even miss them." The plastic balls rustled as Yoshi rolled onto his side. His face was just a few inches from mine, and my gaze landed on his lips as he told me, "I'm saying this because I care about you, Mike: I think it's time to stop hiding from the world and get back out there and date again. You're probably going to tell me you tried a year ago when you went out with Marie, but I think you always knew it'd never work out with her."

"Dante said the same thing."

"Well, maybe we both have a point."

"Maybe."

His voice was so gentle when he said, "I won't pretend to know what it was like when you lost your wife, and I know everyone grieves in their own way. But don't you think it might be time to open your heart to love again, Mike?"

I shifted my gaze from his lips to his eyes. There was my opportunity to be honest with him, quite literally staring me in the face. But I just couldn't tell him how I felt. Not yet.

While I blamed my hesitation on the fact that he had a boyfriend, in truth I was afraid of how everything would change once the words were out of my mouth. So I sat up and said, "Yeah. You're right. Now, come on, let's go find the snack bar and get a drink. Maybe we can ask them for some plastic bags to use as footwear, since our shoes must have been stolen by now."

"Okay, I get it," he said, as we both waded out of the ball pit. "This is none of my business and I should shut up. I didn't mean to push, Mike. I just worry about you, that's all."

"I know, and I appreciate it," I said. "For what it's worth, I do actually plan to get back out there sometime soon." That was very true. I just left out two critical words: *with you*.

Chapter Six

I was pretty sure I was even more nervous than MJ, and he'd nearly thrown up just minutes before. It was the afternoon of the talent show, and somehow my son had been assigned the very last time slot. I didn't know how either of us was going to survive that long.

The large auditorium was crowded, and I shifted in my lumpy, red vinyl seat and looked around. How could so many people want to watch a junior high talent show? It didn't help that over a dozen members of my family had turned up to watch MJ perform. That just added to the pressure.

When I thought of him all alone backstage, I wanted to get up and go to him. More specifically, I wanted to grab my son, tuck him under my arm like a football, and run for the door. But that was crazy.

One way or another, MJ would get through this. He'd been rehearsing every day. He'd also received a lot of coaching from Zan during their twice-weekly video calls. He knew the song inside out, and he sounded great. I just had to have faith, which was proving a bit challenging in the face of overwhelming anxiety.

I swiveled around and scanned the crowd. I was seated on the center aisle in the eleventh row, so I had a pretty good vantage point, and I tried to pick out MJ's crush in the audience. The fact that I had no idea what the mysterious Jude looked like was problematic. MJ had spotted the boy right before he went backstage, but he'd refused to point him out. That had been a good call, actually. I absolutely would have gone over and interviewed the kid if I'd known where to find him.

Yoshi was sitting right beside me, and he patted my thigh and said, "I don't know who's more nervous, you or your son."

"I was just thinking it's probably me."

Elijah was sitting directly in front of me, and Mark and Mitchell were beside him. My sons were already getting antsy, and Mitchell kneeled on the seat so he was facing me and said, "Do we really have to sit through the entire show? MJ's last, so can't we leave and come back? The other kids are going to suck. I saw someone with an accordion. *An accordion*, Dad. Sitting through that's like, cruel and unusual punishment!"

"No, we need to stay here," I told him. "We barely found places to sit as it is, even though we were half an hour early. If we leave, someone will take our seats."

From behind me, Dante grumbled, "The kid has a point about the accordion. I'm way too sober for this shit."

I turned around, shot him a look, and said, "Language." Dante had his arm around his husband Charlie's shoulders. Because my brother-in-law was a better sport than the rest of us, he actually seemed entertained by all the goings-on.

"I'm pretty sure your kids have heard that word before, Mikey," Dante told me.

"You should say poop instead, Uncle Dante," Mitchell called. Meanwhile, Mark got up and started jumping in place. God help us.

"You're right," my brother deadpanned. "I should have said I'm way too sober for this poop. Is this thing ever going to start? We've already been here about two hours."

I said, "We've been here twenty-four minutes, and you're worse than my kids."

Seven or eight rows back, Nana stood up on her seat and waved to me as she yelled, "Yoo-hoo! Hi Mikey! Ollie and I are so excited to see MJ kill it! Too bad he's last. I could give a rat's ass about these other kids. Did you see the scrawny kid with the accordion? That's going to suck donkey balls." When several people around her shot Nana dirty looks, she rolled her eyes and yelled, "Oh excuse me! I didn't realize the accordion lovers' convention was in town!" Her husband helped her down, and after Nana took her seat, she gave the finger to a few people who were still glaring at her.

Meanwhile, I caught sight of my brother Vincent chasing his little daughter Lina down the aisle leading to the main door. Vincent was wearing a nice suit and wildly squeaking a pink teddy bear, which he held over his head. Did he think the toddler was a puppy, and that was going to grab her attention?

I sighed and turned back around in my seat. It was official: the Dombrusos won the prize for craziest family in attendance. No contest.

Eventually, the talent show started, and my family more or less settled down. Then we were all rendered comatose by a seemingly endless line-up of truly average singers, dancers, jugglers, 'comedians,' and musicians. Yoshi summed it up by pantomiming repeatedly bashing his forehead against my shoulder during a particularly cringeworthy performance. Later on, he leaned close and whispered, "I'm not just saying this because I'm biased and I adore your son, but MJ is a million times better than these other kids. On a scale of one to ten, none of them has been above a four, and he's a twelve."

Finally, the second-to-the-last act of the talent show was up, and Mitchell whispered way too loudly, "Oh no, the accordion player."

The skinny kid took center stage, weighed down by the big, black instrument, and plugged in his accordion. It was news to me that there was an electric version. A young girl who looked like the kid's sister lugged in a piece of plywood, which was dotted with maybe a dozen small metal boxes, each containing various nobs and levers. She plugged in a cord extending from one end of the contraption before running off the stage.

Then the boy flipped his long, blond bangs out of his eyes and nodded to Ms. Albrecht, the principal, who'd been acting as the show's emcee. She consulted her index cards and read into the mic, "Ladies and gentlemen, please welcome seventh grader Jude Leno to the stage." I instantly sat up and took notice, while the audience clapped politely.

Jude glanced at the audience, and a lopsided grin curved his lips. Then he flipped a switch by tapping one of the boxes with the toe of his sneaker, and the fingers of his right hand began to fly over the round, white keys on one end of the accordion. As if by magic, heavy metal music thundered through the auditorium. He tapped another box with his foot, which added percussion.

It. Was. Epic. I didn't even like heavy metal, but what he somehow produced from the accordion and that equipment was phenomenal. Jude rocked out for about three minutes, working the keys and bellows while occasionally adding elements by tapping one of the boxes. When he finished, he stepped back and grinned again. Yeah, okay. I got why MJ had a crush on that kid.

For a moment, nothing happened. Then someone (probably a member of my family) exclaimed, "Holy shit!"

In the next instant, the crowd went wild. Jude took a little bow as the audience gave him a standing ovation and seemed surprised by all the fanfare. The girl returned and hauled away the boxes and their plywood base, and the boy unplugged his accordion and blinked at the audience. Finally, he took one more bow and left the stage, even though the standing ovation was still in full swing.

Eventually, the crowd settled down again, and as people took their seats, Mitchell turned to me and yelled, "I *need* an accordion, Dad!"

Mark glanced at me over his shoulder and said, "That was awesome, but it kind of blows too, because how's MJ supposed to follow that?" Good question.

A few moments later, the principal reappeared and said, "Well, that was certainly lively! It's now time for the last act of the night. Please welcome seventh grader MJ Dombruso to the stage." She lowered the microphone to roughly my son's height, and then she exited to the left while MJ entered from the right, accompanied by polite applause from the audience and whoops and cheers from my family.

I could tell right away that he was absolutely panic-stricken, and a knot formed in the pit of my stomach. MJ reached center stage and swallowed hard as he stared out at the crowd. His dark hair looked a bit stringy, probably because like the rest of him, it was drenched in sweat.

He'd decided to sing *a capella*, so he was all alone on that big stage. His chest rose and fell as he took a deep breath, then another. The seconds ticked by. My son just stood there, wide-eyed, as everything he'd feared started to manifest itself. I whispered, "Oh God."

The crowd started to fidget and murmur. When some kid off to my right laughed, my heart bled for MJ. I started to get up to go help him off the stage, but just then the principal reappeared. Her expression was sympathetic, and it looked like she was coming to rescue him, so I sat back down.

A tall figure with long hair appeared behind Ms. Albrecht. The man was holding an acoustic guitar and carrying a chair, and when he whispered something to her and she glanced at him, the principal's mouth fell open. She took a few awkward steps backwards and disappeared behind the curtain as the man stepped into the light.

A buzz of excitement filled the auditorium, and someone stammered, "Oh my God, it's Zan Tillane!"

As the audience applauded wildly, Zan placed the chair beside my son, then bent down and whispered in MJ's ear. When my son smiled, I felt like crying with relief. Eventually, the applause died down, and Zan took a seat and grinned at the audience as he said, "Sorry I'm late. I forgot my guitar, so I had to borrow one from a bloke backstage."

As he was talking, he tuned the instrument, and then he turned to MJ and said, "Apologies for keeping you waiting, mate. Want to start off with 'Valerie,' like we rehearsed?"

MJ nodded, and the auditorium lit up with about two hundred recording cellphones. MJ didn't seem to notice. Instead, he focused on Zan, who began to play the Amy Winehouse song on the guitar. And then my son began to sing.

MJ's voice was beautiful and timeless and full of feeling. It wasn't what you'd expect from a thirteen-year-old kid. Instead, it was the voice of someone who'd lived and lost and been hurt and carried on. There was wisdom in it, and longing, and soul. I felt like I learned about him, and from him, just by listening. My heart swelled with pride.

Someone appeared in the aisle and crouched down right beside me about halfway through the number. I glanced at my brother Gianni in the semi-darkness, and he smiled up at me. I beamed at him and squeezed his shoulder.

After that song and a huge round of applause, MJ and Zan sang together. They performed a gorgeous *a capella* version of a Florence and the Machine song called 'Dog Days are Over,' clapping their hands for the beat. That was followed by another tidal wave of applause. Then Zan said, "We've got one final song for you, folks. Thanks for coming out and supporting all these talented kids, including my dear friend MJ Dombruso."

MJ and Zan conferred quickly, and then Zan began to play one of his own songs on the guitar. It was called 'Belonging,' and he'd written it for Gianni. Zan and MJ harmonized beautifully on the ballad, and when they finished, MJ threw his arms around Zan's neck and gave him a big hug. Then Zan stood up and grasped my son's hand, and the two of them took a bow together while a thunderous standing ovation practically blew the roof off the auditorium.

Finally, Zan and MJ left the stage. All around us, people were talking excitedly, and Yoshi gushed, "That was amazing! MJ was phenomenal!"

I grabbed Gianni in a hug and exclaimed, "What a wonderful surprise!"

My brother said, "After coaching MJ for the past few weeks, Zan decided he just couldn't miss his performance, so we chartered a plane this afternoon and flew up from southern California. We were watching from the wings, because we knew it'd distract people from the talent show if Zan got recognized in the audience. But when he saw MJ freeze up, he decided to jump in."

"I'll never be able to thank him enough for that, and I'm so glad to see you," I murmured. "It's been way too long, Johnny."

When I finally let go of him, Yoshi pulled Gianni into an embrace and said, "You and your boyfriend just won the lifetime achievement award for coolest uncles ever."

As the rest of our family all but tackled Gianni, I stepped back and pulled my phone from my pocket. I'd received a text from Zan, which said: *MJ and I left by the back door to avoid getting mobbed and are headed to your house. He says he has a key, so we'll let ourselves in. See you soon, mate.*

I called over the commotion, "Dombruso family, roll out! There's a victory party at my house!"

Nana exclaimed, "Hot damn, I love a party!" She linked arms with Gianni on one side and her husband Ollie on the other and headed for the door.

In all the chaos of my family coming together, Elijah had retreated a bit and was standing off by himself. As Yoshi herded Mitchell and Mark toward the exit, I went over to my young friend and said, "Come have dinner with us, Eli."

He seemed a bit overwhelmed, but he murmured, "Okay. Thanks."

As the two of us followed Yoshi and the boys, I said, "You're still planning to join us tomorrow for our trip to Catalina, right?"

Elijah nodded. "I'm actually really excited to see the island and spend time with all of you," he said. "You have an incredible family, Mike." I had to agree.

*****

Our group more than doubled in size as the party got under way, which pretty much always happened when my Sicilian-American family got together. A few cousins dropped by, and Zan called his son Christian, who showed up with his husband Shea, his best friend Skye, and Skye's husband Dare. Dante, Vincent, and their families made it, too. It had been a long time since all four Dombruso brothers were together, and Nana got a bit teary-eyed when she snapped a photo of us and gathered us into a group hug.

147

Fortunately, I'd anticipated a big crowd. As soon as we got home, I put two huge lasagnas into the oven and pulled an enormous salad and six trays of appetizers from the refrigerator, all of which I'd made the night before. My cousin Carla helped me. She was several months pregnant, refused to name the baby daddy, and as always, looked like she'd come straight from the Jersey shore with her big hair, high heels, and loads of jewelry. Carla was also one of the most intelligent people I'd ever met, and I absolutely adored her.

MJ appeared in the kitchen just as Carla went to take a tray of appetizers into the living room, and I grabbed him in a hug and said, "You were amazing. I'm so proud of you." He'd gone upstairs to shower and change as soon as he got home, which had been a good call since he'd been dripping with sweat.

He let go of me and frowned a little. "I choked. Thank God Uncle Zan decided to come and watch me perform. If he hadn't swooped in and saved me, it would have been the most embarrassing day of my life."

"You just got a bit nervous, that's all. Once you started to sing, you were absolutely flawless."

"Yeah, well, it's too bad I had to lead off with that deer-in-headlights thing. Zan did a great job covering for me, though. He made it sound like I'd just been waiting for him to show up."

I grinned at my son and said, "You know who else did a great job? Jude Leno. I can see why you like him."

MJ looked embarrassed, but he said, "He's like, the coolest guy in my whole school. Some kids backstage tried to tease him about the accordion, but he just stared them down. And then he went out there and shredded! That was the greatest thing I ever saw in my whole life."

"It was pretty awesome."

MJ fidgeted with one of the cocktail napkins on the kitchen island and told me, "So, I did something kind of brave. Or maybe it was stupid, I don't know. Jude was still backstage when we finished singing. He was in awe of Zan, so I introduced the two of them. People get weird around celebrities, and I don't really understand that, because they're just people. Anyway, I told him we were having a party and invited him to come over tonight. He said he had to ask his mom, and if she said yes, it'd have to be after they dropped off his sister Janet at a slumber party. Now I'm all nervous. I don't know which is worse: if he shows up, or if he doesn't."

"Why would it be bad if he shows up?"

"Because I might say something stupid and blow whatever teeny, tiny chance I have with him. Also, it's like, he wouldn't be coming over because he was interested in me. It would just be because he knows Zan's going to be here."

I said, "But Jude might come over because he wants to get to know you."

MJ frowned again. "I don't think you realize how famous Uncle Zan is. Just now when I came downstairs, Uncle Charlie told me there are already a bunch of videos of Zan and me on the internet. And all that cheering and the standing ovation at the talent show? That wasn't for me, Dad. It was for the famous person."

"Come sit down a minute," I said, as I pulled out two chairs beside the kitchen island. MJ did as I asked, and I took my phone from my pocket and did a quick search. Then I played one of the videos of him and Zan at the talent show. I stopped the video after the first song, the one MJ sang by himself, and said, "Do you see how absolutely phenomenal you are? Your voice literally gave me goosebumps. I'm so proud of you, not just because you're a great singer, but because you were brave enough to get up there and show all those people what you could do. And guess what? That standing ovation was for you, every bit as much as it was for your celebrity uncle."

He grinned, just a little, and said, "I guess I did sound pretty good."

"You sounded fantastic."

He ate a cube of cheese from a tray of appetizers, and after a moment, he said, "I was wondering something. Is Zan really my uncle? I mean, Charlie is, because he's your brother Dante's husband. But Zan and Gianni aren't actually married."

"No they're not, but Zan and Gianni have made a lifetime commitment to each other. They chose not to have a wedding ceremony, but that doesn't change the fact that they're a couple, every bit as much as Dante and Charlie. So, Zan is definitely your uncle and a part of this family."

"Okay, that makes sense. But then, why do we always say Uncle Yoshi?"

"Because he's a member of this family, too."

"He is for sure. But like, if you and he ever got married, would I still call him my uncle?" Well, that had certainly come out of the blue.

I was startled when Yoshi said, "I'm not your dad's type, MJ." He'd been acting as bartender in the living room, and he grinned at me as he carried an armload of glasses into the kitchen.

MJ asked, "Why wouldn't you be his type? You're really nice and super handsome."

"Thanks for the compliment," Yoshi said as he loaded the dishwasher. "But I'm not his type because your dad's straight."

MJ said matter-of-factly, "No he's not, he's bisexual." Just then, the doorbell rang, and he exclaimed, "What if that's Jude?"

"Then you should probably let him in," I said, as I got up and grabbed two bottles of dressing from the refrigerator. My son took a deep breath and bolted from the kitchen. I thought it was a good sign that he actually ran toward the front door, and not away from it.

Yoshi dried his hands on a dishtowel and said, "I wonder where MJ got the idea that you're bi."

"I came out to him a few weeks ago, after he came out to me."

"Wait, so you really are...."

"Bisexual." Why did I feel nervous telling him that?

"Was this a recent revelation?"

I shook my head. "I've known since puberty."

He asked, "So, why did Gianni tell me you were straight when I asked him?"

"When was that?"

"A long time ago, before I started going out with Gale." Yoshi murmured, almost under his breath, "All these years...."

I asked, "Why did you want to know if I was straight?"

He answered my question with another one. "Why didn't you tell me you're bisexual?"

"It's complicated."

Yoshi's voice rose a little. "Is it, though? You just had to say the words: 'I'm bi.' Did you think I'd have a problem with that?" He almost seemed angry.

"That's not the part that's complicated." Before I could try to explain, a nervous-looking MJ returned to the kitchen with Jude and a blond woman who had to be the boy's mother, and Yoshi frowned at me and left the kitchen. Damn it.

Claire Leno did the parental due diligence thing, introducing herself and basically ascertaining that I wasn't a psycho before agreeing to leave her son in my home for an hour. They had plans that night, but apparently Jude had begged and pleaded and they'd reached the compromise of a short visit. I sincerely hoped at least some of his eagerness had to do with MJ, and not just the celebrity in my living room.

Dinner was ready soon after that. I served the lasagna and salad with a mountain of garlic bread, and my family mowed through the food like a pack of starved hyenas. Dessert was next up. I'd hauled my industrial-sized 'family gathering coffee maker' in from the garage, so I got it going, then plated the two massive sheet cakes I'd picked up at Costco.

As was usually the case, most of the party had shifted to the kitchen by that point, and it was total chaos. Mark and Mitchell ran up to me, and Mark exclaimed, "Uncle Gi and Uncle Zan said we can fly back to Long Beach with them and spend the night on their sailboat if it's okay with you. Please say yes!"

I looked around for Gianni to get more details, and MJ appeared beside me and said, "Jude's mom just picked him up." When I asked him how it had gone, he said, "I'll tell you later."

At the same time, Dante waded through the crowd and told me, "You're out of wine glasses."

"Check the dishwasher. I think it just finished."

Mitchell prompted, "Dad, can we go on the plane?"

"I don't know yet. Let me talk to Gianni."

Right in the middle of all of that, Yoshi poked his head in the kitchen and told me, "I'm taking off. See you tomorrow." I'd really wanted to talk to him, but I was up to my eyeballs in family right then, so all I could manage was a nod.

A few minutes after that, Gianni found me in the kitchen, and I asked, "Was flying the kids to Long Beach your idea or theirs?"

"Actually, it was Zan's," he said. "The plane we chartered seats six, and he thought your boys would get a kick out of it. We're going to spend the night on the boat and sail to Catalina in the morning. That should take four or five hours, so we'll probably get there before you do. We need to take off pretty soon though, because the pilot has another flight scheduled later tonight."

Mark ran over to us and clasped his hands as if he was praying. "Please Dad? Say yes! Please oh please oh please!"

When I hesitated, Gianni said, "You don't have a thing to worry about, Mike. You know I'd never let anything happen to my nephews."

The whole thing made me nervous, but I knew there was no good reason for that, so I finally relented. "Yeah, okay. They'll love the plane and the sailboat, and I know the boys are in good hands with you and Zan. Text me when you land so I don't have to worry, and make sure they brush their teeth and eat a good breakfast, especially Mitchell. He's been weirder than usual about food lately."

Mark jumped up and down and yelled, "Woohoo!"

Gianni said, "You're welcome to come with us, Mikey. There's room for one more on the plane."

"I wish I could, but I'm going to need to get all of this cleaned up," I said, as I gestured at my trashed kitchen.

"Plus, I have to work tonight. I have to make sure all my clients are squared away before I take off for a week."

My brother looked sympathetic. "I wish I could stay and help, but our car and driver will be here any minute."

"It's fine." I turned to Mark, who was doing a happy dance, and said, "I need you to find MJ and Mitchell. All three of you need to go upstairs right away, put on your shoes and jackets, and get the duffel bags and backpacks that are in your rooms. You have one of each, and they're all packed for our week on Catalina. Uncle Gianni is almost ready to leave, so if you want to go with him, you can't waste time." Mark gave me a quick salute and sprinted from the kitchen, yelling his brothers' names.

Barely five minutes later, I crushed each of my kids in an embrace before they ran to the waiting town car. "See you tomorrow when you get to Catalina," Gianni said as he gave me a hug. "Expect lots of texts and photos in the meantime."

The rest of my guests took their departure as a cue that the party was over, and they all filtered out with hugs, kisses, and promises to see me soon. Since most of them were coming along to Catalina, soon actually meant ten a.m. the next day, when we'd all be boarding Dante's party bus for the drive to southern California. I waved goodbye before closing the front door behind them, then swept through the living room and gathered stray plates and glasses before heading to the kitchen.

There I found Dante and Charlie cleaning up, and I said, "Thanks for helping, guys."

Charlie took the dishes from me and loaded them into the dishwasher. His green eyes crinkled at the corners as he smiled at me and said, "We're happy to help."

"I noticed Yoshi left early," Dante said as he ran a damp cloth over the counter. "He didn't look very happy. Did you two have a fight or something?"

"I actually don't know what happened. MJ mentioned the fact that I'm bisexual in front of him, and then things got weird for some reason."

Dante asked, "Did you talk to him about it?"

"I didn't have a chance. The party was too hectic, and before I knew it, he took off. We'll have plenty of time to talk tomorrow though, on the drive to Long Beach. What's that going to take, about six hours?"

"More or less, depending on traffic," Dante said as he rolled down his sleeves and buttoned the cuffs of his gray dress shirt. "I'm proud of you for letting the boys fly down with Gi and Zan, by the way. That probably wasn't easy for you, given how overprotective you are."

"I'm not *over*protective, just normal Dad-level protective," I said as I pulled the overstuffed garbage bag out of the trash can. "It did actually make me nervous to send them off without me, but I didn't want them to miss out on a pretty unique experience."

"Well, we'll get out of here and let you enjoy the rarity of a night all to yourself." Dante pulled on his suit jacket and nuzzled his husband's dark hair, and Charlie turned to him and smiled.

As they headed for the door, Charlie asked, "So, how are you going to spend your first kid-free night in ages? I'm picturing you watching R-rated movies, smoking cigars, and drinking whiskey."

"Close. I'm going to make spreadsheets, put together invoices, and break in my new accounting software," I told him.

Dante chuckled and quipped, "Nobody parties like an accountant."

I followed them out and tossed the trash, then gave them a little wave as they headed for their car. When I got back inside, I went around the house and locked up before returning to the kitchen. As I washed my hands, I realized I was absolutely starving, since I'd been too busy to eat anything during the party.

There was a single piece of cake left, which was kind of a miracle given my family, and a little bit of salad. After a quick internal debate about what I should do versus what

I wanted to do, I sat down with the salad at the kitchen island. Then I sighed and looked around.

The house felt so empty with the boys gone, and it was way too quiet. I didn't even have Gizmo to keep me company. I'd checked him into the kennel earlier that day, to give me one less thing to do in the morning before leaving on vacation.

If only Yoshi had stayed after the party ended. That was what normally happened. I hated the fact that things were weird between us, and I still didn't quite understand why finding out I was bi seemed to upset him, unless maybe he'd thought I'd been intentionally keeping secrets from him.

After poking the salad with my fork a couple of times, I pushed it away. Then I picked up the last piece of chocolate cake and carried it upstairs with me. Even though I'd packed my sons' bags days ago, I hadn't even started my own packing. I took a big bite of cake, then left the plate and fork on my nightstand and went to the closet. When I reached over my head and pulled a suitcase from the top shelf, a small piece of paper fluttered to the floor.

I'd forgotten all about the flyer I'd been handed weeks ago in the Castro. The image of a bound, naked guy kneeling before a man in a suit was every bit as electrifying as the first time I saw it. I picked it up and studied the photo closely, as if it held a puzzle that needed to be solved. And in a way, it did. I wanted to understand why it turned me on like that.

There was so much I didn't know about myself, including some pretty basic stuff, like whether I was a top, a bottom, or a bit of both. Was I vanilla, or kinkier than I knew what to do with, as my reaction to that photo might suggest? That lack of knowledge embarrassed me. How could I be thirty-two and still so clueless?

Well, I actually knew the answer to that. All of my adult life, my needs and wants had been my last priority. The only release I'd allowed myself for a very long time was jerking off in the shower some mornings, and even that was done as quickly as possible so I could get on with my day. No wonder I was so out of touch with my own sexuality, after years spent pushing it aside.

If only I could have explained to Yoshi that there were so many reasons I'd never discussed my bisexuality with anyone. It wasn't just because I was a private person, though that was definitely a part of it. I also hadn't brought it up because it revealed a part of myself I'd never explored and barely understood.

I wished I could have told Yoshi I was in love with him, and that being in love with a man for the first time in my life was exhilarating and terrifying in equal measure. It opened a door to a virtual stranger who lived under my skin. Was I really prepared for what would happen once I let him out?

Chapter Seven

I answered my door at a quarter to ten the next morning and found Elijah shifting nervously from foot to foot on the front porch. "Hey," I said as I stepped back to let him in. "I'm glad you're early, because I found out we're one of the first stops on Dante's party bus pick-up route."

Elijah looked around when he stepped into the foyer and asked, "Where are your kids?"

"They went on ahead with Zan Tillane and my brother Gianni. I've been getting texts all morning from the boys' big adventure. At the moment, they're on a sailboat about an hour off the coast."

"That sounds…terrifying, actually, but probably not to most people."

I told him I needed a minute to make sure everything was locked and shut off, and when I completed a last lap around the house, I said, "Maybe we should wait outside. When that bus pulls up, it's going to block the entire street, so I don't want to delay it any longer than I have to."

Elijah nodded, and I grabbed my luggage and locked the deadbolt behind us. We sat side by side on the top step, and after a moment, he said, "I'm sorry I slipped out of the party last night without saying goodbye. It was just a bit…."

"Loud, crazy, and hectic? I get it, believe me. Did you get a chance to meet Zan?"

"No. I was only here for a few minutes, just long enough to congratulate MJ on his talent show performance. I was so scared for him when he froze up, but then he did an amazing job."

I smiled and said, "He really did. We barely had a chance to talk about it, but I hope he feels good about what he accomplished."

There hadn't been an opportunity to find out how it went with Jude either, and I had mixed emotions about that whole thing. On one hand, I wanted my son to be happy. But at the same time, I was having a hard time coming to grips with the idea of my barely-thirteen-year-old venturing out into the dating world.

Five minutes after we stepped outside, a dark blue tour bus pulled up in front of the house, and I said, "Well crap, Yoshi's not here yet." I sent him a quick text, and then Elijah and I jogged down the stairs. He climbed onboard with his backpack, and the driver got off the bus and opened the luggage compartment for me. After I loaded my things, I told her, "I'm still waiting for someone. Can we give him a minute?"

She muttered, "Not a problem," and got back behind the wheel.

I paced for a few moments and checked my phone. The bus really was blocking the whole street, just as I'd predicted, though fortunately there wasn't any traffic right then. A minute later, Yoshi's sleek, black truck rounded the corner and pulled up behind the bus. I didn't know what to make of that. He'd said he was going to take a Lyft, since there was no place to leave the truck for a week in my neighborhood, and my garage was only big enough for one car.

He met me on the sidewalk, and I said, "Hey. Did you decide to drive yourself to Long Beach instead of spending six hours trapped on a bus with my relatives?"

Yoshi said, "I got a text a little while ago. Gale has a layover in San Francisco about an hour from now, so I'm going to meet him by the airport. He's en route to Los Angeles, because his band has been asked to make a guest appearance on one of the late night talk shows."

Anger, jealousy, and a tangle of other emotions welled up in me, and I exclaimed, "Come on, Yoshi! Gale's an asshole, and he treats you like dirt. Why the hell would you drop everything and run to him, just because he snapped his fingers?" I was out of line and I knew it, but the words were out of my mouth before I could stop them.

Not surprisingly, that instantly put Yoshi on the defensive. "That's not what I'm doing, Mike."

"Really? Because that's what it looks like!"

"Why are you angry?"

I yelled, "Because we had plans! But apparently that means nothing to you, not when the total douche bag you call a boyfriend decides to grace you with his presence!"

He lowered his voice and said, "I'll talk to you later, after you've calmed down." Then he strode back to his truck, executed a quick three-point turn in my neighbor's driveway, and sped off down the street. Damn it!

I'd totally botched all of that and I knew it, but it absolutely infuriated me that he'd go running to Gale at the drop of a hat, given the way that jerk treated him. And yes, it hurt like hell that he was willing to cancel our plans to be with that asshole. But then, I'd practically pushed Yoshi into Gale's arms with my anger and jealousy, instead of trying to tell him how I felt.

I boarded the bus with a black cloud hanging over my head and went to the very back, barely acknowledging my relatives on the way. My pregnant cousin Carla was stretched out across the row of seats at the very back with a magazine and a bunch of pillows, and Elijah was sitting in the second-to-the-last row with a thick accounting textbook on his lap. I dropped into the row in front of his and leaned against the window. As the bus rolled down the street, Elijah asked, "Are you alright?"

"Yeah. I suppose you heard all of that."

"Everyone did."

"I totally blew it."

"You're in love with him, aren't you?" I glanced at Elijah, and after a moment, I nodded. "I'm sorry. It must hurt to see him go off with someone else." That was putting it mildly.

*****

The six-hour drive to Long Beach was painfully slow. I texted Yoshi twice, apologizing for the way I'd acted and asking him to message me. When I didn't hear back, I put my phone away and tried to make myself stop obsessing.

The bus was followed by an hour-long ferry ride to Catalina Island. While my relatives laughed and chatted on the upper deck, I sat off by myself and stared out at the water. I sent two more texts and again got no answer from Yoshi. Eventually, the island loomed on the horizon, and a few minutes later, the ferry pulled into Avalon Bay.

I smiled for the first time in hours when the ship docked and I found my sons waiting for me on the pier.

Mark ran up to me, grabbed me in a hug, and said, "Hi Dad. I'm glad you're here."

I gave him a big squeeze and kissed his forehead, and then I said, "Hi Mark. Are you having fun?"

He nodded. "You should have come with us. The plane was super cool! So was the sailboat. Uncle Gi let me hold the wheel. I felt like I was driving a pirate ship!"

"That's awesome."

"Can I get a way-up-high ride?"

He hadn't asked for that in at least a year. I felt a wave of nostalgia as I said, "Sure you can, buddy," then lifted him up and sat him on my shoulders.

Gianni, Mitchell and MJ caught up to us at that point, and the kids all talked at once about their adventure. Finally, when Gianni could get a word in edgewise, he said, "Zan went ahead to the ranch, for obvious reasons, and he texted to let me know they're making a big dinner for us. He took the kids' luggage with him, by the way." By 'obvious reasons,' he meant that his famous boyfriend would have gotten mobbed if he'd been standing on the pier when a boatload of tourists arrived.

I thanked Gianni when he picked up my bags, and then I asked, "Have you seen the place we're staying yet?"

"Nope. We've been exploring Avalon since we arrived."

"It's so pretty here," MJ said. "The whole town looks like a postcard."

He wasn't wrong. White sailboats bobbed in the tranquil, C-shaped bay, which was lined with a sandy beach. On the far right edge of the bay stood the landmark Catalina Casino. The graceful round, white structure with a terra cotta-colored roof looked exactly like I remembered it from my childhood. So did the town of Avalon. Candy-colored buildings, mostly shops, restaurants, and hotels, lined the main street and rose up the hillside, and palm trees swayed in the gentle breeze.

We waited for Elijah to catch up to us, and then we followed the giant pack of our friends and relatives down the pier. Mitchell ran over to the railing and said, "You have to see this, Dad!" I joined him and leaned over the railing carefully, since my nine-year-old was balanced on my shoulders and I really didn't feel like tipping over and chucking him into the bay (though knowing my daredevil son, Mark probably would have loved that).

Three vividly orange fish floated just a couple of feet below the surface of the emerald green water, and I said, "Oh cool. They're called garibaldi, by the way. We should plan to do some snorkeling while we're here, since there's a lot of interesting marine life in these waters."

MJ turned to Mitchell and said, "I told you Dad would know what they were called."

Elijah came up beside me, peered over the railing, and took a look at the fish. Then he murmured, "Oh wow."

We proceeded down the pier, and Mark called from up above me, "Where's Uncle Yoshi?"

I adjusted my grip on his skinny legs and said, "He had a change of plans." That earned me a sympathetic look from Elijah and a disappointed chorus of 'awww' from my kids.

Mitchell turned to me and adjusted his glasses as he asked, "Is he going to miss the whole week?"

"I really don't know." That was a really upsetting thought, but rather than dwell on it, I redoubled my efforts to stop sulking and focus on my kids.

Two white trolleys with open sides and red fabric roofs were waiting for us at the end of the pier, each festooned with a hand-lettered banner which read: 'Welcome Dombruso Family.' I put Mark down so he could run after his brothers and climb aboard. Gianni stuck my bags in the luggage rack behind the driver's seat, and the boys hurried to the back to sit with Nana and Ollie. I called to them to stop hanging over the half-walls, and Gianni and I sat down in front, since the back was full. Elijah sat right behind us, clutching his backpack to his chest and taking in everything with wide eyes.

As I watched my sons, I told Gianni, "I hope they weren't too much of a handful."

He said, "Your kids are great, Mike, and I'm glad you let them come with Zan and me. They're growing up too damn fast, especially MJ, and it meant a lot to us to get to spend time with them." He and his boyfriend had visited San Francisco sporadically over the last three years, and it had been a while since my sons had gotten to spend a significant amount of time with their uncles.

Once the trolley was full, a guy in his mid-twenties climbed aboard. He looked like a model with his light eyes, dark hair, and muscular build, but he was dressed like a cartoon character in lime green skinny jeans, a straw hat that looked like he'd woven it himself out of palm fronds, and a form-fitting yellow T-shirt that featured a hot pink seahorse and the name of the ranch. He picked up a microphone and said, "Welcome, Dombruso family! I'm Beck, and I do a little of everything at Seahorse Ranch, which is owned by my uncle, Ren Medina. If you have any questions or need anything at all during your stay, I'm your man. And right now, I'm your driver, so sit back and relax. It'll take us less than twenty minutes to reach our destination."

As Beck fired up the shuttle and we began to roll down the street, Gianni slid his sunglasses to the top of his head, which pushed his collar-length black hair back from his face. He was dressed in turquoise shorts and a fitted white T-shirt, which emphasized his deep tan, and as he rested his sandaled foot on his knee, he asked, "Is there something happening between you and Yoshi? I know you two have been spending a lot of time together, but I feel like there's more to it than what I've been told."

I filled him in as concisely as I could on what had been happening, including my Valentine's Day revelation. That in turn led to the inevitable discussion of why I'd never told Gianni I was bisexual. I concluded by telling him about that morning's argument and saying, "So, basically, I'm an idiot. I shouldn't have reacted like that when he told me he was going to meet Gale."

"You're right. What you should have done is told him you're in love with him."

"How could I when he has a boyfriend? Even if Gale wasn't in the picture, there's no saying he'd ever want this to be anything more than a friendship."

"Except that he used to have a crush on you," Gianni said.

"When was this?"

"He mentioned it about three years ago, but I think it went back a lot longer than that. This was right around the time I met Zan, and a few months before Yoshi met Gale. He was really into you, but I told him you were straight because that was what you let me believe."

I sighed and looked out at the passing scenery. Colorful painted tiles decorated fountains, benches, and some of the buildings, adding to the already considerable charm. All the golf carts were cute, too. Most island residents and a lot of the tourists used them in place of cars, so they were everywhere.

We were climbing steadily. Once we left the downtown shopping district, the tidy residential area reminded me a bit of San Francisco, in the way the houses were nestled close together on the hilly terrain. The eclectic mix of architectural styles in Easter egg colors were also similar. Farther up, the hill turned steeper and the homes became mansions with sweeping views of the town and the harbor below.

It took just a few minutes to cross all of Avalon. Shortly after the land opened up around us, we turned left onto a private drive, passing beneath a wooden sign which read 'Seahorse Ranch.' From the back of the trolley, Mitchell shrieked, "Look at the horses!"

A corral and stables were off to our right, and straight ahead was the ranch. Two large, Spanish-style buildings were fronted with a series of graceful arches. They formed an 'L' around a spacious, terra cotta-tiled courtyard, which was dotted with several seating areas and raised planting beds. A dry fountain topped with a five-foot-tall seahorse sculpture stood in the very center of the space, and a waist-high wrought iron fence spanned the left-hand edge of the property, where the land fell away and revealed a panoramic view of Avalon and the bay.

Behind the main building to the right of the courtyard, several little cottages dotted the hillside, nestled amid trees and shrubs which looked like they were native to the island. All the buildings were white stucco with terra cotta tile roofs, and they were accented with painted decorative tiles similar to those produced on the island in the 1920s. The whole thing was just beautiful.

As soon as the trolley came to a stop, my kids dashed to the front, and Mark asked, "Can we go see the horses, Dad?"

I said, "Sure, but wait for me," as I pulled my luggage off the rack.

Nana and Ollie were right behind the boys, and she said, "We'll keep an eye on the kiddos, Mikey. You go ahead and get yourself settled." When I said okay, my sons and their great-grandparents hurried off the trolley and headed for the corral.

Dante, Charlie, and their fifteen-year-old son Jayden had flown down first thing that morning to make sure everything was set up for the rest of us before we arrived. Apparently their son Joely and his pregnant girlfriend Maya were supposed to arrive at the end of the week. I'd believe that when I saw it, since the nineteen-year-old wasn't much for family gatherings.

Dante and Charlie looked right at home. They sat at a table in the shade of a big umbrella, sipping drinks with Zan and a handsome man of about forty with a short beard and dark, collar-length hair that was just beginning to turn gray. Gianni, Elijah and I joined them. Meanwhile, Beck bounded off the shuttle with a clipboard and started assigning rooms to the rest of our party.

Gianni sat on his boyfriend's lap and kissed him like they'd been apart for days, instead of a few hours, and Dante said, "Ren Medina, I'd like you to meet two of my brothers, Mike and Gianni Dombruso, and one of our guests, Elijah Everett." Dante told us, "Ren owns this place. He built it from the ground-up, and I have to say I'm really impressed with it."

As Ren and I shook hands, he said, "A huge box was delivered for you yesterday, Mike. It's in my office."

"Thanks. That's almost everything I'll need for Easter, aside from some candy, which I figured I could buy on the island. I thought it'd be easiest to send it on ahead." I turned to my travel companion and said, "I just realized you haven't been properly introduced to Zan yet. Zan Tillane, I'd like you to meet Elijah Everett. You and MJ sang with him on a video call a few weeks back."

Zan smiled and said, "I remember. You have a wonderful voice, Elijah. I'm planning to do some vocal coaching and guitar lessons with MJ this week, and I hope you'll join us." Elijah was so starstruck that all he could manage was a quick nod. His dark eyes were as big as saucers, and I noticed for the first time that they were actually a unique shade of indigo blue, and not brown like I'd always thought.

I scanned the crowd that was milling around the courtyard and asked, "What happened to Vincent and his family? They weren't on the tour bus."

"They decided to drive down to Long Beach and catch the ferry on their own. They figured that would be easiest with two teens, two toddlers, and all their gear. Since they're not here yet, I'm going to guess they were wrong about that." Dante pulled a key from the pocket of his suit jacket and handed it to me as he added, "Speaking of kids, I reserved one of the biggest casitas for you and the boys.

They're the little houses up on the hillside. You can cut through the lobby to get there." He gestured at the two-story main building.

I pocketed the key and said, "Thanks. I'm going to drop off my luggage and get cleaned up before dinner. I doubt my kids will come looking for me since the horses have their full attention, but if they do, tell them I'll be right back." Then I turned to Elijah and asked, "Want to bunk with my kids and me? It sounds like we have plenty of room."

Elijah looked a bit lost and murmured, "Yeah…I mean, if that's alright."

"Absolutely."

He and I cut through the building, as Dante had suggested. On the outside, it looked a bit like one of California's Spanish missions. Each of my kids in turn had to build a model of a mission in the third grade, and I twitched a little as I remembered the mess that resulted from gluing sand onto cardboard to simulate plaster.

Inside, the building was decidedly posh. The focal point of the spacious, high-ceilinged lobby was an enormous double-sided fireplace, and beyond that was a bar and dining room. Orange upholstered furniture added spots of color to the white-and-neutral color palette. We exited through a set of glass doors at the back of the building and followed a meandering brick path up the hill to the third casita on the right. Beside each of the dozen little houses was a pair of hammocks. My kids were going to love them.

I let us in and cut through the cozy, earth-toned living room, then found the boys' luggage lined up in one of the three bedrooms, which held two sets of bunk beds. Elijah ducked into a room with two twin beds, right across from the kids' room. After I put my luggage in the master bedroom at the end of the hall, I checked my phone for about the five hundredth time that day.

I'd sent Yoshi several texts over the past few hours, apologizing and asking him to call me. Sending yet another message would be pathetic. Since he hadn't responded, that had to mean he was either pissed off at me or busy with Gale. The latter made me cringe.

I made myself put away the phone, and then I used the facilities and washed my face and hands. I'd decided to forego shaving since I was on vacation and frowned at my reflection in the mirror above the sink. At the rate my beard grew, I'd look like a lumberjack by the end of the week.

After I pulled a jacket over my white polo shirt, I found Elijah in the living room, studying a painting of cowboys, which was above the fireplace. I said, "Are you okay with these arrangements? It's perfectly fine if you'd prefer a room by yourself in one of the main buildings."

"No, this is good," he said. "I'm more comfortable staying with you guys than on my own."

"Great. In that case, come help me round up my kids. It's close to dinnertime, and it won't be easy to pry them away from the horses."

My young friend followed me out of the little house and back down the hill. When we returned to the courtyard, I spotted my brother Vincent. He and his husband Trevor were schlepping huge armloads of luggage and following their son Josh and Josh's boyfriend Darwin, who were each carrying a sleeping toddler. Elijah said, "Looks like your family's complete now."

I murmured, "Almost," and fought the urge to check my phone yet again to see if Yoshi had sent me a message.

*****

Later that night, after the rest of my family went to bed, I wandered to the edge of the property. Three steps led down to a narrow patio, which was softly lit by rustic-looking electric lanterns hung from wrought iron posts. The patio extended over the cliff's edge and overlooked all of Avalon in the distance, and the beautiful Catalina Casino stood like a beacon on the opposite side of the C-shaped bay.

A light breeze stirred my hair as I sighed quietly. It had been a nearly flawless evening. I got to spend time with my family in an absolutely wonderful setting. We'd feasted and visited and shared stories while my kids played tag and hide and seek, like they used to when they were younger. It would have been the perfect start to our vacation, if not for one thing.

Once again, I took my phone from my jacket pocket and checked my messages. I hadn't heard a word from Yoshi all day, and with every hour that passed, I grew more worried that I'd done real damage to our friendship by the way I'd acted. After a pause, I dialed his number. I knew it was pathetic to leave that many messages in one day, but I had to try to make things right between us.

The call went straight to voicemail, and I said, "Please call me, Yoshi. We need to talk, not just about this morning, but about a lot of things. I'm sorry for losing my temper. Please…just call me."

That had sounded fairly desperate, but I didn't care. I stared at the phone for a few seconds after I disconnected, willing it to ring. Finally, I returned it to my pocket and leaned against the iron railing at the edge of the patio, staring unseeingly at that panoramic view.

A few minutes later, a cab pulled into the circular driveway twenty feet to my left. I was stunned when Yoshi climbed out of the backseat. He smiled when he spotted me and slung a black leather duffel bag over his shoulder. As the cab pulled away, he walked over to me and said, "I just got quite the island history lesson from the cab driver. Did you know the casino has never actually been used for gambling? The word casino means 'gathering place' in Italian. There's a ballroom and a movie theater in the building, but no gaming tables, damn it. I was all set to get my Monte Carlo on."

He came to a stop at the top of the stairs, and I murmured, "I just tried calling you."

"I forgot my charging cord at home, so my phone died sometime around noon. I'll have to buy a new one while we're here. Or maybe I won't. I'm not sure I care what the outside world has to say this week."

I asked, "How did you get here? The last ferry from the mainland left hours ago."

"I found a guy with a boat and paid him two hundred bucks to bring me over."

"Oh." I was nervous, maybe because I didn't know where we stood after that morning, and I flailed around for something to say. After a moment, I asked, "So, how did it go with Gale?" Why did I say that? It was the last thing I wanted to talk about.

"It went great." That felt like a kick in the gut, but then he said, "After I broke up with him, we talked for nearly three hours. It was actually the best conversation we ever had, and I think we're going to end up being good friends."

I repeated, "You broke up with him?" Yoshi nodded. As my pulse sped up, I wandered to the foot of the stairs and stammered, "Why?"

"Because I want to be with someone else, Mike."

He put his bag on the ground and descended two of the three steps. Then he stopped and grinned a little. My heart was pounding in my ears, and I looked up at him and murmured, "You do?"

"Yeah, I really do. I've known this person forever, and I've always thought he was absolutely extraordinary. But I also thought I had to put aside my feelings for him, because I wasn't his type. I found out recently that I might actually have a shot with this guy, and since I want to take that shot more than anything, I knew it was time for Gale and me to go our separate ways."

I whispered, "God, I hope that guy is me."

Yoshi took my face between his hands and said, "Of course it's you, Mike. It's always been you." And then his lips met mine.

That kiss was a revelation. It was like the first vital breath of air after being underwater far too long. It was everything.

Yoshi took his time. He kissed me as if he was savoring me, and I sank into it. I lost myself in that kiss. I found myself in it, too.

I'd never been kissed like that. Not once. What set it apart wasn't that it was my first kiss with a man, but that it was uniquely Yoshi. He kissed me the same way he did everything, with bold confidence, and the message behind it was as clear as if he'd actually said the words: *you're mine.*

When the kiss finally ended and he drew me into his arms, I murmured, "I'm sorry about this morning. I didn't mean to yell."

"I get why you were upset."

I nuzzled his neck as I held onto him. His clean scent was both familiar and comforting, and I breathed him in. "This changes everything," I said after a while, as I put my head on his shoulder. "You know that, right?"

"I know." He kissed my hair and asked, "Are you ready for that?"

I met his gaze in the soft glow of the lantern light. "I want to be. I'd be lying if I said I wasn't scared, though."

Yoshi took my hand and said, "Come on, let's find a place to sit and talk."

He picked up his bag, and we circled around behind the buildings, then climbed the hill to my little cottage. Instead of going inside, we went to the pair of hammocks. Yoshi put his bag in one, and we tried to climb into the other. It was pretty unstable, and we had to hold back our laughter to avoid waking my family as we rocked and swayed and tried not to flip over.

When we were finally settled in, I slipped my hand under the open flap of his black leather jacket and felt his heartbeat through the thin fabric of his T-shirt. Yoshi put his arm around my shoulders and kissed me again, and then he murmured, "I wanted to do that for such a long time."

"I did, too."

"Why didn't you tell me how you felt?" We spoke softly, because it was so quiet. The only sound was the breeze rustling the palm trees overhead.

I said, "Because you had a boyfriend."

"Kind of, but that wasn't a real relationship by most definitions."

"I'm curious why you stayed with him that long, even though he was always disappointing you."

"For the first two years, I was fine with the way things were," he said. "We got together whenever we could, and in between, I had plenty of time to devote to my business and do whatever I wanted. I guess I was a bit starstruck too, and flattered that a big celebrity chose me, when he could have had almost anyone. It wasn't until this last year that I began to realize I wasn't getting what I needed from him. But I stuck with it, because…."

"Why?"

"I guess I figured, if I couldn't have the man I really wanted, at least I had something." Yoshi met my gaze and asked, "Why the hell didn't you tell me you were bi, Mike? I thought we told each other everything."

"I've always had a hard time coming to terms with my sexuality. I don't just mean my attraction to men. Sometimes, I get turned on by things that surprise me, and I don't even know what to do with that."

"Can you give me an example?" Even though I felt embarrassed, I lowered my voice to a whisper and told him about the photo on the flyer hidden in my closet, and Yoshi said, "It sounds like you're a submissive."

"I don't know. Maybe."

He stroked my hair and held me a little more securely as he asked, "Didn't you ever experiment with any of the women you went out with?"

"No. I've only slept with one person in my life, and Jenny and I were both really shy when it came to sex, so there were no bells and whistles."

"Didn't you sleep with Marie? You two went out for quite a while."

"After a couple of very awkward failed attempts at being intimate with each other, Marie and I mutually agreed to limit it to kissing and cuddling. Somehow, we just didn't click as lovers."

Yoshi murmured, "Holy shit. I figured you were pretty innocent, but this is beyond what I imagined. It's not just that you've never been with a man. You've never gotten to explore your sexuality or figure out who you are."

I looked up at him and asked, "Is that a problem?"

He grinned and said, "It's an opportunity. We're going to have so much fun, Mike." An embarrassed laugh slipped from me, and I returned my head to his shoulder.

After a pause, he said, "It's weird. I feel like we're stepping right into the middle of a long-term relationship. Since we've known each other forever, it's as if all those awkward first dates and the getting-to-know-you period are already behind us."

"I know what you mean. Apparently Dante and some other people have thought of you and me as a couple for years."

His grin got wider. "You talked to your brother about me?" I nodded, and after a pause, Yoshi mused, "I wonder how your kids are going to react to this."

"They adore you, so I think they'll be thrilled."

"Speaking of your sons, do you want to go in and check on them? I assume this is where you're staying." He gestured at the little guesthouse to our right.

"It is, but I know the boys are fine. They convinced Gianni and Zan to do a sleepover. Elijah's staying with us too, so that's a one-to-one kid-to-adult ratio."

"That's good news. It means we can keep doing this all night long." He kissed me again, and I smiled against his lips.

Chapter Eight

We hadn't intended to fall asleep in the hammock, so I was a bit surprised when I woke up outside the next morning. I shifted slightly and noticed someone had covered us with a blanket. Yoshi stirred a few moments later, and when he opened his eyes and saw me, he smiled and murmured, "Good morning."

We realized we weren't alone when someone said, "Aw, they're so cute."

Someone else said, "It's about damn time those two hooked up. What the hell were they waiting for?"

Yoshi and I raised our heads to see who was speaking. Several of my family members were headed down the hill, presumably on their way to breakfast, and all of them were grinning at us. A striped brown cat was strolling past too, and even he stared at us on the way by.

A faint bell was ringing in the distance, and when Nana and Ollie stepped out of the little house immediately to our left, dressed in matching red track suits, she called, "That's the sound of the chuck wagon, boys! Put on some pants and come have breakfast. It's nice to see you finally realized you're supposed to be together, by the way. If you didn't bring enough condoms, let me know. I always travel with a big box, in case any of my boys need them. You know what I always say, wrap it before you tap it!" Oh lord. My cousins Carla and Rachel burst out laughing as they clicked past us in their high heels.

A few seconds later, the door to our casita opened, and Gianni and Zan stepped outside hand-in-hand. Since they didn't seem even remotely surprised to see Yoshi and me waking up together, I assumed they'd spotted us earlier and were probably responsible for the blanket. I got up and patted my pockets as I muttered, "What did I do with my glasses?"

"You weren't wearing them when I found you last night," Yoshi said. He got up too, and then he reached out and caressed my cheek. It was such a simple gesture, but it meant everything to me, because it was a reminder that we really had just transitioned from friends to something more.

My kids burst through the door, followed by Elijah, and Mitchell yelled, "Uncle Yoshi's here!"

He and Mark tackle-hugged Yoshi as I headed inside and called, "I need to get cleaned up, so go on down to breakfast with Johnny and Zan, kids, and we'll catch up. Also, try not to squish Yoshi."

I went back to the bathroom, used the facilities, and brushed my teeth, and then I stepped into the master bedroom and pulled a change of clothes from my luggage. The bed was rumpled because I'd given it to my brother and his boyfriend the night before, and I'd intended to sleep on the fourth bunk bed in my kids' room. I smoothed the covers before sitting down and taking off my sneakers. A minute later, Yoshi came in carrying his bag and asked, "How are we going to handle the sleeping arrangements? As much as I loved holding you all night, it might seem weird to your kids if you and I started sharing a bed all of a sudden."

"I'm not sure what to do about that, but I think we should talk to the boys at breakfast and tell them we're...dating? Is that what we're doing? The word seems a little too casual, don't you think?"

Yoshi came right up to me and stood between my knees, and as he brushed my hair back, he said, "We're redefining our relationship, but I suppose that's an odd explanation for kids. I do want to take you on a date, though. How about tonight? I know you're here with your family, but do you think I could steal you for a few hours?"

"Absolutely."

"Great. So, let's plan on having dinner, then doing whatever people do when they're on a date."

"You tell me. It's not like I have much experience with that."

"I don't either."

I said, "Really? But you've been dating since your teens, haven't you?"

Yoshi traced my lower lip. "That's a long story, and since a lot of people are expecting us at breakfast, we should discuss it later. Are you planning to shower before we go down to the dining room?"

"I showered last night, so I was just going to change my clothes."

He asked, "In that case, mind if I use your shower?"

"Go right ahead."

He took off his jacket and tossed it on the bed, and when he peeled off his T-shirt, a little sound of longing slipped from me. As my cock stiffened, I wrapped my hands around his narrow hips and rested my forehead against his chest. Yoshi stroked my hair and murmured, "God, I need some time alone with you." I nodded in agreement and rubbed my cheek against his smooth skin. "I'd ask you to join me in the shower, but then we'll never make it to breakfast." He flashed me a flirtatious smile before heading to the bathroom. Holy. Shit.

I changed my clothes quickly, went outside, and tried to calm down. Yoshi found me out there less than ten minutes later. As was often the case, he was dressed in a fitted T-shirt and jeans, both black, and he looked so sexy I could barely stand it. He pushed his damp hair off his forehead and said, "I thought you ran off."

As we headed down the hill together, I told him, "I didn't think I'd survive seeing you wet and naked after your shower." Yoshi chuckled at that and took my hand.

An enormous buffet had been set up in the sunny, high-ceilinged dining room. My kids were seated front and center at a big, round table, packing away pancakes like they'd never seen such a thing before. Elijah, Gianni, and Zan sat with my boys, and they were soon joined by another child and a couple named Quinn and Duke.

They were part of the extended circle of gay men Nana had brought into the family over the years, and they were a beautiful couple. Both men were blond with light eyes, but there ended the similarities. Quinn was a small, thin ballet dancer, and his husband was a very tall, very muscular police officer. Though physical opposites, somehow they seemed like two halves of a whole.

At Christmas, Quinn and Duke had taken in a little blond runaway named Aiden. Ever since then, the couple had been mired in the complex process of trying to legally adopt the twelve-year-old, whose parents had disowned him when he came out. The situation was complicated by the fact that he had some relatives who might be willing to take him, although from everything I'd heard, those relatives and the rest of the boy's birth family was completely toxic. I'd seen Quinn, Duke and Aiden at a few get-togethers over the past several months, and I knew for a fact that the three of them were meant to be a family. The thought of anything coming between them made my heart hurt.

That day, all three of them seemed perfectly happy, and that was so nice to see. Quinn and Elijah were friends, and they talked animatedly while Quinn leaned against his husband and Duke wrapped a huge arm around Quinn's shoulders. Meanwhile, Aiden and my sons laughed and joked as they ate. When we reached the table, Mitchell exclaimed, "Aiden and his dads are going to come horseback riding with us after breakfast! Duke doesn't think he should ride, because he's so big he might squish the horse. But you're pretty big too and you're going to ride, aren't you, Dad?"

"Um, I don't know," I hedged.

Gianni chimed in, "A horse traumatized your dad when he was about your age, Mitchell. Mikey and I were supposed to take riding lessons together, but on the first day, he became convinced that one of the horses was out to get him."

I exclaimed, "It was! That horse was vicious."

"Her name was Cupcake, and she was a Shetland pony," Gianni said, which gave everyone a good laugh.

Before I could offer a rebuttal, Mark turned to look at me, and then he asked, "How come you and Uncle Yoshi are holding hands?"

"Well, because Yoshi and I have decided we want to be more than friends. Actually, we're going to go on a date tonight. But first, we're going to spend the whole day with you guys."

MJ and Mitchell both looked happy, but Mark startled me when he yelled, "No! You're going to ruin everything!" He pushed back from the table and ran from the dining room. A hush fell over the crowd, and everyone watched him go before turning their attention to me.

Yoshi and I exchanged worried looks, and I murmured, "Be right back," before taking off at a jog after my youngest son. When I got outside, I spotted Mark just as he ducked into the stables. I slowed to a walk, because I wanted to give him a few moments to get himself together.

A skinny kid in his early twenties with shoulder-length dark hair was saddling a horse in the corral, and he glared at me as I approached. Awesome. I ignored the sullen stranger and entered the long, wooden building. The center aisle was lit with a row of rustic-looking light fixtures, which gave the place a soft, golden glow. It smelled like fresh hay, and a breeze blew through the building, since the half-doors to each of the twenty stables were open to the outside. A dozen horses shifted in their pens, watching me with intelligent, dark eyes as I passed.

Mark was at the end of the row, petting the muzzle of a medium-sized brown horse with a white stripe down its face. The animal leaned over the gate and nuzzled Mark gently. I stopped a couple of feet from my son and knelt down so we were closer to the same height, and then I said, "Hey. Can we talk?" He shook his head and kept focusing on the horse. "I need to know why you're so upset, Mark. I thought you liked Yoshi."

"I do," he said. "That's why I don't want you to date him."

"I don't understand."

He turned to look at me. "Can you promise you and Yoshi will never break up?"

"Nobody can make a promise like that," I said quietly. "Are you afraid Yoshi will leave like Marie did if things don't work out between us?"

"I don't want Yoshi to go away." Mark's voice shook. "He's a part of our family. Why can't you just leave everything the way it is?"

I tried to put it in terms a nine-year-old could understand. "Because the feelings I have for him aren't like the feelings you have for a friend. I don't know what's going to happen down the road, but I do know this: I'm going to try so hard to make sure things work out between Yoshi and me."

"But you could still break up."

"Even if we did, and I'm not saying we will, Yoshi would never disappear from your life, Mark. He just wouldn't. I know Marie promised to keep in touch, and then she didn't. Yoshi's not like that. He loves you and your brothers, and he'll always be a part of your life."

He muttered, "I don't like it when things change."

"I can understand that."

After a pause, he said, "I want to be alone for a while. Is our cottage unlocked?"

I handed him the key and said, "I'll have someone come get you when it's time to go horseback riding, okay?" Mark took the key from me and nodded, and then he left the stable.

I stood up and brushed some straw from my jeans. When the brown horse with the stripe bumped my shoulder, it startled me. I turned to face the creature and studied it for a moment. He studied me just as closely. When I tentatively held out my hand, palm up and fingers flat like I'd been taught as a child, the horse butted my hand with his nose. "Sorry," I said. "I don't have any apples." The horse bobbed his head up and down, as if he understood me and was nodding in agreement.

My moment of bonding with the big animal was interrupted when the sullen kid entered the building. He opened two of the stable doors and led a pair of horses out by their bridles, but not before glaring at me again. I frowned at him, then left by a side door and went to rejoin my family.

MJ and Mitchell were chatting happily with Aiden when I returned, and I was pleasantly surprised to see Elijah and Zan deep in conversation on the other side of the table. A few moments after I sat down, Yoshi appeared at my side and put a cup of coffee and a big plate of food in front of me. I glanced up at him, and he said, "You have a tendency to skip breakfast, so I wanted to make sure you ate." He bent down and kissed my forehead, and I murmured a thank you. It felt unfamiliar but also really nice to have someone take care of me, when that was usually my role. Then he asked, "Is Mark alright?"

"He will be. Right now, he's just afraid of what might happen if things don't work out between you and me. He thinks you might disappear like Marie did."

"That's what I figured. If you want, I'll talk to him after he's had a chance to process this a bit. I'm going to tell him the same thing you probably just did, that I'm not going to disappear from his life, no matter what."

"I think that'd mean a lot, coming from you."

He ran his knuckles down my cheek and said, "I need to talk to Gianni for a minute. I'll be right back."

Gi was across the room, chatting with Dante and Ren Medina. As I ate some scrambled eggs, I watched Yoshi move among the tables, chatting amiably with several of my family members along the way. He knew all of them. Ever since he and Gi became best friends in college, Yoshi had joined us for countless Thanksgivings, Sunday dinners, Easter brunches, and other holidays and family get-togethers, because he said his parents weren't the type to celebrate. I wondered if Gianni had met Yoshi's family, and what they were like.

My train of thought was interrupted when Beck appeared, holding a bunch of carrots by their lacy, green tops. He was dressed vividly once again, this time in neon yellow shorts, a purple Seahorse Ranch T-shirt, and red cowboy boots. The thing that really made his outfit though was the white, sequined cowboy hat.

He came over to my sons and Aiden and said, "Hey, mini dudes. Our ranch hand is getting the horses all saddled up for your ride. I'm going to be your trail guide. If you want to head over to the corral, I'll introduce you to your horses, and you can feed them a carrot. Once you do that, you've got a friend for life."

Aiden leapt out of his seat, his big blue eyes sparkling with excitement. Even though he was just a couple of months younger than MJ, I noticed he was nearly a head shorter. "I can't wait," he gushed. "I love horses! I love all animals, actually. I have a pet skunk at home. She's staying with Xavier while we're on vacation. That's our next-door neighbor."

Mitchell exclaimed, "Oh wow! Can I come visit and see your skunk when we're back home?"

"For sure!"

The two of them followed Beck out the door, but MJ came over to me and said, "I'm happy about you and Yoshi, Dad. Mark will come around too, just give him some time. Where is he, anyway?"

"He went to our cottage for a few minutes. If he doesn't come out on his own, will you go get him before the trail ride?" MJ nodded, and I said, "You know what? The last couple of days have been so crazy that we've barely had a chance to talk. How did it go with Jude when he came over on Friday night?"

He shrugged and said, "I found out he has a girlfriend, so that was a bummer. But he's super cool and a really nice guy, and I think we're friends now. I'm happy about that.

It'll be nice to have someone to hang out with at school."

That was so totally MJ. Even when life knocked him down, he still looked for the silver lining.

"That's definitely a good thing."

He said, "I'm going to go see the horses. You're riding with us, right?"

"If you really want me to, then sure." He flashed me a thumbs up before leaving the dining room. Once he was gone, I muttered, "Ugh, horseback riding. That's gonna suck."

When Zan went to join his boyfriend, Elijah moved around the table to sit beside me and I asked, "Are you going horseback riding with us?"

"No. I'm terrified of horses."

"I get that. So, what're you up to today?"

"I'm planning to read in one of those hammocks. They look comfortable."

"Did you bring along anything lighter than the accounting textbook?" He shook his head, and I asked, "Are you taking a class?"

"No. I just wanted to supplement what you taught me, so I can try to find a job as a bookkeeper when we get back home."

"Try to actually relax a bit, too," I told him. "Don't forget that you're on vacation."

Elijah grinned a little. "This is how I relax."

"Fair enough. Hey, by the way, I was happy to see you and Zan hitting it off."

"He's so nice. It's surreal talking to him, though. It's like, there's the face from my album covers, right beside me." Elijah looked self-conscious when he added, "He's trying to encourage me to sing, and he offered to do some vocal coaching with me this week. He thinks I'm talented."

"You are."

He wrapped his ever-present light blue cardigan around his shoulders a bit more securely and said, "There's no point in learning to sing, though. I could never get up and perform in front of an audience. The thought makes me physically ill."

"I totally understand the stage fright thing, but maybe take him up on his offer anyway," I said. "Do it for yourself. After all, how often are you going to have the opportunity to learn from a famous singer?"

"That's true. I guess I'll think about it."

Yoshi joined us a minute later. He was carrying a large shopping bag, and he stuck a white cowboy hat on my head, presumably to go with the black one he was wearing. "I don't know about y'all," he said, with a country accent, "but I'm ready to get on out there and ride those dusty trails. What do you say?"

I got up and said, "I don't think there's a way out of this, so let's do it. I'll see you later, Elijah. Have fun today." The blond gave me a little wave. As Yoshi and I headed for the door, I asked, "Where'd you get the hats?"

"There's a gift shop. I got hats for the boys, too. I was tempted to get myself a pair of leather chaps, but maybe those should wait for tonight." Yoshi wiggled his brows suggestively, and an embarrassed bark of laughter slipped from me.

A dozen saddled horses were lined up in the shade of an ancient-looking oak tree, arranged by size. Since Duke had decided to stay behind, I was the biggest rider by far. I assessed the largest animal in the line-up and asked Beck, "Are there any bigger horses? That one over there, maybe? I don't want to squash this poor guy." A huge black stallion was in a corral by himself, some distance away.

He said, "Sorry Mike, the black horse is wild. Nobody but Cassidy, our ranch hand, can even go near him. But this fellow right here can do the job, I promise you." He patted the neck of the big, brown horse closest to us.

"Are you sure? Because I can sit this one out if I'm too heavy."

He ran his gaze down my body and said, "You're what, six-foot-four, two-forty?"

"Just about."

Beck fanned himself with his clipboard and said, "Lord have mercy. You went back twice when they were handing out the hotness, didn't you?" He flashed me a flirtatious smile, but then when Yoshi joined us and took my hand, Beck said, "Oops, my bad. I didn't know you two were a couple, but it figures that you're both taken. The gorgeous ones always are. Oh well, some day my prince will come. Multiple times, hopefully." He winked at us, then crossed the corral and went back to the task of assigning horses to riders.

I turned to Yoshi and said, "I wasn't flirting, I swear."

"We might have just started dating, but I know you Mike, and I trust you implicitly. You never have to explain yourself to me." It felt good to hear that.

Mark joined us a few minutes later. He didn't really look at us, but he mumbled a thank you when Yoshi gave him his hat. Then he climbed on his horse effortlessly and trotted over to his brothers and Aiden, who were doing a few practice laps around the corral. The horses all seemed docile and perfectly trained, so I wasn't really worried about how this little adventure was going to go for the boys, who'd all had riding lessons. Me, on the other hand....

Beck held my horse's bridle as I stuck my foot in the stirrup and tried to swing myself onto the saddle. But I had way too much momentum going, so I tipped over and fell off the other side, where I landed on my back in the dirt with an, "Oof."

Yoshi appeared above me and grinned a little as he asked, "Are you alright?"

I chuckled as I got up and brushed myself off. "Well, at least I've gotten falling off the horse out of the way. Things can really only improve from here, right?"

Wrong.

I spent the next three hours flailing, bouncing, and generally botching horseback riding in every way possible. Despite my misery, I was still glad I went along, because I loved seeing my sons' excitement. They adored the horses and were absolutely delighted when we came across the resident buffalo herd.

It was surprising to discover that most of the island was wild and undeveloped, and when I mentioned that to Beck, he said, "A lot of people think Avalon is all there is to Catalina, but there's so much more to it. This is actually the part I fell in love with." He gestured around us. We were in a small valley between the hills. Yellow and purple wildflowers added splashes of color to the low-growing scrub and fairly dry environment.

I shifted in my saddle and gripped the reins tightly as I asked, "How many people live on Catalina?"

"Just over four thousand. Ninety percent live in Avalon, and most of the rest live in Two Harbors, northwest of here." Beck gestured with his left hand, perfectly at ease on horseback. "There are a couple of marine research and educational facilities outside the populated areas, but not much else. Around a million tourists a year visit the island, but the vast majority of them stick to Avalon. I like that, because it means I can come out here just about any time of year and find some solitude."

Just then, Mitchell rode up to us and exclaimed, "I saw a lizard!" Beck seemed as excited about that as my son and promised to take the kids on a nature walk later that day, claiming he knew the best place to spot reptiles. I tried to muster some enthusiasm and smiled at them as I prayed for the ride to just end already.

*****

When we finally returned to the ranch, my back and legs were killing me. I dismounted awkwardly and hunched over, then reached up and patted the horse as I said, "Good job, buddy. Sorry I weighed a ton."

Yoshi dismounted gracefully and rubbed my shoulder as he said, "Aw. I guess horseback riding really isn't your thing."

As the sullen ranch hand led our horses to the corral, Beck asked me, "Dude, are you alright?"

"More or less." I winced as I tried to straighten up and stretch my back.

"I know what you need." Beck produced a ring of keys, disconnected one of them, and handed it to me. "There's a spa on-property, but we can't afford to hire anyone to work in it, so it's just sitting empty. There's a Jacuzzi tub in there, so if you and your boyfriend want to go and soak for a while, I'll take your kids to the dining room for lunch and on that nature hike I promised them."

"You're a lifesaver, Beck," I said as I pocketed the key.

"I do what I can. The spa's on the ground floor in the smaller of the two main buildings. Take your time and have fun." He grinned and shot a knowing look at Yoshi and me.

"Thanks. Hey, maybe see if Elijah wants to join you guys for lunch and that hike," I said as I gestured up the hill. My friend was sitting outside our casita in a hammock with his big textbook, where he'd probably been all morning.

"On it." Beck jogged across the field and up the hill. I couldn't hear what was said, but I watched as he made several animated hand-gestures, and I was glad to see Elijah laugh and set aside the textbook.

I turned to the kids and said, "I need to go recover for a little while, but Beck's going to take you to have some lunch, and then you guys are going to go hunting for lizards." I handed MJ my phone and said, "Your mission is to get pictures of as many reptiles as possible."

MJ said, "Will do," and gave me a salute. Mark was still basically ignoring Yoshi and me, but I wasn't going to push it. He'd come around when he was ready. In the meantime, at least he was having fun with his brothers and Aiden.

Duke joined us and kissed Quinn's forehead. Then he asked Aiden, "Can we tag along on your next adventure?"

The boy's face lit up, and he said, "For sure! Come on Dads, let's go eat, and then we're going to go look for lizards."

My kids joined their little family. A moment later, Elijah and Beck fell into step with them, and they all headed for the dining room. Quinn challenged Duke and Aiden to a race, and the boy burst out laughing when Quinn cheated and took off before the count of three.

I watched them until they disappeared into the main building, and Yoshi touched my arm and asked, "Why do you look so sad all of a sudden?"

"I was just thinking how tragic it'll be if the courts end up denying Quinn and Duke's petition to adopt Aiden.

They're so happy together, and it breaks my heart to think about anything coming between them." Yoshi stretched up and kissed me gently, and I smiled at him and asked, "What was that for?"

"That's for being a kind, good-hearted person who cares deeply about others. Now come on, we need to get you into that tub, stat."

We waved to a few of my family members as we cut across the courtyard, and when I let us into the spa, I murmured, "Oh wow."

The space was tranquil and beautiful, with sand-colored marble floors and walls, high ceilings and soft light filtering in through sheer, white curtains. We found the Jacuzzi tub in a private room at the back of the spa, and while I got the water running, Yoshi went in search of towels. He returned a minute later with an armload of them and two bottles of water, and he asked, "After we soak, can I give you a massage? I found a table and supplies in the next room."

"You don't have to do that."

He put the towels on a teak bench and crossed the room to me. I was seated on the edge of the tub, and Yoshi took off my cowboy hat and brushed my hair back. "Because you don't like massages?"

"I don't know. I've never had one."

"So, you just don't want me to have to do any work."
When I nodded, he told me, "You need to learn to let me take care of you, Mike."

"I'll work on it." I checked the water temperature, then pulled off my shirt and said, "You're joining me in that tub, right?"

"I was wondering if you were ready for that."

"More than ready. Do you know how long I've been fantasizing about getting you naked?"

"Well, in that case...." Yoshi took off his hat, peeled off his T-shirt and tossed it aside, and put the hat back on.

"It's very cute that you're embracing your inner cowboy."

His dark eyes sparkled mischievously. "Glad you like it."

He tossed aside his boots and socks and unfastened his belt. I tried not to drool as he made a show of slowly unzipping his black jeans, then dropping them to the floor and stepping out of them. That left him in just the hat and a tiny pair of black briefs, which barely covered his swelling cock. I was so turned on by the sight of him that I had to adjust my own hard-on, which was straining against my jeans.

When Yoshi stripped off the briefs, his thick erection sprang up against his stomach. He was shaved everywhere, which was so damn sexy. I felt a little self-conscious about the fact that I was wearing tightie whities and was *au naturel* below the belt, but I was way too aroused to let that stop me from stripping myself quickly and slipping into the warm water with him. Still, I couldn't stop myself from murmuring, "I need to step up my game."

Yoshi turned on the jets, which frothed the water with a low whirr, and asked, "What do you mean?"

"You and I both look like we're ready to make a porno movie, but mine's from 1978." He chuckled at that, and I added, "If I'd had any inkling you and I were going to end up naked together this weekend, I would have made an effort."

"No need to change a thing. I think you're perfect. Stop frowning, I mean it." Yoshi drew me into his arms and kissed the crease between my brows before his lips found mine.

I totally forgot what I'd been talking about. As he reclined against the side of the tub, I straddled him, and when he rocked his hips a little, his cock brushed mine. I reached out tentatively and stroked his erection. Aside from some fun new equipment to play with, I realized in that moment that being with a man for the first time wasn't nearly as different or disorienting as I'd expected it to be.

Maybe that was partly because I loved and trusted Yoshi, so feeling comfortable with him was easy.

He tossed his hat aside, then nuzzled my ear and kissed my neck as his hand slid down my back. When he cupped my ass and pulled me close, I rubbed my hard-on against his, and he reached down and grasped our cocks with one hand. I kissed him and moaned against his lips as he began to jerk us off with his length pressed to mine. He let go after just a few minutes though, and I sounded breathless when I asked, "Why'd you stop?"

"Because I don't want either of us to finish too soon, and I was already getting close."

Yoshi dialed it back a bit, switching positions with me and kissing me deeply while he straddled my hips. I tangled my fingers in his hair as I tasted his mouth and marveled at the feeling of his body on mine. After a while, he leaned back and looked in my eyes as he asked me, "Are you ready for phase two? The bad news is, it means getting out of the tub. The good news: I took three massage classes, so I'm pretty good at it, if I say so myself."

"You sure you want to go to all that trouble?"

He kissed the tip of my nose and said, "It's my pleasure."

I smiled at that and followed him out of the tub. After we dried ourselves, I wandered out into the hall, still rubbing my hair with the towel, and asked, "Which way is the massage table?"

When I glanced over my shoulder, I caught Yoshi completely staring at my butt. He grinned and said, "I have no idea what you just said, because I was mesmerized by your bare ass." Then he caught up to me and took my hand, and he led me to a little room at the back of the spa with soft lighting and a little tabletop fountain that sounded like rain.

I tossed the towel on a chair and stretched out face-down on the comfortable padded table, which had been covered with a clean sheet. Yoshi squirted some oil on his palm and rubbed his hands together, and then he went to work on my upper body. As he kneaded the tension from my shoulders, I murmured, "That feels amazing."

I loved the feeling of his strong hands on my skin. He was thorough and meticulous, working every muscle group with just the right amount of pressure. I exhaled slowly and let myself relax in his care.

After my back and shoulders, he massaged my arms and legs. He finished up by massaging my ass. Even though he was no-nonsense about it, I started getting hard again. When he told me to roll over, I did as he asked and colored slightly because my dick was pointed at the ceiling. Yoshi met my gaze, and we both started chuckling.

Then he oiled his hands again and slid his palms down my abdomen. He slipped right past my cock and massaged the tops of my thighs before swooping back up and running both hands over my erection. A wave of pleasure surged through me, and I drew in a sharp breath. He asked, "Is this okay?"

I murmured, "Better than okay."

He caressed my balls with one hand as he began to jerk me off with the other. I bucked into his palm, loving the feeling of his firm grip on my cock and the added sensation of the slippery oil. After a while he asked, "Can I try something?" I nodded, breathing hard as I gripped the sheet.

His voice was low and steady when he said, "Put your hands above your head, Mike, and cross your wrists."

I opened my eyes and watched him while I did what he told me. He kept stroking me as he gripped my wrists and lightly pinned them down, and my cock jumped in his hand. My heart had already been racing, but it sped up even more the moment he held me down, and a little sound slipped from me that I couldn't begin to explain.

Yoshi varied the strokes on my oiled-up cock, working me faster, then slower. My head was spinning, and I couldn't form words. He brought me right to the edge of orgasm, then eased off. When he did that twice more, I cried out and writhed on the table. His voice was surprisingly soft when he said, "Look at me, Mike." When our eyes met, he said, "Don't cum until I tell you to."

I managed to whisper, "Okay," and then I moaned when he started jerking me off hard and fast.

My orgasm built and built, my balls tightening, my cock throbbing and pulsating, but I fought the urge to cum with everything I had. My body shook, and an inhuman cry slipped from me. I bucked my hips again but made no move to free my hands from his grasp. Finally, *finally*, he said, "Cum for me, Mike."

I yelled and arched off the table as the most powerful orgasm of my life tore from me. My toes curled and my vision was reduced to pops of color as I shot again and again, all over my stomach and chest. My body nearly convulsed as it just kept rolling through me.

By the time it ebbed, I was trembling, drenched with sweat, and gasping for breath. As I sprawled on the table, I felt Yoshi wipe me down with a damp towel, then a dry one. I didn't have enough energy to open my eyes. A moment later, I felt a soft sheet cover me, and Yoshi began to stroke my hair and speak to me in quiet, soothing tones. I couldn't quite focus on what he was saying, but the sound of his voice was reassuring.

It was a few minutes before I came back to myself enough to open my eyes and focus on him. Yoshi smiled sweetly, and I murmured, "Holy shit."

His smile got wider. "I think that's the first time I've heard you swear."

I smiled too and said, "I swear all the time."

"Hell and damn don't count."

"I guess I don't say the rest of it out loud." I sat up shakily, and Yoshi produced a bottle of water from underneath the table, unscrewed the lid, and handed it to me.

After I chugged half of it, I said, "I need to know: are you just extraordinarily gifted, or is gay sex always like that?"

"Unfortunately, the answer to both questions is no. Do you feel steady enough to return to the Jacuzzi tub? I used a lot of oil on you, so it might be an idea to wash off before getting dressed."

I swung my feet off the table, then stood up slowly on shaky legs. "I feel as if I just completed a biathlon." Then I snort-laughed and said, "*Bi*-athlon. That's the worst joke ever. In my defense, I didn't even mean to say it." Yoshi chuckled and shook his head.

For some reason, I dragged the sheet with me, wearing it like a sash as we returned to the other room. Yoshi added hot water and turned on the jets again, and as soon as we were back in the tub, he gathered me in his arms and held me securely. After I settled in comfortably with my head on his chest, I asked, "How could you possibly make me cum that hard?"

"I'm going to guess it was a combination of a few things, including the fact that you obviously hadn't orgasmed in a while, coupled with a dash of letting your submissive side out to play for the first time. Mostly though, I think you and I just have amazing chemistry."

"Can't argue with that." I kissed him and said, "It was one-sided, though. You didn't even get to cum."

"I really wanted the focus to be on you."

"It was. Now it's your turn."

I pulled him into a kiss, which soon turned from tender to urgent. When Yoshi responded, I ran my hand down his body and massaged his cock, which made his breath catch. As I felt him harden, I said, "Sit up on the edge of the tub, okay? I really want to suck you, but I don't want to drown."

Yoshi did as I asked. As the water ran off his strong body, I knelt between his legs and jerked him off for a minute before taking his tip in my mouth. I sucked him tentatively at first, but then I picked up the pace as I heard and felt him respond.

I caressed his balls as my lips slid up and down his shaft, and when our eyes met, his cock twitched. That encouraged me to suck him harder, and I tried to take an extra inch or two. Yoshi ran his fingers into my hair and rocked his hips slightly, which made me moan. He seemed to like that.

What I lacked in experience, apparently I made up for in enthusiasm, because in just a few minutes, he murmured, "I'm about to cum, Mike." He might have been expecting me to pull back. Instead, I sucked him harder and was soon rewarded with a sexy moan and a mouthful of cum. I grasped his hips and swallowed as he shot a second and third time.

When I released his spent cock from my lips, I felt a tremor go through him. Yoshi slipped back into the tub and kissed me. Then he cupped my cheek and rested his forehead against mine as he whispered, "You amaze me."

All I could manage was, "Right back at you," which didn't even begin to cover it.

Eventually, we drained the tub, dried off, and got dressed. We cleaned up after ourselves, depositing the sheet and towels in a laundry hamper on the way out the door. I locked up behind us, and then we both paused and looked at each other as I ran my fingertips over his cheek.

The day was bright and sunny, the sky impossibly blue. Several people were in the courtyard, just a few yards away. Their voices carried over to us. It felt like an intrusion, all of it.

I tried to shut out the light and sound and motion, the rest of the world, just for one more minute. I focused on Yoshi, concentrating on him intently. There was so much longing in his eyes as he looked into mine. He probably saw the same thing reflected back at him.

Everything had changed. *I'd* changed. My whole world had realigned in that quiet refuge. The unspoken thing between Yoshi and me, the thing that had been there, waiting, such a long time, had been transformed from fantasy to reality. We went in there as two individuals, as friends on the cusp of becoming so much more. We left as a couple, all that potential fully and finally realized.

I almost didn't know what to do now. I didn't know how to go back to the same world when I'd been completely remade. *We'd* been remade, he and I.

I wanted to tell him all of that, but I didn't know how. Somehow though, it seemed like he understood. Yoshi took my hand, and when he smiled at me, I felt a crazy surge of optimism.

Then we went to rejoin our family and friends, together.

Chapter Nine

That afternoon, Yoshi told me he had to get ready for our date and headed to town in one of the ranch's golf carts. Gianni was obviously in on whatever Yoshi was planning, given the fact that he wouldn't stop grinning. But he refused to divulge any information when I pressed him.

While my sons played a ranch-wide game of ultimate hide-and-seek with Aiden, I sat in the courtyard and sipped spiked iced tea with Dante and Charlie, and Gianni and Zan. The striped cat sat under the table, lazily grooming itself by licking its paw, then batting at the same ear over and over.

Eventually, Vincent and his husband Trevor joined us. Their son Josh and his boyfriend were babysitting Trey and Lina, the twin toddlers, for the afternoon. As I poured them some iced tea, Vincent adjusted his wire-framed glasses and murmured, "This is nice, all of us in the same place at the same time."

Trevor brushed his shaggy, dark hair out of his eyes and said, "Now that Gi and Zan are dropping anchor, maybe we'll have more afternoons like this to look forward to. Have you given some thought to where you might want to settle?"

Gianni nodded. "We're loving Catalina, so we decided to look at a few houses while we're here. We're keeping the boat, so we want someplace near a harbor but off the beaten path. This seems to fit the bill. Plus, it's beautiful here, don't you think?"

"It really is," I said. "Plus, you can sail up the coast and visit us whenever you'd like."

"Exactly. Or if we need to get there in a hurry, it's fifteen minutes by helicopter to the mainland, then less than two hours by plane to San Francisco," Zan added.

"If you do end up buying here, Charlie and I might be seeing a lot of you," Dante told him. "Ren Medina is looking for an investor to keep this place afloat, and we're seriously considering it. If we buy in, we'll be visiting the ranch a few times a year, since we'll want to be more than silent partners."

I offered to prepare a summary of the ranch's financial records, so they'd know exactly what they were getting themselves into, and Dante said, "Thanks, Mikey. Hopefully that won't take too long. I don't want to cut into your and Yoshi's vacation love fest."

Vincent looked confused. "What's this about Mikey and Yoshi? I thought Mikey was straight."

Dante shook his head. "Man, you're really out of the loop."

"That's your fault," Vincent told him. "You're supposed to keep me up-to-date on all the family gossip while Trevor and I are busy potty training twins and generally trying to keep a grip on our sanity."

I glanced from Dante to Vincent and grinned as they bickered. I loved the way Vinny was evolving. For most of his life, he'd been closed off and stoic. Some might have even described him as sullen. But ever since he met his husband Trevor, he'd gradually been opening up. He seemed so much happier and freer now, and I never would have applied those words to him in the past.

I watched as Vinny picked up the slender brunet's hand without a glance, as if he was hyperaware of Trevor at all times, and his husband said, "So, of the four brothers, two ended up being gay, and the other two are bi. Nana must be beside herself with glee."

I looked around and asked, "Where is she, anyway?"

"Nana and Ollie took Carla and Rachel into town for a full day of spa treatments," Gianni said. "She seems to be having a great time."

"That reminds me, she chartered a fishing boat for tomorrow," Dante said. "Everyone's invited. Since I despise fishing, I'll be bringing a full bar."

"Cheers to that," Vincent said, as he raised his glass. Then he asked, "So, how long has the Mikey and Yoshi thing been going on?"

Dante answered for me. "Unofficially? For fucking ever, although neither of them realized it until recently. *Very* recently, by the looks of it. I'm pretty sure they finally traded in their 'just friends' card during a visit to the magic Jacuzzi tub of love this afternoon. Am I right, Mikey?"

Vincent perked up and echoed, "Jacuzzi tub?"

"It's amazing," I told him. "You and Trevor need to check it out. There's a massage table too, and I glimpsed a steam room on our way out."

Trevor said, "Oh yeah, that definitely needs to happen. So, where is this Shangri La?"

I pointed at the building on the far side of the courtyard and said, "Right there. I returned the key to Beck, but I bet he'll give it to you if you ask him."

Vincent and Trevor were both up like a shot. "We still have two hours before the kids are back," Vincent told his husband.

Trevor flashed him a huge smile. "I think Beck is in the dining room. Race you." The couple took off running while the rest of us laughed. They disappeared into the main building, then reappeared a minute later, ran to the other building, and let themselves in.

Gianni raised his hand. "Zan and I call dibs on the spa when those two are done with it."

"Go right ahead," Dante said. "Charlie and I will take the overnight shift." His husband smiled and snuggled closer.

A few minutes later, my very sweaty youngest son flung himself onto my lap and announced dramatically, "I need juice or I'm gonna die of thirst."

"What's the magic word?"

"Please before I die."

I got up and followed him inside. Since Dante had reserved the entire kitchen for our family when he booked the ranch, I went back and helped myself to some apple juice, and then Mark and I joined Beck and Elijah in the dining room. As I sat down beside him, Beck beamed at my son and said, "Hey kidlet, are you having fun?" He was wearing a red velvet fez with his T-shirt and shorts. Obviously, hats were a thing with him.

Mark took a long drink of juice, then caught his breath and said, "Yeah, but I'm all hide-and-seeked out. I spent like, an hour trying to find MJ. It turned out he was in our cottage reading a book, which I don't think is a fair hiding place. How was I supposed to know to look inside there?"

I asked, "What happened to Mitchell and Aiden?"

"They decided to visit the horses again. I mean, I like horses and all, but those two are completely obsessed." Mark put his empty glass on the table and said, "Thanks for the juice. I think I might not die after all. I'm going to try to get MJ to put his book down and come outside and not be boring."

I called, "See you later," as he left the dining room by the back door.

When he was gone, Beck told us, "I have a surprise for the kids tonight. We have this huge, inflatable screen, and I'm going to set it up in the courtyard so we can watch movies." I thanked him for all he'd been doing for the boys, and he said, "I've had a great time. We don't get many visitors, so it's been incredible to see this place full of life and energy."

Elijah said, "I don't know why the ranch isn't sold out every night. It's absolutely beautiful."

"Nobody knows we exist. We need to advertise and build a website, but money's been too tight to do much of anything. Before Dante rented the place for a week, we didn't even know how we were going to pay this month's bills."

"There's a lot you can do for free though, like posting on social media," I said.

"I've suggested that and all kinds of other stuff, but Ren's response is always, why bother? His heart's just not in it. But don't worry, once Dante comes on board, it'll be two against one and Ren will have to start making an effort."

"Why is he so apathetic?"

Beck said, "Don't tell him I said anything, but my uncle built the ranch with his boyfriend, this guy named Simon. They were supposed to run it together. But after less than a year, Simon decided he was bored with all of it, and he left Ren and returned to acting. He's on some stupid sitcom now, as if that's better than building a future with my uncle."

"I'm surprised Ren didn't sell it," Elijah said. "The ranch must hold a lot of bad memories."

"Sometimes I think he stays out of sheer stubbornness," Beck told us. "Also though, he sank a fortune into building this place, far more than he'd ever recoup if he tried to sell it, and that was even before he bought out Simon's share. I don't think he can afford to do anything else at this point."

"Speaking of Dante, I told him I'd take a look at your financial records and prepare a summary for him, since I'm his accountant. Let me know when that would be convenient for you."

Beck looked worried. "You can do that any time you want, but I have to warn you, they're a disorganized mess. I've been acting as our bookkeeper since we can't afford to hire anyone, and I'm terrible at it."

"If you want, I can help you get your records in order," Elijah offered shyly. "I've been studying bookkeeping and accounting, and Mike taught me quite a bit. I think I'd be able to get you organized."

"That'd be amazing," Beck exclaimed. "Are you sure you want to spend part of your vacation doing something that boring, though?"

Elijah said, "This is going to sound dumb, but it'd actually be fun for me. I think everyone's going fishing tomorrow, which I really don't want to do. Maybe I can work on the books then." Beck readily agreed.

We chatted for a few more minutes, and then I got up from the table and told my companions, "I'd better go get ready. I have a date tonight."

Beck said, "I know, and it's going to be super sweet. I helped Yoshi with a couple of the details. I hope you have a great time, and don't worry about your kids. I know you have like, thirty family members here to babysit them, but I went ahead and planned a bunch of stuff to keep them entertained. We're going to cook dinner together, and then after we watch Willy Wonka, I'm hosting an invent-your-own-candy contest. They're probably going to be pretty sugared up. I hope that's okay."

I grinned at that. "I won't be here, so that cause and effect is all yours, Beck."

*****

Yoshi had asked me to be ready by six, and at 5:45, I was pacing at the edge of the courtyard and second-guessing my outfit. I'd gone with khakis, a light blue polo shirt, white sneakers, and a dark blue canvas jacket. I was pretty sure every single part of that was wrong.

Gianni came over to me and asked, "Why are you so nervous, Mikey? You've known Yoshi forever."

"But this is our first real date, and that's a lot of pressure. Also, look at me! I'm dressed like I'm going to do his taxes. I should have gone shopping and bought something sexy."

"Like what, a negligee? You look good, Mikey. You even unfastened the top two buttons on your polo shirt, which for you is practically risqué."

I adjusted my glasses and asked, "Is this outfit okay for wherever he's taking me? If we're going to a restaurant, I should change into a button-down and a tie."

"You're dressed perfectly, and you're not just going to a restaurant. Yoshi wanted to do something special for your date, because he's crazy about you, Mike."

"Is he?"

"Isn't it obvious?"

I stopped pacing and turned to Gianni. "But he just came out of a three-year relationship. Maybe he's on the rebound."

"He's not. You and I both know that wasn't really a relationship, it was an ongoing booty call."

After a pause, I asked my brother, "Do you think he and I have a shot at making this work long-term? It's almost impossible to imagine a man like Yoshi driving carpool, or packing sack lunches, or spending his weekends loading up the cart at Costco. How would his life and mine ever actually fit together?"

Gianni looked sympathetic. "You're overthinking this, Mikey. Tonight's your first date. One thing at a time, alright?"

"This is just how I am, I have to look at the big picture. I can't help it. I'm a dad with three young kids, and everything I do affects them."

"Your nerves are getting the better of you. Just breathe, and try to relax. If this is meant to be, you two will figure it out." I nodded and shook out my hands to try to release some tension.

A few minutes later, Yoshi and his golf cart pulled into the circular driveway. He was dressed all in black in a fitted V-neck T-shirt and jeans, and as usual he made them look effortlessly sophisticated. But he'd actually dressed down a bit too, at least by his standards. He'd replaced the boots he normally wore with black Chucks, and instead of leather, he was wearing a zip-up athletic jacket. That made me feel slightly better about my casual outfit, even though he looked like a model and I looked like a soccer dad.

He got out and handed me a pretty blue flower, which I couldn't name. Then he pulled me down to his height and kissed my cheek. His eyes were sparkling with anticipation as he asked, "Are you ready to go?"

I nodded. "I already said goodbye to my kids. They're in the kitchen with Beck, making homemade pasta. It looks like a flour bomb went off."

Gianni called, "Have a great time, guys. I won't wait up." Then he went to join our family in the courtyard.

It couldn't be that easy, though. Dante yelled, "Have fun, Mikey! Remember, lube is your friend! Did you bring enough rubbers? If not, Nana has some!"

My grandmother leapt up and exclaimed, "Shit, I almost forgot!" Then she rushed over to me, dug in the pockets of her red track suit, and produced two enormous handfuls of condoms. She thrust them at me and said, "These claim to be one size fits most, but I don't know. I remember when you were a boy, you had a tiny tootsie roll, much smaller than your brothers. So, these might be too big. Then again, maybe Yoshi will be the one wearing them. I'm not gonna make any assumptions about which of you is the peanut and which is the M and M." I had to take a minute to absorb her analogy.

Across the courtyard, Dante nearly fell off his chair laughing, and I turned crimson as I shoved the condoms in my pockets. I muttered a thank you and boarded the golf cart, and as Yoshi pulled away, he smiled and said, "I love your grandmother. Talk about accepting. She couldn't be more wrong about your size, though. Maybe I should tell her you're actually very well-endowed. Normally, it'd be super weird to say something like that to someone's grandmother, but I bet Nana would take it in stride. Hell, she might even throw you a party. Everything would be themed, of course. There'd be foot-long hotdogs, giant salamis, maybe even a pecker-shaped rainbow piñata full of XXL condoms."

"Oh God."

Yoshi glanced at me as the golf cart puttered down the private drive and said, "Don't be embarrassed, Mike. Nana's just Nana."

"I know. This just isn't how I envisioned our first date starting off."

Yoshi stopped the golf cart at the end of the driveway. Then he picked up the flower, which had been on my lap, and said, "Hop out for a minute, okay?"

"Sure, but…why?"

"You'll see."

I did as he asked and was confused when he drove off and left me there. But when he hit the street, he executed a U-turn and came back to where I was standing. Then he cut the engine, hopped out and handed me the flower again, and he said, "Hi Mike. You look great." He stretched up and kissed my cheek. "I'm really looking forward to our date tonight, so let's get going. Your chariot awaits." He gestured at the golf cart with a grand flourish, and I grinned and climbed on board.

"Much better," he said as he got behind the wheel again and started the engine. "I needed a do-over, too. I think I was much more suave this time." That made me chuckle.

He did a three-point turn and drove back out onto the street. As we rolled down the hill at about fifteen miles per hour, which was probably the golf cart's top speed, I asked, "Do I get to know where we're going yet?"

"If I tell you, it'll sound lackluster. You need to see it all come together to fully appreciate my vision for this date."

I left it at that and watched the scenery roll by. In just a few minutes, we were in the heart of Avalon, which was crowded with tourists. I said, "Oh look, a kite store. I need to remember that, so I can bring the boys here." Then I glanced at Yoshi and murmured, "I never actually stop sounding like a parent, do I?"

"It's sweet. I've always loved the fact that you're such a dedicated dad."

Eventually, we parked near the beach and walked to the water's edge, where a guy with a little motorboat was waiting for us. I considered it a major victory when I managed to climb onboard without tipping over. He ferried us out to Zan and Gianni's forty-two foot sailboat, which bobbed in the tranquil harbor, and I said, "Oh, nice. I'm glad we're having dinner on the Mariposa."

The elegant wooden boat dated from the 1920s, and it was a thing of beauty. The Mariposa had obviously been cherished by each of its owners. It was perfectly maintained, and despite some updates over the years, it retained all of its vintage charm.

We climbed aboard, and I was surprised when Yoshi unhooked the mooring line and started the engine. I asked, "Wait, are we sailing this thing? I thought we were just having dinner in the harbor."

"We're most definitely sailing. In a minute. I'm a little rusty, so I want to use the engine until we're clear of the harbor."

"Um, if you're rusty, maybe we shouldn't be doing this." I could hear the nervousness in my voice, and I was sure he could, too.

Yoshi took the wheel and smiled at me. "Have faith, Mike. If Gianni and Zan trust me with their baby, you can, too."

He had a point there, but I still felt nervous. That was amplified when we cleared the harbor and he asked me to take the wheel while he let out the sails. "Just hold it steady," he said, and I white-knuckled the grips.

He cut the engine, and then he unfurled the sails quickly and efficiently and tied them off. The boat surged forward as they caught the wind. My death-grip on the wheel tightened when it pulled hard to the left. After adjusting the sails (which probably had some cool nautical term that I was unaware of), Yoshi took over the task of steering. As he competently guided us forward, my anxiety began to trickle away.

There was something almost transcendent about sailing and the way it connected you to the raw power of the wind and the ocean. There was beauty in it too, from the graceful boat with its fluttering white sails to the wide-open sky and the endless green-blue Pacific. When a pod of dolphins leapt out of the water off our port bow, I felt exhilarated.

After an hour or so spent flying over the water and circling the island in a wide arc, Yoshi lowered the sails and went below deck. He returned moments later with a picnic basket, and as the ocean rolled beneath us and the boat gently rose and fell, he popped the cork on a bottle of champagne and filled two delicate glasses. Then he handed me one of them and said, "To us."

I clinked my champagne flute to his and took a sip, enjoying the sensation of the bubbles on my tongue. Yoshi and I settled onto a padded bench on the deck, and as the sun began to sink behind the horizon and the sky turned orange, I said, "Thank you for all of this. It's perfect."

"I'm glad you like it."

I took another sip of champagne and said, "I'm beginning to think there's nothing you can't do. When did you learn to sail?"

"I took sailing lessons with your brother in my mid-twenties, mostly because Gianni wanted the company. He always loved boats."

"Oh, right. I remember that now."

"Since then, I've kept in practice by renting boats once or twice a year and traveling along the coast when I need a break from it all," he said. "Nothing I rent is ever as nice as the Mariposa, though. This boat is a work of art." It really was.

He rested his hand on my knee as we sipped champagne and watched the sunset. The sleeves of his jacket were pushed up to his elbows, and after a while, I ran my fingertips over the black ink on his left arm and said, "You're the only tattoo artist I've ever met with just a single tattoo." I knew he'd done it himself and it was beautifully drawn, though admittedly, I'd never paid a lot of attention to it.

Yoshi glanced at me and asked, "Have you met a lot of tattoo artists?"

"Yup. I know ten of them. They work at your studio, and they're all running out of places on their bodies to add more ink. Though I'll admit, I've only seen them fully dressed. Now that I've seen you fully *un*dressed, I'm surprised you only have the one."

"I'm pretty atypical, I'll give you that. But I don't just have one tattoo. I have well over twenty."

"Are the rest in invisible ink?"

Yoshi grinned at me and indicated San Francisco's jagged skyline, which ringed his arm just below the elbow. "My first three tattoos made up this part of my sleeve. The rest of them have slowly been filling in the cityscape." Below the skyline, an angled aerial view of the city showed finely detailed buildings, streets, trees, and even tiny people. He turned over his arm, which still had a little open space at his wrist, and said, "It's a bit problematic, because I'm running out of room, and I'm only thirty-three."

"What do you mean?"

"This was supposed to be my entire life story." He turned his arm over again and began trailing a fingertip down one of the streets. "It begins here, with the studio apartment in the Tenderloin where I was born."

"Were you literally born in the apartment?"

He nodded. "My mom gave birth to me at home, with the help of a doula. When I was six, we moved down the street to this one-bedroom apartment, because the studio was too crowded. Here's the shop they used to own, and around the corner is the one they own now."

"I never realized everything in your sleeve has meaning. I just thought it was a cool rendering of San Francisco. What else is happening in your tattoo?"

He trailed his fingertip around his arm and said, "When I was a kid, I used to play in this park all the time. I

fell out of this tree when I was seven and broke my arm."
There was a miniscule silhouette of a child amid the
branches of a tiny tree. "Also, every school I attended is
represented, from kindergarten through college. Here's
where I met Gianni and we became friends." Two little
figures were walking across a portion of the San Francisco
State campus.

"This is amazing."

He turned his arm palm-up and continued the tour.
"This is my mentor's tattoo shop, and that's my tattoo
studio." He slid his fingers down a few inches. "There's
your grandmother's house. The only time I've ever been
tempted to add color to my tattoo was when she painted
that huge rainbow down the front of it, but I decided to
stick to my aesthetic."

I had to lean in close, and when I did, I spotted Nana's
Queen Anne Victorian, beautifully rendered and about an
inch high, nestled among trees and other buildings on his
inner arm. I asked, "What made you include her house?"

"Your family's been important to me for a long time.
Gianni started inviting me to dinners and holidays at
Nana's house within days of meeting me. My own family
never really accepted me, but yours did, right from the
start."

"They didn't accept you because you're gay?"

"My parents weren't thrilled about that, but I think it wouldn't have been much of an issue if the rest of my life had gone the way they wanted it to. Now it's just one more checkmark on the very long list of ways I've disappointed them. But let's not talk about that now. It's too nice a night to depress ourselves."

I returned my gaze to the tattoo, studying the details as I murmured, "How did I never know all of this was here?"

His tone was playful when he said, "Because you hate tattoos, so you've never paid attention to mine."

"I don't!"

"Would you ever get one?"

"Well no, but that's just a personal preference."

"It's because you hate them. Remember when I used to babysit your kids and draw pictures on their arms with those wash-off tattoo pens? It made you so twitchy." He seemed amused by that.

"Okay, I'll admit I don't fully understand the tattoo thing. But I want to, because this is a big part of your life. I really do like yours though, especially now that I know what it means to you, and because it tells a story. I just don't get it when people have random things permanently inked onto their bodies. Like, the other day, I was standing in line behind this guy at the grocery store, and he had a tattoo of a scissor jabbing into his neck, complete with spurting blood. Why would anyone do that?"

Yoshi shrugged. "Probably for shock value."

"Mission accomplished." I drained my glass, then said, "You know, I've never asked what made you decide to become a tattoo artist."

"I always loved to draw, and I was good at it, even from a young age. My parents thought it was completely frivolous and tried to discourage me, and I guess part of me listened, because I ended up majoring in business when I got to college. But then, after I graduated, I just couldn't make myself go through with the plan of getting an MBA and a job behind a desk. Around the same time, I became involved with a guy who was a tattoo artist, and I fell in love with the idea of creating art that meant something to people, that became a part of them, and that they carried with them all their lives."

I asked, "Had you ever considered it before then?"

"Just in passing. But through him, I met a sensational teacher, and everything fell into place. She became my mentor, and years later she ended up helping me open my own studio. I thought I'd found my life's calling."

"Are you and that guy still friends?"

He shook his head. "He moved to Seattle six months after we met, and we didn't keep in touch. It's funny how some people can be a part of your life for just a short time, but still make a big impact."

He refilled my glass, and I took a sip of champagne before asking, "Do you still think being a tattoo artist is your calling?"

Yoshi considered the question for a long moment before saying, "There are some things I still really like about it. I love the freedom of owning my own business and not answering to anyone, and I'm grateful that it's been successful. I'm a little burned out on applying tattoos after all these years, but I still enjoy going to work. I especially like the little family I've created at the shop."

"They seem like nice people. I've always appreciated the fact that they don't treat me like an oddity whenever I come in to do the books, even though it's hard to imagine a place where I fit in less."

"You don't feel like you fit in there?"

I answered his question with a question. "How many nerdy, soccer dad accountants come in for tattoos?"

"More than you might imagine. In the last few years, getting inked has become much more mainstream, especially here on the west coast."

"I guess it's just me then. I'm hopelessly out of style."

Yoshi smiled as he took off my glasses and slipped them in my jacket pocket. "No you're not. You're still just trying to blend in. I suppose getting a tattoo would work against you there, because it might draw attention to you."

He got up and kissed my forehead, and then he crossed the deck to the boat's cabin and stepped through the doorway. A moment later, soft lights came on inside and around the edge of the deck, and instrumental music began to play from hidden speakers. When he returned, he spread out a blanket on the deck and served the picnic he'd prepared.

We feasted on gourmet antipasto, open-faced sandwiches on thick French bread, and fresh fruit, and then we shared a thermos of hot tea, which went perfectly with the lemon cookies he'd brought for dessert. After he packed away the dishes, we stretched out on the blanket side-by-side and held hands as we gazed up at the stars.

The rolling motion of the boat on the water lulled me, and I murmured, "I could fall asleep right now." Then I turned my head to look at his profile and blurted, "I don't mean that this is boring. I'm just full and relaxed, and the boat is rocking me to sleep. That was a dumb thing to say."

Yoshi rolled onto his side and propped his head up with his hand. He rested his other hand on my chest as he said, "I knew what you meant."

I searched his face in the soft glow of the running lights that ringed the deck, and after a moment I admitted quietly, "I'm so afraid of messing this up."

"You can't."

I grinned, just a little. "I'm pretty sure I can prove you wrong."

He brushed my hair back from my forehead and said, "It's me, Mike. I'm the same guy you've known for twelve years, so there's no pressure here. I know we're calling this a date, but just think of the countless nights you and I hung out together in your family room, after your kids went to sleep."

"This feels completely different."

"Yeah, it does. But in a good way, don't you think?"

I nodded. "I love this. But I guess I just wouldn't be me if I didn't make it a bit awkward."

"You're too hard on yourself."

After a pause, I said, "You told me earlier that you hadn't dated much. How can that be?"

"Most of my adult life has been a series of pseudo-relationships, some of them fairly long-term. Actually, calling them relationships is giving them way too much credit."

"What do you mean?"

"I guess I should start at the beginning," he said. "I lost my virginity at nineteen with one of my college professors. Our tryst lasted nearly two years, but I was nothing to him, just a cute piece of ass. I broke it off eventually, but then I started a similar relationship with a guy my age. After that, I guess a pattern developed.

"I kept getting involved with emotionally unavailable men who didn't really want me for more than sex. When I met Gale, I thought I'd finally broken the cycle and found a man who truly wanted me." Yoshi laughed and said, "How stupid is that? I wasn't his boyfriend. I was just some guy he was fucking. But I let myself believe it was more than that."

"I don't understand why you'd do that. You could have anyone you want."

He said, "Not anyone. Not my best friend's gorgeous, allegedly straight brother."

"You mean me?"

Yoshi chuckled. "Of course I mean you, Mike. I was attracted to you from the day I met you, but you were married to Jenny, so I needed to get over it. After she died, your heart still belonged to her. It took years and years for you to finally let her go enough to even consider dating. But I still didn't make my move, because I thought you were straight."

"So really, I fit your pattern perfectly," I said. "I was just one more unavailable guy to fall for."

"Actually, yeah. You're right."

I asked, "And what am I now?"

"I hope to God you're the guy who finally breaks the cycle." He leaned in and kissed me, and then he got up and held out his hand. "Dance with me, Mike."

I let him pull me to my feet, and he drew me into his arms. We held each other tight, and Yoshi put his head on my shoulder. As we swayed, the boat did too, almost as if it was joining in. I tilted his chin up and kissed him, and when he smiled up at me, my heart felt so full.

*****

We returned to the ranch around ten p.m. and Gianni greeted us with, "Oops. I meant to try again to get your kids to go to bed. They had really compelling arguments for staying up when I tried to get them to go a little while ago."

"It's fine." Yoshi and I took a look at the huge, inflatable screen in the courtyard. About a dozen members of my family were laughing, visiting, and half-watching a movie on three uneven rows of seats, while Mitchell and Mark played tag around the seahorse fountain. MJ and

Aiden sat off to the side, deep in conversation, and MJ gave me a little wave when I caught his eye.

Yoshi said, "Aren't you going to ask if we sank your boat?"

Gianni grinned at that. "Your clothes are dry, so I'm going to assume you made it back to port safely."

Mitchell ran up to us and exclaimed, "Beck said we can sleep outside on the rooftop patio if you say it's okay! Quinn and Duke already said Aiden could do it. Jayden, Josh and Darwin are going to spend the night up there, too. Please say yes, Dad!"

"As long as you promise to listen to your cousins and actually get some sleep, then it's fine with me. Round up your brothers, then brush your teeth and change into some sweats. It might be too cold to sleep outside in pajamas." He shrieked with delight, then went to tell Mark the news.

Yoshi gestured at the picnic basket he was carrying and said, "I'm going to go unpack this in the kitchen. See you in a bit." We exchanged smiles before he headed toward the dining room.

"So, it looks like date night was a success," Gianni said.

"It really was. Thanks for the use of your boat."

"It's always been magical for Zan and me. I thought some of it might rub off on you, too."

A few minutes later, after the kids had been tucked in under thick blankets on the roof of the main building, I joined Yoshi at the bar. He was chatting with Elijah and a handsome African-American guy with interesting gray eyes, who wore his hair in gorgeous, tousled curls. Beck was working behind the bar, and he exclaimed, "Hey Mike! Meet my friend Sage. He's a grad student at the marine lab on the other side of the island."

I shook his hand and echoed, "Sage?" I wasn't quite sure I'd heard it right.

"What can I say, my parents are a bit bohemian," he told me with a grin.

"I think it's a really nice name," Elijah murmured. Then his gaze strayed to a slim figure in a flannel shirt, who was using a microwave in the adjacent dining room. I recognized the surly ranch hand and had to take a moment to recall his name, which I finally remembered was Cassidy. Elijah kept watching until the person took his food and left the building. He seemed strangely fascinated, and I didn't quite know what to make of that.

Beck tipped back his straw hat and interrupted my train of thought by asking, "What can I make you, Mike?"

I slipped my arm around Yoshi's shoulders and said, "I'll have what he's having."

Yoshi looked up at me and smiled. "This is whiskey on the rocks. You hate that."

"Oh. I do, actually. Make it a red wine."

After he filled my glass and I paid for the drink, Beck said, "Now that the kids have gone to bed, want to watch a more grown-up movie? I had a request for Jaws."

"One of my brothers requested that, right?"

Beck nodded. "It was Dante's suggestion."

"Figures. They think horror movies are hilarious."

All of us got up and headed for the makeshift movie theater. Ren Medina was coming into the building as we filtered out, and Sage's entire face lit up as he said, "Hi Ren."

The man muttered, "Hey kid," without breaking his stride.

When we were outside, Sage complained, "I'm twenty-five, not twelve. That 'kid' thing crushes my soul."

Yoshi and I got comfortable in the last row of seats while Beck cued up the movie. Meanwhile, Elijah and Sage went to start a fresh batch of popcorn in the movie theater-worthy red popcorn machine that had been set up to the left of the screen. A bunch of my relatives were gathered around a table in the far corner of the courtyard, where Nana was telling a story that had everyone in stitches.

I draped my arm along the back of the bench as we sipped our drinks, and Yoshi slid closer to me. After a minute, Beck announced, "Jaws is all cued up and ready to roll, folks," and my family members filled the seats in front of the screen. They were loud and enthusiastic, and they applauded when the movie started.

I was far more interested in the person beside me than the film, and after a while Yoshi took my hand and led me out of the courtyard and down the private drive. The gravel crunched under foot, and a breeze rustled the scrub brush on either side of the road, which looked silvery in the moonlight. The sound of laughter and applause drifted to us from the courtyard, which made me roll my eyes and mutter, "They always root for the shark."

Yoshi grinned at that. "Your family is truly one of a kind."

After a minute, I said, "I'm sorry we didn't have more time for our date tonight. I thought I should get back to the kids, but as it turns out, they didn't really need me to be here. I guess it's just hard for me to step out of dad mode for very long."

He stopped walking, and when I turned to face him, Yoshi told me, "You're amazing in 'dad mode,' and the love you have for your kids is beautiful. In fact, it's one of my favorite things about you. If the trade-off is less time for the two of us, then it just means we need to make the most of every minute we do have."

"I must seem so boring though, especially after dating a rock star."

"There's absolutely no comparison between you and Gale."

I muttered, "That's what I figured," and tried to turn away.

But Yoshi didn't let go of my hand. "There's no comparison because this is a thousand times better. I can be myself with you. It doesn't matter if I say or do something stupid, because you're not going to judge me for it."

I glanced at him and said, "That's nice to hear. You never say or do anything stupid, though."

"That makes me think you haven't been paying attention. I guess I need to turn it up a notch, so it's impossible to miss." He stuck out our joined hands and pulled me into an embrace, and then he started dancing the tango with me as he belted out 'Let it Go' in Japanese.

I burst out laughing. "What are you doing?"

"Embracing my inner dork." He sang the next stanza loudly and badly as we tangoed in zig-zags across the driveway, and then he said, "Mentally prepare yourself. I'm going in for the dip."

Before I could explain what was wrong with that idea, Yoshi swung me around and tipped me back. Since I weighed a hell of a lot more than he did, I fell over with a yelp and landed between two bushes on the side of the road, and Yoshi landed on top of me. He looked at me with concern, but when I started laughing again, he did, too.

When we caught our breath, I said, "You made your point. I really can't imagine you doing any of that with Gale."

"See?" He straddled me, and I pulled him close and kissed him.

We were still kissing a couple of minutes later, when a golf cart pulled up beside us and Dante said, "The family decided to send out a search party after we witnessed you keeling over and disappearing into the bushes following that…tango, was it? I drew the short straw, so I'm here to see if you're alright."

We got up and dusted ourselves off, and Yoshi told him, "We're fine, but we need to commandeer your vehicle."

Dante raised an eyebrow, and I went around to the driver's side and said, "You heard him. Hop out."

My brother stepped out of the golf cart with a little frown, and as I got behind the wheel, he asked, "Where are you going?"

"It's still date night, so we need to go do some datey stuff." I started the engine, and Yoshi climbed onboard.

My brother's frown deepened. "Datey isn't a word."

"But hey, look at that! You knew what I meant." I smiled at him, then left Dante standing there as we took off down the driveway and swung onto the street.

As we sped down the hill, as much as the golf cart could speed, Yoshi asked, "Where should we go?"

"Anywhere, really. I'm taking what you said to heart about making the most of every minute we have together."

We puttered through town, which was considerably quieter now that the last ferry of the evening and its day-trippers had returned to the mainland. I ended up parking near the little beach at the edge of the harbor. We left our shoes and socks in the golf cart and walked hand-in-hand across the soft sand. When we reached the water's edge, I pulled Yoshi to me and kissed him. He felt so good in my arms.

Yoshi swayed with me when I started to slow dance with him, and I said, "We need music."

"I got the last one. It's your turn."

"I don't know what to sing."

"Just go with the first thing that comes to mind."

I said, "If you insist," and started belting out an old song I used to sing to my kids about an ant moving a rubber tree plant. Yoshi burst out laughing, and then he began to sing with me while we attempted a gangly ballroom dance routine, box-stepping and swirling across the sand. Some people stopped and stared. Normally, that would have bothered me, but I was having too much fun to care.

Chapter Ten

By Friday night, after several very full days which included snorkeling, kayaking, boating, several horseback rides (ugh), and hiking, I was exhausted. So were the boys. Mitchell and Mark were piled on top of me in one of the hammocks beside our casita, and I told them, "Beck's cueing up a Pixar film festival in the courtyard. Think we can scrape up enough energy to make it down there?"

MJ and Aiden were in the hammock beside us, at opposite ends with their feet in the middle, and MJ muttered, "I can't move. You guys should go on ahead, though. Beck's starting with 'The Incredibles.' Mark and Mitchell love that movie."

"About the only thing that's motivating me to ever get up again is the fact that Beck is also setting up a make-your-own-sundae bar," Aiden said. "I guess I can walk for sixty seconds if it means ice cream."

Mark and Mitchell both perked up at that and tumbled out of the hammock, and Mark exclaimed, "I definitely have enough energy for a sundae!"

Aiden got up too, but MJ said, "You guys go on ahead. Dad and I will catch up in a few minutes. Try not to eat all the ice cream before we get there."

Mitchell called, "We can't make any promises," as the three of them headed down the hill.

Once they were out of earshot, MJ sat up and said, "I want to ask your opinion on something."

"Okay."

He hesitated before asking, "What do you think about Aiden?"

"I think he's a wonderful kid. Why do you ask?"

"Do you think he's too young for me?"

I sat up facing MJ with my legs dangling over the edge of the hammock and said, "No, he's not too young. You're only a few months older than he is, and you're in the same grade. Maybe he seems younger because he's short for his age and you're really tall."

"Maybe. So, you don't think it'd be weird if I asked him out on a date?"

After a pause, I said, "I'm going to play devil's advocate for a minute. Are you thinking about asking Aiden out because you know for a fact he's gay? Or is it because you really like him?"

"Both. I mean, he could still say no, but it'd be nice if the first time I asked someone out, it didn't result in me getting punched in the face."

"I get that."

MJ said, "I'm not just using him to practice dating, if that's what you're suggesting. He's been on my mind all week, which was surprising at first. I used to always think about Jude, but now all I keep thinking about is Aiden, and I really want to get to know him better."

"I'll talk to his dads and make sure they're okay with him going on a date. Then if you ask him out and he says yes, I could drive you two into town tomorrow. There's a movie theater in that casino building, and that might be a good first date."

"Actually…maybe we should wait until we're back home in San Francisco." He chewed his lower lip for a moment before saying, "This is going to make me sound like a total dork, but do you think you and Yoshi might want to double date with us? I just…I was thinking, what if someone says something when they see two boys on a date? Or what if they try to start trouble? I mean, I can defend myself and Aiden, but I guess I might feel better knowing some grown-ups were nearby."

It broke my heart that my son would have to worry about something like that. "Of course, MJ. Yoshi and I would be happy to double date with you."

"Speaking of Yoshi, shouldn't he have been back by now from his errand with Gianni and Zan?"

"He texted a little while ago and said they were going to stop off and look at a house. I guess their real estate agent called them about a place that's about to go on the market, and they're getting an early preview." There wasn't a lot of available housing on the island, and over the past three days, my brother and his boyfriend had already looked at everything for sale that met their criteria.

"I'm glad they're buying a house on the island," he said. "Between that and Uncle Dante buying a share of Seahorse Ranch, I hope that means we'll be coming back here a lot."

"For sure."

After a pause, MJ asked, "When we get back home, is Yoshi moving in with us?"

"No. We just started dating."

"Do you think he will eventually? Or will we move in with him? Maybe you'll buy a new house together...."

I told him, "We haven't thought that far into the future. For now, we're just taking it day by day and enjoying each other's company."

"Come on, Dad. You're a total planner, so I know you've given this some thought. What do you think is going to happen?"

"I honestly don't know, MJ. I wish I did."

He frowned and said, "I don't like not knowing."

"Well, as soon as we figure it out, you and your brothers will be the first to know."

He murmured, "Yeah, okay."

I got up and asked him, "Want to go get some ice cream?"

"No thanks. I kind of just want to hang out here by myself. I feel like I'm all peopled out after this week, if you know what I mean."

As a fellow introvert, I totally got it. I gave his shoulder a gentle squeeze and said, "Tell you what. I'll go down and make you a sundae, and then I'll bring it to you. I bet you want chocolate on top of chocolate on top of chocolate. Am I right?"

He nodded. "Thanks, Dad."

"I'll be back in a few minutes."

When I reached the courtyard, I found Gianni and Zan talking excitedly and showing some of our family members pictures on their phone. Yoshi came up to me and said, "They put in an offer on the place we just saw! It's gorgeous, and it has sweeping views of Avalon and the harbor. Best of all, it has total privacy, so it's perfect for them."

"Sounds fantastic." I kissed his forehead and told him, "I'm on a mission to bring MJ some ice cream, so I'll come find you in a few minutes."

"Carry on with your mission. I'm going to keep helping with 'Operation Shut Up About It,' so I'll probably be in the secret lair."

That was the ridiculous code name Dante had come up with for Nana's surprise not-birthday party, which was happening the following afternoon. Yoshi, Gianni, and Zan had stepped in to help with the last-minute details, and from what I'd seen, everyone had gotten completely carried away. But as long as it made Nana happy, that was all that mattered.

I took a look at Gianni's photos of a modern, elegant mansion in the hills above Avalon, and then I assembled and delivered a sundae to MJ. When I returned to the courtyard, I noticed Mark and Mitchell were both sound asleep in a pile of pillows in front of the movie screen. I covered them with a blanket and went to check on the party planning, but I was intercepted by Nana on my way to the staging area.

She put her hands on her skinny hips and said, "Something's afoot, and nobody will tell me what it is. I know you can't lie to save your life, so tell me the truth, Mikey: are they planning a surprise birthday party for me? Because I made it clear after seventy-five of those fuckers that I was done with that shit!"

I looked in her dark eyes and said, "I promise no one is planning a birthday party, Nana." Fortunately, I had the loophole of it being a 'not-birthday' party, so technically, I wasn't lying to my grandmother.

She actually looked a little disappointed. "Oh. Well, okay then." Nana perked up a bit and linked her arm with mine. "Come to the bar with me. I want to get one of Beck's specialty tropical drinks and talk about you and Yoshi." Oh man.

When we reached the bar, Nana climbed up on one of the barstools, and then she waved her bony finger at me. "Don't screw this up, Mikey. You and Yoshi are perfect for each other. I know you're Mr. Cautious, but there comes a time when you just need to take the plunge. I'm talking about sex here. I asked Dante about it, and he says you've never been with a man before. Do you need your big brother to give you a sex talk? I'd do it myself, but I gotta be honest: I'm not totally clear on all the particulars of gay homosexual lovemaking. I mean, I've watched some porn and read several gay romance novels to get myself up to speed, so I get most of it. But then there are a few terms I'm hazy on, like 'power bottom.' Do you know what that means?"

I muttered, "Oh God," and glanced at Beck, who was behind the bar trying to keep a straight face. He'd opted for a white canvas sailor's cap for that night's offbeat fashion statement.

Nana waved her hand dismissively and said, "Look who I'm asking. It's like expecting a nun to give me directions to a sex shop."

Beck offered helpfully, "To answer your question, Mrs. Dombruso, it's a person who prefers to bottom during sex, but also likes to take control. It's, um, actually what I am. Sorry if that's TMI."

"Call me Nana," she said, "and you're part of the family now, Beck, especially since my grandson Dante and your uncle are going into business together. You'll soon learn there's no such thing as TMI with us."

"That's way too true," I muttered.

Beck actually seemed a little emotional when he told her, "Thank you, Nana. Ren's been the only family I've had for a very long time, so that means a lot to me."

Partly to get Nana to stop talking about sex and partly because I was curious, I asked him, "What made you decide to follow your uncle to Catalina?"

He'd been mixing up a big, colorful cocktail ever since we'd walked into the bar, and he stuck a fruit garnish in it and placed the beverage in front of Nana. Judging by her delighted expression as she tucked into the drink, it seemed he'd predicted her order perfectly. Then he said, "There are primarily two types of people who live on this island: those who were born here, and those who are running from something."

I asked, "Is that true for both you and your uncle?"

Beck nodded. "Ren was trying to escape the pressure of running an IT company in the insanely competitive Silicon Valley. Me…well, I moved here to start fresh. I made some big mistakes in my early twenties. I don't really want to elaborate on that, but I was so grateful when Ren offered me a job and an opportunity to leave my old life behind."

Beck glanced out the windows at the back of the bar and continued, "I have no idea what our ranch hand Cassidy was running from, but I think it must have been pretty dark. He's amazing with animals, but he doesn't trust people at all. That includes Ren and me, even after three years, and after we've made every effort to reach out to him."

"Yeah, I'd noticed he wasn't exactly a people person."

While Nana happily sipped her drink, Beck said, "Speaking of moving to the island, I wanted to ask your opinion on something, Mike. Your friend Elijah did a terrific job getting our financial records in order this past week, so I'm thinking about offering him a position as our bookkeeper. I know you're an accountant, so what do you think? Is he up to the task, even though he's never worked in the field before? I guess I'm asking because he seems so young."

"Elijah might be young, but he's in no way a typical twenty-year-old. He skipped a couple of grades in high school and recently graduated with a degree in mathematics from a prestigious university. He was there on a full scholarship created specifically for him, because he's literally a genius. Don't ever call him that though, because it makes him uncomfortable. Could he do the job as your bookkeeper? Without a doubt. He can do absolutely anything he puts his mind to. Just don't expect him to stick around forever, because Elijah was meant for far greater things than accounting. It'd actually be tragic if he ended up like me."

I felt a light touch on my shoulder, and when I turned around, I was surprised to see Elijah standing there. He said softly, "I'd be lucky to end up like you, Mike. I really admire you."

I murmured, "I didn't know you were there."

"I just came in. I was helping Dante and Charlie with a few things." He glanced at Nana, but she was still engrossed in that huge cocktail. Then he asked, "Why were you guys talking about me?"

Beck said, "Because I want to offer you a job as our bookkeeper, and since Mike's known you a lot longer than I have, I thought I'd get his opinion on that. Sorry to talk about you behind your back, that wasn't very cool of me."

"It's fine." Elijah looked surprised. "You really want to offer me a job?"

Beck nodded. "It'd be part-time, room and board included. We can negotiate the salary, if you're interested. Since we finally have an investor, Ren agreed that we need to hire a few people, including a cook, a housekeeper, and someone to handle the books. We might even be able to get the spa up and running. That's all in anticipation of finally being able to advertise and hopefully start bringing in some customers."

"Thanks for the offer," Elijah said. "I'll have to think about it, but I'll let you know soon, okay?" Then he glanced out the window, toward the stables. I knew the horses didn't hold any interest for him, so I wondered if his thoughts had turned to the dark-haired ranch hand.

Beck told him to take his time, and Nana finished her drink and exclaimed, "That was fantastic! You know, you're quite the mixologist. What else do you have up your sleeve?"

While he went to work on another cocktail, I put a couple of bills on the bar to cover my grandmother's tab and said, "I'm going to go see what Yoshi's up to. I'll talk to you both later. Elijah, could you show me where he is?"

My friend and I left the bar, and as we headed to the other building, he asked, "Do you really think I could do that job? It was pretty easy to get their financial records in order this week, because all I really had to do was plug the information into that accounting software you told me about. But you know how inexperienced I am. What will I do if I run into a problem and don't know how to solve it?"

"You'll call me," I said. "I'm always available to lend a hand."

"Thanks, Mike. But what happens when it's tax time? I wouldn't even know where to begin."

"They probably already have someone who prepares their taxes, so I assume they just want you for the day-to-day recordkeeping." I glanced at him and said, "The real question is, do you want the job?"

"Maybe. I love the ranch, and I feel good here. Also, I really like Beck. He's become a good friend over this past week."

"It's a huge change, though. Do you think you're ready for that?"

"Even though I'll miss the family I live with, I always had a hard time coping with San Francisco. It's just too much of everything: too many people, too much noise, too much traffic. Catalina is like a different world. I know Avalon gets crowded during the tourist season, but the ranch and the island's interior are so peaceful."

"It might seem less peaceful once the ranch starts advertising. Would you like it as much if it was sold out every night?"

"It's been busy with your family here, but when it's gotten to be too much, all I've had to do was take a short walk, and then I was all by myself out in nature. That's impossible in San Francisco."

"It sounds like you're going to take the job."

"I'm definitely considering it." Elijah glanced at me and grinned a little. "But you know I never make decisions quickly."

"Which is good," I told him, as we headed to the second floor of the building. "This one's definitely life-changing."

"Completely. But maybe that's exactly what I need."

When we reached the hotel room that had become the staging area for Nana's party, I did the secret knock and rolled my eyes. Dante let us in, and Elijah immediately veered off to the left to help Jayden wrestle a big picture into a frame. I headed right and wrapped my arms around Yoshi's shoulders, and I told him, "I've seen far too little of you today."

He turned to face me and slid his hands around my waist. "We need a midnight rendezvous. Come to my hotel room tonight, after the kids are asleep."

I smiled and said, "Yes, please."

*****

A couple of hours later, all three boys were tucked in and sound asleep in our little cottage. Elijah was reading on the sofa and agreed to keep an eye on things, so I slipped out quietly and headed to the second floor of the main building. As much as I'd wanted Yoshi to share my bed during our vacation, we'd decided for the kids' sake to stick to separate accommodations. That night, it proved to be a very good decision, because it meant we had someplace private to meet up.

As soon as I knocked on his door, Yoshi swung it open, dragged me into the room, and pushed me against the wall. Lust flared in me as he pulled me down to his height and claimed my mouth with a passionate kiss. He stripped off my jacket, and I grasped the hem of his T-shirt and yanked it over his head, then quickly shucked off his shorts and briefs.

Once he was naked, Yoshi led me to the bed and wasted no time undressing me. He climbed on top of me, and I shuddered with pleasure as skin met skin. I ran my hands down his back as he licked and kissed my neck, and when he started stroking my swelling cock, I murmured, "Fuck me, Yoshi."

He kissed me before saying, in a rough whisper, "Not tonight, Mike."

"Why not?"

"The first time I fuck you, I plan to take my time, and I want to make sure we're not interrupted. If you want to, you can fuck me instead."

"God yes, but I still want you to be in charge."

Yoshi grinned and said, "Not a problem."

He laced his fingers with mine and pinned my hands to the mattress on either side of my head. His kiss was demanding, and as he slid his tongue between my lips and ground against my cock, I moaned and rocked my hips. After a while, he asked, "How do you feel about a little light bondage?"

My cock twitched at those words, and I stammered, "Do anything you want to me."

"Now, there's an erotic thought."

When he climbed off me, I instantly missed the heat of his body. He pulled the sash from the white robe that hung from the bathroom door and returned to the bed with it. As he ran the strip of fabric over my thigh and up the length of my cock, I shook with pleasure.

His voice was low and even when he said, "I want you on your back with your hands here, Mike."

He touched one of the posts at the foot of the bed, and I rushed to comply. I loved the way he took control. There was no need to bark orders. Instead, he guided me with quiet confidence, and that was such a turn-on.

Once I was splayed out diagonally across the white duvet, I raised my hands over my head. He bound my wrists together and tied the ends of the sash to the bedpost, and then he met my gaze and asked, "Too tight?"

"It's perfect."

He caressed my cheek. "If any of this gets to be too much, or if I do something you don't like, I need you to tell me, Mike. Do you promise to do that?" I nodded.

Yoshi took a bottle of lube, some tissues, and a condom from the drawer of his nightstand and tossed them on the mattress. Then he climbed on top of me and proceeded to drive me absolutely wild. He alternated between sucking my cock and jerking me off while he licked, kissed, and caressed every part of me.

By the time he slipped the condom over my achingly hard cock and slicked it with lube, I was panting, sweating, and writhing beneath him. I raised my head and watched as he worked some lube into himself. He took a moment to wipe his hands before straddling me. Then he positioned the tip of my cock against his opening and held my gaze as he slowly eased himself onto it.

He took every inch of me, and when he was sitting on my hips, I rasped, "Oh God." He was so tight and warm. I thought nothing could feel better than that...until he started to move.

Yoshi proceeded to show me exactly what the phrase 'power bottom' meant. He rode me hard, driving his ass onto my cock again and again as I pulled against my restraints and arched off the bed. He jerked himself off as my orgasm built, and in just a few minutes, I cried out and came almost violently, thrusting up into him as pleasure flooded my senses. Soon after, he grunted and shot across my stomach and chest.

Afterwards, he untied me and cleaned me up while I caught my breath. Then he put a pillow under my head and curled up right beside me, and as he pulled a blanket over both of us, I murmured, "That was so intense."

He wrapped an arm around me and kissed my jaw. "Was your first time with a man like you thought it'd be?"

"It was much better than I'd ever imagined, because it was with you. Thanks for taking care of me like that."

"Always."

I wrapped my arms around him, and he settled in comfortably with his head on my chest. After a while, I said, "I think we've pretty well established that I have submissive tendencies. But are you actually a dominant, or are you just humoring me? For that matter, are you usually a top or a bottom?"

"I'm versatile. Beyond that, I guess I've always been whatever my partner needed me to be."

"That's exactly what you're doing now. What about your needs, Yoshi?"

"Oh, they're being met, believe me. After ending up with a lot of sexually aggressive men, it feels fantastic to be in control for once."

I asked, "Is there anything you've always wanted to try but never have? I'd love it if we checked off a few firsts for you, too."

"We are. This is the first time I've ever been with someone I trust implicitly and am totally comfortable with. I don't have to worry how you'll react when I throw out suggestions, like tying you to a bedpost. That's not usually part of my repertoire, by the way, but wow was it fun."

I grinned and said, "It really was."

He grinned, too. "As for your question about what else I might like to try, you know what sounds fun? Going to a sex shop with you, browsing around, and seeing what grabs us. I've never done that with anyone. But if it's outside your comfort zone, I understand."

I thought about it for a few moments before saying, "Normally, I'd be mortified. But I really want to do that with you when we get back to San Francisco."

"You do?"

I nodded. "I'm curious about what I might respond to in a sex shop."

"I'm so lucky that I get to be a part of your sexual awakening," he said, as he held me a little tighter. "I love watching you make discoveries about yourself, not to mention the fact that you're incredibly sexy when you give yourself over to your desires. Actually, you're sexy all the time, but especially then."

"You think I'm sexy?"

"I know it for a fact."

I said quietly, "For the first time in my life, I'm actually okay with just accepting that compliment, instead of trying to talk you out of it." Yoshi looked happy as he stretched up and kissed me.

Chapter Eleven

Needless to say, I was exhausted the next day. I'd slipped back to my own bed around three a.m., and then the kids woke me at seven. Those hours with Yoshi had been totally worth it, though.

There wasn't much time to dwell on how tired I was, not when there was so much to do to get ready for Nana's party and Easter. After breakfast, Gianni and Zan took Nana and Ollie and my sons and Aiden sailing. Elijah went along too, because Zan had promised him and MJ one final singing lesson before we headed home the next day. I accompanied them into town, then headed to the grocery store in the golf cart while the Mariposa pulled out of the harbor.

By the time I returned to the ranch with several bags of Easter candy, the party decorating was well under way. Two dozen three-by-four-foot framed photos of Nana and our family stood on easels around the edge of the patio, and everywhere I looked, garlands and huge bunches of beautiful Mexican paper flowers provided cheery splashes of color. A long, red banner had been hung between two second-story windows on the main building, above the dining room and lobby, and it read: *Happy Nana Dombruso Appreciation Day.*

Ren and Dante were busy trying to get the dry fountain going. Meanwhile, Vincent and Trevor were setting up a sound system, and Duke and Yoshi were assembling a stage for the band that Dante had imported from the mainland. When Yoshi caught my eye, I flashed him a big, dopey smile. The delighted squeal of toddlers filled the air, and the twin brother and sister darted across the courtyard, with Josh and Darwin in hot pursuit.

Since they seemed to have the party prep well in hand, I took my shopping bags to the dining room and retrieved the huge box I'd shipped to the island. I assembled Easter baskets for my kids, Aiden, and Trey and Lina, the twin toddlers, and then I lined up a row of gold foil-wrapped chocolate rabbits and tied ribbons and name tags around them. Those were for the teenagers. I'd even gotten a pair for Joely and his girlfriend Maya, because I was trying to be optimistic about them joining the family for the weekend.

After that, I sat down at one of the dining room tables and began the time-consuming process of stuffing five hundred plastic eggs. The first batch was just for the twins. After I filled the larger eggs with toddler-safe goodies, I set them aside and started on the rest.

Quinn came into the dining room a few minutes later. He was wearing red shorts and a bright yellow T-shirt with a cartoon unicorn on it. I thought it was very cute that Aiden had a matching shirt. When he saw the basket with Aiden's name on it, he threw his arms around my neck and kissed the top of my head. "Thank you so much for including him," he said. "I have an Easter basket waiting for Aiden at our house, which I'm planning to give him tomorrow night when we get home, but I should have brought it along."

"You're welcome. I hope he decides to do the egg hunt, too. As you can see, there's plenty to go around."

"You might have gotten slightly carried away."

Quinn sat down and started filling eggs with me, and I explained, "There are two reasons for that. First, I suspect this will be the last time MJ hunts for eggs. He'll probably decide he's too old for it next year, so I want this Easter to be epic. The other reason is that the adults in my family are unapologetically immature, so I know for a fact they'll be pilfering a lot of the eggs."

"I just love your family. We've felt really lucky to get to spend time with all of you this week."

"Well, we've loved having you here."

"I'm so happy that Aiden and your boys hit it off," Quinn said. "He's had a hard time fitting in at his new school, so it's great that he'll have some friends when we get back home."

"It means a lot to my boys too, especially MJ. He and his group of friends drifted apart this year, and I know he's been lonely."

"Poor kid. Junior high is the worst."

"Yeah, no kidding." As I angled a toy car to try to get a purple plastic egg to close around it, I said, "MJ's become pretty smitten with Aiden."

"It's mutual. All I keep hearing is MJ this and MJ that."

"I actually wanted to talk to you about the two of them. MJ wants to ask Aiden on a movie date, so I told him I'd see how you felt about that."

Quinn looked startled. After a moment, he brushed his blond hair back from his forehead and blurted, "I gotta be honest here: I have no idea what to do in this situation. The past few months have been a crash course in parenting. I've tried so hard to get myself together for Aiden's sake. I stopped eating junk food, and drinking, and I'm trying to be a good role model for him. Duke and I both are. But there's so much I don't know, like whether twelve is too young to start dating. I mean, I totally trust MJ and I know they're not going to mess around or anything. Holy crap, I'm definitely not ready for that! But it still seems young. Doesn't it?"

"It seems young to me too, but what do I know? I found out a while back that my nine-year-old had a girlfriend."

"Did he really?"

"Well, kind of. It lasted less than two weeks, and it just meant they got to use each other's skateboards, but it still threw me for a loop."

Quinn chewed his lower lip for a few moments before saying, "I guess if you're okay with this, then I am, too. I trust your judgement, because you're a fantastic dad. You're what Duke and I aspire to be."

I grinned at that and reached for another plastic egg. "I'll let you in on a little secret: I'm making this up as I go along. Don't worry if you feel like you don't know what you're doing, because most parents feel that way, pretty much all the time."

"It's reassuring to hear that from someone who seems like Superdad."

After a pause, I said, "I hope you won't be insulted by this, but can I make a contribution to your legal fund? I know how expensive lawyers can be, and I really want you and Duke to get custody of Aiden. The three of you are absolutely meant to be a family."

Quinn smiled at me. "I really appreciate the offer, but we're okay. My mom and dad have actually been paying our legal fees. They've been wonderfully supportive throughout this whole thing, and the lawyer they found us is phenomenal. I'm sure she's the only reason we've been allowed to keep Aiden with us while the custody case is in progress."

"I'm happy to hear you have that support."

"I'm very lucky, and I'm trying so hard to be optimistic," he told me. "Aiden's parents don't want him back, but his aunt and uncle could potentially get custody. The court almost always goes with blood relatives, unless there's a highly compelling reason not to. We found out they have a long history of abusing their own kids, so we're trying to prove they're unfit. It would be so awful if Aiden ended up with them. I don't even know what I'd do."

His voice broke a little, and I rubbed his back. "Think positive, Quinn. This is going to work out."

He nodded and sat up straight. "You're right. I get scared sometimes, but I make sure Aiden never sees that because I need to be strong for him. I love that kid so much, Mike."

"I know you do, and that's why you're already a great dad." By the expression on his face, it seemed like I'd just paid him the world's highest compliment.

A few minutes later, we were joined by Yoshi, Duke, and Jayden. Yoshi kissed my cheek and sat beside me, and as Dante's son sat down across from me I said, "Hi Jay. I feel like I've barely seen you this whole vacation."

Jayden was a good-looking African-American kid who wasn't quite a man yet, but he wasn't a boy, either. He looked younger than fifteen, except for his dark eyes, which were wise beyond his years. As he polished his glasses on the hem of his baggy green T-shirt, he said, "That's because I was trying to finish a present for Nana. I had the idea to paint her a family portrait for her not-birthday celebration, but there are a heck of a lot of us Dombrusos, so it took forever." After he put his glasses back on, he adjusted the bandana that held his short dreads back from his face.

It made me happy to hear him refer to himself as a Dombruso. Trust hadn't come easily with either him or his sibling, and even after Dante and Charlie adopted the brothers, it had been a long, slow process for the four of them to really come together as a family. Joely was still a work-in-progress.

"It's nice of you to do that for her," I told him. "I'm just sorry to hear it ate up so much of your vacation."

"It's alright," he said, as he picked up a plastic egg and stuffed it with a mini candy bar. "I still managed to do all kinds of fun stuff this week, like horseback riding and snorkeling."

The egg-stuffing went a lot quicker with five of us, and we chatted about our week of adventures as we worked. When we were almost done, I noticed about twenty people filtering into the courtyard, and I told my companions, "It looks like Beck's back from his ferry run with Nana's surprise guests." I spotted my grandmother's best friends, a little old lady named Kiki, who was rocking what appeared to be a neon yellow prom dress, and Mr. Mario, who looked dapper in a white linen suit.

Jayden craned his neck and scanned the crowd. Then his face lit up and he exclaimed, "Joely's here!" He raced from the dining room and practically tackled his older brother. Joely's girlfriend Maya had come along too, and she also got a big hug.

I spotted my cousin Nico and said, "Hey, Nicky's here. I'm going to go say hello."

When I got outside, Nico and I grabbed each other in a back-slapping bear hug, and I told him, "I'm so happy you made it! I wasn't sure if you and Luca would be able to get away."

"Time off is rare these days," Nico said, "but there was no way we'd miss Nana's celebration."

My cousin and his partner were a gorgeous couple, both tall and muscular with dark hair and olive complexions, and both looked wonderfully happy. Though they lived in San Francisco, I didn't see them all that often, because Nico was in medical school and insanely busy. When I let go of him, I gave Luca a hug and congratulated him on his new job. "I was impressed when I heard you'd begun teaching art history at Berkeley. Are you enjoying it?"

Luca spoke with a subtle Italian accent, and he said, "I really am. It's been a big change, but one for the better. I love being there every night for Nico, when he drags himself home exhausted from the hospital. His residency can't end too soon, as far as I'm concerned." When he and my cousin first met, Luca had been traveling the world acquiring artwork for wealthy clients, so 'a big change' was an understatement.

I saw some parallels between Nico and Luca's relationship and what I hoped was developing between Yoshi and me, and I would have loved to pull my cousin aside and ask him how they made it work. Nico was a lot like me, quiet and bookish, while Luca had been accustomed to a far more glamorous life when they first met. Yet somehow, they fit together beautifully. That conversation would have to wait for another time though, because we were soon inundated with family members.

Dante weaved through the crowd and greeted the newcomers with, "Welcome, everyone! I'd like you all to

meet our host and my new business partner, Ren Medina."
Ren gave a self-conscious wave, then seemed startled when
the fountain in the center of the courtyard suddenly
sputtered to life. Dante added, "Nana will be back soon,
and in the meantime, come and have a drink!"

As he headed to the bar that had been set up in the
corner, Kiki yelled, "You don't have to tell me twice!" She
linked arms with Mr. Mario, and they rushed to be first in
line.

Vincent turned on a stereo system, and as dance music
filled the courtyard, Yoshi came up to me and slipped his
arm around my waist. "Looks like a party."

"It sure does. Let me finish those eggs, and then I'll
join in."

"I just did, and then I packed them up and hid
everything in the pantry. You're all set for tomorrow."

"Thank you, Yoshi."

"I told you I'd always take care of you, Mike. That
includes supporting you in your efforts to go completely
bat shit crazy for every holiday."

I grinned and kissed him, and Nico glanced over at us
and asked, "Wait, what's happening right now? Why is
Mike making out with Yoshi?"

"Here's the short version," Vincent told our cousin.
"Mikey's bi. Surprise! He just never bothered to tell

anyone, because apparently his sexuality is a bigger secret than the formula for Coca Cola."

Nico pulled out his wallet and handed Vincent a five-dollar bill, and I asked, "What's that for?"

"We made a bet when we were in high school. I thought you were totally hetero, but Dante and Vinny had no doubt you were bisexual. Looks like I lost."

"Seriously? My family's been placing bets on my sexuality?"

"It's your own fault," Vincent told me. "If you'd just opened up to us, there would have been no need for speculation."

I muttered, "All of you suck."

Nico beamed at me and replied, "And oh look, so do you. Welcome to team peen, Mike."

I couldn't help but laugh at that. "Team peen? Really? Why is it that all of us regress to about fifteen years old whenever we get together?"

"Because we can," Nico said. "Who else is going to accept our inner dorks, except for our family?" He had a point.

A moment later, Dante yelled, "Nana's going to be here in fifteen minutes! Gianni just texted."

Someone asked, "Should we hide?"

"No, just don't wander off. I need to go tell Charlie. He's in the kitchen giving the caterers a hand." Dante jogged into the dining room.

A pair of golf carts pulled into the driveway a few minutes later, and Nana got out and exclaimed, "What the hell is this?" About fifty people yelled surprise, and she scowled and put her hands on her hips. "What did I tell you people about not throwing me any more birthday parties?"

Dante stepped through the crowd with a sash and a tiara, and he told her, "It's not a birthday party. In fact, your birthday isn't even until tomorrow. This is Nana Dombruso Appreciation Day. See the banner?"

Nana stuck her big, round glasses on her face and looked at the sign. After a moment, she nodded. "Seems legit. Give me my crown, and let's party!" Everyone breathed a sigh of relief.

Dante placed the tiara on her head and draped the sash over her yellow velour track suit. It read: *The Queen of Everything.* When Charlie handed her a big bouquet of pink roses, she held them in the crook of her arm and said, "I feel like Miss America."

Her husband joined her, and as Nana and Ollie made their way through the crowd, she greeted her guests. My sons followed, along with Gianni and Zan, and said hello to the newcomers. Meanwhile, Elijah hung back and took it all in with an amused expression.

Nana and Ollie went around and looked at the framed photos, which spanned decades of Nana's life. In the first picture, she was about nineteen. She wore a modest, white dress, and her thick, dark hair reached her waist. Nana exclaimed, "I was a fox!"

To that, Ollie replied, "What do you mean, was? You're even sexier now, hot stuff." That earned him a kiss on the cheek.

Yoshi and I trailed behind them hand-in-hand and studied each picture in turn. One was of Nana with her three sons and their wives, taken sometime around 1980. The heartache I felt at the sight of my mom and dad was as familiar to me as my own name. They were virtual strangers, faces I recognized only from photographs. Knowing that was the way my sons remembered their mom sharpened the ache to a knifepoint.

We moved down the line, and there was Jenny, in a photo taken twelve years ago. She and I stood beside a sparkling Christmas tree, along with Nana and my brothers. Jenny was beaming at the camera and holding nine-month-old MJ in her arms. Yoshi whispered, "You both look so young."

"We were."

The photos were arranged in chronological order. Toward the end was a picture taken at the dinner table during Thanksgiving, maybe six years ago. Yoshi murmured, "Hey, there I am." Nana was seated at the head of the table. Yoshi sat beside Gianni, directly across from me.

I chuckled softly and said, "It looks like you're checking me out." Everyone at the table was facing the camera, except for Yoshi. He was looking at me with a wistful expression.

"I was." I glanced at him, and he grinned a little.

The last photo was Nana and Ollie's wedding picture, and it was followed by Jayden's painting of our family. He'd included all of us on the five-foot-wide canvas, not just blood relatives, but all the people Nana had brought into the fold over the years. She was in the very center of the painting, right beside Ollie, and the two of them were surrounded by maybe fifty people, most of whom had come with us to Catalina.

Appropriately, Yoshi stood beside my boys and me in the painting, and I leaned close and gestured at the canvas as I whispered, "You're right where you belong." He swallowed a lump in his throat and nodded as he squeezed my hand.

Meanwhile, Nana took off her glasses and wiped a tear from her dark eyes. "This is the best present anyone's ever given me. Thank you, Jayden. It's going right above the fireplace when I get home." The teen looked so proud.

Nana turned to face the crowd and told us, "I love the hell out of all of you. Now somebody get me a drink, because I see a lot of you fuckers have started without me." She had a big smile on her face as she and Ollie headed to the bar.

*****

Later that night, Yoshi and I sat side-by-side on a bench in a corner of the courtyard. The band was playing a slow song, and Nana and Ollie were dancing in front of the makeshift stage, along with Josh and Darwin. The seniors and the teens both gazed at their partners with pure adoration.

All around us, groups of people laughed and chatted. Everyone seemed to be having a great time, but I couldn't help but feel a bit blue. As Yoshi and I leaned against each other, I looked at his hand in mine and murmured, "How can the week be over already? I feel like we just got here, but we're going home tomorrow."

"It really flew by."

I turned to watch Mark and Mitchell, who were trailing behind the ranch cat on the opposite side of the patio in a game of follow the leader, and after a moment I asked, "What happens when we leave here?"

Yoshi sat up a bit and looked at me. "What do you mean?"

"We're about to go back to our normal routines, our jobs and responsibilities, and our separate lives. But after all that's happened this week, I can't be satisfied with hanging out on Mondays and inviting you over for dinner one night a week. I need more, Yoshi. I need *you*."

He kissed me before saying, "We'll figure this out, Mike."

A minute later, Mark and Mitchell joined us. Both kids wedged themselves onto the bench, and Mitchell asked, "Do we really have to go home tomorrow?"

I nodded. "I bet you're looking forward to seeing Gizmo."

"Yeah, but that's the only thing I'm looking forward to. I don't want to leave the ranch, and I really don't want to go back to school on Monday."

I said, "Let's plan on coming back here this summer."

Mark exclaimed, "For sure!" Then he glanced at Yoshi and asked, "Are you coming, too?"

"Do you want me to?" When Mark nodded, he said, "In that case, I promise I'll be here."

Elijah drifted over to us a few minutes later, and when I asked if he'd made a decision about the job, he nodded. "I decided to take it. I just need to go back home to pack my stuff and tell the family I live with that I'm moving out. Then I'll be back here in about a week." He looked to the right and said, "Aw, that's really cute."

I followed his gaze and spotted MJ and Aiden slow-dancing. They stood about two feet apart with their hands on each other's shoulders and awkwardly shuffled from foot to foot. Mark murmured, "Wow. So much has changed this week." No kidding.

*****

Yoshi spent the night in our little cottage. He started on the couch, but after the kids fell asleep, he slipped into my bed, and we slept in each other's arms. When my alarm went off at six a.m., he got up with me, and we both dressed quickly. Elijah opened his bedroom door as we tried to sneak out of the house, and he whispered, "Can I help you hide the Easter eggs?" He was already fully dressed, and when I nodded, he followed us outside.

We set up a designated toddler area and dotted it with eggs for the twins, and then we fanned out and hid the rest all over the property. When Elijah placed a few near the stable, the ranch hand watched him warily.

From my vantage point a few yards away, I saw Elijah approach the corral, where Cassidy was brushing out a dappled mare. He held up a bright green egg and called, "This is for you. I'm going to leave it out here so the horses don't eat it."

Cassidy just stared at him. Elijah balanced it on a post before heading to the dining room. The slender brunet watched him go. Once Elijah was inside the building, Cassidy retrieved the egg and opened it to reveal a toy car. He turned it over in his hands for a moment. Then he slipped the egg and the toy into the pocket of his baggy plaid shirt and returned to work. I grinned and went back to the task at hand.

Yoshi joined me a minute later and told me, "I'm out of eggs, how about you?"

I placed a pink egg in the crook of a tree. "That was my last one."

"Alright, then let's get going on phase two of your over-the-top holiday extravaganza."

I kissed his forehead and said, "Thanks for humoring me."

*****

Easter morning passed in a blur. The egg hunt was a big hit with kids and adults alike, and the boys were delighted with their Easter baskets. After enjoying a hearty brunch made by Elijah, Yoshi, and me, everyone went off to pack. Later on, as we gathered at the curb to board the shuttles, Gianni came up to me and grabbed me in a big hug. "You need to promise me you'll come back here soon," he said. "We just got a call from our real estate agent, who apparently never takes a day off. Our offer on that gorgeous house with the great view was accepted, so Zan and I are the two newest residents of Catalina Island."

"Congratulations! I already told the boys we're coming back this summer, and now there's even more reason to look forward to that."

My brother pulled back to look at me and grasped my shoulders. "I can't begin to tell you how happy I am about you and Yoshi. I think I'm as emotionally invested in this as the two of you are." I grinned at that as Beck pulled up with one of the two trolleys.

When Gianni hugged me again, I told him, "I wish I didn't have to go."

"Me too."

The second shuttle pulled up behind the first, driven by one of Beck's friends. As people began to board, I looked around for my kids and spotted them with Aiden at the corral, saying goodbye to the horses. Yoshi joined us a moment later, and he and Gianni gave each other a big hug and promised to talk soon.

I called the boys over, and Mitchell looked at me with teary eyes and said, "I don't want to go." I brushed his hair from his forehead and reminded him we'd be back soon, and then he exclaimed, "I almost forgot to say goodbye to Gerald!" I had no idea who that was. Mitchell ran across the courtyard with his backpack bouncing on his slender shoulders, and then he scooped up the striped cat and kissed its head.

Eventually, we all boarded the trolleys. As we started down the gravel road, the kids called goodbye to everything they saw, including each horse by name. I took a last look back at the ranch and whispered, "See you soon."

When we arrived at the dock several minutes later, my sons tackle-hugged Beck, and Mark said, "I wish you could come with us."

"We'll see you this summer," I told him as I shook Beck's hand. "Thank you for everything. You truly went above and beyond for my kids and the rest of my family, and we're all really grateful for that."

"It was my absolute pleasure, and I'm so glad you guys are coming back," he said. "This was one of the best weeks of my life." He seemed perfectly sincere.

"Don't forget what Nana said. You're an honorary Dombruso now, Beck." That put a smile on his face.

We boarded the ferry and settled in for the hour ride back to the mainland. My kids were uncharacteristically subdued. They sat with Yoshi and me and stared out at the water. After a while, Mitchell curled up in his seat and fell asleep, and Mark climbed on me and did the same thing. MJ and Aiden wandered off to the back of the boat.

Yoshi leaned against me and laced his fingers with mine. So much had changed over the last week. *I'd* changed. How was I supposed to step back into my old life after all of that? I grasped Yoshi's hand a little tighter and took a deep breath.

Chapter Twelve

The house was cold when we stepped through the front door around nine that night. I turned up the thermostat as I told the boys, "I need you to do two things for me. First, everyone get a shower, so we don't have to worry about it in the morning. Then after you put on your pajamas, find your school backpack and make sure you have everything you need for tomorrow."

Mitchell pointed out, "That's three things, if you count putting on our PJs."

Mark grumbled, "I'm starving, Dad. Dinner was like, a million hours ago."

"We all are," I said, as I scooped up six pieces of luggage and schlepped them down the hall. "I'll make us a snack while you shower. One of you can use my bathroom, so it'll go faster."

I couldn't face all that laundry, so I left the bags in front of the washing machine and went to the kitchen to consult my refrigerator. I'd purposely let almost everything run out before vacation, which meant I'd have to go to the market before breakfast. I recalled a T-shirt I'd seen recently, which said, 'I'm already tired tomorrow.' That summed up my life perfectly.

The best I could do for a snack was some cheese and crackers. I frowned at the sad little platter, and then I opened a can of black olives and put them in a bowl. It still didn't look like much, so I started randomly dishing up everything I could find that might qualify as finger food.

When MJ came downstairs, dressed in Spider-Man pajamas with his wet hair slicked back, he said, "Well, this is definitely eclectic." He sat down at the kitchen island and popped a maraschino cherry in his mouth.

"I know. I desperately need to go to the store."

"I'm not complaining. It's fun." He took a bite of a dill pickle and made a face. "Pickle and cherry is a bad combination, though."

Eventually, all three kids were fed and tucked into bed. I left my clothes in a pile on the bathroom floor and stood under a not particularly hot shower for a while. Then I toweled off, threw on an old T-shirt and a pair of sweatpants, and crawled into bed. I was beyond exhausted, but of course I couldn't fall asleep.

After a while, I sent Yoshi a text that said: *Hey. I hope you made it back okay.* Since he'd driven down, he hadn't returned with us on the rented tour bus.

He replied a moment later with: *I was just about to message you and say the same thing. How are you?*

I typed: *So very, very tired, and yet, I don't seem to be falling asleep. Instead, I'm making mental lists of everything I have to do tomorrow, including ten loads of laundry, freeing the dog from the kennel, and buying food. I fed my sons maraschino cherries when we got home.*

Yoshi answered with: *Promise me you'll try to get some rest. I know how little you've slept the last few days, and I'm worried about you.*

I replied: *I'll be alright. Since tomorrow's hooky Monday, I hope to see you at some point, in between the errands and general insanity.*

He wrote: *For sure. Talk to you soon.*

I sent back a good night and plugged in my phone on the nightstand, and then I turned off the light and stared at the darkness for a while. Even though my body was totally done, my mind kept racing. Eventually, I gave up and turned the light on again. Then I decided I might as well do something productive, so I retrieved my laptop, got back in bed and started checking my work emails.

I was startled when I heard a key in the lock downstairs, but then a text from Yoshi popped up on my phone: *What happened to sleeping? I'm downstairs, and I see your light is on. Stay in bed, I'll be up in about five minutes.*

I heard him moving around downstairs. He headed to the kitchen, and after that I lost track of him for a bit. But then the pipes rattled quietly, in a way that told me the washing machine was running.

Yoshi appeared in my bedroom doorway a minute later and clicked his tongue. "What are you doing with your laptop when you're supposed to be sleeping?" He clicked the door shut behind him, and then he crossed the room and handed me a steaming mug. "That's herbal tea with honey. It'll help you relax." He traded the cup for the laptop and sighed when he looked at the screen. "Work emails shouldn't take priority over getting some rest, Mike."

"I know, but I wasn't sleeping anyway." I blew on the hot liquid and took a cautious sip. "This is really good. Thank you."

He shut the computer and slid it under the bed, and then he took off my glasses and gently brushed back my hair. "You're welcome. I want you to try to sleep after you finish that."

I took a long drink from the mug before asking, "Are you doing laundry?"

"I am, just because I knew those unpacked bags of dirty clothes would be weighing on you. I'm running a load of the kids' stuff first, in case they need any of it for school tomorrow. I'll stay until it's dried and folded. I brought you some groceries, too. You'll still have to make a trip to the store, but now you have some essentials, including everything you'll need for tomorrow's breakfast and the kids' lunches." He cupped my cheek and asked, "Why do you look like you want to cry?"

"I can't believe you did all that for me." I put the cup on the nightstand and grabbed him in a hug.

"I'm planning to come back in the morning, so I can make the kids some breakfast and take them to school. That way, you can sleep in."

"You don't have to do that. You must be as tired as I am."

He rubbed my back and said, "I got home way before you did and took a two-hour nap, so I'm fine."

I looked up at him and touched the other side of the mattress. "Why don't you spend the night?"

"You sure? The last thing I want is to keep you up."

"Please?"

"Alright, as long as you promise to sleep."

He was dressed in a T-shirt and track pants, so once he took off his jacket and sneakers, he was ready for bed. Yoshi slipped under the white duvet, and I adjusted the pillows and turned off the light. When I burrowed into his arms, I sighed with pleasure, and then I whispered, "You're the kindest, most wonderful man in all the world. You know that, right?"

"You'd do the same for me if the situation were reversed."

"Just take the compliment, Yoshiro. You're so bad at that!"

He grinned and said, "Uh oh, my full name. I must be in trouble."

I grinned too. "It's a beautiful name. I just felt like taking it out for a spin."

"Spin away."

"Does it mean something?"

"Yes and no. It means 'happy individual' but that's not why my parents selected it. God knows my happiness was never of concern to them. I was actually named for some long-deceased distant relative, who was supposedly a huge success back in Japan. In the picture I saw of him, the last thing he looked like was a happy individual. The name can also mean 'good son' with a slightly different kanji, by the way, but I was spared that irony."

I asked, "Do you think you'll ever introduce me to your parents?"

"No, because I like you."

"What does that mean?"

"It means I don't want to subject you to their endless complaints and criticisms."

"I know you don't really get along, but I'm curious about them, and about where you grew up."

He said, "Well, next time we accidentally drive through the Tenderloin, we can do a lap around my old neighborhood."

"Do you ever visit your parents?"

"Yup, once a week. I swing by their store to drop off some money, and they grill me for about fifteen minutes, presumably so they can verify that I'm still a disappointment. Their shop manages to keep them afloat, but money's tight, so I help out."

"I'm surprised I never knew about those weekly visits."

"Well, I generally avoid conversations about my parents. Now, you need to get some sleep, Michael. No more stalling."

I grinned and said, "You're right, the full name thing does accompany a feeling of being in trouble. And I'm not stalling, I just got my second wind. It happened when this super hot guy showed up at my house with some groceries."

Yoshi chuckled at that. "You're so easy to please."

"Oh, I know. Forget candlelight and flowers. The key to any exhausted single parent's heart is showing up at their house with bread and milk and saving them a trip to the market. They'll love you forever."

"You deserve both, the romance and the support," he said. "I'm going to try my damnedest to strike that balance."

"But that's just all about me, so it seems one-sided. What do you get in return?"

Yoshi tilted my chin up with his fingertip, and I met his gaze. "I get you, Mike."

"That's the most romantic thing anyone's ever said to me."

He smiled and said, "Balance achieved."

We talked for few more minutes as he held me, and when his phone beeped, he said, "I'll be right back."

"Where are you going?"

He got out of bed and headed for the door. "I want to put the clothes in the dryer and start another load."

I started to get up too as I said, "Let me do that."

Yoshi tried to look stern, but he didn't really pull it off. "Don't even think about it, Mike. I'll tie you to the bed if I have to." I shuddered with pleasure, and he smiled at me. "Hold that thought. And stay here, I mean it." Then he jogged out of the bedroom.

When he returned just a few minutes later, he said, "Speaking of tying you up, can I see that photo you mentioned? The ad for the BDSM club, I mean."

"It's on the top shelf of my closet, to the left of the shoe boxes."

Yoshi retrieved the flyer, turned on the lamp on the nightstand, and studied the photo carefully before saying, "I like everything about this."

"Really?"

He nodded. "It's actually beautiful. I love that gentle touch, and the way the man on his knees has his face upturned, as if he's totally focused on the man in the suit. I also like the fact that you can't see their faces, so they could be anyone. It's easy to imagine them as you and me actually, given their body types." When he turned the picture toward me, I exhaled slowly and adjusted my growing hard-on. Yoshi said softly, "I'm doing the worst job ever of letting you get some rest."

"It's okay." I studied the photo, and after a moment I murmured, "I wish I understood why I like this so much."

"Not that you need a reason, but this actually makes a lot of sense. You're always in control, in every aspect of your life. You run your household and your business and everything else, and I know it gets exhausting. I can certainly see the appeal of relinquishing control in this one aspect of your life." He leaned the photo against the lamp on the nightstand, and then he added, as he got up and headed to the door, "Then again, maybe you just like it because it's fucking hot."

He clicked the door shut and turned the lock, and I asked, "What are you up to?"

"You'll see." Yoshi pulled a tiny packet of lube from his wallet and ripped it open, and I grinned as I put two and two together.

He climbed into bed and folded back the covers, and then he pulled down the front of my sweats, exposing my cock. After he squirted the lube into his palm, he jerked me off with quick, sure strokes. The feeling of his firm grip on my shaft was sensational, and I moaned softly as pleasure coursed through me. In just a few minutes, I was right on the brink of orgasm, and Yoshi whispered, "Cum for me, Mike." That was all it took to send me over the edge. I bit back a yell and gripped the sheets, thrusting into his palm as I came.

I was completely spent after that. Fortunately, Yoshi wasn't done taking care of me. He cleaned me up, and after he tucked me back in, he returned the flyer to my closet. I was almost asleep when he slipped under the covers and turned off the light. I murmured a good night, and he kissed my forehead and whispered, "Good night, my beautiful

Michael." I drifted off a moment later with a smile on my face.

*****

The next morning, I was awakened by gentle kisses along my jawline, which was infinitely better than my screeching alarm clock. When I raised my eyelids, Yoshi brushed his lips to mine. Then he said, "Everything's ready for breakfast downstairs. I prepped the ingredients for French toast, and there are four bowls of fresh berries in the fridge. Please eat when you feed your kids. Their lunches are already made, so you'll have time."

"Thank you for doing all of that."

"I was happy to help. Call me after you drop the boys at school." He got up and started to reach for his jacket.

I sat up and asked, "Aren't you staying for breakfast?"

Yoshi said, "I didn't think you'd want the boys to know I slept over."

"You've spent the night here countless times."

"Yeah, but before, I was a friend crashing on the couch. Now I'm the person their dad is dating."

I slipped out of bed and took his hand. "I think it was the right call to play it cool while we were on vacation. But now that we're back, I want the boys to start getting used to the idea that you and I are a couple. Plus, you've joined us for breakfast before, so I don't think it's going to throw anyone for a loop."

Apparently I was right, because the kids didn't bat an eye when they found Yoshi flipping French toast in the kitchen a few minutes later. That included Mark. Even though he still hadn't fully warmed up to the idea that Yoshi and I were dating, he asked Yoshi if he could come over every morning, because his French toast was 'the bomb.'

The morning went remarkably smoothly, especially for a Monday following a week off, which normally would have been utter chaos. I dropped the boys at school with a few minutes to spare, then swung by the kennel to pick up Gizmo. When I got home, I found Yoshi folding the last of my family's vacation laundry into neat little piles. I pulled him into an embrace while the dog raced around the house like a maniac and asked, "Did you sleep at all last night, or did you stay up doing ten loads of laundry?"

"It was only seven loads, and I got plenty of sleep."

"I said it before and I'll say it again. You're the kindest, most considerate man in the world."

"No I'm not. It just feels really good to take care of you."

I pulled him onto the couch, and Yoshi stretched out on top of me. While we kissed, Gizmo ran into the room, jumped on the couch, and nested in the small of Yoshi's back. We both laughed at that. Then Yoshi traced the side of my face and said, "No glasses. You've been wearing them less and less lately."

"Well, I mostly just need them for driving."

He ran his fingertip along my furry jaw. "I like this short, tidy beard. Is it staying?"

"I'm glad you like it," I said. "It was supposed to just be a break from shaving while I was on vacation, but I've decided to keep it for a while."

He kissed me again, then asked, "Since it's Monday, are you meeting Dante for coffee like you usually do? I need to do a few things at my studio, so I can drop you off at the café and meet you afterwards if you want me to."

"He's still on Catalina, finalizing the purchase of his share of the ranch. Charlie came back with Jayden because their son had to be back in school today, and Dante should get back Friday or Saturday. I'll go with you to the studio if you want me to. Then I have an idea for what we can do afterwards."

When I smiled at him, he said, "That grin can only be described as mischievous. What did you have in mind?"

"Remember how we talked about visiting a sex shop together? I think we should do that today."

It was his turn to smile mischievously. "We can definitely do that, and I know just the place."

*****

Since we had over an hour before the shop opened, we went to Yoshi's tattoo studio first. On the way, we dropped off Gizmo for a play date at my grandmother's house. I didn't have the heart to stick the dog in daycare right after a week at the kennel.

The studio was closed on Mondays, and we were assaulted by deafening heavy metal music when we stepped through the door. Yoshi's apprentice Max was tattooing one of his coworkers, a guy with green hair whose name I couldn't remember. They both waved. Yoshi veered off to the right to turn down the sound system while I looked around.

The shop was spacious and modern, with polished concrete floors, a high ceiling, and sleek workstations. Well, they'd started out sleek, anyway. Apparently the art of tattooing required a hell of a lot of stuff, from bottles of ink and jugs of cleanser to things I didn't recognize, and most of the counters were crowded.

On top of that, each of the artists who worked in Yoshi's shop had personalized his or her space in some pretty unique ways, from concert posters to hideous collectible clowns and everything in between. The only exception was Yoshi's work station. It was clutter-free to the point of seeming almost austere. Aside from some things he needed to do his job, like the machine and a row of identical black binders on a low shelf, there was nothing personal in his space, and most of the surfaces were empty.

His apartment was much the same way. It managed to feel warmer, thanks to its wood floors, artwork, and exposed brick, whereas the studio was all chrome, glass, black leather, and concrete. I tried to keep my house in order, but there was always some junk scattered around despite my best efforts, and all my shelves were covered in photos, books, toys, and random ephemera. I wondered if all that stuff grated on him, given his very obvious aesthetic.

Once the music was turned to a level where we could actually hear ourselves think, Yoshi and I went to say hello to his colleagues. Max was a young Asian guy of about twenty-five with a lot of piercings and several tattoos, whose long hair was gathered up in a messy bun of sorts. He smiled at us when we approached and said, "Hi boss and boss's accountant. How was your island getaway?"

"It was great." Yoshi leaned in and took a good look at what Max was tattooing. Since the skull tatt was being applied to the green-haired guy's butt cheek and his pants were around his knees, I was instantly uncomfortable. Everyone else took the bare ass in stride, though. "This is looking great," Yoshi said. "You're pulling some nice, consistent lines."

Max lit up at the compliment. When Yoshi straightened up and took my hand, the guy with green hair glanced at him and said, "Dude, did you and your accountant hook up on vacation?" He glanced at me and added, "Sorry, I don't remember your name."

Yoshi answered for me. "His name's Mike. How do you not know that? He's been coming in here for years." He seemed annoyed, which wasn't something I saw from him very often.

I said, "I don't actually know his name, either."

The guy with green hair stuck his hand out. "I'm Marvin. So are you two like, dating or something?"

I shook his hand, still trying to avoid looking directly at his half-hairy, half-shaved butt, and said, "Yeah. We are." I wondered if the job of shaving that ass cheek had fallen to Max.

"Right on." Marvin scratched the butt cheek that wasn't getting a tattoo. Gross.

Max glanced at Yoshi and asked, "What happened to Gale?"

"We broke up."

The apprentice's expression became sympathetic. "I'm sorry. Are you okay? I hate getting dumped, it's just the worst."

"Actually, I broke up with him." Marvin and Max both stared at him like he was insane, and Yoshi frowned and said, "I have a few things to do in the office, so I'll talk to you later."

He turned to go, but Max called, "Hey, so are we still going to New York? Please say yes." He reminded me of one of my kids.

Yoshi nodded. "I forgot to buy plane tickets before vacation, but I'll do that now. Thanks for reminding me."

As we headed to the office, I asked, "Why are you going to New York?"

"I promised my apprentice I'd take him to an exhibit at one of the museums. It's about tattoos as fine art, and I hope he'll find it inspiring."

"Wow, that's really nice of you."

"Max is a good kid, and he has a lot of talent. He doesn't have much confidence in his ability though, so I'm always trying to think of ways to encourage him."

When we reached the office, Yoshi picked up a big stack of mail and flipped through it, and I asked, "How long will you be gone?"

"Thursday through Sunday. I wanted to spend a couple of extra days there, so I could visit some friends. One of them is playing a gig with her new band, and I wanted to check it out."

"Thursday of this week?"

He nodded, then sat at his desk and fired up his sleek, silver laptop as I murmured, "Sounds fun." I dropped into the chair in front of his desk and idly rifled through the stack of invoices cluttering his in-box, a reminder of just how much work I had waiting for me now that vacation was over.

Yoshi asked me, "Want to come? I'm just about to book our flight, so I could buy a ticket for you."

"I can't."

"If it's the money, I'll pay for everything."

"It's not that," I said. "I can't just drop everything and fly to New York."

"One of your relatives could watch the boys, Nana maybe, or—"

But I shook my head and told him, "I'm already going to be swamped with work after a week away, and the kids need to settle back into a normal routine with school and their activities. The last thing they need right now is that kind of disruption."

"I'd push the trip back, but the art exhibit closes on Sunday."

"Go and have fun with Max. It sounds like a terrific weekend."

He studied me carefully and asked, "Are you upset?"

"No. I'm fine." I was the king of 'I'm fine.' I'd probably say that even if I was on fire.

"You sure?"

I tried to sound cheerful as I said, "Yeah. Another time, alright? It's not like this will be your last trip to New York."

"True. I usually go two or three times a year." And there was yet another reminder of how utterly different our lives were.

*****

The sex shop was about a million miles outside my comfort zone, and yet it was interesting. By that I meant interesting from an anthropological standpoint, not a sexual one. I had yet to find anything even sort of erotic on the racks and shelves.

One entire wall was lined with dildos, arranged in size from petite to Oh My God. There was a section with shoes and clothing, including costumes, lingerie, and some things made of rubber and latex, which looked uncomfortable. There was even some furniture. A huge, padded table with built-in tie-downs seemed pretty appealing, but where the hell would someone put such a thing?

And then there was a room devoted entirely to leather, from whips and harnesses to some items I really didn't get. I pointed questioningly at a black leather mask that looked like a dog, complete with a muzzle and floppy ears, and Yoshi said, "Please don't ask me to explain why people are into puppy play, because I'm not sure I can."

I glanced at the selection of butt plugs with tails attached and asked him, "Is there a novice section in this shop? I feel like we've jumped right into advanced kink, and I'm having a hard time processing all of this."

Yoshi turned and scanned the leather room. We'd told the young guy working behind the counter that we wanted to browse on our own, so he'd left us unsupervised. But since the shop was big and crowded with merchandise, it was hard to find what we were looking for…especially since we didn't really know what that was.

After a moment, Yoshi said, "I thought you might randomly find things that appealed to you if we just wandered through the shop, but it's pretty overwhelming, isn't it?"

"Definitely."

"Let's try to narrow it down. Does any of this stuff appeal to you?" He indicated a wall full of whips, floggers, and paddles, and I shook my head. "Okay. We know you like to be tied down, right? So maybe we should look for restraints."

I gestured at a pair of handcuffs and frowned. "These just seem cheesy, like we're playing cops and robbers or something."

Yoshi held up a leather cuff with metal hardware on it and asked, "What about this?"

"That'd go nicely with the Wonder Woman costume in the other room. Think I can pull off a gold bustier?"

He chuckled and said, "Come over here and sit down. I think you need to try these on to get the full effect."

I did as he asked and held out my hands once I was seated. Yoshi buckled on a pair of cuffs, and I imitated the sound of a firing gun and held up my wrist Wonder Woman-style to stop the imaginary bullet. Then I said, "I don't know. It just feels silly." I was so glad we were the only customers in the shop.

Yoshi surprised me by grabbing my hands and pushing them against the wall above my head. He clicked the

312

hardware on each cuff to a metal grate, and then he pushed my knees apart with his leg, stepped between my thighs and asked, "How about now?"

It was like flipping a switch. My cock immediately started to swell, and my heartbeat sped up as I murmured, "Okay, so, these are actually really good."

He unhooked the cuffs from the grate and asked, "Do you want me to buy them for you?"

"I don't know. That was a definite turn-on, but where would I even keep something like this? And if the boys ever discovered them, how could I possibly explain what they're for?"

"You could keep them in my apartment."

"Except that we never spend the night there." I started to unbuckle one of the cuffs.

Yoshi removed the cuffs for me as he said, "We could start spending hooky Mondays there. And you *could* sleep over occasionally, you know. Your kids spend the night at Nana's or one of your brothers' houses now and then."

"True."

"So, what do you think? Do you want these? If they're not right, we can keep looking."

I ran my hand over the black leather, and after a moment I admitted, "I really do want them. I think I'm just making excuses, because this is pretty much the last thing I ever thought I'd own."

Yoshi smiled at me. "I'm proud of you for stepping out of your comfort zone. There are a few other things I want to buy you to go with these. Do you trust me?"

"Of course I do. I'm curious though, what kinds of things?"

He browsed the shelves and picked up a larger pair of cuffs, which matched the ones he was holding. "These are for your ankles. There are two...possibly three more things I want to find." He spent another couple of minutes looking around and ended up with a pair of leather straps and a long, black bar with fasteners at each end.

I asked, "What do those do?"

"The spreader bar is meant to hold your ankles apart, and the straps go around your thighs. The cuffs can be hooked to them to hold you in position with your knees bent and legs spread." I must have looked confused, because he added, "It's easiest if I show you. Let's plan on going to my apartment after this."

"Alright." I rearranged the bulge in my jeans as Yoshi turned back to the displays.

After a moment, he said, "You might not like this idea, and that's fine. I'm just going to throw it out there. Feel free to say no."

He held up a big, black leather collar with silver hardware, which looked like it was meant for a Great Dane, and I frowned, even as my cock throbbed. I studied it for a long moment and finally said, "I'd probably say no to that if I wasn't already horny."

"Does that mean you want to give it a try?" I started to reach for the price tag to help make up my mind, but he said, "Don't worry about the cost. If you think you might like it, I'll get it for you."

"I feel like buying that will take this whole submission thing to another level."

"So, you think it's too much?"

I studied the collar and chewed my lower lip for a moment. Then I took a leash from the wall and handed it to Yoshi. "I think if we're going to do this, then let's do it." He looked pleased, which made me happy.

We started to head to the register. Along the way, Yoshi plucked a black box off one of the shelves and brought it with us, and I asked, "What's that?"

He was very matter-of-fact when he replied, "A set of butt plugs in four different sizes. They vibrate and come with a remote control."

I mumbled, "Oh," as my cock strained against my jeans, and I rearranged myself yet again.

It was a relief that the young guy working behind the counter was all-business. He rang up the items without comment, and without even a single curious glance at the two of us. I was stunned at the total, but Yoshi handed over his credit card and remarked, "That's less than I was anticipating."

"All our leather products are twenty percent off this month," the cashier noted, as if we were in a grocery store, commenting on the price of bread. The whole transaction was just so *normal*. The items were wrapped in tissue paper and packed in a large, craft paper shopping bag with handles. It was all very discreet, aside from the metal bar, which jutted out of the top of the bag. Not that most people would know at a glance what that was used for…probably.

I fully expected to run into a dozen family members as we walked the three blocks to Yoshi's truck, but we got lucky. He drove us to his apartment, and as we pulled into his space in the underground parking garage, he said, "As of right now, you have less than four hours before you need to pick up your kids from school. I want to hold off on fucking you until we have an entire night together, but there's still a lot we could do with these new toys. We can also save them for a later date. It's up to you."

"I think some of this stuff should wait until we have that night together. But you, me, and those cuffs have a date upstairs in about three minutes."

Yoshi flashed me a big smile as he shut off the engine and said, "Sounds like a plan." I grabbed the shopping bag, and we both rushed to the elevator.

From the moment we tumbled into the apartment, we were all over each other. Both of us had gotten pretty worked up during our shopping expedition, so a slow build-up just wasn't going to happen. We pulled each other's clothes off, then landed in a tangle of arms and legs in the middle of his living room floor.

Yoshi kissed me roughly, demandingly, and my cock throbbed against his hip. I fumbled for the bag and dumped out the contents, and he flipped us over so he was on top and quickly fastened the leather cuffs to my wrists. Then he stood up and said, "On your knees." I immediately complied.

He circled behind me and fastened the cuffs together at my lower back. A shockwave of pleasure reverberated through me. He bent down and licked and nipped my shoulder before stepping around to the front of me again and slipping his cock between my lips.

I sucked him frantically while my cock throbbed and leaked precum. Yoshi thrust into my mouth, just enough to drive me wild, and held my head between his palms. He came in just a few minutes, and I moaned as I swallowed his load.

When he unfastened my wrists, I thought we might be done. But then he helped me up and said, "Follow me." We crossed the apartment, and he touched the long, cement counter that separated the living area from the kitchen. "I want you up here, on your back, with your hands over your head." Just like the last time, he didn't bark orders. Instead, his tone was calm and confident.

I did as he asked and stretched out naked on the counter, which was cool against my skin. It was far more erotic than I could have predicted to be put on display like that. When I raised my hands over my head, they hung off the edge of the counter. Yoshi circled around me slowly, trailing his fingers over my body. He retrieved a broom from a narrow closet at one end of the kitchen, slipped it between the cuffs and the edge of the counter, and stood it upright. My bound wrists held it in place, and the broom handle prevented me from lowering my arms.

I grinned and said, "Clever." He grinned too, and then he held my gaze as he wrapped his hand around my cock.

Yoshi edged me for what had to be a solid hour, licking, sucking and stroking my cock until I was just about to cum, then easing me down again. And again. And again.

When he finally took me to the edge and whispered, "Cum for me, Mike," before wrapping his warm, wet mouth around my tip, my orgasm tore from my body, and I yelled and arched off the counter.

I came so hard my vision faltered. I shot again and again, and even when I was empty, my body tried to shoot some more. By the time it was over, I was covered in sweat and shaking violently.

Yoshi unhooked my cuffs and helped me off the counter. I couldn't go very far, so he brought me a blanket and wrapped it and himself around me as I curled up on the floor and tried to catch my breath. When I could finally speak again, I managed, "It was even more intense than last time. I didn't think that was possible."

A few minutes later, he noticed me studying my cuffed wrists and asked, "Do you want me to take those off for you?"

"Not yet. You know, it's a shame I can't pull off a punk rock aesthetic. If I could, then I'd be able to wear these all day long and claim they were a fashion statement."

He smiled at me. "I'd love to see that. Maybe you and I and the boys could dress like a punk band for Halloween."

"That'd be really cute." I glanced around and asked, "What time is it?"

"Just after one. You have plenty of time." I relaxed again, and after a pause, he asked, "Are you hungry? If so, I'll make us some lunch."

"I'm starving, actually. Can I use your shower while you do that?" When he nodded, I sat up and said, "I guess that means I have to take these cuffs off after all."

I held out my hands, and after Yoshi unfastened the cuffs, he rubbed my wrists and examined them closely. They were a little red, but I hadn't really pulled against the restraints and the suede lining had provided cushioning, so I probably wasn't going to end up with any tell-tale marks.

While he headed to the refrigerator, I climbed the spiral staircase and cut through the tidy bedroom to the master bathroom, both of which were modern and sophisticated with a gray and black color palette. I lingered in the hot shower and thoroughly enjoyed his obviously expensive body wash, which enveloped me in the clean, citrus scent I'd long associated with Yoshi.

Afterwards, I stood in the doorway as I dried off and looked around. Even though I'd been in his apartment many times, I very rarely had a reason to go upstairs. I took the opportunity to study his bedroom and tried to decide what it said about Yoshi.

The low platform bed looked like a piece of art with its modern, black, wood frame, and it was neatly made with crisp, charcoal gray linens. The wall behind the bed was exposed red brick, adding warmth and color to the beautiful but impersonal room. Two matching nightstands flanked the bed, each topped with an identical chrome lamp and nothing else. There were closet doors to the right of the bed and a low dresser to the left, in front of the railing at the edge of the loft. The surface of the dresser was empty. It all reminded me of a very expensive hotel room.

I wrapped the towel around my waist and finger-combed my wet hair as I went back downstairs. Yoshi smiled when he saw me and said, "I'm making a tofu and veggie stir fry. I can't recall if I've ever seen you eat tofu, so I hope you like it." I noticed he'd gotten dressed, and my clothes were draped over the back of the couch. He'd also put away the sex toys. I glanced around the room and wondered where they'd ended up.

Instead of asking, I told him, "I love it, but for some reason two of my sons don't, so I never make it. I think I need to try again with them. By now, they might have forgotten that they hate it."

I got dressed and sat at the counter, the one I'd been tied to minutes earlier. As I ran my palm over the polished concrete surface, Yoshi glanced at me and said, "That probably got uncomfortable, especially considering how long I left you up there. Sorry about that."

"Oh believe me, the last thing I was thinking about was the countertop. And actually, it was perfect. I liked the fact that it wasn't warm and snuggly."

"Well, that's good. Please tell me if my next attempt at creativity misses the mark though, okay?"

"I will." He set a glass of ice water in front of me and started to dish up the stir fry, which smelled wonderful. I took a sip of water before asking, "Does it seem like we have sex a lot? I mean, more than other people? I'm not complaining. I'm just wondering if this is typical for most couples."

"I have no idea what's typical." Yoshi put two steaming plates of food and a bottle of soy sauce on the counter and added, "But this hasn't just been about you and me coming together as lovers. It's also been about you exploring your sexuality, and I'm thrilled to be along for the ride." I grinned shyly and picked up my fork.

"There's literally no one else on earth I could have done this with," I told him. "It had to be my best friend. I never would have trusted anyone else or felt safe or comfortable enough to do the things we've done."

"I'm honored, both that you trust me, and that you just called me your best friend. You're mine too, you know."

"You don't have to say that. I know Gianni's been your best friend since you were in college."

"I think of Gianni as the brother I never had. My feelings for you definitely aren't brotherly."

I grinned at that and tried a bite of the stir-fry. Then I told him, "This is delicious. Thank you."

"I'm glad you like it."

He stepped around the counter and sat beside me, and we spent a few minutes eating in comfortable silence. After a while, I said, "We still have some time before I need to pick up the boys from school. What would you like to do?"

Yoshi glanced at me, and then he quickly looked away. "One thing just came to mind, but maybe it's kind of weird."

"What is it?"

"I'll tell you after lunch."

I didn't know what to expect when Yoshi took my hand after we'd finished eating and led me upstairs. He looked up at me and seemed embarrassed when he asked, "Will you just hold me for a while?"

I climbed onto the bed and drew him into my arms, and he curled up with his head on my chest and held on tight. I'd never seen Yoshi show such stark vulnerability, not to me or anyone else. The fact that he trusted me with that part of himself felt like a gift.

After maybe fifteen minutes, he kissed me, and then he got up and glanced at me self-consciously as he said, "Thanks for humoring me."

"You don't have to thank me, Yoshi."

He murmured, "I hate it when I get needy like that." Then he pulled up his usual veneer of confidence and took control of the situation. "If we leave now, we'll have time to make it to the market before you have to pick up your boys. I only brought you enough groceries to last a couple of days, so we really should get that done."

I caught his arm as he started to leave the bedroom, and when he turned back to me, I kissed him deeply. Then I said, "Lead the way."

Chapter Thirteen

On Friday afternoon, MJ was a bundle of nerves. I'd agreed to invite Aiden and his dads to dinner, and my oldest son was helping me cook. The boys had talked on the phone every day since returning from Catalina the weekend before, and my son planned to ask Aiden out on a date that evening. So far, he'd changed his shirt four times and was second-guessing everything, right down to the meal we were making. "Maybe we should put all the tomatoes and junk on the side, in case they don't like it in their salad," he said, as he eyed the vegetables I was chopping.

"We can do that."

"Okay, good. Also, I think the shrimp scampi was a mistake. What if someone has a seafood allergy? Or what if they just don't like shrimp?"

"I texted Quinn and asked, and all three of them are fine with it."

MJ transferred the chopped lettuce to a big serving bowl and told me, "Please don't use a ton of garlic like you usually do. I don't want to stink."

"The good news about the garlic is that everyone will be eating it, including Aiden, so you'll smell the same."

"You never smell your own breath, Dad, just other people's."

"Fine, I'll cut back on the garlic."

MJ moved to the sink and dumped some cherry tomatoes into a colander. After a few moments, he said, "So, I want to talk to you about something. I've been thinking about recording some songs and uploading them to the internet."

"Really?"

He nodded and began fidgeting with a dish towel. "The videos of Zan and me at the talent show got a ton of views, and most of the comments were really nice. I mean, I know everyone was only interested in them because Zan's super famous, but...I don't know. When I watched them, I kind of thought I did okay."

"You did great, MJ, and I'm proud of you for wanting to put yourself out there again. I know that's not easy."

"It's really not," he said. "It actually scares me to death. But I've been giving it a lot of thought, and if anything's ever going to come of my singing, then I have to be brave and take some chances, don't you think?"

"You're absolutely right."

After a pause, he muttered, "I hate the fact that I'm such a coward."

"You're not even sort of a coward. Just the opposite. You're one of the strongest and bravest people I know."

"I don't feel strong and brave," he said. "Remember how petrified I was at the talent show? That was only two weeks ago, and I haven't changed since then."

"The talent show is a great example of your bravery. It would have been so easy to just decide not to sign up in the first place. But you did it."

"I froze like a deer in headlights, Dad."

"Okay, so stage fright got the better of you for a minute. But even so, you didn't run, and when Zan showed up, you sang beautifully, in front of that entire, crowded auditorium. That's something to be proud of."

MJ said, "But I couldn't have done it without Uncle Zan."

"There's nothing wrong with letting people help you. That also doesn't change the fact that you truly have a gift. You're better at singing than I've ever been at anything in my entire life. That's why I think you should go ahead and make those videos. People will love them."

"I hope you're right."

"I know I am."

After a pause, he said, "I think I need to be reminded to be brave sometimes. Actually, maybe you do too, Dad. Let's promise to remind each other."

"Deal."

MJ looked down at himself and set aside the dish towel. "I'm going to go change my shirt. Last time, I swear. Thanks for listening."

"Always, MJ."

I was surprised when he grabbed me in a hug and said, "You know, you don't think you're good at anything, but you are. You're great at being a dad." He let go of me and left the kitchen, and I had to swallow a lump in my throat. That was the best thing he could have possibly said to me.

Our guests arrived a few minutes later. I loved the fact that the whole family matched. They all wore jeans, and Quinn had paired his with a red sweater that featured a dancing unicorn. Duke was wearing a red Henley, and Aiden wore a red sweatshirt with a ninja cat on the front. When I mentioned how cute it was that they'd color coordinated, they seemed genuinely surprised, and they looked at each other and chuckled.

In addition to their day jobs, Quinn and Duke ran a cookie business, and they'd brought a gorgeous sugar cookie bouquet for dessert, made up of clouds, suns, and rainbows, arranged in a decorative flower pot. My kids and the dog barreled down the stairs, and Mark and Mitchell shrieked when they saw the cookie pops. MJ and Aiden exchanged shy smiles, and our little blond guest laughed delightedly as Gizmo tried to tackle him.

I led Quinn and Duke to the kitchen, where nonalcoholic drinks and a big antipasto tray were waiting on the island. Mitchell and Mark followed us and tried to make a case for before-dinner cookies, but when I shot them down, they turned their attention to the antipasto. As Mark stuffed his face with cheese cubes, Mitchell said, in a loud stage whisper, "See, Dad? We're giving MJ and Aiden some space, just like you asked us to."

"That's good," I said. "Thank you." The two older boys still lingered near the front door.

Mark mused, around a mouthful of cheese, "It seems weird that like, MJ wants to get all romantical with our friend. Do you think they're going to kiss and stuff?"

"Romantical isn't a word," Mitchell told him. "And don't be gross and talk with your mouth full. We have guests, so use your manners."

I said, "Mitchell, stop parenting your brother." But then I added, "He's actually right about all of that though, Mark."

My youngest son busted out his patented frown/eye roll combination. "Fine. But really though, doesn't it seem weird?"

"Nobody's getting romantic," I said. "We're all just hanging out together."

"And you're being hypocritical, since you used to have a girlfriend," Mitchell said. Bonus points for using the big word correctly.

"Yeah, but I don't anymore, since she wanted to 'keep her options open,' whatever that meant. Besides, we never did gross stuff like kiss. I don't get why anyone would want to mash their mouth against another person's and swap spit." Mark shuddered dramatically.

When MJ and Aiden joined us in the kitchen a minute later, the dog was tucked under Aiden's arm. Duke and Aiden exchanged a stealthy down-low thumbs up, which seemed to be code for 'it's off to a good start.' Meanwhile, Quinn drained his glass and said, "I heard from Max a little while ago. He told me he and Yoshi are having a great time in New York." Quinn had been adopted by an Asian family when he was little, and he and Max were related to each other, though I wasn't quite sure how.

I refilled his glass from a pitcher on the counter and muttered, "Yeah. Sounds like it."

Mark said, "Must be nice, getting to fly off to New York whenever you want to."

Mitchell shot him a look. "Shut up about that. You know Dad's sad because he had to stay behind." And here

I'd thought I'd been doing a great job of acting like I was fine with sitting out that trip.

When the boys took Aiden to show him the family room, I murmured embarrassedly, "Kids are way too observant sometimes."

"They really are. Aiden is totally attuned to our every mood. If one of us is even slightly upset about something, he's right there, asking what's wrong." Quinn lowered his voice and added, "We're both trying not to let him see how stressed we are about the custody case. If he knew we were worried, the poor kid would be beside himself with anxiety."

"Have you heard anything since you've been back from vacation?"

Duke told me, "We have a court date, but it's not until June. The wait is going to be tough. But the good news is, we're all insanely busy, so hopefully the next couple of months will pass quickly." He scooped up his husband's small hand in his huge one, and there was so much love in the look they exchanged.

*****

After dinner and dessert, we broke into teams and played movie title charades. MJ was slightly horrified at first as we all got up and took turns acting like idiots, but when he saw that Aiden was enjoying himself, he relaxed and seemed to have fun, too. He and Aiden were on the same team. Quinn and Duke were another. The three-person team of Mitchell, Mark and me didn't really have an advantage, because I was terrible at trying to act out the movie titles, and MJ and Aiden ended up winning (though I suspected Quinn and Duke let them win).

After that, we all settled in and watched a movie, and when it ended, Duke said, "I hate to break up the party, but it's getting late and we should head home. Aiden's pet skunk has probably eaten the furniture by now."

MJ looked at me in a panic. He'd planned to ask Aiden on a date (with Duke and Quinn's blessing), but it hadn't happened yet. As everyone got up, I said, "MJ, you forgot to show Aiden your room. Why don't you run up and do that real quick?" That probably would have been more subtle if Mitchell hadn't flashed MJ a cartoonish, exaggerated wink.

We took our time heading to the front door and made plans to get together again soon, next time at Quinn and Duke's house. Then Mark said, "Mitchell and I should go wait in the family room. If Aiden says no when MJ asks him out, it's going to be super embarrassing for our brother if we're all standing here staring at him." I thought that showed an admirable bit of empathy.

But before Mark and Mitchell made it down the hall, Aiden and MJ came bounding downstairs. Aiden was holding a handmade card and a little toy skunk that MJ had bought for him, and he smiled sweetly at MJ and said, "I'll talk to you tomorrow, okay?"

MJ was all smiles, too. "Definitely."

After a round of thank yous and good nights, their little family took off, and I turned to MJ and said, "That obviously went well."

He was elated. "We're going to the movies next weekend. Remember a long time ago, when I asked if you and Yoshi could come along?"

"I remember. Do you still want us to do that?"

"No, that's okay. I've got this. Could you drive us, though?"

"Sure thing."

I sent the kids to get ready for bed, and after I cleaned up the kitchen, I went upstairs to tuck them in. I said good night to Mark and Mitchell first, and then I stuck my head in MJ's room and said, "Asking Aiden on a date was another example of you being brave tonight."

MJ looked up from the book in his lap. "I was a little worried. I didn't really expect him to say no, because I was pretty sure he liked me. But he's gotten to be a good friend, and I didn't want to mess that up. Then I thought about you and Yoshi. You two have been friends forever, but you were still willing to take a chance. I figured if you could do that, I could too."

"I'm glad you and I both took those chances."

"You should call Yoshi. I know you miss him."

"It's three hours later there," I said. "I should probably wait until tomorrow."

MJ shot me a look. "It's Friday night and he's in New York, Dad. I guarantee he's not asleep. Just give him a call."

"Okay, I will. Good night, MJ."

"Good night, Dad."

I paused on my way out the door and turned back to him. "I'd tell you not to stay up reading, but you know what? Go ahead and finish your book. I can see you're close to the end."

MJ beamed at me. "Thanks, Dad. I really wanted to finish it tonight. Now I won't have to do that in secret, with a flashlight under my blanket."

"That's exactly what I used to do as a kid," I admitted.

When I got to my room, I sat on the edge of the bed and looked at my phone. It was one a.m. in New York, but

MJ was right, Yoshi wouldn't be asleep. He never even went to sleep before one when he was at home.

I selected his name in my list of contacts and put the phone on speaker, and a few moments later, Yoshi answered with, "Hey Mike!" Techno music was blaring in the background.

"Hey! It sounds like you're at a club," I said loudly. "I just wanted to check in and see how you're doing."

"I'm at a club," he yelled. "I can't really hear you, but I'm glad you called! Is everything okay with you and the boys?"

"Great!"

"That sounded like a yes. That's good! I'll talk to you tomorrow, okay?" Someone in the background said something to him that I couldn't make out, and he laughed.

I murmured, "I miss you, Yoshi." And then I yelled into the phone, "Have fun! I'll talk to you tomorrow!"

When I disconnected the call, I felt deflated. I changed into a white T-shirt and pajama pants, but instead of going to bed, I went into my home office, which was basically a little alcove off my bedroom. I was already depressed, so I figured I might as well get some work done. After putting in late nights the past few days to make up for taking a week off, I was just about caught up with all my clients, though there was always more to do.

I fired up my computer, but then I just sat at the desk for a while, lost in thought. I really wondered how a man like Yoshi could ever be happy with someone like me. He was dancing the night away at a club in New York, while I was staring at spreadsheets. I didn't even think it was possible that I could be more boring. I sighed quietly and tried to make myself focus on the column of numbers in front of me.

*****

The next afternoon, the boys and I returned from Mark's basketball league playoffs and a trip to Costco to find Dante's black SUV parked in front of the house. As I pulled into the garage, I fired off instructions quickly, because I knew the kids would scatter like roaches the moment the vehicle came to a stop. "Mitchell, grab Gizmo's carrier and take him into the backyard before he explodes. Mark and MJ, I want you both to help me bring in groceries. After that, you need to take a shower, Mark."

My youngest son complained, "I'm starving to death, Dad."

"Since you just ate a granola bar, you'll probably manage to cling to life long enough to help with the groceries and get cleaned up. Please wash your hair this time, don't just wet it."

I lugged a massive 48-pack of toilet paper into the house and found Dante sitting at my kitchen island, sipping coffee. He was wearing an immaculate and clearly expensive black suit, along with a black shirt and tie, which seemed like total overkill for a Saturday afternoon, but whatever.

He looked up from his phone, and when he saw what I was carrying, he quipped, "Jesus, Mikey. Maybe lay off the fiber."

"Hilarious. When did you get back from Catalina?"

"I got back about an hour ago and came straight here from the airport. I need to talk to you about something." Mark and MJ came into the kitchen with some groceries and gave their uncle a hug before heading upstairs.

I asked, "Was there a problem with the Seahorse Ranch transaction?"

"No, that went great. I now own forty percent of a failing island resort, which is something I never thought I'd say. Gianni and Zan are about to close on that house too, so all's well on Catalina."

"Great. Give me just a minute," I said. "I need to bring in a few more things from the garage."

"Want my help?"

"No."

"Good."

Once my SUV was empty and all three kids were upstairs, I grabbed the ingredients for peanut butter and jelly sandwiches and told my brother, "You have about three minutes before my boys come barreling back down here demanding food, so what did you want to talk to me about?"

Dante said, "You know I think the world of Yoshi. He's been a part of this family for a long time. But still, there's something you should see."

"What is it?"

"The TV in the airport was tuned to one of those sleazy gossip shows, and they aired some photos that were taken last night in Manhattan."

He pulled up something on his phone and handed it to me. I frowned at the picture of Yoshi with his ex-boyfriend Gale Goodwin and said, "That could have been taken a year ago."

"It wasn't. I looked into it, and that band in the background was playing their debut show last night."

I studied the trio of photos closely. They'd been taken in a crowded club, and Yoshi and Gale clearly hadn't known they were being photographed. In one, they were dancing. In another, Gale's arm was around Yoshi's shoulders, and he was whispering in his ear. Both of those might have been perfectly innocent, but the final picture made me see red. In it, Gale held Yoshi in an embrace, which also might have been okay, except for one little detail: Gale's hand was cupping Yoshi's ass. The caption read: *Mayday Lead Singer Gale Goodwin Sharing Passionate Moment with Sexy Boy Toy.* I'd never had a stronger urge to punch someone in the face.

The longer I looked at that photo, the angrier I got. Not at Yoshi, because I knew I could trust him. But Gale Goodwin was a douche, and it seemed pretty obvious that he'd decided to make a play for his ex-boyfriend, even though Yoshi must have told him he was seeing someone.

Dante was saying, "For the record, I really don't believe Yoshi would cheat on you. But as your big brother, I felt it was my duty to bring those to your attention. Why don't you call him and get the story behind the pictures? I bet there's a good explanation."

I handed Dante his phone and called Yoshi on mine. Gale answered on the second ring. There was loud music in the background, and he said, "Well, look who it is. Yoshi's busy, Mikey. Now run along." Then he hung up on me. I was *livid*.

My voice was a low growl when I said, "Gale Goodwin needs a lesson in manners. He also needs to be made to understand that Yoshi is mine."

A burst of surprised laughter slipped from my brother, and he said, "I've never seen Caveman Mike before. I like him."

"I can't even tell you how much I wish I could confront Goodwin. That arrogant prick needs an attitude adjustment."

"I totally agree. So, go do it." Dante picked up his phone and sent a quick text, and then he tapped his screen a few times.

"God I want to, but I can't just fly to New York. What about my kids?"

My brother said, "I'll watch them, obviously. I just asked Charlie and Jayden to pack a bag and join me, and we'll stay here until you get back. You won't have a thing to worry about." He turned his attention back to the phone and scrolled through some sort of list, then tapped the screen again.

"It's sorely tempting," I said, "but do you know how expensive a last-minute flight to New York would be?"

Dante tapped his screen once more and told me, "I know exactly how much it is, because I just bought you a ticket. Your plane leaves in a little over two hours. I left the return trip open-ended, so you can come back whenever you want to."

"Did you really?"

Dante's phone buzzed with an incoming message, and after he read it, he said, "Charlie and Jayden will be here in twenty minutes. So, are you doing this, or what?"

"I've never done anything this impulsive in my entire life. Not even close."

From behind us, MJ said, "Remember how we were supposed to remind each other to be brave? This is your reminder, Dad."

I turned to face my son. "I didn't know you were there. How much did you overhear?"

"Enough to know this is important and you need to go."

"I really do," I said, "not just because Gale needs to be put in his place. I need to do this for Yoshi. I have to show him what he means to me, and that I'm willing to fight for him."

MJ raised his fist in the air and exclaimed, "Go get your man, Dad!"

Dante pulled MJ close and kissed the top of the boy's head. Then he whispered, "You're my favorite nephew. Don't tell the others."

That made MJ smile, and he asked, "How can I help, Dad?"

I gestured at the loaf of bread on the counter. "Could you please make peanut butter and jelly sandwiches for yourself and your brothers? I need to pack a bag and change my clothes."

"On it." MJ went to the cupboard to grab some plates.

I looked down at my jeans and white polo shirt and sighed. "For the first time in my life, I wish I had a ridiculously expensive suit like yours, Dante. A man like Gale Goodwin would notice something like that."

My brother got to his feet and gestured at the doorway. "Let's go upstairs and see what we can do."

As we left the kitchen, I told him, "You won't like what you find in my closet. All I have are the dull 'Accountants R Us' suits you're always teasing me about."

Mark met us at the top of the stairs and asked, "What happened to lunch?"

"MJ is making sandwiches. Find Mitchell, and then both of you help him put together the rest of the meal," I said. "This is going to sound weird, but I need to fly to New York this afternoon. I'll be back tomorrow, and Uncle Dante, Uncle Charlie, and Jayden are spending the night here."

The boy took it completely in stride, as if that was something that happened every day in our family. As he headed down the stairs, Mark said, "Cool, I've been wanting to show Jayden my new video game. Bring me back a present." That was the sum total of his reaction.

When we reached my room, Dante emptied his pockets, took off his suit jacket, and held it out to me as he told me to try it on. Not surprisingly, it was a perfect fit, since we were the same height with the same big build. "It looks like it was made for you. Let's trade outfits."

He tossed his things on the mattress as I stripped off my clothes. When I took off my jeans, my brother muttered, "Oh, come on."

"What?"

He pulled my polo shirt on and gestured at my underwear. "You're a grown man, Mike. Why are you wearing the same style of tightie whities that we wore as kids?"

I buttoned up his black shirt as I said, "It doesn't matter. Nobody's going to see my underwear."

"Then you're doing this wrong."

"What does that mean?"

"You're flying cross-country to stake a claim on your man," he said. "If an act that primal doesn't land you two in bed, I don't know what will."

I considered that for a beat. Then I went to my dresser and grabbed a pair of black socks, followed by a new pair of miniscule briefs that I'd tucked away for my next date night with Yoshi. They were black with red piping, and the entire backside was cut out in a big, butt-framing oval, trimmed in crimson. I was hoping Dante wouldn't notice, but he muttered, "There's no middle ground with you, apparently. You just went from saint to stripper in three seconds."

"I bought these because I wanted to make an impression on Yoshi."

"Yeah, I'm pretty sure you'll meet your objective."

Once I got dressed, I sat on the edge of my bed and put on the black socks, followed by Dante's Italian dress shoes. I wiggled my toes and told him, "My sneakers are going to be too small on you."

He rummaged around in my closet and ended up with a pair of oversized fuzzy slippers that my sons had given me, which looked like green monster feet. "That really completes the look," I said with a smile.

"That's what I thought." Dante looked down at himself and chuckled. "This reminds me of that movie 'Freaky Friday,' where two people change places with each other." He unfastened his wristwatch and handed it to me, and when I told him I had one, he said, "I know. But if the goal here is to make that fucker Gale Goodwin feel like an inferior little turd blossom, then wear this one."

I took the watch from him and fastened it to my wrist. "Should I ask how much something like this costs?"

"No, because if I tell you the truth, you'll judge me for spending too extravagantly and make one of those pinched faces." He contorted his features into an exaggeratedly pained expression.

I turned my arm and admired the timepiece. "Not this time. It's gorgeous. Thanks for the whole Cinderella treatment, Dante, including the plane ticket. You need to let me know how much I owe you for that."

"It's my treat."

"I can't let you do that."

"C'mon, Cinderella, take some help when it's offered. I thought you were learning to let people do things for you now and then."

I considered that for a few moments before saying, "Well, okay. Thank you again." I adjusted my cuffs, and as I stood in front of the full-length mirror on the back of my bathroom door, I decided that suit was worth every penny. No wonder Dante spent so much on clothes.

"No need to keep thanking me."

I turned to face him and said, "You'd tell me if I was acting nuts, right?"

"Oh, you are. In fact, what you're about to do is bat shit crazy. That's what's so great about it."

"Wait...what?"

"I know you adore Yoshi," my brother said, "but it seems like you've been holding a part of yourself back, probably because you're afraid of getting hurt again. But love isn't careful and planned out. Just the opposite! It's passionate and spontaneous, and a little bit crazy. It's exactly what you're doing right now, and I'm proud of you, Mike."

"And apparently doing something dumb finally allowed me to graduate from Mikey to Mike. That's ironic."

Dante grinned at me. "You need to pack, and I'll arrange a Lyft to take you to the airport. I'd drive you myself, but I'm not sure how long it'll take my husband and son to get here, and I don't want to keep you waiting. Actually, I should do that now, since you don't have all that long before your flight." He pulled up the app on his phone and typed in some information.

Meanwhile, I stuck my phone, a charging cord, a little plastic comb, and my wallet in the pockets of that gorgeous suit, and then I put on my glasses and announced, "I'm ready." While the glasses might not have been necessary, I felt more like myself in them, and that was reassuring at a time when I felt almost unrecognizable.

"Really? No luggage?"

"I'm planning to go straight from the airport to wherever Gale is, and I don't want to be weighed down."

We headed for the stairs, and Dante asked me where Yoshi was staying. When I told him, he said, "I'm going to book you a room at the same hotel. No matter what ends up happening, you'll probably want to spend the night, so I'll make sure you have a place to stay."

"If we're thinking positive, I'll be staying with Yoshi tonight."

"He's there with his apprentice. I'm thinking very positively and assuming you and Yoshi are going to need a lot of privacy, so this way you two will have a room of your own. I'm also going to track down Gale's whereabouts during your flight, and I'll text you with details on where to find him."

"What if he's already gone by the time I get there?"

Dante tapped his phone a few times, then said, "According to his band's website, Gale has an interview tomorrow with one of the morning shows, so he'll still be in New York tonight."

"And surrounded by bodyguards, no doubt."

Dante slipped something into my hand. "So, figure out who you need to bribe to either look the other way or create a distraction."

I glanced at the fat money clip in my palm and raised an eyebrow. "You and I are profoundly different people, Dante."

"Only on the outside. Underneath, we're exactly the same. We're both men who adore our families and would do absolutely anything for the people we love."

"You know what? You're right about that." I tried to hand back the money, and when he wouldn't take it I asked, "You're not seriously giving this to me, are you?"

"Of course I am. It's good to have cash on hand when you travel."

I grinned a little. "For bribes and whatnot."

"Exactly."

When we reached the kitchen, my kids stared at us in disbelief. "That's so weird," Mitchell stammered. "It's like you and Uncle Dante were a part of some kind of freaky experiment and partially morphed into each other."

I chuckled at that, then stepped around the island and gathered the boys in a group hug. "Mitchell, I need to go to New York tonight. I'll be back tomorrow."

"I know. MJ caught Mark and me up to speed. Go and bring home Yoshi, Dad, for all of us. That overrated rock star can't have him."

"That's the plan." After a beat, I added, "You know I'm not going to New York to beat up his ex-boyfriend, right? I'm just going to have a talk with him."

"Sure Dad, have a nice, long *talk* with him." Mark made air quotes with his fingers.

"I mean it. I don't want you boys to think violence solves problems, because it doesn't."

Dante muttered under his breath, so only I could hear it, "Except when it does." Then he glanced at his phone and told me, "Your ride's just a couple of minutes away, Mike. I'll walk you out, so I can give you the overcoat that's in the back of my SUV. It's cold in New York right now."

I kissed each of my sons on the forehead. "I love you guys. You know that, right?"

"We love you too, Dad," Mark said.

Gizmo started to jump on me, but Dante snapped, "Don't even think about putting your paws on that suit, you little maniac." To my surprise, the animal sat right down and watched Dante expectantly, and I scratched the dog behind his ears.

I gave each boy another hug in turn and asked, "Does anyone need anything before I go?"

"Don't worry Dad, we've got this," MJ told me.

"Alright, then I'll see you tomorrow."

I started to head for the door, but Mitchell called, "Wait, I almost forgot. This is for you." When I turned around, he handed me a brown paper bag with 'Dad' written on it. "You didn't have time to eat, and we thought you might get hungry on your trip." I felt a little choked up as I thanked him and took the sack lunch.

When Dante and I reached the sidewalk, he rummaged through a few dry cleaning bags that hung from a hook in the backseat. After a moment, he pulled a gorgeous, black cashmere overcoat from its wrapping and handed it to me. Then he went back to rifling through a few more bags. "I checked, and it's been getting down to the thirties at night in New York. Fortunately, Charlie just had some of our cold weather things cleaned so we could pack them away for the season. Ah, here we go."

My brother produced a soft, charcoal gray knit scarf and draped it around my neck. He grinned a little as he did that, and I said, "I just flashed on every winter when we were kids, and the way you'd always bundle me up when I wanted to play outside."

"I just thought of the same thing."

I pulled my brother into a bear hug and murmured, "Thank you for always having my back, Dante. Literally always. I can't remember a time when you weren't right there, making sure I was okay."

"I told you to stop thanking me." He tried to sound cranky, but he held me tight.

"Since when have I ever listened?"

"Be safe, little brother, and if you need anything at all, don't hesitate to call me. I know a lot of people in New York, and they're all at your disposal."

My ride arrived a minute later. After I settled into the backseat with my lunch bag on my lap and we began to drive away, I glanced over my shoulder and watched my usually sophisticated brother head back inside wearing those huge green slippers. I smiled fondly.

I knew I was damn lucky to have such a loving and supportive family. I couldn't even imagine who I'd be without them. That made me think of Yoshi. He'd grown up without any of that, but he'd become a part of my family. He belonged not only with me, but with all of us, and fuck that asshole Gale for trying to come between us.

Ever since I'd seen those pictures, I'd let anger guide me. I tried to focus on that and hold on to it, so it would drown out that tiny but insistent voice in my head, the one telling me I could never hope to compete with a man like Gale Goodwin. It was a voice I knew well, because it was always right there, ready to remind me I wasn't enough.

But that wasn't a day for insecurity. I knew Yoshi cared about me, and he'd already chosen me over Gale. That nagging little voice could go to hell.

*****

Of course, Dante had splurged on first class. I settled into the comfortable seat, and we soon took off for the five-and-a-half-hour nonstop flight to New York. We were offered a meal in the front cabin, but I turned it down. I did say yes to a glass of champagne, though. Then I spread my sack lunch out in front of me and smiled when I saw that my sons had cut my sandwich into a heart shape. They'd also sent along a baggie of fruit salad that someone (probably Mitchell) had tossed with colorful sprinkles, a second baggie with goldfish crackers, and a note that said: *We love you, Dad. We love Yoshi too, so kick Gale's butt and bring him home.*

The uptight business-douche sitting beside me glanced at my lunch, then shot me a look of disdain. I stared him down and hissed, "I have the best kids in the whole goddamn world, and they made this for me, so you can take your attitude and shove it up your ass." He ignored me for the rest of the flight, which was exactly what I wanted.

*****

It was nearly eleven p.m. local time when I landed in New York. I read a text from Dante as I strode through the terminal at LaGuardia, which said: *Goodwin is staying in the same hotel as Yoshi, room 1026. I booked you a suite on the same floor, so you can use your keycard to access the elevator. Best of luck. By the way, I have an excellent lawyer on retainer in New York, but it'd be good if you proceeded cautiously and didn't end up needing her.*

I messaged him on the cab ride into Manhattan and thanked Dante for the first class ticket and the hotel room. I also mentioned I wasn't planning to do anything that would require a lawyer. That was good to know, though.

In truth, I had absolutely no idea what I was going to do. I'd never been in a fight before, and I didn't relish the thought of landing in jail for assault. I mostly just wanted to yell at Goodwin for a solid minute and let him know in no uncertain terms that Yoshi was taken, but I couldn't really imagine him standing still for that.

When I reached the hotel, I pulled up the collar of Dante's cashmere overcoat against the cold breeze and rushed inside, through an elaborate wood and brass door held open by a uniformed doorman. The opulent lobby was decorated in dark reds and golds, but I only got a vague impression of it. I was totally focused on a lone figure talking on a phone off to the right: Gale Goodwin.

Yes! I'd totally lucked out. He was by himself too, without a single beefy bodyguard in sight.

I strode across the lobby, keeping my gaze fixed on Gale. I'd met him twice while he and Yoshi were dating, though I doubted he remembered me. I'd forgotten some things too, including the fact that Goodwin was enormous. He was about my height, but even more muscular with huge, tatted up arms and wide shoulders. There was every chance he was going to beat me to a pulp in the next two minutes. I didn't care.

He noticed me a moment before I reached him, and Gale's blue eyes went wide. I plucked the phone from his fingers and tossed it aside, and then I shoved him against the tinted glass wall behind him. I balled up the front of his T-shirt in my fist, got right in his face, and growled, "You had your chance with Yoshi, you asshole. He's with me now, and you're going to keep your goddamn hands off of him, understood?"

He stammered, "Wh—what?"

I shook him a little and slammed him back against the wall. "I said you're going to keep your fucking mitts off Yoshiro Miyazaki."

"Who the fuck are you?"

"His boyfriend."

He thought about that for a moment, and then he asked, "Mikey?"

"It's Mike, you prick. Mike Dombruso. Remember that name, because if you fucking touch Yoshi again, you'll be answering to me."

Three huge guys with buzz cuts, dark suits, and earpieces rushed up to us. To my surprise, Gale held up a hand and told them, "It's alright, boys. I got this."

They backed up a couple of feet, though each of them remained totally on edge and seemed ready to rip me limb from limb. I let go of Gale's T-shirt and took a step back, and he said, "You wasted a trip. Yoshi already told me to go fuck myself."

"Well, now I'm telling you, too."

Yoshi stepped through a doorway ten feet to my left and blurted, "Mike? What are you doing here?"

Right about then, I noticed the wall was actually a tinted window fronting the hotel bar. Max was on the other side of the glass, along with a group of people I didn't recognize. Several of them were holding up their phones and filming.

Gale said, "This is about those tabloid photos, isn't it?" He turned to Yoshi and called, "I told you they might be an issue, Yo."

Yoshi's brow was creased into a sharp frown. He came up to us, staring me down as he muttered, "And I said they wouldn't matter, because my boyfriend trusted me."

"I do trust you," I said. "But I don't trust Gale, and his hands were all over you."

"I admit I crossed a line when I grabbed Yo's ass. He reminded me of that by kneeing me in the nuts. Message received," Gale said.

I snapped, "And when you answered Yoshi's phone earlier, told me to run along, and hung up on me? Was I just supposed to laugh that off?"

Gale pushed his shaggy, dyed black hair out of his eyes and shrugged. "I'm kind of a douche when I've been drinking, and I'd been tossing back Bloody Marys all afternoon. Sorry, man."

"You're kind of a douche all the time," I countered. He frowned at that but let it go.

Yoshi's expression was grim as he muttered, "I didn't know you'd called, since Gale failed to deliver the message."

"I forgot all about it. That was when Max was puking and you were holding his hair," Gale told him. "That kid needs to stay the fuck away from Bloody Marys. Seriously. Like, forever."

"He's pretty drunk again, so I'm going to take him up to the room." Yoshi pointed at me and added, "Then you and I are going to have a talk."

"I can take him upstairs if you want me to." Gale looked around and asked, "What happened to my phone?"

One of the bodyguards picked it up and checked the screen. Fortunately, it had landed on an area rug and was still intact. The man handed it back to Gale as Yoshi told him, "Max is my responsibility, and I've got this."

"I'll be in my room," I said. "I'll text you the number after I check in." Yoshi nodded and went to retrieve his apprentice.

Gale started to return to the bar with his trio of bodyguards, but then he turned to me and said, "For the record, you're right. I did try to make a play for Yoshi this weekend. That's actually why I came to New York a couple of days early, because I wanted him back. Just so you know, he shot me down. Hard. Like, seriously, he rejected the hell out of me. It was pretty brutal. Anyway, it was a dick move on my part since I knew he was seeing someone, but I didn't think it was anything serious. I found out I was dead wrong. He's crazy about you."

"It's mutual."

"I'm impressed that you came all this way to fight for Yoshi. I was never really there for him, I know that. He deserves someone who'll make him a priority."

I stared him down and muttered, "I don't give a shit that you're impressed."

Gale grinned a little and said, "You're stone cold, man. I like it." Then he turned and went back to the bar, flanked by his own, personal army.

I was checking in at the front desk a couple of minutes later when Yoshi and Max passed me on their way to the elevator. Max was saying, "But it's our last night in New York, and the hotel bar was just supposed to be the warm-up! We were going to hit like, six clubs tonight!" He swayed a bit, and Yoshi caught his arm. Then Max noticed me and waved as he yelled, "Hi Mike! You look fucking hot! Damn it, why are all the good ones taken?" Yoshi just kept propelling him forward with an exasperated expression.

When I reached the beautiful, royal blue and gold suite that my generous brother had clearly overspent on, I texted Yoshi my room number. Then I messaged Dante with: *I have good news and bad news. The good news is, I'm not going to jail. The bad news: Yoshi's pissed off at me, because he thinks I don't trust him. Guess I should have predicted that.*

He replied with: *Yoshi's nuts about you, so he'll get over it.*

He'd better be right. I asked: *How are the boys?*

Dante wrote: *They're great. We're making popcorn and watching a double feature, 'Poltergeist' and 'The Exorcist.'*

I immediately fired back: *What the hell!*

Dante replied with a row of emojis that were laughing so hard they were crying and the words: *God, you're an easy mark. I'm kidding. They're torturing Charlie and me by making us watch Disney movies. Go patch things up with Yoshi, I'll talk to you later.*

I sighed and plugged in the phone on the nightstand, then hung the overcoat and scarf in the closet. After I used the restroom, washed up a bit, and combed my hair, I was totally out of things to do. That left me with pacing a crease into the carpeting until Yoshi showed up.

It was a solid fifteen minutes before he knocked on my door. I'd planned to apologize, but when he stepped into the room, I blurted, "Gale deserved that. He deserved a lot worse, actually. Nobody gets to grab your ass and treat you like a piece of meat, least of all Gale Goodwin."

"I handled it, Mike."

"I know. And now, I've handled it, too. I had to. You're mine, Yoshi, and I want everyone to know that, including your douchey ex."

Yoshi tried to fight back a smile as he grumbled, "Fucking caveman in a three thousand dollar suit. Damn it. You look hot as hell, and seeing you put Gale in his place was a huge turn-on, but I shouldn't encourage this type of behavior." As he said that, he walked up to me and ran his hand down my chest.

I lightly trailed my fingertips down his arm. "It's probably a bad idea to encourage a caveman. Dangerous, even."

His gaze dropped to my lips, and he murmured, "I was all set to be furious with you."

Now it was my turn to try to suppress a smile. "That doesn't seem to be going very well."

"You're right, it's not. I was going to make the argument that you must not trust me, but I know you do. You show me all the time."

"I trust you with every part of me."

"It also occurred to me, as I was trying to get Max to settle down and go to sleep, that you left your boys to come here and fight for me," he said. "That tells me how important this was to you, because you'd never do that lightly."

"Right again."

"And here's the clincher: if the situation were reversed, I absolutely would have taken the first flight I could find so I could come here and fight for you. I would have done that because you're mine, and you're worth fighting for. The fact that I trust you more than anyone I've ever known is beside the point. I would have done exactly what you did."

"I'm glad we understand each other." When I kissed him, Yoshi leaned into me, and I ran my fingers into his hair.

He looked up at me, and his voice was rough when he whispered, "I need you to show me I'm yours tonight."

"That was the plan even before you asked." His breath caught, and he parted his lips as he met my gaze. The raw lust in his eyes ignited my desire like a match to gunpowder. When I claimed his mouth with a demanding kiss, a tremor rolled through his strong, slender body.

There was no going slowly, not that night. I carried him into the bedroom and tossed him on the mattress. Yoshi murmured, "Fuck yes," and I could see his cock straining against his black jeans.

I stripped him quickly, then explored his body with my mouth and tongue before pausing to undress for him. I made a show of it, holding his gaze while I tossed aside one piece of clothing after another. When I was down to just those racy black and red briefs, he murmured, "You're full of surprises, Mike."

To make sure he thoroughly enjoyed the rear view, I grinned and said, "Be right back," before sauntering to the bathroom. When he got a look at the oval cut-out that framed my ass, Yoshi moaned and told me to hurry.

Fortunately, he always kept packets of lube and condoms in his wallet, and when I returned from the bathroom with a couple of towels, he had some supplies ready for me on the nightstand. I worked him open as I jerked him off, and then he got on his knees and arched his back, offering himself to me. I pulled down the briefs to just below my balls and rolled on a condom, wiped the lube from my fingers, and grasped his hips as I slid into him. His ass was so warm and tight around my cock, and I murmured, "You feel so good." Total understatement.

I tried to start off slow, but Yoshi drove himself onto me. Even when I started pounding his ass, he ground out, "Harder." I gave him what he asked for. The sound of our bodies slamming together filled that luxurious suite as pleasure radiated through me.

In just a few minutes, my orgasm tore from me, and a moment later, Yoshi's ass tightened around my cock. He cried out and shot onto one of the towels as he jerked himself off with quick, hard strokes. I held him tight and kissed his shoulder as his orgasm shook him. Finally, when he was completely spent, I eased my cock from his body and cleaned us up with one of the towels, and then I cradled him in my arms.

Yoshi kissed my chest before looking up at me and whispering, "I'm so glad you're here. I missed you like crazy these past few days."

"I missed you, too."

After a while, he asked, "Do you want to go out? You came all the way to New York, so you should make the most of it."

"I'm already making the most of it." He grinned at that and curled up in the crook of my arm. But a few moments later, I said, "Just because I don't want to do anything doesn't mean you're obligated to cancel your plans."

Yoshi sat up and met my gaze. "Are you trying to tell me to go out and leave you here, and if so, why?"

"I just don't want you to miss out on anything because of me."

"There's more to it than that."

I tried to find the words to tell him what was on my mind, but all I came up with was, "You and I are very different people, Yoshi, and I don't expect you to want to stay in just because I do. Case in point, over the last three days, you've been partying with a rock star on a whirlwind, spontaneous trip to New York. During that same time period, my biggest accomplishment was removing dog barf from the area rug in the living room without it leaving a stain."

"There's a hell of a lot more to your life than that."

"Okay, maybe. The bottom line, though, is that my world is pretty ordinary, so I can't really expect to hold your interest."

"You've held my interest for twelve years, Mike. That's how long I've been mesmerized by you," Yoshi said. "As for that whole partying thing, Max wanted to check out the New York club scene, so I let him drag me out every night. And guess what? I hated it. I might only be eight years older than him, but I've spent this whole trip feeling like Max's dad and getting frustrated because he makes such stupid decisions. Incidentally, the aforementioned rock star is even more annoying. Gale's actually a year older than me, but he acts like a drunken, emotionally stunted teenager. I don't want this life, Mike. It had a certain appeal when I was twenty-one, but at thirty-three? No thanks."

"Okay, so you've outgrown the club scene. But our lives are still completely different."

"How do you figure?"

"You have so much freedom," I said. "You can be spontaneous and run off to New York for an art show, or take off and sail along the coast, or do anything you want, really. Why would you trade that for someone like me?"

"Someone like you? Don't you get it, Mike? All my life, I wanted two things: a wonderful man, and a loving family. You're all of that and more. You're *everything.*"

"But after a while, wouldn't I start to feel like an anchor and drag you down?"

"I'd love it if you were my anchor. Think about that word. You say it like it's a negative, but you're wrong. Anchors don't drag you down, they hold you safely and securely. They...never mind."

Yoshi got out of bed and fumbled for his briefs, and as he pulled them on and started to reach for his jeans, I asked, "Where are you going?"

"To my room, before I make a complete fool out of myself."

I climbed out of bed and caught him by his shoulders, and he tucked his face into my chest. I wrapped my arms around him, and after a moment, I asked, "What's wrong?"

"I'm right on the verge of saying a whole bunch of stuff you're probably not ready to hear, so I need to go before I mess this up."

"Say it anyway, even if you think I'm not ready for it."

There was so much emotion in his dark eyes when he looked up at me and whispered, "I'm afraid to."

"Maybe it'll help if I go first." I cupped his cheek and told him, "I'm completely, madly, wildly in love with you, Yoshi. I'm not sure when it changed from loving you as my best friend to being in love. I just know it happened long before I was able to admit it to myself.

"I wasn't sure I'd ever be able to let someone in again, but then it wasn't even a choice. It just happened. You claimed a piece of my heart, and it's yours forever. That actually scares the hell out of me, because I'm worried about not being enough for you. I'm also worried that our lives are too different to ever really fit together. But none of that changes the fact that I absolutely adore you."

Yoshi held my gaze and said, so quietly, "I can't even remember a time when I wasn't in love with you. I was ashamed of myself, because you were married when we met, but I fell in love with you anyway. Ironically, it happened when I saw you with Jenny and your baby. MJ was about a year old when Gianni started bringing me to Sunday dinners at Nana's house. You were the most gentle, loving, devoted husband and father I'd ever seen in my life. It was absolutely beautiful, and so were you, inside and out.

"I never intended to act on my feelings for you. It was just going to be my secret. But by some miracle, we're actually together now! Everything I ever wanted is right here, within my grasp, and I'm fucking terrified, Mike. I keep thinking, what if I mess this up? What if I ruin the only chance I'll ever get with the man I've wanted all of my adult life? How would I ever get over something like that?"

I was stunned by his revelation, and I whispered, "You never said anything."

"Of course not. How could I? You were totally unavailable, at first because you were married, and for years after that because you were both in mourning and totally focused on raising your kids. Never mind the fact that I thought you were straight. I tried to move on by dating Gale and other equally inadequate people, but I never loved any of them. How could I, when my heart belonged to someone else?"

I murmured, "All these years."

He grinned a little. "I believe that's exactly what I said when I finally found out you were bi, right before we went to Catalina. But this thing between us really couldn't have happened any sooner. You weren't ready. Even when you let your family convince you to start dating again and got involved with Marie, I could tell you were just going through the motions."

"You're right. We really couldn't have done this any sooner."

I led Yoshi back to bed, and when we were curled up under the covers again, he said, "I'm going to throw an idea out there, and you can take it or leave it. You've commented for years that you think my life is exciting, while yours seems dull by comparison. But I'm not really doing anything all that interesting. I work way too much, and maybe once a month, I take a long weekend and travel somewhere, or I take a class and learn a new skill. That's about it.

"The thing is, you could do that too, Mike. You're so used to putting everyone else first that you never do anything for yourself. That makes you a sensational dad, but I think it also leaves you feeling a bit dissatisfied with your own life. Maybe that's why the things I do really stand out to you. And maybe, if you figure out how to find time to do things for yourself, you'll stop seeing this huge divide between my life and yours."

I admitted, "You may have a point, but I'm not going to find more hours in the day. My schedule is jam-packed, and that's just the way it is."

"There's plenty of time, as long as you're willing to make one key change."

"What's that?"

He said, "Accept help. You and I are a couple now, so let me take over some of your responsibilities. For example, I could run your errands while I'm running mine, or take over the job of picking up the boys after school, or I could drive them to their activities. Or hell, all of the above."

"I couldn't ask you to do that."

"You're not asking me Mike, I'm asking you. I want to be more involved in the boys' lives, not just as a guest who drops by for dinner and a movie occasionally, but as someone who's there day-to-day as a real part of your family. You have a resource in me. You also have your brothers and Nana. They'd gladly step in and become more involved in your boys' lives if you let them. If they did that regularly, you'd have a block of time all to yourself."

"To do what?"

"Anything you want! You could take a class, or visit a bookstore, or see a movie that doesn't have animated characters in it, or whatever. It doesn't really matter what you do. The important part is regularly scheduling time for yourself, not just a few stolen minutes here and there. And that all comes down to relinquishing a little bit of control and deciding you don't have to do everything yourself."

"What I really want is more time with my gorgeous boyfriend."

"You can have both, time for me and time for yourself."

I thought about that, and after a few moments I said, "You're right about the control thing. For such a long time, I felt like I had to handle everything myself, to make sure it not only got done, but done right. I wasn't like that before Jenny died. But afterwards…losing her triggered something in me. I didn't have control over the way she was taken from me and our sons, but I made damn sure I could control everything else. I felt like that was the only way I could hold myself and my family together."

Yoshi trailed his fingers over the short beard along my jawline and whispered, "These past few years must have been exhausting."

"That's putting it mildly."

He turned my chin so I was looking in his eyes and said, "You're not alone anymore, Mike. I'm here now, so you don't have to do everything by yourself."

Until he said those words, I hadn't even realized how badly I needed to hear them. It felt like a tremendous weight was being lifted off, one that had become such a part of me that I barely even realized it was there anymore. I was flooded with emotion, and whatever Yoshi saw in my expression made him crush me in an embrace.

We both knew I wasn't going to change overnight. That need to feel like I was in control had become deeply engrained. But that day marked a turning point. It was when I began the process of learning to let go.

Chapter Fourteen

About a month later, on a sunny Saturday in May, I brushed some sawdust off my jeans and stepped back to admire the object in front of me. With Yoshi's encouragement, I'd decided to take a class through the city's Parks and Rec Department called 'Introduction to Art.' Over the last three weeks, I'd learned I had absolutely no natural talent, but I really enjoyed making things. So far, I'd brought home a wonky ceramic vase and a cheesy landscape painting, and I now had a lopsided wooden sculpture to add to the little gallery my boys had made for me in our family room.

After I cleaned up my workspace and called goodbye to my instructor and classmates, I carried the sculpture to my SUV and put it in the passenger seat. Then, for good measure, I fastened the seatbelt around it to keep it secure. It might look like crap, but I was proud of it, mostly for what it represented: a chance to step outside my comfort zone, learn some new skills, and do something just for me.

The class was held in a converted warehouse on a pier in the Embarcadero, at the opposite end of San Francisco from where I lived. On the way home, I cut through the Financial District, which was ever in shadow amid its towering skyscrapers. In just a few blocks, the business center gave way to the Tenderloin, one of the rougher neighborhoods in the city. All of a sudden, I was hit with an overwhelming sense of déjà vu.

Even though I was pretty sure I'd never been on that particular street before, it was startlingly familiar. The feeling was so persistent that I pulled to the curb and got out so I could take a better look at my surroundings. Unremarkable businesses lined the street, topped with equally unremarkable apartments. Like the rest of the city, the street and sidewalk were crowded with a hell of a lot of people who all seemed to be in a hurry, even on the weekend.

Then I suddenly got it: I was on one of the streets Yoshi had included in his tattoo. He'd pared it down to just a few buildings, but I was able to piece it together. After a minute or two, I located the apartment where he'd been born. I started walking north and soon found the apartment where his family had moved after they outgrew their studio. From there, I was able to identify the convenience store they used to own. That meant the one they owned now was right around the corner.

Curiosity propelled me around the block, and I came to a stop in front of a small market with a produce display out front. When I went inside, it felt like stepping through time. Though clean and tidy, the place looked like it hadn't been

updated in twenty years, maybe longer. The back of the
shop was lined with refrigerated cases topped with outdated
soda company logos, and the wall space that wasn't
covered with shelves featured faded, decades-old posters
advertising cereal and candy bars, some of which I was
pretty sure weren't even made anymore.

Yoshi had mentioned spending a lot of time in that
shop as a kid. His parents couldn't afford babysitters, so
when they both had to be at work, so did he. He'd told me
his favorite spot was the fort he made for himself
underneath the sale table.

When I bent down to glance beneath the scarred
wooden tabletop, which was heaped with an array of
marked-down products, I discovered dozens of stickers on
its underside. Some were colorful images of cartoon
characters, including Transformers, ThunderCats, and
Ninja Turtles. He-Man was particularly well-represented,
and that made me grin. The rest were product labels,
including at least a hundred blue and yellow Chiquita
banana stickers. I tried to picture Yoshi under there as a
little kid, doing his best to entertain himself and to make
the shop feel like home.

The register was to my left, and I studied the slender
woman behind the counter as I approached. She was clearly
Yoshi's mom, with the same strong cheekbones, slightly

prominent nose, and quick smile. Cheryl Miyazaki was younger than I'd expected. She was probably just over fifty with long hair that was just beginning to turn gray and outdated glasses that aged her a bit. She asked, "May I help you find something?"

"Um, I just wanted to introduce myself. My name is Mike Dombruso."

Her smile faltered, just a little, and she said, "You're Yoshi's boyfriend."

"That's right. I'd wondered if he'd mentioned me."

"You're all he talks about, you and those three boys of yours."

On impulse, I asked, "Will you and your husband come to dinner at my house one night next week? I'd love it if we could get to know each other."

The rest of her smile faded. "Yoshi doesn't know you're here, does he?"

I shook my head. "I was just driving through the neighborhood and decided to drop in."

"That's what I figured," she said. "I don't think dinner would be a good idea, but thank you for the invitation."

"Are you sure?"

"You seem like a nice guy, and it's nothing personal. My son and I just have a very strained relationship. It's the same with him and his father. We love Yoshi, but we can't seem to go longer than five minutes without arguing."

I said, "He thinks he's a disappointment to you."

"I know he thinks that."

I couldn't help but notice she didn't bother to correct me. "So, that's it? You're not even going to try?"

"I've tried for thirty-three years, Mike. My son thinks I'm a terrible parent, but all I've ever wanted is a good life for him, better than what I was able to provide." She gestured at the faded shop almost apologetically.

"He has a good life, Mrs. Miyazaki. Great, even. I get that it's not the life you wanted for him, but he's still a huge success, in every way that counts."

"He could have done so much more." She said it quietly, with no malice behind those words, but they cut like a knife. I understood Yoshi so well in that moment.

"That's true for every single one of us," I told her. "I could have done more than becoming an accountant. You could have done more than running a shop. But that doesn't mean any of us failed, not by a long shot."

"But he had so much potential."

"The irony is that he's actually doing everything right. He's not only a kind, intelligent, wonderful human being, he's a financial success. Between his investment in that apartment and his flourishing business, Yoshi is doing great. What more do you want?"

She held my gaze and asked, "Do you have any tattoos, Mike?"

"Well, no. They're not really my style. Why do you ask?"

"Because you're obviously a nice, clean-cut boy, and by the looks of you I suspect you find tattoos as distasteful as I do. I'm glad Yoshi ended up with someone like you, and not the riff-raff that frequent his tattoo parlor."

I asked her, "Is your low opinion of what he does for a living really worth destroying your relationship with your son?"

"You'll understand when your boys are older. Every parent wants their child to reach his full potential. We can't just sit back and watch them waste their lives on some ridiculous whim. We owe them more than that."

"I already understand," I said quietly. "All we owe our kids is unconditional love. That's it. I hope you realize that someday and mend your relationship with Yoshi. Until then, I'll keep loving him enough for both of us." I turned and left the shop with an aching heart and an overwhelming urge to give my boyfriend a hug.

*****

When I returned home, MJ met me in the garage. "I need to show you something, Dad. Do you have a minute?" He was clutching Yoshi's laptop with both hands.

As I unfastened the belt that held my sculpture in place on the passenger seat, I said, "Sure. Want to go inside?"

He shook his head. "I'm not ready to show this to Mark and Mitchell. Everything's a big joke to them."

"Okay, then have a seat in here. What did you want to show me?"

He climbed in the SUV and said, "I need brutal honesty here, Dad. Pretend I'm not your son and tell me if this is any good, for real."

He opened the laptop and played a video of him singing a pretty ballad I didn't recognize, accompanied by his boyfriend Aiden on the acoustic guitar and his friend Jude on drums. It had been filmed at Jude's house, in the makeshift studio the boy's mom had set up for him in the garage. The two musicians were good, but MJ was phenomenal. When the song concluded, I told him, "That's absolutely terrific."

"Do you swear?" I crossed my heart and held up my hand. After a pause, he told me, "I was thinking about posting this on YouTube, but I don't want people to laugh at me."

"They won't, MJ. You sound great."

"Thanks. I mean, I get that some people will laugh or make fun of me anyway. There's no way around that on the internet, but I don't want to let my fear of getting hurt stop me. I need to be brave, like you."

I asked, "You think I'm brave?"

"Absolutely. You flew to New York last month and fought for Yoshi, and ever since then you've been going out and making art, and it doesn't even matter that you're terrible at it. You're doing it anyway, and you're obviously having a lot of fun with it."

I chuckled at his assessment and held up my latest creation. "Today was wood sculpture day."

"I see that. What's it supposed to be?"

"It's us, you and me and your brothers and Yoshi. Oh, and Gizmo. He's that little block at the bottom. It's meant to be abstract."

He deadpanned, "Oh, it is."

As we got out of the SUV and headed for the stairs, I said, "I didn't recognize that song you were singing. Who's it by?"

"Michael Dombruso, Junior."

"You wrote it?"

MJ nodded. "That makes putting it out there a thousand times scarier, by the way. It's tough enough when it's someone else's words. Now that they're mine, it makes me feel super vulnerable."

"I'm even more impressed now that I know you wrote it."

"I'm not that great at it. The song's pretty basic, but you get better by doing, right? I figure if I start now, then by the time I'm ready to make a career of my singing, I'll probably be pretty good."

We found Yoshi in the kitchen, cooking with Mark and Mitchell. My youngest son exclaimed, "Hi Dad! What did you make today?"

I held up the statue, and MJ explained, "It's supposed to be us. The cube is Gizmo." The dog was splayed out on the floor, and he wagged his tail at the sound of his name.

Mitchell came over, and when I handed him the statue, he studied it carefully before saying, "I see what you were going for, Dad, and it's actually pretty good. Which one is me?"

"That one." I pointed to each of the wooden rectangles in turn. "And that one's MJ, that's Mark, this one is Yoshi, and that's me."

I came up behind Yoshi, kissed his shoulder, and murmured, "Hello, gorgeous."

"Hi handsome. Did you have fun?"

"I had a great time." I turned to Mark and asked him, "How was your judo lesson?" Basketball season had ended with victory, and now Mark was on to another sport in his never-ending cycle. I intended to be there for the matches, but we'd decided Yoshi would take him to practice to give me time to take a few classes.

"It was awesome, and now Yoshi's teaching us how to make Greek food. I know that spinach looks super gross, but give it a chance, Dad. We're making something called spank-a-dopida and it's got cheese and puff pastry and stuff. I think it's going to be pretty tasty."

"It's called spanakopita," MJ corrected. Then he said, "Thanks for lending me your computer, Yoshi. Can I keep using it for a few more minutes? I want to upload a video."

When Yoshi agreed, MJ sat down at the kitchen island and opened the laptop. Meanwhile, Mitchell told me, "I'm going to add your latest masterpiece to the gallery, Dad," and carried my sculpture to the family room.

As Yoshi transferred the sautéed spinach to a bowl, Mark whispered loudly, "Mitchell and I finished our part of the surprise, Dad. Do you have your part ready?"

That made MJ sigh in exasperation, and he reminded his brother, "You're not supposed to talk about it!"

"I'm not talking about it," Mark countered. "I just said 'surprise.' I didn't say what it was." Yoshi grinned and pretended not to notice the conversation.

MJ rolled his eyes. A minute later, he said, "Okay, my video is up. I'm so nervous I could puke. Dad, can I call Aiden from the phone in your office and tell him it's live?" Over the past month, MJ and Aiden had talked on the phone every day and gone out on four movie dates, one each weekend. They were both very shy and careful with each other, and even though I still had a hard time accepting the fact that my first born was old enough to date, the innocence of their blossoming relationship was actually very sweet.

When I nodded, MJ hurried from the room, and Mark asked, "What video?"

"Your brother uploaded a video of him singing."

Mark rolled his eyes. "Ugh, boring. What do we need to do next, Yoshi?"

"We have to let the filling cool before we assemble the layers," Yoshi told him. "It'll take about fifteen minutes."

"In that case, I'll be in the backyard practicing my judo moves. Come get me when it's time for phase two of the spank-a-coppa. Peace out!" Mark left the kitchen as Yoshi stuck the covered bowl in the refrigerator.

When he crossed the room to me, I scooped my boyfriend into my arms and murmured, "Alone at last." We kissed for a long moment, and then I said, "I need to talk to you about something, before the kids come back."

"The super secret surprise, I'm guessing."

"Do you know what it is?" Yoshi shook his head. "Well, I'm about to ruin the surprise, because I don't want you to be put on the spot this afternoon. You know I adore you, Yoshi, and I want you to move in with us. You've been a part of this family for years, and over the last month, you've spent all your free time and every night here. You've been living out of a duffle bag, and it shouldn't be that way. This should be your home. It's where you belong."

He whispered, "Oh wow."

"Since it'll mean a big change for all of us, I talked to the boys ahead of time, and they're so excited. They made a big card and a banner, and we're going to ask you officially later today. But I was worried you might think it's too soon, and I didn't want you to feel obligated to say yes in front of the kids, just because you don't want to hurt their feelings. So, this is me ruining the surprise by asking you ahead of time."

His face lit up, and he told me, "As if there's any way I'd say no to that."

"Really?"

"I was actually going to bring up the subject myself tonight, during our date." He studied my expression and asked, "But what about you, Mike? Have you really thought about this, and are you sure you're ready?"

"I've been thinking about it for weeks. I love you so much, Yoshi, and I want you right here, all the time."

We kissed again, and then he buried his face in my chest and murmured, "You don't even know what this means to me. You're my whole world Mike, you and those boys. This house has felt like home for such a long time, and now it really will be."

Mitchell appeared in the doorway a moment later and asked, "What are you guys talking about?"

We'd planned on getting Yoshi out of the house for a few minutes that afternoon, to give the boys a chance to set up their surprise, so I said, "I was just telling Yoshi we should take the dog for a walk after lunch. It's a beautiful day."

Mitchell beamed at me and winked. "Great idea, Dad." All my kids were as subtle as a heart attack.

I kissed my boyfriend's forehead before saying, "Okay Yoshi, put me to work. It looks like we're going to the Mediterranean for lunch today, so how can I help with this culinary journey?"

Mark returned a few minutes later and helped assemble the spanakopita, which was a dish layered with puff pastry, spinach, and feta cheese, baked to a golden brown. Meanwhile, Mitchell and I went to work on the Greek salad. I thanked Yoshi as I tossed a handful of Kalamata olives in the bowl, and he asked, "What are you thanking me for?"

"For teaching my kids to cook, for sharing your culinary skills with us, and for broadening our horizons with this ongoing global feast. Every time you make us something, it's different and interesting and wonderful, and I want to make sure you know how much we appreciate it."

He smiled and murmured, "It's nice to feel appreciated."

After lunch, we harnessed up the dog and clipped on Gizmo's chew-proof chain link leash, and then Yoshi and I walked the few blocks to the ocean, hand-in-hand. When we reached the water's edge, we turned right, and I took a deep breath of the cool, briny sea air. Ocean Beach was surprisingly uncrowded, with just a few surfers enjoying that perfect spring day. I actually recognized one of them and waved at Jamie, a member of my grandmother's extended family, as Yoshi and I strolled at a leisurely pace.

After a while, I asked my boyfriend, "Will you do something for me this evening, either before or after our date?"

"Of course. Anything."

"I want you to give me a tattoo. I'm thinking I'd like to put our family motto right here." I touched a spot on my inner arm, a few inches below my elbow.

"I didn't know we had a family motto."

"It's new. MJ and I have been taking it to heart over the past few weeks. It's just two words: be brave."

He glanced at me and asked, "Did you forget that you hate tattoos?"

"I really don't. They didn't fit with the way I used to see myself, but I'm evolving, and I think a tattoo will help reflect that."

Yoshi stopped walking and turned to me, and Gizmo sat at his feet with his tail wagging and watched us expectantly. "While I can totally respect the personal evolution thing, I can't help but think there's more to it than that."

"There are a lot of reasons behind it," I said. "You're an artist, Yoshi, and I want to carry a piece of your art with me, always. I want to be able to look at it and think of you. I also want to honor you and show you how much I respect what you do."

"Thank you for all of that. I still feel like there's something you're not telling me, though. Why today, of all days, have you suddenly decided you want some ink?"

I admitted, "I'm totally serious about all of those reasons, but I guess the thing that pushed me over the edge is the fact that I met your mother today. I was cutting through the Tenderloin on the way home from my art class, and all of a sudden, I started recognizing things from your tattoo. I went into your parents' shop because I knew you spent a lot of your childhood there, and I wanted to see it. Your mom was working behind the counter, and after I introduced myself, we had a very brief conversation."

"Now I get it. You feel sorry for me."

"It's not that. She's so misguided about everything. Somehow, she really seems to think she's helping you by trying to push your life in another direction, even though she also seems to understand how much it's damaging your relationship. At one point, she asked me if I had any tattoos, and she seemed to take it as validation of her point of view when I said I didn't. Don't get me wrong, I'm not asking for the tattoo to spite your mom. But I completely disagree with her, and this is my way of making that point. Plus, there's still the long list of other reasons for getting this tattoo, which I just mentioned."

Yoshi pulled me down to his height and kissed my cheek, and then he said, "Thank you for wanting to do this. Are you sure it should be today, though? If you change your mind after the fact, it's a pain in the ass to get a tattoo lasered off."

"There's no chance I'll change my mind later. Once I commit to something, it's forever." Yoshi grinned at me and squeezed my hand.

When we got back home half an hour later, I whispered, "Try to look surprised," as we stepped through the front door. We freed Gizmo from his harness and leash, and he took off running down the hall. We followed him to the family room, and the boys yelled, "Surprise!"

They'd draped a colorful banner across the room, which read: *Please move in with us, Yoshi.* They'd also picked every flower in the backyard, which Mark presented to him in a charmingly messy bouquet. Mitchell stepped forward and held up a card that was easily three feet high. He'd drawn a picture of our house on the outside, and inside were the words: *We love you so please say yes,* followed by all of our names.

I pulled a package from the game cupboard and said, "I wanted to give you something to mark the occasion. It would have made sense to present you with your own set of keys, but you've actually had those for a few years now. So instead, I had this made for you." I gave Yoshi the flat package, and when he tore off the wrapping paper, a little sob slipped from him.

The round, wooden plaque was about fourteen inches in diameter and painted glossy white. The words 'Love Makes a Family' were written in a graceful script in the center of the plaque. Forming a circle around that sentiment were five names: MJ, Mark, Mitchell, Mike and Yoshi. Each name was separated from the one before it with a small red heart.

Yoshi carefully put the present on the couch, and then he grabbed me in an embrace. Mark asked, "Is that a yes?" Yoshi nodded as I held him tight, and the boys cheered and surrounded us in a group hug.

Next, we found a place of honor to hang the plaque. We decided as a group that it belonged in the kitchen, because that was the heart of our home. After we hung it on the wall, we all stepped back to admire it. Then the boys went off to do their own thing, and I told Yoshi, "I'm going to go upstairs and bag up half my wardrobe so I can donate it to charity. Do you want more than half the closet and dresser? I can easily get rid of two-thirds if you think you'll need the room."

"You don't have to do that, Mike. We can figure out how to combine our households without tossing out so much of your stuff."

I took his hand as we headed upstairs and said, "I've been wanting to go through and purge my wardrobe anyway. Most of it is just so blah, and I'm not feeling it anymore. Actually, I wanted to ask if you'll go shopping with me sometime soon and help me pick out some new things."

"Wow. A tattoo, new wardrobe, and a live-in boyfriend, all in one day," he teased. "What's come over you, Mike?"

"He got woke," MJ called from his room, as we passed his open door. "If you're getting a tattoo, Dad, can I have one too?"

"Sure, just as soon as you turn eighteen," I called as we continued down the hall. That was met with a dramatic groan. I grinned at Yoshi and said, "Apparently I 'got woke.' Grammatically, that makes me twitchy, but I get the gist of what it means, and I think MJ hit the nail on the head. I feel like you've brought me back to life, Yoshi, after way too many years just spent getting through each day."

He leaned in and kissed my shoulder, and then he told me, "I feel the same way too, you know. You snapped me out of my routine and gave me a reason to look forward to each new day." It felt good knowing it was mutual.

We emptied the dresser when we reached the bedroom, and then we grabbed big armloads of the clothes hanging in my closet and piled them on the bed. Yoshi located the flyer from the sex club on the top shelf, and he tucked it in the back pocket of his black jeans as he said, "I'll give this back later. For now, let's make sure it doesn't get lost in the shuffle."

"Good idea." We turned to the pile of clothes, and I said, "Let's toss everything I'm getting rid of on the floor, and then later, I can sort it into trash or donations." I grabbed the entire stack of my old, saggy briefs, the ones everyone referred to as 'tightie whities,' and dumped them onto the area rug.

Yoshi grinned at that and told me, "You know that only leaves you with about three pairs of underwear."

"So we'd better go shopping soon."

When I tossed all of my suits on the floor, he asked, "Aren't you going to need those for work?"

"I want to get myself one nice suit. It won't be quite as high-end as Dante's, because come on. But I can do better than these cheap pieces of crap. I'm self-employed and have known most of my clients for years, so it's not like I have to wear a suit every time I go see them. I just need one for special occasions."

"True."

Yoshi started to sort my clothes, and as he grouped all the polo shirts together, I muttered, "I literally have two types of outfits: soccer dad, and accountant. Also, I don't even remember the last time I cleaned out my closet, but I know it's been years." I picked up a pink button-down shirt and said, "Jenny bought this for me."

He looked sympathetic as he rested his hand on my arm. "We can keep the stuff that has sentimental value."

"I don't have the heart to throw this on the floor, but I'm not going to keep it. This shirt hasn't fit me in years, not since I started working out, and I don't need to hang on to it to remember Jenny. It's not as though I'd ever forget her."

Yoshi slipped his hands around my waist. "Since you and Jenny bought this house together, does it feel weird to you on some level that someone else is moving in?"

I draped my arms around his shoulders and shook my head. "Jenny will always be a part of me, this house, and our family. But you're my future, Yoshi, and this is our home now, yours and mine and the boys'. I want us to redecorate it together to reflect that."

"Just so you know, you've never made me feel like I'm living in her shadow. Not once. In fact, what you show me every single day is just how big your heart is, Mike. I know there's plenty of room in there for Jenny, and me, and your boys, and your big, crazy, extended family." I smiled at him, and Yoshi kissed me before turning back to the clothes on the bed. "Now let's talk about why any one person would possibly need twenty white polo shirts."

*****

After dinner that evening, I pulled up in front of Dante and Charlie's house with the boys and the dog and told my kids, "I want you to be on your best behavior tonight, okay? And keep an eye on Gizmo. Don't let him eat the furniture. Or anything else, actually."

"We've spent the night here a bagillion times, Dad," Mark said. "We know the routine." He had a point.

Once inside, we found Jayden at the kitchen island, chatting with Vincent's son Josh and Josh's boyfriend Darwin. Dante was making popcorn while Charlie lined up a bunch of bowls on the counter. I gave my brother and Charlie a hug and said, "It looks like your house is the happening place to be tonight."

"Joely and his girlfriend are home too, and they said they'll be joining us for movie night," Charlie said happily. "It's nice to have a full house."

Dante asked, "Where's Yoshi taking you for date night?"

"I have no idea. He just told me to dress casually and meet him at his apartment at seven. He left an hour ago to get ready."

Mark put his backpack on the kitchen counter and blurted, "Yoshi is living with us now! We asked him today, and he said yes!"

"And there's my big news," I said.

Dante slapped my back and exclaimed, "Wow Mike, way to commit. I was hoping you wouldn't spend the next year or three overthinking the hell out of that."

Meanwhile, MJ sat down at the kitchen island with the teenagers and asked to borrow Josh's phone. He pulled up his video, then returned the phone to his cousin and said shyly, "Tell me what you think. This only has like, fifty views so far, so it's not exactly going viral, but at least nobody's shredded it yet in the comments."

"If they do, just ignore them," Darwin told him, as he pushed his long, black bangs out of his eyes. "People can be really awful sometimes. Believe me, I know. I've been attacked more times than I can count because I'm transgender, and what I've learned is this: when people act cruel and hateful, that's all about them, not you. Just keep being yourself and focusing on the positive."

I was surprised when Mark went up to Darwin and threw his skinny arms around him. "I'm sorry that people are mean to you," my son said. "I hope you and Josh get married, because I want you to be a part of our family forever, so we can all keep you safe."

Darwin looked a little emotional as he hugged the child, and Josh grinned shyly and pushed his thick, black-framed glasses up the bridge of his nose as he said, "That's the plan, but I need to graduate from high school first. Don't tell my dads I said that, though. They both get twitchy whenever I mention the word marriage." Josh and Darwin had gotten together a couple of years ago, when my nephew was a high school freshman and Darwin was a senior. While their age difference had been a point of contention with Vincent and Trevor, the teenagers had slowly been wearing them down, basically by being the most loving, devoted, and surprisingly innocent couple imaginable.

I kissed the top of Mark's head when he let go of Darwin and told him, "I'd better get going. Have a great night everyone, and I'll see you in the morning."

When I kissed the top of Mitchell's head, he said, "MJ told me you're getting a tattoo tonight. Is that true, Dad?"

Dante's head snapped up like a startled deer, and he stared at me as I said, "Maybe. I'm not sure what Yoshi has on the agenda, so we might not have time for that. But if not tonight, then hopefully it'll happen in the next day or two."

"It's like I'm suddenly in a bizarre parallel universe, where my baby brother has forgotten how to nerd. You're getting inked, seem to have permanently misplaced your glasses, and you're not even wearing a polo shirt," Dante muttered, as he gestured at my black T-shirt. "I don't have any idea what to do with you now."

"What you can do is come with me when I go shopping next week. I'm donating all my cheap suits to charity, and I'm going to meet with your tailor to have a new one made. I don't want to spend as much as you do though, because I'm not insane."

"Or maybe you are," Dante deadpanned, "but I'm not complaining. New, insane Mike seems like a pretty fun guy."

I kissed the top of MJ's head, and he smiled at me. Then Josh started playing the video, and everyone gathered around the phone. I paused to watch for a minute before leaving the kitchen. On the way out, I scratched Gizmo's ears and told him not to be an asshole. The last thing I heard before the front door closed behind me was everyone cheering and applauding MJ, and I grinned happily.

*****

When I reached Yoshi's apartment building, I pulled into a guest space in the underground parking lot and cut the engine. I was a few minutes early, so I got out of the SUV and paced a bit to try to burn off some excess energy. Yoshi and I had decided that tonight would finally be the night he fucked me, and I was equal parts nervous and excited.

I'd spent some pretty awkward moments locked in my bathroom that afternoon with a new douching kit, in anticipation of what was going to happen on our date. After that, I'd showered and gotten dressed in one of my new pairs of underwear, followed by jeans and a T-shirt. Then I'd tried my damnedest to act casual while watching the minutes tick by. I was ready for this and absolutely trusted Yoshi to take care of me, but there was still a little apprehension, because I fully expected it to hurt like hell. I basically just wanted to get my first time bottoming over with.

As soon as I rode the elevator to my boyfriend's apartment and found a folded note taped to his door, I was reminded that Yoshi always defied expectations. The note had my name written on the front, and inside, it said: *Let yourself in with your key, take off all your clothes, and go upstairs to the bedroom. Then kneel on the pillow, put on the blindfold, and wait for me.*

Lust shot through me, drowning out the worry that had been nagging at me all day. After I let myself in, I started to put my keys and the note on the little table just inside the door, and my breath caught. He'd framed the sex club flyer and left it on the table for me to find. As always, the sight of the naked guy kneeling before the man in the suit made my cock throb.

I undressed quickly as I looked around. The lighting was low on the main floor and only slightly brighter up in the loft. Yoshi was nowhere to be seen, and the apartment was perfectly still.

I left my clothes on a chair and hurried upstairs. He'd arranged everything we'd bought at the sex shop in a tidy display on top of his dresser. So far, we'd only used the wrist cuffs, but clearly that was going to change tonight.

Lube, condoms, and a gray hand towel were lined up on the nightstand, beside two bottles of water. On the second nightstand, he'd arranged the collection of four butt plugs according to size, along with their remote. He'd prepared the bed, too. The blankets had been removed and were neatly folded in a corner of the room, and a dark towel was centered on the charcoal sheets. This was going to get messy. I grinned at that as I dropped to my knees on the pillow in the center of the floor.

There was a black blindfold beside the pillow, and my heartbeat sped up as I slid it over my eyes. My cock was leaking precum by that point and aching for some stimulation, but I ignored it. Instead, I put my hands behind my back and grasped my left wrist with my right hand.

Yoshi didn't keep me waiting very long, and when I heard his key in the lock, my cock twitched. I straightened my posture as he climbed the stairs, and I concentrated on his quiet footsteps as he went to the dresser. A slight shuffling sound told me he'd picked something up.

Every nerve ending crackled in anticipation. My back was to the stairs, and when he crossed the room, I could sense him right behind me. All I could hear was my own breathing, which was fast and jagged in the quiet of that apartment. My hard-on throbbed, demanding attention, and my heart raced.

He crouched behind me and lightly ran his hands down my arms. I had to fight back a moan. Every part of me craved his touch, and that little taste of it was like kindling on a fire. He kissed my shoulder, and then he fastened the leather cuffs around my wrists and hooked them together. I let my arms relax, secure in my bonds. When he leaned in and nuzzled my cheek, I caught a hint of his clean scent. It was wonderfully reassuring.

Yoshi got up and walked around the pillow. When he was standing directly in front of me, I tilted my head toward him, and he cupped my cheek and ran his thumb over my beard. Then he kissed me before removing the blindfold.

My jaw dropped when I got my first look at him. Yoshi was dressed exactly like the man on the flyer, in an impeccable black suit, along with a dark shirt and tie. There was so much love in his eyes as he reached out and gently stroked my hair. He was giving me exactly what I wanted, the fantasy in that photo down to the last detail, and I was overcome with emotion as I whispered, "Thank you."

He bent down and kissed me again, and then he whispered in my ear, "I adore you, Mike. Now, this is going to get intense fast. Are you ready for that?"

He leaned back to meet my gaze, and I smiled at him and said, "Bring it on."

"If this first part gets to be too much, let me know by raising both shoulders. Okay?"

"I will." I looked up at him and whispered, "Please use me hard. Show me I belong to you."

That was all he needed to hear. Yoshi stepped forward and pushed his bulge against my lips, and I rubbed my face against it through the fabric of that dark suit. When he unzipped his fly and pulled out his cock, I lunged for it and sucked it eagerly as my own cock throbbed. He grasped my head with both hands and began to fuck my mouth, and I moaned and opened wide for him.

As he slid down my throat I gagged a little, and he backed off. I worked on relaxing as he began to fuck my mouth again, and I looked up and met his gaze. He picked up his pace, thrusting harder and deeper in increments, and I felt a sense of pride when I was able to take his length.

I was so aroused that precum ran down my cock, and I moaned around his shaft. In a few minutes, I was rewarded with a load of his cum, which I swallowed without hesitation. He zipped up, then bent and kissed me again, tasting himself on my lips.

Before Yoshi helped me up, he fastened the collar around my neck, and then he led me to the bed. I literally shook with desire. When I was seated on the edge of the mattress, he added the ankle restraints and a set of straps that buckled around each thigh. He worked slowly and meticulously, and he smiled at me when our eyes met.

I was struck by how perfectly normal it all seemed and how comfortable I was, even though we were taking our sex life to a place it had never been before, at least not to that extent. The love and trust I felt for Yoshi made it easy to relinquish control. All I had to do was relax and let him guide me.

I lost all track of time as Yoshi completely took over. He sucked and stroked my cock while fingering me open, and when he started to massage my prostate, I writhed with pleasure. Later on, he used the butt plugs on me, working me up to the biggest one, sometimes with the vibration feature, sometimes without.

Throughout all of that, he kept varying my restraints. Sometimes my hands were bound above my head. At other times, my wrists were hooked to my thigh restraints. At one point, he bent my legs and fastened my wrists to my ankles, and then he spread my thighs and drove me crazy by tonguing my hole as he jerked me off.

All rational thought left me. I was distilled down to pure instinct and pleasure and sensation. After edging me so long that I pleaded for release, he finally let me cum. The orgasm was unbelievably intense, but the relief was short-lived. He gave me a drink of water and took the time to get undressed, and as soon as I caught my breath, he started working me right back up again.

By the time he was ready to fuck me, I was begging for his cock. He positioned me face-down with my knees bent and placed a folded pillow under my belly, and then he fastened the spreader bar to my ankles, which held my feet apart. Next, he hooked my wrists to the straps around my thighs and clicked the leash onto my collar. I smiled as I rested my cheek against the cool, clean sheets and relaxed for him as he worked more lube into me with two fingers.

Yoshi knelt behind me and put on a condom, and then he positioned the tip of his cock against my hole. He told me to bear down, and I followed his instructions, pushing back as he began to enter me. It was a tight fit, even after all that time spent working me open. As predicted, it hurt, but I was too turned on to care. My cock throbbed, and I moaned as he slid his length into me.

As much as I'd enjoyed all that lead-up, it paled in comparison to Yoshi fucking me. His cock began to pound my prostate, and waves of pleasure overwhelmed me. I rasped, "Harder. Please," and he did as I asked. Soon my entire body was rocking under the force of his thrusts.

I felt so wonderfully, totally full. Yoshi's hips slapped against my ass as he fucked me, and his strong hands grasped my waist and pulled me back onto him. The fact that I was restrained and could do nothing but take it was utter perfection.

He picked up the leash and held it securely, pulling just enough to remind me it was there. When he reached beneath me and started jerking me off, it was almost sensory overload. I yelled as I came, aware of nothing but the pleasure flooding my senses and my boyfriend's cock filling my ass. A minute later, Yoshi came too, thrusting hard and fast until he was completely satisfied.

I whimpered when he slid his cock from me. He gently moved me onto my side, took off all the restraints, and cleaned me up before covering me with a blanket. I was too exhausted to move. Yoshi went into the bathroom for a minute or two, and I forced myself to stay awake until I knew he was back in bed with me. He murmured, "I absolutely adore you, Mike," and kissed my forehead, and I burrowed into his arms and fell asleep in the next instant.

*****

It was dark when I awoke. Yoshi was sitting right beside me with one hand resting on my shoulder, and he was lit by the soft glow of an e-reader. I sat up and mumbled, "What time is it?"

"Almost one a.m. How do you feel?"

I grinned and leaned against him. "So ridiculously good." That made him grin, too.

He put the e-reader on the nightstand and brushed my hair back as he asked, "So…did that live up to expectations?"

"Live up to them? Hell no. It shattered them. Tonight was utterly amazing, Yoshi. We need to start doing that *a lot.*"

He chuckled softly. "Fine with me."

I draped my arm over his stomach, and after a moment, I asked, "Since you're moving in with me, are you going to sell this apartment? If so, I'll be sorry to see it go."

"I've been thinking about that," he said, "and I'm actually going to hold onto it as an investment. I'd already looked into renting it out on one of those vacation property websites, and I should be able to generate a pretty substantial second income that way. The best part is, I can block out days in the rental schedule, so we can keep using it as our own, personal retreat."

"That's the best idea ever."

"It also means we can keep storing our sex toys here. We'll obviously stash them in a locked closet, so the tourists don't stumble across them."

"Perfect." I kissed his shoulder, and then I said, "I know we talked about doing my tattoo tonight, but can we do it first thing in the morning instead? I really don't want to get out of this bed."

"Sure." When my stomach rumbled, Yoshi grinned and said, "I was just about to ask if you were hungry. I'll bring you a snack." When he got up, I noticed he'd put on a pair of black pajama bottoms.

He turned back to me and hesitated for a moment before saying, "This is probably going to sound stupid, but thank you."

"For what?"

"For trusting me tonight. I kept expecting you to reach a limit or hold part of yourself back, but you never did. Instead, you showed me in such a profound way how much faith you have in me, and it felt like the most wonderful gift imaginable."

"I adore you, Yoshi."

"It's mutual." He grinned embarrassedly and muttered, "Anyway, I'll be right back with something to eat."

"I should help."

I started to get up, but he stopped me with a gentle hand on my shoulder. "Please let me take care of you, Mike."

I settled back onto the pillows and said, "I can do that."

*****

The next morning, I got comfortable on the leather chaise in Yoshi's studio and watched with fascination as he prepared to apply my tattoo. It was about nine a.m. on Sunday, and we had the shop to ourselves. Sunlight streamed in through the plate glass window, and pop music played at a low volume.

We'd already talked about size, appearance, and placement of my tattoo, and he'd meticulously prepped the area before readying his machine and dispensing black ink into a little plastic pot. He'd printed a visual reference for himself with the old-fashioned typewriter font I'd requested, but he'd opted to freehand it, rather than work from a stencil applied to my skin. I was totally fine with that.

"Are you sure? Most people get nervous when I say I want to ink them without a stencil," he'd said.

"I trust you with my life, Yoshi," I'd told him. "Given that, I have no problem trusting you with three inches of my skin."

He met my gaze when his work station was ready and said, "Last chance to back out."

I smiled at him. "Let's do this."

He flipped a switch, and the machine started up with a low whirr. Yoshi dipped the tip into the little pot of ink, and when the needles made contact with my skin, it felt horrible. But after a few minutes, I began to get used to it, and I turned my attention to my gorgeous boyfriend.

Yoshi was a study in perfect concentration. He held my skin taught with one gloved hand while he continually repositioned the needles with the other. It was a slow process, even with a small tattoo, and it required a hell of a lot of patience on both our parts. After a while, I settled into it and actually started to enjoy the process, even though the feeling of my skin being pierced remained unpleasant.

But there was something almost lulling about it, and since I was madly in love with the person applying my tattoo, it was also really intimate. When he turned off the machine and wiped the excess ink from my skin for the last time, I murmured, "Aw, are you done already?"

"You know, most people say, 'thank God that's over.' Did you actually enjoy it?"

"I did. Don't get me wrong, the needles felt horrible. But I loved watching you work, and the end result is fantastic." I held up my arm and admired the two perfect little words spelled out in lower case letters: *be brave.*

He said, "I'm glad you like it."

"When can I get another one?"

Yoshi grinned at me. "I never expected you to say that."

"That's because you thought I was either humoring you or trying to make a point, right?"

"Maybe."

"Nope. I really wanted a tattoo, and now that I've gotten a taste of it, I want more."

He started to clean up his workstation as he said, "Let's give this one a chance to heal and go from there. You know, there's really no hurry on the next one. I'm not going anywhere." That last sentence put a huge smile on my face.

Chapter Fifteen

There was something so reassuring about waking up next to Yoshi every morning. Nearly a month after we'd officially moved in together, I shut off the alarm a few minutes before it was set to go off one Thursday morning. He raised an eyelid and caught me watching him sleep, and then he grinned and pulled me into his arms.

We spent a few minutes wrapped up in each other before we finally tumbled out of bed and started our day. After we worked out together, I headed to the shower and Yoshi went downstairs to make breakfast. By the time I got the kids up, he had a fantastic meal on the table, and we all ate together. Afterwards, I cleaned the kitchen while the kids got ready, and I drove them to school while Yoshi took a shower.

I knew it was slightly nuts to derive so much happiness from a morning routine, but I really did. It was just so tranquil, and almost totally devoid of stress. When I thought back to the way life had been before Yoshi and I became a couple, I wondered how I'd managed to survive it with even a shred of sanity.

That particular day was a little unusual, because after I drove Mark and Mitchell to school and dropped off Gizmo at daycare, I went home and put on my new, black suit, and then I helped MJ put together his best outfit. Yoshi joined us, wearing a dark suit that normally would have given me all sorts of bad ideas, but we had a serious day ahead.

We'd allowed MJ to skip school so he could attend his boyfriend's custody hearing, and the three of us were quiet as we drove to the courthouse. But at one point, my son blurted, "What if the judge sends Aiden back to Oregon to live with his horrible relatives, and what if they're mean to him?"

"His lawyer thinks they have a solid case and that Aiden will get to stay with Quinn and Duke." I tried to keep my tone upbeat, despite the knot in my stomach.

"It's her job to say that." MJ's voice was shaking. "She can't just tell her clients they don't have a snowball's chance in hell." He had a point, but I repeated my reassurances.

Even though MJ was a wreck, he put on a brave face when we entered the building and he spotted Aiden. Then he ran across the lobby to give him a hug. Quinn and Duke were acting confident too, but the strain showed around their eyes, and they both fidgeted uncomfortably in their gray suits. Their lawyer, on the other hand, was utterly self-assured. The tall brunette, whose name was Monica, told her clients more than once, "We've got this. You'll see."

Over the next few minutes, we were joined first by Quinn's large family and then by dozens and dozens of friends and relatives. Nana and Ollie were among them, and so were Dante and Charlie. I hugged my family members and waved at several familiar faces in the crowd. Duke and Quinn both seemed overwhelmed, and Quinn's voice shook when he called, "Thank you so much for being here. I can't tell you what this means to us."

Nana was one step ahead of the game, as usual. She'd had large buttons made, and she and Ollie distributed them to everyone in our party. They came in a rainbow of colors, and each featured the same two words: Team Aiden. I pinned a red button to my jacket, and Yoshi pinned a green one to his before helping MJ pin on a purple one.

When their case was called, we all followed Aiden and his dads into the courtroom. They sat at the front, and we filled in every single seat behind them on the right-hand side of the gallery. It was so crowded that a few people had to stand in the back. The left side remained completely empty.

We sat in the first row, because Aiden and MJ wanted to be close to each other. Aiden looked like he was on the verge of tears. He turned around in his seat and reached across the railing to hold MJ's hand, and I noticed the disapproving looks from his aunt and uncle across the courtroom. They were the ones trying to obtain custody, and I knew at a glance that would be a *huge* mistake. I stared daggers at them until they both shifted uncomfortably and looked away.

The judge was an African-American woman of about sixty, who looked unimpressed by pretty much everything. She listened to both lawyers' opening remarks with a poker face. The relatives' lawyer made the argument that Aiden belonged with family and mentioned several laws and precedents that should have made this an open-and-shut case in their favor. But then Monica stood up and made an impassioned plea. She talked about Aiden's condemnation by his family over his sexual orientation, and how it had gotten so bad that the child had chosen life on the street over remaining with them. The judge barely blinked.

The uncle and aunt both took the stand and pled their case, quoting the Bible more than once. They made the argument that because Aiden was a blood relative, he belonged with them, according to the law and the 'will of God.' They also called Quinn and Duke 'a morally questionable pair of homosexuals' who would try to corrupt the boy. I watched a flush rise from under Duke's collar, and his huge hands curled into fists.

Later on, Monica called a surprise witness. We all turned to watch as the door at the back of the courtroom was opened by a bailiff and a petite, blonde woman of about twenty entered. She turned out to be Aiden's cousin Ellie, who'd come from Oregon to testify against her parents.

At one point, Ellie told the judge, "My parents verbally abused me all my life, and it'll be a hundred times worse for Aiden. Please don't make him live with them. They use their religion as an excuse to be hateful bigots, and because he's gay, they'll make his life a living hell. No kid should have to go through that." I had to swallow a lump in my throat, but the judge remained as expressionless as ever.

Then it was Aiden's turn to take the stand. He answered a long series of questions from the opposition's lawyer and was visibly rattled as the man tried to get him to admit he had an unstable home life with Duke and Quinn. Tears streamed down MJ's face as he watched his boyfriend's distress, and when I put my arm around my son's shoulders, I felt him trembling.

Duke took the stand next, followed by Quinn. The opposing lawyer tried his damnedest to discredit them. He brought up the fact that Quinn used to work as a go-go boy, and that although Duke was a police officer, he had a mark on his record from a bar fight. But both men held their ground and answered every question honestly, while emphatically maintaining that they were what was best for Aiden.

After Monica cross-examined him, Quinn made an impassioned speech. "My husband and I aren't perfect," he said, "but that's not what it takes to raise a child. All Aiden needs is love and acceptance, and that's what we've provided, every single day since we found him alone, half-starved, and trying to find shelter on Christmas Eve.

"I know what it's like to grow up gay, and I'm lucky, because I have a great family." He smiled at his parents, who were seated near the center of the courtroom. "They adopted me when I was little and taught me what it means to be loved unconditionally. They've always been in my corner, and now they're in Aiden's corner, too. If you let him stay with us, Aiden won't just have my husband and me to love and support him. He'll also have a big, extended family and an entire community of friends and loved ones. Many of them are here today."

He gestured at the crowd on the right side of the courtroom, and from somewhere behind me, Nana yelled, "Damn right!" I was impressed that she'd gone that long without causing a scene.

Quinn continued, "None of us will ever judge Aiden for being gay. Just the opposite. We'll all remind him to be proud of who he is, and we'll help him grow into a strong, confident young man." He turned to the judge and concluded with, "Family isn't blood, it's the people in your life who love and support you unconditionally. Aiden is a part of our family, and this is where he belongs. Please give him the best shot at a happy life by letting him grow up surrounded by love. I'm begging you, your honor, don't take him away from us."

When Quinn returned to his seat, Aiden grabbed him in a hug and said, "I love you, Dad." MJ sobbed silently as I held him, and Yoshi reached over and wiped a tear from my cheek.

The judge spent several long moments looking through some documents. Finally, she said, "In my sixteen years on the bench, only twice have I denied custody to a child's blood relatives." All of us held our breath. Then she said, "Today marks the third time. That little boy is right where he belongs." The judge granted Quinn and Duke custody of Aiden, and everyone on our side of the courtroom cheered as the brand new family of three grabbed each other in a hug.

Our group waited until we were outside the courthouse to go absolutely crazy. Quinn and Duke both tossed aside their ties, dress shirts and suit jackets to reveal matching red T-shirts that said 'Aiden's Dad' in rainbow letters, and Quinn yelled, "Let's all officially welcome Aiden to the family!" Then he and about forty people threw handfuls of glitter confetti into the air.

Aiden and MJ jumped and danced in the center of the crowd as glitter rained down on them, and Nana yelled, "Victory celebration at my house! Come on, everybody, it's party time!"

MJ asked to ride with Aiden, and after they left together and the crowd began to disperse, I turned to Yoshi and said, "Let's spring Mark and Mitchell from school a couple of hours early. It's two days before summer vacation, so it's not like they're going to miss anything important, right?"

Yoshi flashed me a big smile. "Anything they're doing in school today isn't half as important as a Dombruso party."

*****

We ended up springing not only Mark and Mitchell, but our dog, too. When we reached my grandmother's house, Gizmo teamed up with Nana and Ollie's mismatched dogs, the Wookie and the Chihuahua. Then a neighbor arrived with Aiden's pet skunk, Mrs. Nesbitt, and she also joined the pack. As the menagerie ran past us, I said, "Somehow, that seems oddly appropriate for this family."

The kids went to form a pack of their own in the backyard, and Yoshi and I turned toward the sound of my grandmother cussing someone out in the living room. When we went to investigate, we found Nana pointing her finger accusingly at some sort of cylindrical speaker, which had 1980s David Hasselhoff's face taped to it, for reasons I couldn't begin to explain. I asked what she was doing, and she said, "This is the Hoff, my new electronic assistant. I started off with that bitch from that shopping website, but she and I didn't get along, so Vincent got me this programmable one instead, and Darwin hacked it for me so it'd do what I wanted. It's still a shithead, though. Watch this. Hoff, play my party songs!"

The male, robotic voice said, "Ordering you one case of thongs."

Nana yelled, "No you shithead, songs!"

It replied, "I found nine listings for bongs. Shall I text you a map?"

Nana threw her hands in the air. "See what I have to put up with? Anyone know how to fire an electronic assistant?"

The Hoff said, "Calling 911 and dispatching the fire department."

Nana started to protest, but then she shrugged. "I'm good with that one, actually." Someone knocked on the door just then, and Nana exclaimed, "Hot damn, that was quick! Mikey, go let in the firemen while I call my girlfriends and tell them to hurry up and get their asses over here." She pulled out her phone and looked at the screen, then exclaimed, "Why are there pictures of thongs all over my screen, and how many is a gross?"

When I opened the door, I found two delivery drivers on the porch, each with a fully loaded hand truck. I instructed them to stack everything just inside the entryway, and when Nana came into the foyer a minute later, I asked her, "Have you been doing some online shopping?"

"About ten percent of that is stuff I ordered on purpose. The rest is shit the Hoff dreamt up to buy me."

I started to close the door, but one of the drivers informed me, "That's just the first half. We'll be right back."

Yoshi and I started to look through the extremely miscellaneous assortment of items while the drivers returned to the truck. They were back a minute later with two blue, plastic fifty-five gallon drums, and I asked, "What is that?"

The first driver managed to keep a straight face as he told me, "Personal lubricant."

Just then, a van double-parked in the street, and a purple-haired woman in a T-shirt that read 'Speed Demon Delivery' jogged up to the front door. She handed me a small pet carrier labeled 'caution: live animals,' and I glanced through the air holes as I asked, "What the hell is this?"

She shrugged and said, "A weasel of some sort."

I exclaimed, "All of you have to take this stuff back!"

The first driver shook his head as the speed demon jogged back to her van. "No can do. You gotta go through the websites where everything was purchased to get a return authorization."

"But all of this stuff was obviously ordered by mistake."

"Not our problem."

My voice rose. "Come on! What do you think I'm going to do with a hundred and ten gallons of lube and a live weasel?"

The man grinned, just a little, and told me, "That's none of my business, sir." Then both drivers turned and left.

Dante had been watching from the kitchen doorway, and he started laughing and said, "This is awesome. For once, you get to deal with Nanageddon, not me." Dante raised a glass in a toast and returned to the kitchen.

Yoshi took the pet carrier from me and peered through the vents, then said, "Aw, I think it's a ferret. The poor thing's probably scared. I'm going to take it out and give it some food and water."

Before I could stop him, he flipped the latch. The weasel shot out of the cage and ran down the hall, and I chuckled and told him, "You just turned a weasel loose in my grandmother's house. You're such a Dombruso."

"Being called a Dombruso is a compliment. I'm sorry about the rodent, though. Wait, are weasels rodents?"

"No idea. Ask Mitchell, he'll know."

Mark wandered into the entryway eating a Popsicle and asked, "Mitchell will know what?"

"If weasels are rodents. Yoshi just turned one loose in the house."

Mark's eyes lit up, and he exclaimed, "Awesome! I'm gonna go get my brothers. If we catch it, can we keep it?"

I muttered, "I guess somebody'll have to take it home," as I leaned over and peered down the hallway.

Mark yelled, "That's totally a yes," before running off to find backup.

I turned to Yoshi and asked, "Did I accidentally just tell my youngest child that he could keep a feral weasel as a pet?"

"Pretty much."

"I need a drink." We started to head to the kitchen, but a moment later, a piercing siren pulled up in front of the house, and I changed direction and added, "Right after I deal with the fire department."

*****

Later that evening, I crossed one sneakered foot over the other as I rested my head on my boyfriend's shoulder. The party had broken up about an hour earlier, and we were sitting around the backyard fire pit with a few family members. I'd gone home long enough to grab a change of clothes for Yoshi, MJ, and myself, and when I pulled up the zipper on Yoshi's hoodie because I thought he might be cold, he grinned at me.

Mark and Mitchell were sprawled out on the patio a few yards to my left, surrounded by three tired dogs, a skunk, and a ferret. The latter had actually proven to be pretty tame, once we caught him and Nana fashioned a tiny harness and leash for him out of a string bikini. Meanwhile, Aiden and MJ were slow-dancing. They stood more than a

422

foot apart with their hands on each other's shoulders as they did an awkward box step to an instrumental song I didn't recognize, and I called, "Is that one of your songs, MJ?"

He nodded. "Jude recorded the melody last weekend. I still need to come up with some lyrics for it."

Dante stepped outside just then, eating a Popsicle like the one Mark had earlier, and asked, "How many followers are you up to on YouTube now, MJ?"

My son looked embarrassed as he answered, "Almost twenty thousand."

Dante said, "That's fantastic. You're getting famous." He dropped onto a chair on the other side of the fire pit, broke his Popsicle in two, and gave half to Charlie. Beside them, Quinn and Duke snuggled happily, looking like they didn't have a care in the world. Vincent and Trevor were also a part of our little circle, and both were sound asleep, pinned down by a pair of napping toddlers.

"Not quite," MJ said. "It's cool to have some fans, though. When we're on Catalina next month, Uncle Zan said he's going to help Aiden and me record some stuff in his brand new home studio. Some of our followers are looking forward to that, which is nice."

Dante squinted at me around the glowing fire and asked, "Did you get another tattoo, Mike?" I was wearing shorts, and the ink in question was on my left shin. It was Yoshi's name and mine in Japanese kanji, and when I nodded, he said, "How many is that now?"

"Just four. Yoshi only lets me get one a week."

I grinned at my boyfriend, who sighed and shook his head as he murmured, "I've created a monster."

"Yoshi also got a new tattoo," I said, as Nana and Ollie stepped out the back door and joined our fire circle. I pushed back the cuff of my boyfriend's sweatshirt and kissed the inside of his left wrist, where he'd filled in all the remaining space on his sleeve with a picture of our house and our family of five.

Dante asked, "So Mike, a couple of years from now, is every inch of your skin going to be covered in ink, like a circus side show?"

I shook my head. "Now that I've gotten the hearts, there's just one more that I really want." I'd asked Yoshi to tattoo five interlocking hearts in a row on my left bicep, each a different color of the rainbow to represent Yoshi, our boys, and me. On my right bicep, I'd gotten a heart in white ink. It represented Jenny, and I'd chosen white because it looked ethereal and made me think of an angel in heaven.

I added, "But Yoshi has to be willing to get a matching tattoo, and that means straying from his city-sleeve for the first time."

Yoshi turned to me with a curious expression. "This is the first I've heard about matching tattoos. What did you have in mind?"

I held up his left hand and traced a line around the base of his ring finger as I said, "Wedding bands."

"What?" He looked startled.

"You know I adore you," I told him, as I got down on one knee. The boys all gathered around, and Dante took off his shoe and threw it at Vincent. Vinny woke with a start and knocked the shoe into the blazing fire pit, and when he realized what was happening, he shook Trevor, who awoke with an unflattering snort.

I watched my brothers with a raised eyebrow, and then I turned my attention back to Yoshi and took his hand in both of mine. "As I was saying, I adore you, and I can't imagine life without you by my side. More than anything, I want to be your husband and spend the rest of forever making you as happy as you make me, so will you marry me, Yoshi?"

He blurted, "Of course I will." I was overcome with joy as he grabbed me in an embrace, and we kissed passionately.

Mark and Mitchell jumped up and down and screamed with delight, which made the dogs leap up and start barking. The ferret ran in a circle at the end of his bikini leash, and the skunk hunkered down, raised her tail, and gassed the entire lot of us. We all jumped up and ran in different directions, and Duke exclaimed, "I'd always wondered if the de-scenting procedure the vet performed actually worked. Now I have my answer!"

As Yoshi and I ran into the house hand-in-hand, I bent down and scooped up the ferret, who'd escaped in the melee. We stopped running when we reached the foyer, and as our sons caught up to us, MJ exclaimed, "Oh man, we all reek!" Fortunately, none of us had taken a direct hit, but we were definitely pungent.

"This is the worst smell ever," Mitchell complained. "It's like old cheese, Mark's socks, and puke, all mixed together."

Mark pinched his nose shut, and then he noticed the twin barrels of lube and asked, "What's that stuff for?"

I laughed and pulled my husband-to-be into my arms, and as the ferret stuffed itself inside his jacket, I said, "Welcome to the family, Yoshi."

Epilogue

Our friend Quinn was a very different person now that the worry of the custody battle was behind him, and he'd found a kindred spirit in Beck Medina. Duke sat in the shade and grinned as Quinn taught Beck a dance number for that afternoon's 'Dombruso family and friends talent show.' They were decked out in body glitter, booty shorts, sparkly tank tops, and high heels, and Beck was doing a surprisingly good job keeping up, considering Quinn was a professional dancer.

After a minute, Quinn jumped off the stage, ran over to Duke, and threw all his weight into dragging his husband out of his chair as he told him, "I see you over here tapping your toes to the music, and you're not going to sit this one out. You can dance, even though you say you can't, and since you've been watching us practice, I bet you already have the routine memorized. Now come on sexy, shake your money maker!" Duke let himself get pulled to his feet and joined his husband and their friend on the makeshift stage.

When they started twerking, Nana ran over to show them how it was done, but then she exclaimed, "Why am I helping you? You're my competition! Now where did Dante and Vincent go? We gotta rehearse!" She grabbed her husband's hand, and they hurried into the main building.

A minute later, Yoshi joined me with a pair of tropical drinks, and my face lit up with a huge smile. He sat on my lap and handed me a cocktail as he said, "It feels so good to be back on Catalina. We need to make this an annual tradition."

"Definitely. I'm sure the boys won't complain about that." Our sons and Aiden were across the courtyard, trying to rehearse a musical number for the talent show. They were slightly impeded by the fact that Mark had only been playing the drums for two weeks, and Mitchell kept going off on improvisational tambourine riffs.

Yoshi leaned down and kissed my bare shoulder. I was wearing a red tank top with the name of the ranch and a picture of a seahorse on it, along with a pair of white shorts, and he said, "Have I mentioned how sexy you look today?"

"You're biased, but thank you."

He put his drink on the table beside us and draped his arms around my shoulders. "I'm so glad we're here. It really is the perfect place for us to get married." Yoshi looked around wistfully. "After all, this is where we took the leap from friends to so much more."

"Can you believe the ceremony's tonight? The last month just flew by."

Yoshi kissed me and ran his fingertips over my beard. "Good, because I can't wait to be your husband."

Elijah joined us a few minutes later and said, "I'm so happy you guys decided to get married here. I mean, I would have come to San Francisco for the wedding, obviously, but I love having you and your family back at the ranch."

I asked, "How do you like living here? Is it everything you'd hoped it would be?"

"It's been really good. I love the ranch, and Beck and Ren treat me like family. I'm at the point now where I feel confident about the job, too." He didn't mention the young ranch hand, but I'd noticed them watching each other from a distance when we arrived the day before. Maybe that one was still a work in progress.

After a while, Elijah went to help Ren with something, and Yoshi and I moved closer to the kids, so we could watch them rehearse. Aiden looked up from his electric guitar and said, "You guys should totally do something in the talent show. I know you're both focused on the wedding, but I bet you'd have fun!"

MJ exclaimed, "I just had the perfect idea for you two: lip sync battle! You could go head-to-head, and it wouldn't take a lot of rehearsing. Just pick songs you already know.

Beck has a ton of costumes in his prop closet, so I'm sure you'd find something."

Yoshi and I glanced at each other, and he grinned and said, "I call dibs on Britney."

I kissed his forehead. "She's all yours."

A moment later, we were tackle-hugged by Gianni, for at least the tenth time since we'd arrived on the island. My brother kissed us both on the cheek and gushed, "I still can't believe my baby brother is marrying my best friend! You've been my brother forever, Yoshi, but now it's going to be official. I'm so happy!"

I put my arm around Gi's shoulders and said, "You may have mentioned this once or twice."

"I know. I'm just excited."

I said, "Come help me find a costume for the talent show. And don't tell Yoshi what it is when we find something, because I'm going to use the element of surprise to win our lip sync battle."

Yoshi smiled at me and turned his attention back to the boys as Gianni and I crossed the courtyard, and my brother said, "I know I keep going on about it, but this really is one of the happiest days of my life. You and Yoshi are amazing together, and he's so great with your kids. It feels like this was just meant to be."

"They adore him, and you're right, it was meant to be. It was such an easy transition when he moved in with us, because he was already a huge part of our lives. This next step feels so easy too, like it's just our natural progression."

"You both seem so relaxed. I remember the day you married Jenny, you were a bundle of nerves." Gianni glanced at me and asked, "Is it weird to bring that up? If so, I'm sorry."

"It's fine. I've been thinking about it a lot today. You're right that I was nervous, and no wonder. We were both kids, fresh out of high school. It was the right call for us though, and I'm grateful for the time we had together. I'm also so grateful that a part of her is here today in those three wonderful little people we created."

Gianni swiped at his eyes. "If I make it through today without ugly-crying, it's going to be a damn miracle."

"Yeah, it really will be." He chuckled at that, and then I murmured, "Oh wow, they actually came." Yoshi's mom and dad had just climbed out of a cab, and they were looking a bit lost.

"Holy shit, I wasn't expecting that."

"Neither was Yoshi." When we joined them, we shook hands as I said, "Welcome, Mr. and Mrs. Miyazaki. I'm so glad you could make it, and I know your son will be, too."

His mom smoothed the skirt of her flowered sundress and said, "Thanks for inviting us," as she took in the controlled pandemonium of the courtyard. Her husband also murmured a thank you. He had tidy, graying hair and a cardigan sweater, and he reminded me of an Asian Mr. Rogers.

"We're doing a family talent show this afternoon, so a lot of people are rehearsing," I explained. "Then the wedding ceremony will be happening at sunset."

She said, "You have a huge family."

"I do. You know my brother Gianni, right?" They shook hands and exchanged greetings, and I added, "My brothers Dante and Vincent are off doing some sort of secret rehearsal with my grandmother, so I'll introduce you when they come out of hiding. Yoshi's right over there with our sons, let's go say hello."

His mom echoed, "Our…somehow, I hadn't thought about that, that my son is becoming a father with this wedding."

"He's been a dad to those boys for a long time," I told her.

Yoshi looked shocked when he saw his parents, and he crossed the courtyard to meet us in the middle. He hugged them both, which probably wasn't something that happened very often, considering how awkward it seemed. Then he said, "Thank you for coming. This means a lot to me."

"To both of us," I added.

Mrs. Miyazaki was standing right beside me, and I was surprised when I felt her hand on my left arm. "This looks nice," she said, indicating the row of rainbow hearts on my bicep. "Did my son do it?" That was an olive branch if ever I saw one. Yoshi noticed, too.

"He did. It represents us and our three boys." I held up my left hand and said, "He designed and drew our wedding bands, too. We wanted to give them a chance to heal before the ceremony, so he did them a couple of weeks ago."

She leaned in and took a look at the graceful, swirling tendrils of black ink that ringed my finger, and she said, "That's very nice. Isn't it, Bob?" Her husband took his cue and echoed her sentiment. They'd clearly made a decision to try to get along, and judging by Yoshi's expression, their efforts weren't wasted.

"Come on, Mom and Dad," Yoshi said, as he took the little overnight bag from his father. "Let me introduce you to the boys, and then we'll get you a room and some refreshments. We also need to talk about what you're going to do in the talent show."

I expected them to balk at that idea, but his mom said, "If only I'd known, I would have brought my tap shoes. I guess we can throw something together, though. Can't we, Bob?" Her husband nodded as we all headed toward the little band practicing in the far corner.

Yoshi took my hand and squeezed it. There were unshed tears in his eyes when I glanced at him, and I kissed his cheek as he whispered, "This day is perfect."

*****

Almost everyone in my family believed they had some sort of talent. Most of them were wrong. But that didn't stop them from getting up on that stage and having a great time.

My cousin Carla started the talent show by massacring an Adele song. As she left the stage to cat-calls and enthusiastic applause, she waved to her three-week-old daughter and her baby daddy Julian. We'd all just met the man that weekend. At twenty-two, the redhead was nearly ten years younger than Carla, so everyone teased her mercilessly for being a total cougar. That was our job, of course, but we also welcomed Julian to the family with open arms.

I noticed Joely and his girlfriend Maya standing with Julian. Joely cradled his four-week-old son in his arms, and the two young dads seemed to be comparing notes. I'd been trying to go easy on teasing the hell out of Dante for being a grandpa, though it really did delight me to no end.

Over the next hour, act after act went up and did their thing. MJ and the Meerkats (which was the name Mitchell came up with for their band) was a bright spot, and they got a standing ovation for one of MJ's original songs. Later, Gianni and Zan performed an instrumental calypso song on the steel drum and maracas (Zan was obviously holding back, because he could have won the whole thing with absolutely no effort). Yoshi's parents also did surprisingly well with a soft-shoe routine to 'Singin' in the Rain,' which they'd clearly performed before, and they both looked pleased with the huge round of applause.

When it was almost our turn, Yoshi and I both ran off to quickly get ready. He went first, striding onto the stage in a blonde wig, a white, sequined tank top, and white satin shorts, along with some high-heeled white ankle boots that were actually very sexy on him. MJ, Mark and Mitchell were his backup dancers, and my fiancé totally slayed with a fully committed rendition of Britney's song 'Baby One More Time.' I noticed his parents applauding politely in the audience and still making an effort, which was nice.

Then it was my turn in our head-to-head battle. My heart was pounding, because I actually had terrible stage fright, but I wasn't going to let that get in the way of having a good time. When the song 'I'm Sexy and I Know It' began to play, I took center stage dressed like He-Man from Yoshi's favorite childhood cartoon, complete with blond bob, little brown shorts, a blue harness, and a foam sword. My costume was met by screams, applause, and cat-calls from my family.

I spent the next two-and-a-half minutes dancing, strutting around, and badly lip syncing. I felt like an idiot, but when I caught a glimpse of Yoshi and saw he was laughing so hard he was crying, it was all worth it. When the song ended, I was joined by Yoshi and the boys onstage. We all held hands and took a bow, and MJ exclaimed, "That was epic, Dad! I think it's a tie in your lip sync battle, but you did great! Way to be brave."

Yoshi told me, "That was the best thing ever! I had the biggest crush on He-Man when I was a kid."

"I know. Why do you think I'm dressed like this?" He seemed surprised, and then he started laughing again.

The final act of the afternoon brought the house down. Nana, Ollie, Mr. Mario, Dante, and Vincent took the stage dressed as the Spice Girls in full drag, and lip synced to 'Wannabe.' They'd clearly planned it ahead of time, because their wigs, makeup, and costumes were flawless. I fell over laughing as Dante and Vincent danced around awkwardly as Ginger Spice and Baby Spice, complete with massive platform heels.

When the song ended, MJ ran over and grabbed the big trophy, which he presented to Sporty Spice Nana. She beamed with pride as we all gave her a standing ovation. As Dante and Vincent stepped off the stage, I pulled out my phone and snapped a picture of them, and Dante tried to look stern as he grumbled, "If you show that to anyone outside of the family, you're toast."

I tapped my screen a few times and asked, "What did you say? I was busy uploading that picture to social media, so I didn't hear you." My oldest brother sighed dramatically.

I was still chuckling when I found Yoshi in the crowd. He tossed his blond wig aside and said, "I should have known your entire family would go bat shit crazy and totally outdo one another. How soon before we can have a rematch?"

"Oh believe me, in this family, full drag lip sync competitions can happen any time, any place."

Someone tapped me on the shoulder, and I turned to find a little old man with a friendly face, who was holding a sheaf of papers. "Excuse me," he said. "I seem to have made a mistake. I'm supposed to be officiating a wedding at this hotel, but I've gotten the time wrong, haven't I?"

"Yeah, but maybe that's okay." I turned to Yoshi and asked, "What do you think? Should we wait until tonight, or get married right now?"

He ran his fingers along my cheek and met my gaze with so much love in his eyes. "Now's good. That way, I won't have to wait two more hours to be your husband."

I told the official, "Actually, your timing is perfect. Everyone's here, so let's hold the ceremony right now."

MJ was standing nearby, and he asked, "Don't you guys want to change into your suits?"

I looked at Yoshi again, and he smiled and said, "I'm good like this if you are."

When I nodded in agreement, MJ shrieked and ran to the stage, where he grabbed the mic and said, "Everyone, please take your seats! My dads are getting married right now!" A murmur of excitement rumbled through the crowd, and our family and friends quickly rushed to get settled.

MJ, Mark, and Mitchell came up on the stage with us and the little old man. We brought my brothers and Nana up with us, too. The fact that Dante and Vincent were still dressed like the Spice Girls was priceless.

The ceremony was short and sweet. I pledged to love my sweet, gorgeous Yoshi forever, and he promised to love me in return. When the official pronounced us married, I brushed a tear of happiness from my husband's cheek and whispered, "I absolutely adore you." We kissed passionately, as the audience cheered and applauded and our sons threw glitter confetti.

Yoshi and I gathered our boys into a group hug, and Mark exclaimed, "It's totally, one hundred percent official! You're a Dombruso, Yoshi, now and forever."

My heart felt so full as my husband and I looked around at our big, crazy, loving family and all our friends, who'd become family, too. The past, the present, and the future were represented in those smiling faces, from our sons and our dear Nana to those two little newborn babies, and every generation in between. I could tell he was as overcome as I was, and Yoshi held me tight as he whispered, "I'm finally home."

The End

Thank you for reading!

Elijah's story is next up.
It begins a spin-off series set at
Seahorse Ranch on Catalina Island

Made in the USA
San Bernardino, CA
18 June 2018